S0-AES-115

JAN COFFEY

THE
DEADLIEST STRAIN

MIRA®

MIRA

ISBN-13: 978-0-7783-2458-4
ISBN-10:   0-7783-2458-3

THE DEADLIEST STRAIN

www.MIRABooks.com

Printed in U.S.A.

To our sons: Cyrus & Sam

You are our Firishte

One

Moosehead Lake, Maine

As the sun rose, setting the eastern sky ablaze, the north-western hills ahead of them grew bright against the deep blue to the west. It had been three hours since they'd started out from her sister's house in Portland. Haley knew they should be getting close to the lake now.

The sunny weather forecasted for the week had sounded like a good omen to her. She glanced at her husband, but Neil was focused on the road ahead. With good weather, Haley knew the two teenagers in the backseat would soon get over their complaining about being taken away on this "forced" family vacation. Their friends and sports and the zillion electronic gadgets were so important now.

Still, they'd been coming to this same island, renting the same cabin, for eight years now. The boys had been five and seven when they first started. Eager for a week of hiking, fishing, swimming—and having a hundred percent of their father's attention—the boys had always regarded this vacation as a special treat. That made it worth it to Haley. Neil needed this more than any of them. He traveled nearly fifty-one weeks a year for his job, and going to an island in the middle of nowhere in Maine, with no electricity or Internet or cell phone service, was the only way he knew of getting a full week to devote just to his family.

"I think you should wake them up," Neil said in a low voice as he turned onto the familiar road that took them to the lake's edge in Greenville. From there, they would take a rental boat out to the cottage.

Haley looked over her shoulder and smiled. At the sound of Neil's voice, their eight-month-old Lab was doing the job for her, stepping all over the boys, going from one window to the other.

"What the heck!" the younger one whined, waking abruptly. "Mom, Trouble's gotta pee. He'd better not go on me." At thirteen, Stevie was in the throes of a love/hate relationship with their dog.

"Be nice to him, moron," Bobby snapped at his younger brother. "He's not going to pee on you."

The silence of a moment earlier erupted into a full-fledged brawl as the dog joined in, barking louder than the boys could argue.

In a few minutes the van pulled into a space in the gravel lot by the docks, and Haley scrambled out, taking the excited animal with her and leaving the peacemaking to Neil. She stretched and took a deep breath as the dog darted toward the water.

The cool scent of the lake and the pines was welcome

and familiar. Haley followed the dog to the water's edge and marveled. It still affected her, just as it had when she'd first seen it eight years ago. The morning sky was a deep, cloudless blue, the air crisp and fresh, the water dark and clean. To her left, the sun was shining, bright and warm, on the trees and cottages along the Point. Here and there, the light flashed off a cottage window or a boat tied to a dock. Beyond the Point, where the lake extended for forty miles or more, pockets of mist could be seen rising off the water as the sun chased the darkness from the tree-lined eastern edge. Moosehead Lake was so different from the South Jersey suburb where they lived the rest of the year. Over the years, there'd been some development in Greenville, but not much seemed to change really. And almost nothing ever changed on the dozens of islands that dotted the huge body of water.

The dog ran back toward the car. Haley saw Judd McCabe's pickup truck had pulled in next to their van.

Judd was the owner of the cottage they rented. He also owned about fifteen other rental places scattered over the area. Every year, he made a point of meeting them at this very spot the first morning they arrived.

Now he was pointing out to Neil the boat he'd arranged for them to rent. Haley looked out at the dock.

As Neil and the boys started unloading the car, Haley clipped the leash on the dog's collar to keep him from getting in the way. She walked over and said hello to the older man.

"So, this is the new addition to the family," Judd said, petting the playful animal. "What's his name?"

"Trouble," she replied. Seeing the older man's wry grin, she nodded wholeheartedly. "It really is the beast's name.

The boys named him Trouble, and it fits him like a glove. A well-chewed glove, but a glove nonetheless."

"Looks like a happy bit o' trouble, Mrs. Murray."

"He is, actually," she said, smiling. "By the way, thanks so much for not minding us taking him out to the cottage."

He waved a hand in the air. "Not at all. In fact, the people who are renting the other cabin on the island these two weeks have a dog, too."

"That's great," she said, hiding her disappointment.

There were only two places to stay on the small island, and with the exception of one time about five years ago, the other cottage had always been unoccupied. This year they'd have to share their private island.

"Any kids?" she asked.

"One daughter. I think she's thirteen or fourteen."

"Perfect," she replied. "Friendly, I hope."

"Don't know. Pretty little thing, though." Judd glanced at the boys. "They arrived two days ago, and the girl seemed to be fighting a cold, so she was kinda quiet. With your handsome fellas around, though, I'm sure she'll be getting better and romping around the place in no time."

Having a girl on the island would definitely be an added attraction for the boys, especially Bobby. Haley decided to keep that little bit of news to herself until they got out onto the island.

"And we're in for perfect weather," she commented, watching Neil hand the last cooler to Bobby.

"Seems like it." Judd nodded toward the lake. "That fog hanging out around the Point should burn off pretty quick."

Haley looked across the water and saw the thick pocket

of fog that enveloped the end of the Point. Frowning, she glanced at her husband.

"Why don't you folks stick around town till it lifts?" Judd suggested to Neil. He added with a laugh, "Hate to see you miss the island and end up in Canada somewheres."

Neil smiled at the older man as he locked up the car and shook his head. "No. The boys are excited. It's better to be on our way and get settled in. We'll be fine."

"I can grab another boat and you can follow me out, if you like. With the fog—"

"I can find my way," Neil said, too quickly for Haley's comfort. "After eight summers, I know these waters like the back of my hand. Thanks, anyway, Judd."

Haley shook her head. "Men and directions," she muttered, saying goodbye to the old man.

There was no point in arguing with Neil about it. She knew he wouldn't change his mind and take Judd's offer. After eighteen years of marriage, she knew her husband too well. The twenty-minute boat ride might take three hours, but Neil would never admit that he needed help. Haley let it go. They were taking a boat on a lake. There was only so far they could go before they'd reach one shore or the other.

Their coolers and bags of groceries and luggage and fishing gear were piled high in the middle of the small rental boat. The boys were already in, up at the bow, but it took some coaxing to convince Trouble to climb in. Haley held the dog between her feet in the stern seat, where she sat next to Neil.

"I get the top bunk," Stevie announced argumentatively up front.

"No, you slept there last year. I get the top bunk," Bobby asserted loudly.

The battle started before they'd even left the shore. Haley waved back at Judd, who was standing on the dock, looking after them pensively. He waved back.

The small boat cut through the waters toward the Point, and then moved past it. Haley only half listened to the ongoing argument. When the boat entered the bank of fog, however, the boys stopped abruptly. The fog became much thicker as they moved farther out onto the lake, and Neil slowed the boat. She could tell he was concentrating on going straight ahead. Haley could only see a few feet ahead of the boys, though every now and then she would get a glimpse of some trees to the right or left, or the end of a boat ramp coming down from the unseen shore of one of the islands.

The sudden appearance through the fog of another boat creeping toward them was a relief. The two men in fishing gear waved as they went by. Haley could see no sign of where they'd come from. The thick fog was sticking like a mist to her skin and she felt cold creeping down her back. She looked at the bag that contained her sweatshirt. Naturally, it was buried under everything else.

"Do you know where you're going?" she asked her husband quietly.

"Of course," Neil answered, obviously trying to sound cheerful. "Trust me, will you?"

Well, they weren't the only ones crazy enough to be on the water, she told herself.

Trouble stood up, shook himself, and then sat again against Haley's leg. The dog plunked his head on her lap and looked up at her almost mournfully. She shook her head and petted him, glancing at the shore of another island they were passing. There was something familiar about the boathouse.

"We aren't too far away, are we?" she asked. "I recognize that place."

Neil nodded. "We'll go past one more island, and then you'll see our place."

Haley felt relief wash through her. "You hear that?" she said to the dog, scratching behind his ears. "Daddy led us straight to the cottage. He's a regular Daniel Boone."

"Very funny," Neil said.

Haley called to the boys. "We're almost there."

"What are we going to do first when we dock?" Stevie asked, turning in his seat.

"Are we going fishing?" Bobby chimed in.

The dog sensed the boys' excitement from the pitch of their voices. He stood up and looked around, ready to jump in the lake. Haley had to hold on tight to his collar.

"We'll unload the boat first. No one goes anywhere until we've taken everything out and put it in the cottage," Neil told them. He smiled at Haley. "That doesn't include you, honey. You do whatever you want."

She leaned over and gave him a peck on the cheek. Just getting close to their vacation cottage was making a noticeable difference in everyone's mood. Haley looked around. Even the fog seemed to be lightening. If Judd was right, in another hour the sun would be shining.

Hopefully.

Haley considered that her best move would be to introduce herself to their neighbors first. Only the east side of the island was approachable by boat. The west side was rocky and heavily wooded. Because of that, both cottages had been built on the same side of the island, only a hundred yards or so of grass and pine groves separating them. They'd share the boat dock, as there was only one.

Suddenly, as they rounded the last island, the boat engine sputtered and threatened to go out. She had confidence that Neil would know what to do, though. He revved the gas, gently at first, and the motor responded. Speeding up a little, they again moved smoothly across the water.

Haley looked ahead, peering through the fog. She didn't have long to wait. The southern end of the island abruptly appeared through the mist, then the dark outline of the other cottage. No sign of life there. She looked ahead as the beach and floating wooden dock next to it came into view. Trouble started barking.

"He's never been here, and still he's excited," Neil said, petting the dog's head.

Haley noticed the other power boat tied to the dock. There were water skis piled on the dock, and a canoe and two kayaks on the beach. Their neighbors were definitely on the island. Trouble's barks were becoming more forceful. Haley held on to his collar, wrapping the leash around her hand.

"Quiet, Trouble," she said.

"He's just ready to run," Neil said.

"Judd mentioned that the family in the other cottage has a dog, too," Haley reminded her husband.

Neil shrugged. "You should let him off the leash. The dogs get along much better that way."

"We don't want to startle the neighbors. Especially since they must not have seen us coming. If I let him go and—"

"There'll be a lot of tail wagging and butt sniffing, but that's all," Neil said confidently, glancing up at the other cottage. "And they'll *have* to hear us coming in."

She had a hard time holding on to him. The dog was ready to jump in the water. Waiting until the boat pulled near the dock, she unclipped the leash. With one graceful leap, Trouble left the boat and landed on the wooden planks at a full run. Nose to the ground, he dashed off into the fog.

She shook her head at the disappearing animal and looked up at their own cottage. Haley couldn't even see it, but she knew it would be in good condition. That's the way Judd always operated.

"Where's Trouble going?" Stevie asked, standing up as his older brother jumped out onto the dock and quickly tied the bowline to a nearby cleat.

"I think he's looking for a buddy," Neil answered.

Immediately, there were a dozen questions from the teenagers about the other family on the island. Haley pointed to her husband. "Help your dad. I'll give you the entire scoop in a minute."

She couldn't see or hear the dog. While the boys helped to secure the boat, Haley stepped onto the dock and walked toward the stretch of sand-and-rock beach. The familiar outline of their cottage broke through the fog. The rocking chairs on the porch, the two kayaks lying upside down on the path leading from the beach, the canoe next to it, the outside shower on the side of the cottage, the tire swing hanging from the ancient oak tree in the front yard…these were all familiar sights. She remembered exploring all over the island that first year. The oak was the only non-pine tree on the property. Looking at it always made her smile for some reason.

She looked back at the other cottage through the haze. There was still no one outside, but she noticed now the front door was open, and it looked like the screen door had been propped open, as well.

"Trouble!" she called out, hoping the dog hadn't decided to visit on his own. "Come on, good puppy."

There was no barking, no sound. She shook her head. Haley kicked herself for not asking Judd the other family's name. She guessed they must have gone off fishing, and Trouble had gone off after them.

The island was about half a mile wide and maybe a little bit longer. Neil and the boys liked to fish on the rocks on the west side. That was probably where the other family was. Well, they were in for a surprise when Trouble found them.

She walked up the path toward their own cottage. There were no locks on these houses. There was no crime, no one to intrude on people. Judd boarded the places up for nine months, and mostly the same people came back year after year during the summer. The people before them always left a dozen new paperbacks for the collection on the shelf by the stove. She was glad Judd had never put up more cottages out here.

She stepped on the porch and looked back. The fog was lifting. She could see that the boys had already unloaded everything on the pier. She opened the front door. The faintly musty smell, mingled with lemon wax, brought back more memories. Inside everything looked the same. The rustic furniture, the wood bunk beds in the nook off the sitting area, the little kitchenette with the lime-green fridge, the bedroom that was no bigger than a closet off the living area with the creaky double bed and the tiny bathroom off of that.

"Come over here. Right now. Come here, Trouble."

Neil's shouts brought Haley back out onto the porch. Her husband, juggling a suitcase and two bags of groceries, was standing on the path and looking up at the other cottage.

Trouble was on the neighbors' porch.

"Great," she whispered.

"Come on, good boy," Neil called again.

With a little yelp, the dog ran back inside the place.

"Oh, Christmas," she muttered.

"What is he doing in there?" Neil asked.

"Probably helping himself to their lunch. I'll get him," Haley offered, propping the front door open so her husband could take his load in. She started across to the other cottage.

"Hello," she called as she stopped close near the porch. She felt awkward about walking into their neighbors' place without anyone there. "Come out of there, Trouble."

"Mom, something really stinks over here," Bobby called up from the beach.

Haley turned and saw the two boys near the dock, walking around the neighbors' boats. Her husband was walking back down the path. He could handle it.

"Come on, Trouble!" she called more forcefully.

"Smells like a dead animal," Stevie called out. "I think something is dead under the canoe."

She took another look back. Neil was there. She could hear him moving the boys back.

"Trouble!" Haley called, stepping onto the first step of the porch.

Three pairs of sneakers and an assortment of flip-flops were next to the open door. A paperback book with its pages curled from the rain sat on one of the rocking chairs. There was a half glass of something that looked to be milk on the table between the chairs. A couple of flies were floating on top. A brownie next to it had become a feeding frenzy for ants.

Dread filled the pit of her stomach. She stepped hesitantly onto the porch.

"Trouble!" she called again.

The dog barked from inside. She stepped in. A foul smell she couldn't identify hit her senses. It smelled something like chicken that had gone bad, but not exactly. The layout of the cottage was similar to theirs. Trouble was sniffing and crying next to something on the bottom bunk. Suddenly, Haley realized that someone was sleeping there.

"Hello!" she called. The person wasn't moving. She covered her mouth and nose with her hands.

"Dad, is that an animal?" one of the boys asked loudly from the beach.

"Get back!" Neil's command was sharp.

Feeling faint, Haley looked back outside through the open door. Her husband had pushed the canoe over and let it go upright. It was rocking slightly. He and the boys were moving back and staring at something lying on the ground where the canoe had been.

"There's a collar on him," Bobby shouted, sounding very upset. "It has to be a dog."

Trouble barked and ran into the tiny bedroom off the living area. Haley's eyes had now adjusted to the dim light of the cottage, and her gaze followed the animal. As she saw what was attracting the dog, she felt her stomach heave.

A partially decomposed body lay stretched across the double bed.

Two

The mission had now been upgraded to *Urgent*. Ten fatalities. A large area surrounding Moosehead Lake remained under quarantine.

"That's the only runway, three thousand three meters," the pilot said through the headset. "It's over thirty years old. It was covered with land mines when we first moved in."

Austyn Newman looked out the small window at the rugged Afghan landscape. He believed the answer to the outbreak in Maine lay down here. Austyn had been assigned to this trip because he was specifically trained in countering biological attacks. This was his field of study, what he had trained for most of his career.

Matt Sutton, the agent accompanying him on this trip, was a senior intelligence officer in Homeland Security. Austyn had been able to tie the strand of bacteria they'd seen in Maine to a specific laboratory in prewar Iraq, but finding the suspect had been Matt's doing. Searching through CIA files, he'd somehow come up with the location and the name of the scientist who'd been in charge of the Iraq facility. He'd also been able to come up with a three-inch-thick file the CIA had gathered over the years on Dr. Rahaf Banaz.

Both of them reported to Faas Hanlon, the top intelligence officer at Homeland Security. The deputy director and Hanlon preferred to use small teams to handle different aspects of the investigation. Everyone worked together, and Hanlon insisted on having the latest information at all times; he never knew when the national security adviser or the president's office might be on the phone to him.

The airstrip cut a path in the middle of the rocky desert. There were some buildings, a few of them large enough to be hangars. Other structures spread out on the desert floor, some that looked to be under construction. At one end of the field below, a sea of tents and prefab housing covered two or three acres of ground. U.S. Army units.

"The Soviets built most of the permanent buildings, didn't they?" Matt Sutton asked the pilot.

"Yes, sir. The airbase played a real important role during the Soviet occupation of Afghanistan back in the eighties," the pilot explained. "It was the regional base of operations for troops and supplies. It also was an initial staging point for Soviet forces at the beginning of their invasion, with a number of airborne divisions being deployed here permanently. Well, they *thought* it was permanent."

"They put a lot of work into it," Matt commented. "I'm surprised they didn't level the whole place before they left."

"They cleared out of here in a hurry," the pilot said with a shrug. "There was more than you see now. The Sovs threw up a lot of support buildings and base housing units. Most of them were destroyed by years of fighting between the various warring Afghan factions. We're now putting up some of our own buildings, over there. Being only twenty-five miles north of Kabul, this is a strategic place for us, too."

"What's the smoke I can see beyond that ridge?"

Austyn looked past his partner at the clouds of smoke rising above the pale, reddish-brown ridge of sand and rock.

"There's a makeshift refugee camp there. I'm told they're planning to move the whole camp to the far side of Bagram, away from the airbase."

"I heard there's a serious problem with land mines in this area."

The pilot nodded. "Something else the Sovs left behind. Every time we think we've got them all taken care of, another one goes off. An Afghan worker lost a leg to a mine last week. But that's not all. At the beginning of this week, an air force pilot I know found an unexploded, rocket-propelled grenade half buried just outside his... Hold on." He adjusted his headset and spoke to the air controller on the ground. In a moment he turned back to his passengers. "Looks like we're going to have to circle one more time."

There'd been too many casualties and there was no end in sight, Austyn thought. The Taliban was growing stronger in some sectors with every passing month. He looked at the landscape around the base and airstrip. NATO forces had moved in some thirty thousand troops to Afghanistan to take over areas of the country, but there were large sectors, like this one, that were still run primarily by U.S. troops.

The Brickyard was supposed to be about a half hour driving distance from this base. The existence of the classified facility, run by the Central Intelligence Agency and staffed by special army personnel, was officially denied by the U.S. government. It was what the media back home called a "black site." Austyn and Matt had been briefed on it three days ago. The prison, they were told explicitly, was used solely for the war on terror. At present, the agency was holding twenty-two prisoners—male and female—at this prison. None of the people here had been charged with crimes or convicted. As far as the rest of the world was concerned, these prisoners were ghosts. There was no record of them anywhere. And there never would be.

In the past, Austyn had never been too keen to know about facilities like this. He knew they existed, but even as a senior agent in the science and technology division of Homeland Security, he'd never interrogated a prisoner in his life. He didn't want to know how many black sites were around the world. He didn't want to think about the rights of these prisoners. He definitely didn't want to think about the possibility of an innocent person being held or tortured in such places. He wanted to believe that holding these people was a matter of national security. He knew—no matter what the media reported—that it was a rare occasion when abuses occurred. The agency did a better job overseas, as Homeland Security did stateside, of holding on to the right people than they got credit for.

Whatever Austyn's feelings had been before, however, his involvement with places like the Brickyard prison had changed with the bacteria outbreak in Maine. How he'd felt before no longer mattered. Now he was glad that there was a place such as this, where they could find and question a suspect. The consequences of not learning more about the bacteria they were facing were potentially devastating.

"Over there." Matt motioned to something outside his window. "That must be the Brickyard."

The military jet was now dropping through patches of cloud. Austyn looked where his partner was pointing. A cluster of buildings sat between a pair of hills some distance away from the base.

"I think you're right," Austyn agreed.

They'd been told that an abandoned brick-making factory had been converted for use as the prison. Austyn saw a military supply truck driving along a dirt road, away from the factory. A cloud of dust rose up in its wake. The countryside surrounding the prison was barren, a wasteland of pale rock and dirt and scrub foliage.

The jet started its descent to the runway. Austyn stuffed the files and pictures he'd taken out to review back into his briefcase.

"I guess we're as ready as we'll ever be," Matt commented.

The landing was smooth, and they shook hands with the pilot. As he stepped out of the plane, Austyn's first reaction was that the base looked a lot worse from the ground than it had from the air. The landscape and the tents and uniforms and the faces of the soldiers all blended in with the dust that covered everything.

A corporal met them at the plane, and Austyn listened to him as the escort walked them toward a nearby hangar. It had obviously rained that morning, but with the exception of some puddles, the sun had dried everything. The air was parched, but there was a heaviness in it that you felt deep down in your lungs. A military fuel truck driving along the runway raised more dust and made the air even more difficult to breathe.

Austyn noticed the looks they drew from soldiers they passed. He remembered what he'd heard about the lack of variety in the food here. The service personnel looked forward to any stash of food that visitors brought along. He regretted not having thought ahead.

He focused on two dust-covered Humvees racing along the concrete and pulling up a few yards from them. A woman with captain's bars on the collar of her field jacket climbed out.

"That's Captain Jane Adams," the corporal said as she approached them. "She's in charge of the facility you're going to."

Higher rank didn't spare the officer from the dust. She and the driver were covered with the same dirt as the vehicle they'd arrived in. Matt and Austyn were introduced to their host and hustled into the Humvee.

Captain Adams was barely over five feet tall, and thinly built, but she had an authority in her voice and a sharpness to her gaze that made her seem about six foot six.

Before leaving Washington, Austyn had been told of an ongoing internal investigation at the agency regarding prisoner handling at the Brickyard prison. In an effort to head off action by any oversight committee, there'd been a complete turnover of staff during the past year. Captain Adams was heading up the new crew.

As they left the camp, two more military vehicles joined them, one in front and one in the back, forming a caravan.

They passed through a number of security checkpoints before reaching the open road.

"We have to be careful," Adams told them. "We still have roving gangs of Taliban insurgents that pop up unexpectedly under our noses."

Both agents listened to the captain as she told them briefly about the base and the ancient city of Bagram and the locals. Much of what was being said was similar to what they'd heard from the pilot. Neither agent interrupted, though, and soon Adams was asking about news from stateside. It was clear that the lack of attention the country was giving to Afghanistan was a source of irritation for her.

Austyn pulled on his glasses. Even with the windows shut, they were eating their escort's dust. The slight discomfort they were experiencing, however, was nothing compared to what was going on outside.

The poverty was palpable. The drawn, worn faces of the few ragged Afghanis that they passed after coming through the checkpoints were clear indicators of their suffering. At one point a mob of kids playing in front of a corrugated steel shack started running after the cars, lining the road and chanting something in their native tongue. Many were missing arms and legs, hobbling on crutches behind the others. Austyn remembered what he'd heard about the land mines. The Afghani children formed the largest number of casualties. Outbreaks of a number of epidemics had also been taking their toll over the past few years.

The harsh landscape and the culture of survival here was fascinating to Austyn, but he knew he had to focus. When Captain Adams paused, he broke in with his questions.

"Captain, what have you been told about our visit here?"

"The information has been trickling down too slowly for my liking, but I understand there's been a biological attack in the U.S."

"I hope you were also told that this is classified information," Matt responded. "Unlike the anthrax scare of few years ago, none of the details have been officially released to the press or public."

"Yes, sir. I understand," Adams answered, motioning to the driver. "Sergeant Powell here has all the necessary clearances, but it's up to you what you care to tell us. In fact, no one else at our station has been briefed in any way about the purpose of your visit."

"Begging your pardon, sirs," Sergeant Powell told them, looking in the mirror. "You should know that the secrecy has started a lot of speculation. Everyone working at the Brickyard thinks you're part of that congressional committee focusing on the detention facilities."

"I can live with that," Austyn replied. "About this prisoner. What can you tell me that's not in the files?"

"I don't really know what is and what isn't in the files that were passed on to you," Captain Adams told him. "Rahaf Banaz is thirty-five years old and a Kurd. Why she was working for Saddam's regime is still a mystery. She was captured after the marines raided a laboratory in the eastern Diyala region in Iraq back in 2003. She was moved around to different black sites in Iraq, Turkey, Romania and Latvia, and then brought here eight months ago."

Austyn had read about the moves. Dr. Banaz was well known enough in the international research community that there had been a lot of squawk about her whereabouts.

The U.S. response from the very start was that she'd been killed in the attack when they'd raided her laboratory.

"How has she been treated?" Matt asked.

Captain Adams shrugged. "Off and on solitary confinement. There have been no interrogations for quite some time. None since her arrival here. And there's certainly been no abuse," she added defensively.

"And her cooperation level?" Austyn asked.

"Nonexistent." The captain turned around in her seat. "She never complains. She doesn't speak. In fact, she doesn't respond to anything at all. She has moved into a zone that we see some prisoners go into once they've lost any hope of freedom. Four times since she arrived here eight months ago, she's gone on a hunger strike. Each time, we had to move her to the medical facility at Bagram, hook her up to tubes and force-feed her. But I was told when she arrived not to conduct any more interrogations of her, for the time being."

"Why do you think you were given that order?" Matt asked.

She shrugged again. "I assumed that we had what we needed—that final disposition of her case would be coming down."

"What do you mean?" Austyn asked, alarmed.

"This woman was a scientist in Saddam Hussein's biological warfare program. Our people have collected tons of samples and evidence at the site where she was captured. She was the sole survivor of the air attack. So what are we going to ask? What's she going to confess to? We already know what she was working on. And as far as other facilities like the one she was found in, she was the nuts-and-bolts person—the actual scientist—and that was *her* lab. She wasn't administering any other labs. That much she told her captors at the time of her arrest, and our evidence has confirmed that," Adams explained. "Our understanding is that she is being kept here until it's time to move her again to some other facility…permanently."

Austyn looked out the window of the jeep at the stark countryside. Dust, rocky hills and more dust. Every now and then a lone tree had sprouted in the middle of nowhere. It occurred to him that Rahaf Banaz was one of those lone trees. The difference was that she'd been uprooted from the dry rocky terrain of her native Kurdish Iraq and dropped inside the walls of one prison and then another, probably for the rest of her life.

He tried to shake the image. Thoughts like that wouldn't help him get his job done here. She was a ghost because of her own choices, and there were American lives that could be saved if he stayed focused on his task.

"The intelligence information that *was* passed down to us indicated that the strain of bacteria found in the U.S. seems to match what the prisoner was working on," Captain Adams told them.

"That's correct," Austyn replied, turning his attention back to the occupants of the vehicle. "But considering how long she's been in American hands, we can't accuse her of having a direct connection with any attack."

"What we're hoping to gain is information," Matt continued. "We'd like to find out who else might have had access to her research back then. Who was working with her, besides the scientists we know are dead. We want her cooperation."

"Good luck."

"Even more important, we hope she'll tell us how to produce an antidote."

Captain Adams turned more fully around to face them. "There's none?"

"No," Austyn said. "Not yet. That's why we're here. Dr. Banaz may be the one with the key." He wanted to be hopeful. He wanted to think that their trip might be as simple as asking her the questions, and the scientist offering them all the answers. He wasn't foolish enough to think it would really happen, but it certainly was worth hoping for.

"My communication mentioned a bacteria that produces some kind of flesh-eating disease," Adams said. From her expression, it was obvious that even her years of tough military training didn't offer protection from imagining how horrific a death this could be.

"Necrotizing fasciitis. In extreme circumstances and without medical attention, the flesh-eating disease can claim a life in twelve to twenty-four hours," Austyn explained. "But what we're dealing with now is a super-microbe. The bacteria we've seen in Maine is much worse than anything the medical community has had to deal with in the past."

"That bad?" Captain Adams asked incredulously.

"What we know…what we've seen…is that there are no external wounds, no warning signs. Once contracted, this super-microbe eats away at the internal organs of its victim," Austyn told her. "The disease actually consumes its victim from the inside out. Septic shock and death can occur in less than an hour."

The silence in the Humvee was unbroken for a few minutes. He realized the gravity of the situation hadn't hit the two people riding in front until now.

"And how contagious is it? How does it spread?" Captain Adams asked.

"Very contagious. But as far as how it spreads…there's a *lot* we don't know," Matt explained. "Two families— seven people and their pets—were found in advanced stages of decay in Maine by the owner of the property, who radioed in for help. Unfortunately, he and the two emergency personnel who arrived on the scene contracted the disease at the site. An additional emergency group, already on their way, suspected a disaster and called in for more help."

"We're assuming the disease spreads primarily by contact, but we don't know. It's possible that normal protective gear won't stop the microbe. Insects or even airborne particles may also spread the disease, manifesting themselves in the body of a potential victim," Austyn said, continuing where his partner stopped. "In short, there's too much that we don't know. We have no idea if those ten casualties are all we're dealing with. We have no clue how the first family contracted the bacteria. Maybe they brought it in from some other part of the country, and we're focusing our attention on the wrong source. We don't know if there's an incubation period for the germ in the body before it becomes active."

He could go on and explain everything that he didn't know, but that would take forever. They had hundreds of questions—but that was why they were here.

"How were you ever able to tie this to what was found in Dr. Banaz's laboratory in Iraq?" Captain Adams asked.

"The computers in Washington showed a match in the DNA sequence of this super-microbe to what was in Banaz's lab in Iraq," Matt told them. "A database of billions of combinations, and that's the only match we have identified so far."

Captain Adams adjusted the glasses on the rim of her nose. Her struggle with the information she'd received was obvious in her fisted hands and tight jaw muscles. "There are fifty-two soldiers living in close quarters at the Brickyard. There are thousands of troops stationed in or traveling through Bagram Airbase. I don't want to sound paranoid, but we're very exposed," she said. "Have either of you had any contact with those bodies?"

Austyn perfectly understood her concern. "No, the island has been quarantined."

"How about the samples, the DNA sequence? How was all this collected and tested?" she persisted.

"The protective gear was upgraded to the levels NASA uses in space. The sanitation techniques used are similar to what we use with nuclear spills. We've had no new report of the disease since the initial outbreak," Austyn told her.

Captain Adams didn't look very relieved. She turned around and stared straight ahead.

Austyn had seen the same reluctance back in U.S. The professionals that had finally traveled to the small island to monitor a sample collection had drawn the short straw. Though Austyn and Matt weren't allowed to be part of the on-site investigation, neither had been terribly disappointed. There was so much that they didn't know about the microbe. Despite all the precautions, there was no guarantee that an outbreak might not happen right now.

32 *Jan Coffey*

"In your opinion, do you think Dr. Banaz will cooperate once we tell her what's going on?" Matt asked.

"Are you prepared to offer her a deal?" Captain Adams asked.

"We've come prepared to negotiate," Austyn answered. "We'll do whatever it takes."

The satellite phone attached to the front dashboard came to life. The driver answered it and passed it along to his superior. Captain Adams said very little, but listened intently. Austyn could tell from the tightening of her shoulders that the message was not to her liking. Still, he turned his attention back to the road as the Humvee hit a large pothole. The landscape was beginning to change. The rocks were now interspersed with clumps of greenery. From what he'd seen from above, he suspected they were near their destination.

Captain Adams turned around in his seat to look at them once she'd ended the call. She made no explanations.

"About the prisoner," she said. "You can negotiate with someone who's responsive, who wants something, a person who values life. But as I told you before, your Dr. Banaz is past all that. This woman has lost all hope."

Three

Her body may have grown weaker, but her mind never ceased to weave shelters where she could escape to. These imaginary houses were in a different place and time. There she experienced no pain, no grief…no discomfort at all. Those moments of peace were not memories of exact events from her past. She knew, as well, that they couldn't be any premonition of her future. They were only a confused mélange of reality and dream, of truth and falsehood. She didn't mind the mingling of the real and the unreal; it provided her with a few moments each day of sanctuary.

The people she met and spoke to in those imaginary moments were only those whom she invited. Her sister was a regular visitor. They would often repeat some conversation they'd had some years ago, or there would be some other recollection of the past. Friends' names from long ago would fill her with a sense of well-being. Her sister was good at recalling all of these things, much better than she herself was. Lying alone in one cell or another, she would savor each thin slice of good she could recall, living each moment—smelling it, tasting it—as deeply as she could.

Other times, she would invite her students in her mind. They would surround her with their enthusiasm, with their questions. She was the gardener who sowed the seeds of learning. She'd nurture their thoughts as if they were tiny sprouts of palest green, propping them up and protecting them. She would feed their minds with the gentle mist of experience.

We are indebted equally to our teacher and to God. Her mother's words were always with her. Why was it, though, that she could remember the proverbs, the lips speaking them, but never her mother's face?

There were other moments of sanctuary, too. She'd recall an instance where a warm arm might wrap around her. Sometimes, she could feel the smooth touch on her skin. Was it real or imagined? Was it a memory or a longing? She didn't know. It didn't matter now.

In those moments, though, she'd sometimes feel herself escape out of her own body. A touch on her wrist would open a portal for her spirit, and she'd slide out of her body like a silk scarf from her father's pocket. Floating above herself—her body motionless in the dark below—she would come as close to being alive as she had ever been.

She never knew at that instant if it was really happening or not. It was only in the crushing aftermath of such moments that she knew her life was, now and forever, only the stuff of dreams.

The first days were a blur. Perhaps the first weeks were, as well. She didn't know. Eventually, she'd regained her balance, her sense of time. Months had flowed into years and then she'd lost her bearings once again. In the end, it didn't matter whether it was now or tomorrow or last year. Time means nothing when you are suspended in hell. Sometimes she'd feel as if she almost knew. She'd hear some guard mention a date. She'd focus in on it, try to hold on to it. And then it would slip away until she had no idea, once again, if it was one year or ten years since she'd been a free human being, teaching at the university six days a week, having routines and friends and a busy life.

As her sense of time wavered, though, her ability to concentrate on other things—on inner strengths—had grown. She'd taught herself to be indifferent to pain. Cold, heat, shackles, verbal and physical abuse…none of it meant anything to her. She'd learned to become numb to the physical world. She could close her eyes and shut down everything, retreating in silence to her house of dreams.

God finds a low branch for the bird that cannot fly. Yes, Mother. I know.

Lately, though, more and more, Fahimah was finding it more difficult to concentrate. Her discipline was wavering. She was running across some bumps in the road. The groan of a prisoner, the cry of a night bird, the shaking of the ancient and decrepit walls that were her prison brought reality to her consciousness again and again. Whether it was a mine exploding in the hills or American troops bombing a new target, she didn't know. But she could not ignore them as she once had. Increasingly, she could not block out the stark reality of her situation.

During these new moments, her entire life focused. She knew who she was and she even seemed to know how long she'd been in prison. She remembered how hard she'd

worked in life to get where she'd been before her capture.
She recalled the sacrifices she'd made, how much she'd
achieved. She remembered the respect she'd commanded
of her peers, her students. She felt inside of her the warm
realization that she'd made something of herself, despite
being a woman and a Kurd in a country where one was not
particularly valued and the other was so often seen as the
enemy of Saddam and his regime.

It was during these moments that she'd also recall with
vibrant clarity her sister Rahaf lying on the cot in the
basement, her leg gone, the wound from the amputation
raw and bleeding and exposed to the musty air. She could
still hear her sister retching piteously, her body trying to
puke out the poison that she'd injected into her own bloodstream in an attempt to survive. More clearly than any of
these things, though, she could remember her sister asking
for her help.

These had been the deciding moments. Should she tell
them after all this…or not?

Fahimah knew there was only one possible way that she
could ever end this living hell, but telling the truth wasn't
an option. Over the years there had been two separate
messages passed on to her by other prisoners. Although
there had been no name attached to them, she knew they
were from her sister. The last one had come about nine
months ago, just before they'd moved Fahimah to this
facility. Rahaf was alive and looking for her.

The situation was impossible; Fahimah knew that very
clearly. She had acted to protect her sister, never thinking that
her imprisonment would be so…final. Still, she was committed now. She would never expose her sister to this. Her

captors believed the deceit she had woven. Fahimah would go to her grave before shattering the truth they had accepted.

She opened her eyes and stared into the darkness of the new cell they'd moved her into this morning. She wasn't allowed outside. With the exception of the face of the guard that brought the food, she never saw any other. When they moved her from prison to prison, she'd been either sedated or blindfolded. They never kept her in any one cell too long. She was beginning to believe they moved her every so often just to make sure she was still alive. This new cell had no windows, no lights, only a sliver of daylight creeping in at the base of the door. She remembered being moved into this cell, or one similar to it, a number of times before. She hated it. It felt like a grave in which she had been buried alive.

The cement floor smelled of urine. She sat up. Her eyes were already adjusted to the darkness. The size of the room was perhaps four feet by six feet. She looked up and knew the ceiling wasn't high enough for her to stand.

Fahimah pulled the old wool blanket that they let her keep over her shoulders. The old rag smelled like death. The only other thing in the cell was the hospital chamber pot, glinting dully in the corner. She sat back against a wall, her legs crossed. Waves of panic were clawing their way inside of her. The air in the room was so heavy. She felt that there wasn't enough of it.

She recalled how she'd started calming her mind and body those first weeks after her capture. Fahimah had always been enthralled by the idea of Sufism. She'd read about it and studied it. The great Sufi poet Rabi'a of Basrah was her favorite. One of the many myths surrounding Rabi'a was that she was freed from slavery because her master saw her praying while surrounded by light. He realized that she was a saint and feared for his life if he continued to keep her in captivity.

There had been many times in the darkness of her cell that Fahimah had prayed, chanted quietly and meditated. No one had freed her. What her captors thought of her could not be further from sainthood. Despite it all, she'd been able to reach the peace inside she'd been after. She'd discovered her dreams.

She closed her eyes and started her meditation now. She had to observe, guard and control her thoughts. She had to escape this room…this body.

The noise outside of the cell cut through her concentration with razor sharpness. There was the sound of grinding metal, footsteps, voices. She forced her eyes to remain shut. Somebody was coming. Perhaps they were going to move her again to another cell, perhaps to a different prison. Even though they had just moved her in here, that was the way they worked. They never allowed her to feel settled, especially since she had made trouble for them by refusing food. She inhaled deeply, and the closeness of the cell made her stomach turn slightly.

The door opened loudly on rusty hinges. Even with her eyes closed, Fahimah could feel the light pour over her.

"Dr. Banaz."

It was a new voice. She held her breath. No one had called her that for nearly her entire imprisonment. To them—to the Americans—she was Rahaf. She was called by her sister's first name.

"Dr. Banaz," the man's voice called out gently again. "My name is Austyn Newman."

Another American, she thought. She knew their accents, understood their ways. She would never trust them.

"My partner and I were sent here to make arrangements for your release," the man said in the same quiet tone.

Fahimah wrapped the blanket more tightly around her shoulders and dipped her chin to her chest. Another lie. She willed herself to shut the voice out.

Four

Boynton Canyon consisted of a dry, rugged landscape boxed in by distant buttes and cliffs of varying shades of red rock. Because of its close proximity to Sedona and the paved roads that added to its accessibility, the canyon crawled with visitors who loved walking its trails. In recent years, the beautiful scenery wasn't the only thing that drew the tourists. Boynton Canyon's popularity had grown tenfold since it was included on a flyer identifying it as a local vortex—a sort of energy field emanating from the inner earth. Whether or not one believed in this bit of modern mysticism, locals and tourists alike agreed that some sort of powerful feeling could be experienced here among the buttes, the crimson cliffs and the natural desert gardens.

It was one of those locals who'd called the police at six in the morning about a red pickup truck sitting in a gully beyond the barricades, not too far off the hiking trail.

In twenty minutes a police cruiser skirted a luxury resort and drove past the signs and around the barricades to the canyon floor to a spot designated for emergency vehicles. Last night, there'd been the report of a stolen red pickup truck from the front of the movie theater. It would be too good if this were the stolen vehicle.

The driver of the cruiser radioed in their location as a young officer stepped out of the vehicle. The sky was overcast, giving the cliffs a grayish hue. This was Sedona's rainy season, but nothing kept the tourists away. In another hour, there'd be quite a few out hiking the trail.

"See anything?" The driver opened the door and stood beside the car.

The younger cop glanced back at him. "The caller mentioned he'd seen it from the Kachina Woman rock formation." He looked down. Tire treads were visible, leading off through the brush. He pointed them out to his partner. "You wanna drive it or hike?"

"Let's walk," the driver replied with a grin. "If we have a couple of lovebirds out there, we don't want to shake 'em up too bad."

"Shake 'em up." The younger cop shook his head. "Who're you kidding? You're just hopin' to see a little skin, Floyd, I know you."

The older cop laughed, and the two started following the tracks. They didn't have to go too far to spot the vehicle in a gully edged by scrubby ponderosa pines. As they moved closer, two coyotes, which looked up at them from the far side of the ditch, turned and trotted off into the brush.

"If somebody's sleeping in that truck," Floyd said, "they don't know nothing about the flash floods out here."

The younger cop nodded. "Starting to look like teenagers took it for a joyride last night and dumped it here."

"Long walk back to town," Floyd replied.

The men approached the vehicle cautiously. In a moment, they were close enough to see the license plate.

"It matches," Floyd said, checking it against the notebook he'd taken out of his shirt pocket.

From some twenty or so yards away, no one appeared to be inside the truck. It looked as if the driver had just run it straight down into the ditch. It was hard up against a pine on one side. Both of the windows were open.

"The driver wouldn't be able to open his door," the younger officer noted.

"He might have got out the other way or just climbed through the window."

Both men approached the truck more cautiously.

"What's that stink?" Floyd asked, looking around.

The younger officer approached the passenger side and then froze, his face going white. A second later, he turned away from the truck and emptied the contents of his stomach into the gully.

"What is it?" Floyd asked, approaching the truck and looking through the open window.

The odor was foul, but the sight was worse. The older cop had never seen anything like this. Two partially decomposed bodies were slouched next to each other on the seat.

Both still had their seat belts on.

Five

Brickyard Prison, Afghanistan

Austyn didn't know what kind of reaction he'd expected, but this wasn't it.

"Dr. Banaz," he said again. "Did you hear me?"

She never moved. Her head must have been shaved a month or two ago, he noted. He could see nothing of her face, for she had her chin pressed against her chest. Her frame was small and she appeared to be physically fragile. Except for the lowered head, she appeared to be in a meditation posture. With the old wool blanket around her shoulders, the peacefulness of the pose reminded Austyn of images of Gandhi.

He crouched down just outside the door. The cell looked like a small kennel with a very low ceiling. He'd have to bend down to enter.

"Rahaf?" He called her by her first name. There was still no reaction. He stood up.

Captain Adams had led Matt and Austyn here. She was now giving them a knowing look. She shrugged.

"Would you like us to bring her out of there?" Adams asked quietly. "We can move her to one of the interrogation rooms."

Austyn shook his head. They would never get her to cooperate there. The scientist looked so thin. He looked at her arms and wrists, extending from the cover of the blanket. They were like twigs, he thought, frowning.

"When was the last time she ate?" Matt asked, obviously following the same path of Austyn's thoughts. She looked like she was starving herself to death.

Captain Adams turned to the female guard who was standing by the open door. The young soldier didn't have an answer, since the prisoner was moved into this cell only a few hours earlier. The captain turned to another guard behind them and ordered him to find out when the prisoner last ate.

"What would you like to do?" Adams asked, looking back at the two visitors.

As the ranking investigator, Austyn had been coached on the psychological aspects of interrogation before he left Washington, specifically on the interrogation of women. Despite the fact that the U.S. government had denied Rahaf's rights by hiding her for all these years without a trial, they were abiding by the Geneva Convention IV and Amnesty International guidelines regarding treatment of female detainees. Female guards had to be present during the interrogation of female detainees and prisoners, and they had to be solely responsible for carrying out any body searches to reduce the risk of sexual abuses. He'd been assured by Adams that there was no contact between male guards and Rahaf without the presence of a female guard. When they had to seek medical assistance for her, Rahaf had been put under the care of a female doctor.

Austyn had been loaded up with a pile of manuals to read on the topic during his twelve-hour flight to Afghanistan. None of what he'd read or been told seemed to apply here. She wasn't what he'd expected. Even before talking to her, his instincts told him that this woman was not crazy, just…resigned to fate. He sensed that when he looked into her eyes, he'd know without a doubt if she could create a substance as terrible as the one that had killed in Maine.

"I'd like to speak to her here," he told the prison commander.

She looked up and down the hallway. "I'm afraid not, sir. We have other prisoners in cells along this corridor. It would be disruptive, and there is the problem of security. Every one of them would hear you."

Still, Austyn wanted her to come willingly out of that hole. He wanted to start off on the right foot. He wished they hadn't moved her. He'd hoped they had taken better care of her.

A thought crossed his mind, something that had occurred to him as he'd read Rahaf's files. It was the only useful thing that had come out of the reading that he'd done on the flight over. "When was the last time Dr. Banaz was outside?"

"You mean, out in the open?" Captain Adams asked doubtfully.

Austyn nodded.

"These prisoners are not allowed to exercise in an open

yard, if that's what you mean. She gets thirty minutes of fresh air every day in a special containment unit—"

"And the rest of the time, she's in solitary confinement?"

"These prisoners are here because of special circumstances, sir," Adams replied defensively. "I have specific instructions regarding their handling."

"I know that," Austyn said testily. "When was the last time she saw a horizon, Captain?"

"I can't say, sir. Not since she was moved here. She was blindfolded the times that we had to transfer her to one of the field hospitals because of self-inflicted nutritional issues."

He looked at the pale skin of the prisoner's wrists, the short fuzz covering her skull. If she was listening to anything that was being said, she showed no indication of understanding. "Is there a place outside where I can talk to her?"

The prison commander motioned to him to step away from the open cell.

Austyn complied. She moved to a steel door that they had come through into this section of the prison. Beneath the fluorescent lights of the corridor, he could see she was trying to control her anger. He exchanged a look with Matt, who stood behind her.

"I don't know what you're doing, sir, but you need to keep in mind that this prisoner is a high security risk. Because of her classification, she is not allowed to be seen by other prisoners or by anyone other than a select number of guards. We've had to use extreme caution and use medical staff with a high level of clearance each time that she's had to be hospitalized. She's supposed to be dead, Agent Newman, remember?"

He remembered. "Is there anywhere *private* enough outside that we could take her?"

"You're obviously not hearing what I'm telling you, sir," she said sharply. "My orders regarding this prisoner are clear and specific."

"And do you really think that none of the other prisoners know she's here?" Austyn asked.

"There is absolutely no contact between them."

"Maybe since she's been at the Brickyard," Austyn argued. "But we have information from Iraq that the insurgents there *know* that Rahaf Banaz survived the U.S. attack on her lab. The only people we're trying to fool are the United Nations and Amnesty International."

"Look, Agent Newman, the communiqué I received regarding your visit doesn't change my overall charge."

"Captain Adams, my purpose here is to extract information that Dr. Banaz has not shared in almost five years under other interrogation. I want to try something different. I think it could prove beneficial to take her outside for some fresh air."

She stared at him for a moment. "I'd like to see your orders concerning the prisoner," she responded stubbornly.

"All right, Captain." Austyn motioned to Matt to dig the papers out of the briefcase. "I understand your concern, but as of today, her classification changes. These orders supersede your previous orders. As of this moment, she is to be classified as a Homeland Security detainee."

She took the papers that Matt offered and started looking through them. "Then take her. We can help you with transportation."

"We may take her with us if I deem it necessary, or she

may remain here." Austyn watched her reading the orders. He would do what he felt was necessary, but he didn't want to rub her nose in it. He was after cooperation, not hostility. Captain Adams appeared to be very good at what she did, and there was no telling if their paths wouldn't cross again.

"I'd like to talk to her here in your facility before we make any decisions," Austyn said in a reasonable tone, trying to make her understand. "Because time is critical until we know more about the nature of the bacteria, we don't want to waste time moving her to another facility. According to her files, the one leisure activity that Rahaf pursued while she was studying in the U.S. was hiking, getting outdoors. There were a number of references to how she loved being out in nature. Now, it may be heading up toward 110 degrees outside, but if moving her into the open air can jolt her a little, help her to open up, then I'd like to try it." He paused a moment. "Can you help us out with that, Captain?"

His plea worked. She nodded, satisfied. "We've fenced in an area in the back of the building where they used to dry bricks. It's walled in on two sides by the old kiln and a garage building. It faces the hills. We don't use it, as it doesn't meet security standards. You're welcome to it."

"Could she been seen there?" he asked, not really caring, but at the same time not wanting to make the personnel here feel as if whatever they'd done so far had no significance.

"Probably not," Adams said. "We have guards' housing on the adjacent hill."

"Okay," he said. "We'll talk to her there."

"Agent Newman, as I mentioned before, I don't think

you'll get any cooperation from her. The chances are that she won't go willingly outside with you or answer any of your questions. Do you want to have one of our interrogators work along with you?"

That suggestion had been made back in Washington, too. He was authorized to use whatever resources he needed.

"No." Rahaf Banaz looked like nothing more than a slender bag of bones. There was no way he'd risk losing her under rough interrogation. "Agent Sutton and I will handle it."

"Then would you like to have a couple of guards take her outside?"

So much for letting Rahaf go out willingly, Austyn thought. But he guessed there was probably no chance of that, anyway. He didn't know if she even had the strength to walk. He nodded. "Thanks."

As she relayed the orders to the guards, Matt motioned to Austyn and tapped his watch.

"Captain Adams," Matt said to her. "If you don't mind, I need to use a secure phone to call Washington."

"Of course. You can use the phone in my office. I'll show you."

Austyn decided to stay with Rahaf and make sure he didn't lose her, now that they were this close. As they opened the steel door, the soldier who'd been sent to find information on Rahaf's eating schedule came back. They really couldn't pinpoint the last time she'd eaten.

"All the prisoners are given three meals a day," she told Austyn. "But this one tends to nibble, at best."

The sound of a woman's voice came from the cell. "Come on. Stand up now. Get your legs under you."

Austyn went to the door and saw two female guards bent over at the waist, trying to drag Rahaf onto her feet. Either she was being stubborn, or her legs weren't strong enough to hold her weight. One of the guards jerked at the prisoner's arm.

"Be gentle with her," he found himself saying sternly.

Another guard went in. The room was now almost too crowded to maneuver her. The blanket over her shoulders fell on the threshold as they moved awkwardly through the cell. Rahaf was not helping at all.

Austyn eyed the old rag that once was a jumpsuit. One of the guards lost her grip on Rahaf momentarily and the prisoner collapsed, her chin hitting the cement floor with a loud thud.

After the years of working for Homeland Security, Austyn had thought that he'd snuffed out any sympathy for prisoners. They were enemies of the United States and lawbreakers. He'd always been quite happy putting them behind bars. He had no sympathy, in particular, for the educated and the disillusioned who enjoyed the comforts and freedoms democracy offered, while planning acts that would plant terror in innocent people's hearts.

Something was different here, he thought. Rahaf was different. There was something wrong in what he was witnessing. Her case was nothing like those he'd dealt with before in his career.

She had been an extremely promising student, and the Iraqi government had paid for Rahaf's undergraduate degree at Columbia University in New York City, in spite of her Kurdish heritage. She'd done her graduate work at California Institute of Technology. Her research and publications had been well received from day one. Coming back to Iraq, a fast-track career had been waiting for her. During the following years, she'd been a regular speaker at international symposiums around the world.

And now she was reduced to this.

Two guards on either side, taking hold of Rahaf by each arm, started to drag her to one end of the hall. Austyn had to swallow his objection this time.

He picked up the blanket from the floor. Tucking the folder he'd taken out from his briefcase earlier under his arm, he followed them. Windowless doors lined each side of the hallway. Going past one of them, he heard a man cry out. He hurried along, telling himself that he needed to catch up to Rahaf and the guards. The truth was, he knew, he didn't want to think about who else was in those cells or whether they deserved what was happening to them. He had one task that he needed to focus on.

They went through two sets of steel doors and crossed through a dim space that looked as if it had been a wood-working shop and storage area for the old brick-making facility. The air was warm and musty inside, and Austyn's boots kept sticking to something on the brick floor as they made their way through. Distant hills were visible through small windows, jagged with shards of broken glass. One of the guards unchained a door that opened to a yard of sand and brick.

Outside, an eight-foot chain-link fence with barbed wire along the top served as their only visible barrier to the hills. Beyond the enclosure, there was a short stretch of a man-made clearing with signs warning of land mines and another perimeter fence farther out. Beyond that, rocks and the rugged mountainous terrain took over. Austyn looked up, spotting the guards' station that Captain Adams had spoken of. He could imagine there were many places in the looming mountain where agents of the Taliban could be hidden, spying on what was happening in the old brick factory.

"Where would you like her?" one of the guards asked over her shoulder.

Austyn looked around the enclosed area. Garbage was strewn everywhere. There were no chairs, no benches, nothing to sit on. The yard was small and only a thin section of it by the fence was getting the sun right now.

"The ground by the fence will do," he told them, motioning to the area.

They took Rahaf to the fence and stood her against it. She slid down, her legs folding under her. Austyn quickly spread the blanket over her knees. She was too thin, too weak. Her chin sank to her chest again, her back against the fence.

"You can leave us alone," he told the guards.

"We'll wait by those doors, sir, if you need us."

He wouldn't, but he decided against pursuing it. So long as they were on the other side of the yard, it was fine with him.

Austyn waited until the guards had moved away before sitting cross-legged on the ground near her. He made sure to sit in the shade, as he could already feel the sweat running down his back. The heat here was different than anything he was accustomed to. It was so much more intense. An occasional waft of wind running through the yard didn't cool the skin but only raised the dust, making it harder to breathe. He'd give her ten minutes in the sun, and then help her move into the shade.

She wasn't meditating now. He could see that her eyes were partially open, but she refused to look up. The sun poured over her short-cropped hair and shoulders. He saw her take a deep breath.

"Dr. Banaz," Austyn started. He introduced himself again, identified the department he worked for in Homeland Security. There was no reaction. He told her about his partner and what Matt did, and that he would join them out here very soon.

"I know that you are fluent in English, so I'll just continue to speak. If you need any clarification on anything I say, however, please just ask me. Do you understand me?"

He watched her a moment, but she still made no sign.

"Your classification has changed, Dr. Banaz. I flew here directly from Washington with complete authorization to make you an offer of freedom and to meet any reasonable demand you might have…in return for your cooperation on a medical situation that has arisen."

No movement. Still no acknowledgement that she'd heard or understood anything he was saying. Austyn decided to get to the point. He opened the folder he'd brought along, leafed through it, and found the pictures he was looking for. There were some twenty photos, grotesque, showing bodies in advanced stages of decomposition.

"I know anything I say must come across as totally in-sincere, considering your detention these past few years. You have every right not to want to have anything to do with me…or even to hear what I have to say," Austyn said softly. "Dr. Banaz, I ask you to look at these, though. We're desperate. And by we, I don't mean only Americans. This situation could be happening anywhere in the world today.

It could be happening among your own people. We're afraid it might be the start of something devastating."

He started spreading the photos on the blanket on her lap.

She closed her eyes and turned her head. Austyn was relieved that she'd at least taken a peek at them.

"The same DNA sequence of microbes discovered in your lab in Baquba has been identified in the remains of these bodies," Austyn told her. "This is the first time we've seen anything like this outside of a laboratory environment. We don't know what to do with it or how to stop it…if there is a way to stop it."

A breeze threatened to blow the pictures away; he scooped them up, placing three of them on her lap and holding them there.

"These three bodies you see in the photos were teenagers. The others are their parents and innocent people who went there to help them, volunteer rescue workers. These were civilians, totally innocent of what's going on in the world." He paused, wondering if those words would mean anything to her. "We've never seen anything like this, bacteria this destructive and this fast-acting." He shook the pictures lightly. "These children and these adults…we suspect they died in less than an hour after being exposed."

"Some people are fortunate," she said under her breath. "I've been waiting to die for five years now."

Austyn, struck speechless, stared at her. He'd somehow expected that she might not break her silence. He noticed that she had a slightly British accent. But even more so than her words and the accent, he was stunned that she was looking at the pictures again. This time, her face was lifted enough that he could see her.

Rahaf's green eyes were a startling feature in her pale face. He'd never noticed their color from looking at the old pictures they'd had on file. But they shouldn't have been such a surprise. Unlike so many people from the Middle East, who had more of a Mediterranean look, Kurds were known for their more northern European complexions. The thirty or so pounds that Rahaf had lost while in prison made a difference, too, Austyn thought. With her face thin and pale, her eyes were far more startling than they would have been otherwise.

Without touching his hand, she pushed the pictures away and inched along the fence until she was sitting in the shade. He noticed that she'd not once looked at the mountains or the sky.

Something didn't sit right with Austyn, but he couldn't quite put his finger on it.

"They aren't the Adirondacks," he said, "but I thought you might enjoy being outside."

She was back to being silent, looking at a crumpled knot of cassette tape dangling from a roll of fencing a couple of feet ahead of her in the yard. A loop of the tape hanging down from the rest danced in the dry breeze.

Austyn held the pictures in his hand, keeping them in front of him where they were visible to her. "What we've seen with these bodies is unlike anything on record. The strain is connected to the microbes that were found in your laboratory and the samples that were collected there." He wasn't sure if he was repeating himself or not, but she didn't appear to be affected by the severity or urgency of what they were facing. If she cared at all, she wasn't showing it.

She gathered her knees to her chest and tucked the blanket tighter around her. She leaned her chin on her knees, lost in her own world once again.

Austyn noticed a mark above her left ear just inside her hairline and stared at it. A moon-shaped birthmark. He could see it through the short-cropped hair.

"I have to say, officially, that no one thinks that you have any personal connection to any biological attack…if that's what it is."

Her eyes cut to him for a second, conveying without a word how stupid she thought his statement was. She'd been rotting in prison for exactly that crime for all these years. He let it go.

"At this point we don't know how the microbe reached the United States. We don't know who is responsible for it. There are other agents who have been tasked with getting those answers," Austyn explained methodically, calmly. "My partner and I are here to seek your assistance as a scientist, as an expert. You're the only one with the years of research in this specific area that can possibly help us, to give us answers as far as what we should or shouldn't do. You were able to contain the microbe in a dormant stage in your lab. To start, we're hoping that you can tell us if the steps we've taken are good enough to contain the bacteria to where it is. Dr. Banaz, millions of people are at risk. We're trying to save lives."

Rahaf closed her eyes again.

Austyn wasn't ready to give up. "You're a scientist, one of the smartest in the world in this area. I can't undo the fact that you've been detained and moved around in this way. I'm sure no apology would suffice for the way you've been treated for all these years by my government. But I can, at least, tell you that no charges will be brought against you for your work on behalf of Saddam's regime."

It wasn't much of an apology, and she acted as if he hadn't said a word. The troubling part was that he understood her. There were far better ways to deal with her after her capture than what the CIA had done. Since the days of the Romans, people like Rahaf—with her intelligence and background—had always been considered a prize, part of the spoils of the war. The victorious nation would honor them and buy their cooperation. In any situation but this Iraq war, she'd have long been working in one of the top U.S. government labs, heading some important project, having her own staff of scientists. Austyn couldn't understand what had happened here, how they could have done so many things wrong. There was no excuse for how she'd been lost to them for so long.

"Dr. Banaz, since the execution of Saddam and his closest advisers, the new Iraqi government has been trying to move forward. The U.S. has also been trying to—"

Her eyes locked on his face.

"You didn't know that he was executed."

She looked away, but it didn't appear that she was upset by the news.

Austyn's thoughts turned to what he'd read in Rahaf's files. During her years of studying in the U.S., Rahaf had been a dedicated scholar, but she'd also been active politically. She had been outspoken about women's rights, and involved in a number of clubs. Her high energy level had been repeatedly referred to in college and graduate school files and letters.

When she'd returned to Iraq, someone in Saddam's regime had been smart enough to recognize her talents and interests. It didn't appear that she'd faced any discrimination because of her gender or her Kurd heritage. She'd been given her own staff and facility within a year of her return. Knowing this about her, Austyn could not quite figure out why she hadn't raised more hell during her detention. Transcripts of her CIA interrogations had contained no mention of her making demands regarding her rights.

He glanced at her again. Perhaps she had, and the files had been edited, he thought. It was terrible to think they may have killed the spirit in someone so valuable.

The warm, dry breeze swept through the yard, raising a cloud of dust. Despite the heat, he saw her shiver. He found himself staring at her thin arms, at her pale skin. She was definitely not well.

The sensation that something was off continued to bother him. He looked again at the birthmark above her ear and paged through the file he'd brought outside. He was looking for two pictures of Dr. Banaz that were in this file. One was of Rahaf leaving a conference in Stockholm. It was dated 2000. Large sunglasses hid most of her face. He stared at the shape of her chin, her high cheekbones. In the other photo, she was standing on a podium and delivering a speech during the same conference. There was no telling of the color of her eyes. Austyn held the picture at arm's length and compared it to the woman sitting before him. The same slender build and dark hair. She was simply much thinner now and she looked different with her buzz cut.

The door leading to the building opened. Austyn saw

Matt coming through it. He tucked the photos back inside the file folder, closed it and placed a broken piece of brick on it. Standing, he met his partner halfway across the yard, where they were out of earshot of both Rahaf and the guards.

"Anything?" Austyn asked.

Matt shook his head. "No new cases reported. And they're completely done with the sweep of the locations where each of the Maine victims came from. There's been no sign of the bacteria."

"So the monster was just lying there waiting for them to arrive?" Austyn commented.

His partner shrugged. "The only new info was that there's been a recommendation made by the team working out of the National Institute of Health to have mega quantities of some new antibiotic drug made and ready to go."

"What's the drug?"

Matt looked down at a notepad. "DM8A. I don't really know anything about it. Do you?"

Austyn summarized the information he knew for his partner. DM8A had been awaiting FDA approval for over a year now. It was originally designed to be given intravenously to fight infections resulting from internal injuries. Of everything out there, the antibiotic would be the strongest drug they had to fight resistant strains of necrotizing fasciitis. Still, this was simply a tweak of a basic format. The holdup in approving the drug stemmed from the fact that it was potent enough to shut down the liver of the patient in two to five percent of the cases. Of course, there were other side effects, too, but they were more of a nuisance than dangerous.

"The eggheads at NIH say that the effectiveness of

fighting this strain of bacteria with the DM8A is definitely
questionable," Matt told him. "But they're taking out the
biggest guns they have. They've ordered the pharmaceutical company to crank out as many doses of the antibiotic
as they can. If there's a widespread outbreak, they want it
ready for distribution."

"We've been trying to keep a lid on the situation since
it first showed up ten days ago," Austyn commented. "I
guess that was a wasted effort."

"Only one company is being used," Matt told him,
shaking his head. "Reynolds Pharmaceuticals. They're the
same ones who take care of the vaccines for our troops.
They do government jobs on a regular basis."

Austyn had worked before with a number of engineers
and researchers at Reynolds. He felt better that some confidentiality was being maintained.

"They're more worried that the antibiotic won't work
at all," Matt said, voicing his concern.

"Or if we can distribute it to the victim early enough to
have an effect."

A stronger gust of wind swirled through the yard,
raising dust and debris. Austyn looked over his shoulder
at where Rahaf sat. She had leaned her head back against
the fence, her eyes closed. The white column of her neck
was exposed. Despite all the years of hardship, it was impossible to miss her delicate chin and how well propor-
tioned her face was. In her healthy days, she surely must
have been considered a delicate and beautiful woman. He
glanced through the files containing the old photos of her.
Looking at them, he'd not considered the woman on the
podium beautiful. He knew, though, that many women

working in scientific fields made a point of trying to look plain, trying to be noticed solely for their intelligence and their contributions. It was like you could only be beautiful *or* smart. Not both.

A vague suspicion, not yet fully formed, wouldn't leave him.

He motioned with his head toward the scientist, and they took a couple of steps closer to her. Austyn stopped abruptly, though, and his partner followed suit.

"Did I miss something out here?" Matt asked.

Austyn shook his head and looked at Rahaf again. "You've read everything in Dr. Banaz's files. What color are her eyes?"

The other man shot him a curious look but went along. "Hazel. I expected them to be brown, but her student visa documentation said hazel."

"That's right. The file says hazel." He motioned with his head to the prisoner. "But *her* eyes are green."

"Hazel, green, blue…they're all close," Matt said, looking sharply at the prisoner. "You think this isn't Banaz?"

"I'm not ready to jump to any conclusions," Austyn replied. "How about an English accent? Do you remember reading anything in Dr. Banaz's files that she had a British accent?"

"That's not something that an interrogator would mention." He shook his head, staring at Rahaf. "She spoke to you?"

Austyn nodded.

"And she has a Brit accent? You're sure?"

Austyn nodded again.

"How could she have a British accent? She was educated in the U.S." He lowered his voice, looking suddenly concerned. "Are you saying that we might not have the right person here?"

They weren't far away, and Austyn hoped she heard pieces of their conversation. He *wanted* her to know of his suspicion.

"I don't know. But something doesn't feel right."

Matt shook his head. "How can she not be Banaz? She's undergone dozens of interrogation sessions over the years. We would have picked up the fact that she's the wrong woman."

"You'd think so," Austyn agreed.

"We have her fingerprints," Matt reminded him.

"The fingerprints were taken after her capture," he replied. "In spite of her years studying in the U.S., there was no reason for her to get fingerprinted. Those were pre-9/11 days, and unless she was applying for a green card, she wouldn't have had her prints taken. You know as well as I do that the security guidelines weren't the same as they are now. And as far as comparing it to anything the Iraqi government might have had, I doubt if anything was ever tracked down. Don't forget, we have never admitted that a body was recovered."

If Rahaf was listening to this conversation, she gave no indication of it. She hadn't moved. Austyn wondered if she was even breathing.

"The marines took her out of that lab," Matt argued. "She was wearing Dr. Banaz's badge. She was in possession of her keys. She matches her description. There was no reason to think otherwise."

"You're right," Austyn acknowledged. "There was no reason to think otherwise."

"She admitted that she was the scientist," Matt continued. "Now, why would anyone lie about something like that? Who the hell is crazy enough to spend all these years in jail, pretending to be someone else?"

"Someone who's trying to protect someone else."

He tried to remember some of the details of Banaz's files. There was no mention of parents, other than the fact that the girls were from a Kurdish tribe. He stared at the prisoner.

"The *girls*," he said aloud. "Her sister. They were only a year apart. What was the sister's name?"

Matt opened a folder and browsed through it for a moment. "Fahimah Banaz. There's not much about her here, except that she was a professor of political science at the University of Baghdad. She was only a year older than her sister, Rahaf. Missing. Suspected to have died back in 2003 in a bombing near the Tigris River part of University of Baghdad campus."

"Was her body ever recovered?"

Matt shook his head. "Not that we have any record of."

"What else do you have on Dr. Fahimah Banaz?"

"Nothing here," Matt told him. "I'll get on the captain's computer and find some information…whatever they have on the sister."

"Why don't you do that," Austyn said in a louder tone. "And make sure we have some pictures. Fingerprints would be ideal. It's possible that the university files in Baghdad might have something, too. Probably more than what's left of Saddam's government files. We need our people in Iraq to contact any faculty or students that might have had dealings with Professor Banaz. We can interview them on the phone and fly them over, if necessary."

Austyn looked at the prisoner again. Although her eyes were still closed and her posture was unchanged, she was with them, hearing every word. There was tension in every limb. A vein pulsed near her temple. Her face was suddenly reflecting some new stress. Now they were in business.

"Another piece of information that I want right away is Fahimah Banaz's education. Where did she go to school? I'm curious to know how much time she spent in England. Or whether she attended a British school in Iraq."

Matt and Austyn exchanged a look. There was a lot that didn't need to be said but they both understood. If the forces in Iraq happened to have picked up the wrong person, then there was a possibility that Dr. Rahaf Banaz was out there today, running free. If that were true, then it meant there was a strong chance she had a hand in engineering the bacteria's release. Matt headed toward the door across the yard.

Austyn walked toward the prisoner. He crouched down before her and stared at her face, studying every inch. He was close enough that it was impossible for her not to know he was there. It was a battle of will. It could have been a minute or five minutes, he didn't know. She finally opened her eyes and stared back.

"Another Dr. Banaz," he said flatly. "Which are you?"

Six

Reynolds Pharmaceuticals
Wilmington, Delaware

"They do this to us every time," the Southern California sales manager boomed. "They're yanking our chain again. They know we have a September 1 release date for the Strep-Tester Home Kit. They should know how big this thing is going to be—*if* we get it out there before the sore-throat season starts."

"A delivery shift of one month will hurt us, but it isn't going to kill us," the VP of Sales interrupted. "And Bill and Ned Reynolds have told me personally that the change in production schedules will create a marked improvement in the company's cash flow. The government is making special arrangements."

"Be that as it may, we're undercutting the credibility of our frontline sales guys in not delivering a new product when we promised."

"As a company, we can always use improved cash flow, but I agree with you," another district manager chimed in. "This is a major problem we have—we never say no to a quick buck. Frankly, when it comes to long-term planning, we stink. We don't stick to our strategic plan when we make 'adjustments' like this. I don't even know why we bother to diversify product lines. Whenever the government says jump, we say, How high?"

David Link looked around the room. He'd expected pandemonium, and he wasn't disappointed.

As the second-in-charge for North American sales, he'd had a half day lead over all the regional directors on the breaking company news.

David had been scheduled to be on vacation this week and next. Of course, in his position, no vacation was going to stop the top dogs from calling him on his cell phone. They wanted him at this one o'clock meeting in Wilmington today. The company was dropping a bomb on the sales department, so he'd made the two-hour drive. The good thing was that he and Sally and the kids were staying at his in-laws' beach house in Lewes. Although he was interested on how the sales force would react, he was looking forward to driving back to the beach tonight. These days, it seemed to be an increasingly rare event when they could get their family together under one roof for a dinner.

The uproar continued as management let the steam vent. It seemed that *everyone* wanted to get something off their chest. On the phone to Bill and Ned Reynolds, David himself had done some squawking when they'd told him of the decision to push back the release of their hottest nonmilitary product in two decades in order to accept another government contract.

Reynolds was one of the last privately owned, midsize pharmaceutical companies in North America, and its quarterly sales had been creeping up on $100 million over the past two years, with net profits on a steady twenty to twenty-five percent rise. Since the company's founding back in the 1960s, the majority of Reynolds's business had been government-related, a situation that had gotten them off to a strong start but had created severe shifts in revenues, depending on the administration in Washington and the political affiliation of the founding family. Recent strategic planning by Bill and Ned Reynolds, the second generation running the company, had produced a five-year plan and two major changes. One was for Bill to become a vocal contributor to the Republican party while Ned remained a Democrat. The other was to push a chunk of money into R & D. Their ultimate goal was to expand their prescription and over-the-counter drug production until their government contracts comprised roughly fifty percent of the business.

David looked at his watch. They'd started the meeting an hour ago and they had yet to get anywhere. He did some quick math in his head regarding how long it'd take to make the commute back to Lewes tonight, considering the traffic. He definitely didn't want to miss dinner with the family. Their eldest daughter, Jamie, was heading back to New York tomorrow morning.

"Why doesn't anyone give us a straight answer?" someone in the room asked. "It seems like we're screwing ourselves for no reason."

The grumbling continued as the VP of Sales repeated his position. David knew the guy was in over his head, in spite of having gone to prep school with one of the Reynolds brothers.

Well, David thought, this was as good as any time to chime in and minimize some of the damage. Perhaps, with a little luck, he could even help to wrap things up. While David had been en route to Wilmington today, Bill Reynolds had made a follow-up phone call to him. Bill knew that there would be a lot of objections to the company accepting this new contract, especially on the part of the sales force. He'd asked David to intervene, if necessary.

David had actually been honored by the call. It was reassuring to know that he was highly respected by the Reynolds brothers. Twenty-six years he'd devoted to this company, and it was always good to realize that you were trusted by the people above you on the management ladder, as well as below.

That was a curious thing, for David was seen in the company as a family man. In general, a strong family life always seemed to run counter to success in American business, but not at Reynolds Pharmaceuticals. In fact, Bill and Ned had been vocal about David as a role model for younger executives. They saw it as a strength that he cherished his wife and three children. And Bill had been very supportive recently when David and Sally had gone through some very difficult times. Their youngest son, Josh, was twelve, and nine months ago he'd been diagnosed with leukemia.

Of course, with Sally giving up her job and managing the brunt of Josh's hospital visits and treatments, David's own work hadn't suffered badly this past year. But he'd made some changes. He was now not only a lot more flexible with his own schedule, but also with those of his employees. Working with Human Relations to make his staff a "test case" for the company, David had offered a lot of leeway for working from home or scheduling business trips around family commitments. Since implementing these changes, the sales numbers for his group had gone off the company charts. Initially, Bill and Ned had been cautiously supportive of the changes, but with performance continuing to remain strong, they were now completely on board with his management techniques.

The second reason for David's popularity with the company had to do with his habit of not dictating orders, but explaining a situation clearly and giving his team all the facts. Of course, he'd do a major selling job on the decision he wanted them to make, but in the end his people always felt that they had an input in decisions.

With the situation that had been dropped on his lap here, he wasn't totally sold himself, but he had to give it a try.

"Let's put all the facts on the table," he broke in.

The undercurrent ceased momentarily. The VP of Sales nodded to him gratefully. David pulled out his notepad and conveyed some facts and figures that he'd put together as soon as he'd arrived at his office before the meeting.

"Rather than getting competitive quotes and all the rest of it, the undersecretary of Health and Human Services asks us to produce one million units of DM8A serum in two weeks. They know our production rate, and they're well aware that we're operating now at maximum capacity across the board. It's public knowledge that the Dover plant won't come online with Strep-Tester production until early September. They also know that the Scranton plant is ready to switch over to production of DM8A when FDA approval comes down. The bottom line is this—to come close to filling this order, everything else in the queue—including new orders and the processing of returns—*everything* would have to come to a screeching halt and the focus put on this one order. So why would we do that?"

Someone at the far end of the room responded. "HHS comes to us because they know that every one of our competitors would tell them to go pound sand with that kind of deadline."

David nodded. "You're right. At the same time, we know that with standard lead time for that kind of volume, the unit selling price for DM8A serum is planned at just under two dollars. But HHS is offering to pay us close to *fifty* dollars for each unit, *and* they're throwing in a one-time setup charge *and* authorization for overtime billing to run our facilities 24/7. Overruns are theirs, too. They'll take any extra units we can produce in that amount of time. In addition, the money will turn over net-ten…not the standard sixty to ninety-day payment."

As always, it felt great to work in Sales. David could see pens scribbling on paper and numbers being punched in the calculators.

"That's a lot of money," someone said.

Heads were nodding.

David looked around at the faces. "And who in this room is not part of our profit-sharing?"

The murmurs were starting to take on a more positive note.

"Of course, we all are," the California sales manager said in his booming voice. "But what's the rush? Is there a fire they're trying to put out? We've been hearing that DM8A isn't scheduled for FDA approval for another five months. So what's it about?"

"DM8A is a new antibiotic," David replied. "It's better than anything out there and they want it."

"Yes, but HHS doesn't spend this kind of money without months of red tape…unless there's some emergency disaster relief in the works. What's going on?"

David shook his head and deferred to the VP of Sales, who shrugged his shoulders. No one had the answer to the question…not even Bill or Ned Reynolds, as far as he knew. That did bother him somewhat, but he wasn't about to let his emotions be a distraction here.

David tapped his finger on his open notepad. "The answer to that question falls outside of our purview. The government is insisting on complete confidentiality. This is nothing new. We've done it before. We get paid generously to meet their demands and keep quiet about it. And it's not like we're making some kind of chemical weapon. They're asking for antibiotics. I say we do our part in supporting this large order."

The fight seemed to have seeped out of them. There were a few nods, no objections.

"Since this is obviously a done deal," the East Coast director said calmly, "we should be spending our time now coming up with a strategy on how to deal with preorders on Strep-Tester. Our customers won't be happy."

"Preorders of Strep-Tester aren't the only problem. How about the standing orders on existing products?" another person added.

"We're putting together numbers on warehoused product right now," the VP of Sales replied. "We'll have an impact report later today. With regard to the Strep-Tester, we've arranged for some ten thousand additional sample-size packages of testers to run through this coming week as we gear up for DM8A. Use these as giveaways. We're raising the ceiling on your expense budgets for the next two months. Wine and dine the big accounts. Do what you're good at. District sales managers will provide information sheets to the reps regarding what we'll call a possible delay at this point. Tell them that we'll be shipping production lots before October 1. You all know the drill. Keep them happy, whatever it takes."

In addition to a year's worth of promotional brochures and literature, advertisements in key publications and months of beating the pavement, only five hundred samples of Strep-Tester had been distributed by the sales force. David knew the ten thousand additional samples would definitely be a help.

He also knew that everyone in this room, along with the entire sales force, would have medicine cabinets full of samples of DM8A, in case of an emergency. They weren't fools, and this was one perk that went with being in this line of business. The general public might have to wait in lines and pay an exorbitant price for new medications, but not drug company reps.

"Okay." The VP of Sales stood up. "We all know the routine. Production information is not to leave this room. Now, let's get to work."

Seven

Brickyard Prison, Afghanistan

For five years, she'd kept up the lie and not one person had questioned her identity. There'd never been any hint of a doubt. No one had ever asked if she wasn't the person she claimed to be. Until now.

Rahaf hadn't been found because the Americans thought they had her in their prison. Fahimah had no doubt that if they went searching for her sister, they'd find her. There were so many informers. From the little news that had been trickling inside, she knew the country was in the middle of a civil war. There were so many desperate people that could be bought for so little. There would be no sense of loyalty toward an Iraqi scientist from Saddam's regime, especially when that scientist was a woman and a Kurd.

No one knew how much Rahaf had risked in attempting to save her people. No one knew what she had sacrificed.

Now that the Americans knew, no place would be safe for her sister. Rahaf would never have a chance.

Fahimah pressed her forehead against the wall and closed her eyes, trying to block out the pictures the American agent had shown her. She couldn't forget. She had seen the wounds herself…in real life. She'd seen what that microbe or bacteria or whatever they called it could do to a person in such a short time.

Her sister's leg had been exposed to the bacteria in the lab. As Fahimah watched and listened to her sister's cries, a retired Kurdish doctor had amputated Rahaf's leg. She still would have died from the disease without the serum she had to inject in herself continuously over the following days. If what the agent was saying was true, the same serum could have possibly saved the lives of those American children—the ones in the pictures. Perhaps the same serum could have stopped the bacteria from emerging into something much more contagious.

Abruptly, she turned away from the wall. She didn't want to feel sorry for them. Fahimah told herself she had no sympathy left in her, not after all the years that they had left her to rot in one prison cell after another, left her locked up without ever being charged for any crime. The twisted irony was that Rahaf had never committed any crime, either.

Fahimah had never seen the hallways they'd passed through to get to this room. She looked up at the high ceiling, the whitewashed walls. The door had a small window with some kind of silver glazing that blocked any view of the hallway. She guessed they were probably watching her through it. She looked up. A lightbulb dangled from the middle of the ceiling. The cot in the corner had clean sheets, blankets and a pillow. The room was unlike any cell they had ever locked her in. On the table next to it, a tray of food sat untouched. This was nothing like the food she'd been fed for all these years. It looked like *ghormeh sabsi,* a Persian dish of greens served over rice. The smell made her remember Oxford, of the little restaurant on Cowley Road.

Fahimah hadn't thought of those days for a long while. It seemed like another lifetime.

The photos came into her mind's eye again. She'd been told they were only children. She and her sister had suffered when they were that young. After all that had been done to them and to their family, after all that they had witnessed, she'd had many occasions in her life to wish that they had died. The old anger rose up in her, and she hated her inability to stop it. All her life, Fahimah had forced herself not to feel the past, not to care about it. For longer than she'd been held prisoner by these people, she'd taught herself how to be indifferent, not to remember. But the floodgate was bursting open, the pain was rushing in, the memories were all around her. The helplessness was overwhelming, but she couldn't fight it. The burning in her brain was too much. She couldn't escape it.

The closest thing within her reach was the tray of food. She pushed it from the table with one sweep of her hand, sending everything flying into the middle of the room. Fahimah listened to the clatter of the metal dishes, eyed the scattered food. There was strength in the release of anger.

She'd put up with imprisonment for five years…and for nothing. They would go back to the university in Baghdad.

They would find other professors who would remember
her. They would detain and interrogate students who must
have graduated by now, but who would be able to help
them. They would dig into her personnel files. Fahimah had
studied at Oxford. Yes, she had a British accent, for she'd
spent nine years of her life in England. She'd always been
careful to hide it. Today it had ruined everything. All the
American agents had to do now was just ask. They would
find her sister. And now, with what was going on in
America, the disease caused by the bacteria, they would pin
the entire thing on Rahaf.

The bedding was next. She tore the blanket off. The
sheets ripped in her thin fingers. Her own strength surprised her. She didn't know where it came from, but it was
there. She upended the mattress, ripped the pillow open
using a sharp metallic edge of the cot. Clumps of synthetic
foam spewed out. She wanted to find relief in this destruction. But there was no relief. Her anger only escalated.

Enough was enough. She had paid for the nonexistent
crime that these Americans thought her sister was guilty
of. She and Allah were witnesses to the fact that Rahaf had
paid a stiff penalty, too. Fahimah couldn't take it anymore.

The cot was light, and she lifted it and threw it against
the door. The loud bang echoed through the room. She
looked around wildly, at the chaos she'd created. This
should have made her feel better. But it didn't.

Suddenly, she felt very tired. She crouched against the
wall for a moment and caught her breath.

The agents from the U.S. were here to make a deal, to
convince her to help them. At least, this was what the one
named Newman said. He was clearly in charge. She had

to take advantage of that before they were certain of the truth. They had played her. She could do the same.

Fahimah stood and walked to the door. She raised both fists to the small window and hammered on it.

"Why did you have to show those pictures to me? I had nothing to do with it. I hate you. I'm tired of this. Do you hear me?"

She looked over her shoulder at the cot sitting on its side, at the sharp edge sticking out at the corner. She stepped away from the door, jerked at her sleeve and looked at her wrist. With a grim smile, Fahimah looked back at the cot and started toward it.

They must have been waiting just on the other side of the door, for she didn't have to take more than a couple of steps. There was a click behind her and the door opened. Agent Newman stepped in ahead of two guards.

"Stop right there, Dr. Banaz. We don't want to do anything stupid, now, do we?"

Eight

Faas Hanlon climbed out of the helicopter and moved quickly out from under the whirling blades. Two of his top people were waiting for him near three black SUVs parked at the edge of the cliff overlooking Boynton Canyon. Agents were on phones and laptops in each of the vehicles.

The site below was something out of a Steven Spielberg film set. Large silver-and-white tents covered sections of the canyon. Police tape and ropes had been set up all along the parameter. Dozens of police cars parked in the vicinity of the resort kept away curiosity-seekers. Crime labs set up inside trucks and vans were parked everywhere inside the restricted area. The tents hid most of the foot traffic, but the occasional glimpse of people from this view revealed that they were dressed in some kind of protective gear and masks.

"Give me the status, Bea," Faas demanded of the woman standing beside him.

"We've contained the site, sir," Bea Devera shouted back, pointing out the perimeter. Her Homeland Security jacket flapped in the wind caused by the chopper.

"I can see that. What about casualties?"

The situation was more critical than any disaster they'd encountered as yet in this administration. Every investigative department in the government was working together to figure out exactly what it was that they were facing. The potential damage was unknown, but the speed with which the disease struck was stunning.

"Five confirmed dead so far. The two occupants of the truck, the two police officers who found them, and one jogger who got too close to the scene before our search-and-rescue teams arrived."

"Where are the bodies?"

"They just airlifted the last one out of here. The others are en route to our facility in Phoenix."

Faas looked at the folder Bea held under one arm. "Pictures?"

"They're not pretty," she said grimly. She handed him the folder. "There are two Polaroids here. We took a lot more with the digital cameras. They should already be available to view online. You can look at them when we go down to the site."

Faas looked hard at the photos. The pictures were taken from outside of the truck. A dead police officer, showing early signs of decomposition on his face, was sitting against the door.

"Do we know exactly how fast the bacteria killed?"

"No, we don't. From the time the police officers called in after finding the bodies in the truck to the time when our people started arriving on the scene was two hours and fifteen minutes. By then, all five were dead."

"But I was told the officers called in when they realized they were infected."

"Yes, sir. But we lost contact with them about ninety minutes before arriving on the scene. These canyons do funny things to communication devices. The locals say there's a vortex here—"

"Two hours to respond," Faas snapped unhappily. "That's too slow. These people don't understand the severity of what we're facing yet."

"They do now, sir," Bea said in defense. "Most of our equipment and experts were on the East Coast. We were operating under the mistaken premise that the bacteria had been localized to Maine. We had to fly most of these people in from L.A. The mobile crime labs came in from Phoenix, but they couldn't get on the site until the proper protective gear arrived."

Faas appreciated Devera's loyalty to her team.

"How about the local emergency response?" he asked.

"They were instructed not to approach the victims," the other agent explained. "Local police were tasked with closing the trails and keeping the gawkers away."

Without divulging specifics, Homeland Security had communicated these instructions overnight to every law enforcement agency across the country.

"Beyond the initial five people, we're certain that no one else has been infected?" he asked.

Bea exchanged a look with the other agent.

"We can't say that for certain. We don't know where the two teenagers in the truck were before stealing the vehicle.

We haven't even been able to positively ID the two," she explained. "There were a couple of backpacks and wallets in there, but we're not sure if they're stolen property, as well."

Faas turned as a command control van pulled up behind the SUVs. This was a new method of investigating. The agents in charge weren't being allowed on-site.

"As far as our people being infected," the other agent told him, glancing toward the van, "they seem to have everything under control down there. The protocol we're following is similar to that for an Ebola outbreak."

Bea broke in. "Now that the van has arrived, we'll be directing operations from up here."

A remote-control investigation. They were expected to work like surgeons who use computers to operate on patients lying in hospitals on the other side of the country. Faas grimaced at the thought, not for an instant wanting to be on an operating table under those conditions.

"Maine and now Arizona," he said aloud. "Any connections between the victims? Any similar places they visited? Things they ate or drank? Anything that ties them together? This folder is empty. I need a lot more." He handed the manila folder back to Bea.

"As I said, we don't even have a positive ID. Everything has been taken away to the lab. We're hoping that in a couple of hours we'll have more to report."

"Hoping isn't enough. You'd better be sure that you have a *lot* to report," Faas said impatiently. He was frustrated and snapping at his people, not that it made him feel any better.

"Have you been in contact with Agents Newman and Sutton about this?" he asked her, softening his tone.

"Yes, I spoke to Agent Sutton just before you landed."

He'd spoken to Matt a couple of hours ago. They'd located Dr. Banaz but they didn't have any information yet.

Faas noticed a news helicopter had appeared over the canyon. Two military choppers approached the newcomer and the media aircraft swung around and started back the way it came.

"What the hell are they doing here?"

"I'm afraid it's already out," Bea said, frowning. "I assumed you knew. The dead jogger took a picture of the truck and bodies with his cell phone and sent it to KPHO in Phoenix. I just heard that they showed it on the air about five minutes ago. It's just a matter of time before the national media is camped out here."

Faas squinted his eyes against the bright sun and watched the news chopper disappear behind a distant red rock butte. He had to warn the president. He'd been involved with the decision to keep the news of the disease a secret from the beginning. The shots of the site that this news crew was carrying back wouldn't help.

Creating mass hysteria had been a primary concern from the start. The president and his advisers had decided that containment, preparation for other outbreaks, and vigilance were the best course of action. Now, having appeared to have contained the disease within each outbreak location, they needed to track the microbe to its source. As far as Faas was concerned, that was exactly what Austyn Newman would accomplish.

Even in handling the potential source of the microbe, however, this president was so different from the last. President Penn's position was that the U.S.'s sometimes justifiable fears about Middle Easterners had been exploited too much for political advantage. Penn felt that immigrants here had suffered enough this past decade. There was enough hatred and prejudice as it was. They didn't need fingers pointed at them without substantial proof.

Faas understood the president's sentiments. He was an immigrant himself. His father was Danish, his mother from Curaçao. An only child from a broken marriage, he was shipped off to the U.S. to live with a great-uncle when he'd been in the sixth grade.

As he'd grown up here, discrimination and prejudice had been immediate and deliberate at school, at the jobs he'd held during high school, and on the playing fields. He was black to some, white to others, a foreigner to all of them. He was smart, spoke English with an accent, worked hard, didn't break the rules, and that made him an outsider. He was everything other kids didn't want him to be. It was only when he'd gotten into the Foreign Service program at Georgetown that things had begun to change for him personally.

His youth had prepared him well for life, though. Faas's position as intelligence chief at Homeland Security dictated that he suspect *everyone,* and he believed that it would be inexcusable for him to overlook the forest as he searched for the poisoned tree. He had a job to do, and he would do it.

In the president's desire for secrecy at this point, however, he was entirely supportive. Faas Hanlon was the last person who wanted to be going before news cameras once an hour to tell the American public that they still didn't know anything.

They'd done a good job so far of keeping the lid on the

outbreak in Maine. Sedona, a more wide-open area, would be a different story. In the canyon, where the police crews were holding back the crowds, a news van had moved in and was raising its broadcast antenna. Yes, Sedona was going to be a problem.

The cell phone vibrated in his pocket. Faas stepped away from the others and looked at the display. Well, he thought with a sigh, he wouldn't have to call the president.

John Penn was calling *him*.

Nine

Brickyard Prison, Afghanistan

"There's nothing else." Matt frowned, his fingers flying over the keyboard as his eyes scanned the screen. "This is all duplication. There is virtually nothing about her online, other than occasional references to her as missing."

"What about the University of Baghdad Web site?"

"Same thing. The links go to the new Web sites set up over the past three or four years. Everything took a while to rebuild after Saddam's regime fell and the civil war started. The new sites have nothing we want." He clicked over the classified intelligence Internet engines. "Look, even the archived Web presences going back the past decade show very little. These are the pages that were in existence during the years she was on the faculty."

Austyn's eyes ran over the pages. "How about the political science department Web page?" he asked.

"Just her name on the list of faculty. No pictures, no in-dividual pages, nothing."

"Go to the last year. What shows up on the faculty list?"

"This is it." Matt clicked back to the main page of the university. There were a few pictures of the buildings and some links to the different departments, but nothing useful. "They were worrying about other things at this point."

"Like 'shock and awe.'" Austyn, looking over his partner's shoulder, frowned at the screen. "And the Brits had nothing from her time at Oxford?"

"Grades and evaluations. Not a picture, not a fingerprint, nada. We could hunt up roommates and professors, but there's nothing online."

"So what you're saying is that we're wasting our time looking for Fahimah Banaz on the net."

"You got it." Matt nodded. "She just predates the era of the 'information superhighway,' as you old guys like to call it."

"Yeah, the Dark Ages," Austyn retorted.

The younger agent got serious again. "We've got agents in Baghdad. We can send a couple of them over to the university and have them physically go through what's left of the old personnel files."

"Let's get the ball rolling on that."

"Also, we could have our field people start some discreet inquiries about Rahaf."

"If the initial queries turn up nothing, we'll have to move quickly past the 'discreet' part. We don't have time to waste if she's out there and behind this."

"If we get nothing right away, we'll offer rewards for any information about her," Matt suggested. "If she's out there, someone will know something. Offer U.S. dollars, and the locals tend to talk."

"Good."

Austyn straightened up and moved to the wire-reinforced window separating them from Dr. Banaz in the other room. He raised the blinds and looked in at the woman.

He'd had her moved after she'd torn up the other cell. Through the window, they could both see each other. This room was furnished with a cot, as well. A new tray with food and drinks had been brought in, but she had yet to touch it. Austyn had positioned two female guards inside the room with her. He wouldn't risk having her hurt herself.

She was sitting cross-legged on the floor, her back against one of the walls. Her eyes were closed. The old blanket was spread across her lap. She was back to her meditation pose. He wondered if she really did have the ability to escape her surroundings mentally. She had to. How else could she have survived and kept her sanity for all these years? If the hole in which he'd found her was any indication of the type of cells she'd been kept in, it was amazing that she hadn't tried to take her own life a hundred times.

Inside the room, one of the guards said something to the other. Each room was sound-proofed. Austyn didn't hear what they said, but he could see that they both were watching the prisoner. It was obvious from their wariness and overt bravado that they were a little afraid of her.

Not a muscle moved on the prisoner's face. Her hands rested calmly on her knees. She looked to be totally at peace. He was a window-shopper when it came to things like meditation. He admired those who could do it. But to him meditation was almost the same as relaxing, and that

was something that he lacked in the gene pool. His parents
were the same way, and his siblings. No one in his family
took vacations. They took on projects.

He wished he knew more about her. Matt and Austyn had
left Washington with hundreds of pages of files on Rahaf, but
there was nothing worthwhile in any of them about Fahimah.
Matt had logged into the CIA and FBI files, archived files
from the NSA, MI5, Interpol, Scotland Yard, everywhere.
He'd even queried the FSB in the Kremlin. Nothing of any
use. She was a nonthreat, and that made her nonexistent. She
didn't even warrant a picture or a fingerprint anywhere they'd
looked. If it wasn't for the bio at the end of an article published in London back in the late nineties, Austyn would
have pushed aside the suspicion he had of the two sisters
switching places. The article was about some Sufi poet, "In
the Light of Rabi'a of Basrah," and it had a short biography
of Fahimah Banaz. Educated at Oxford. This was the only
piece of information that existed on her on the Internet. As
far as Austyn was concerned, though, it was enough.

Her eyes opened. Through the glass divider, their gazes
locked for a couple of seconds before she closed them
again. She was no criminal. Austyn could feel it in his gut.
She was lying, possibly sacrificing herself. A martyr,
maybe. It was a stereotype, but if she was Fahimah, then
she had given up everything for a sister. But if she was
Rahaf, was she capable of the type of destruction that was
happening in the U.S.? No, he didn't think so.

All he really knew for sure was that this woman was all
they had, and Austyn had to win her cooperation somehow.

"I just received some pictures of the Sedona incident,"
Matt told him.

Austyn walked back to the computer. They'd heard the news only an hour ago. This was their worst nightmare. It meant that the bacteria could pop up anywhere at any time. The ten days in between had given them a false sense of security. Austyn had known what they'd seen in Maine couldn't have been a onetime thing.

His gut twisted as Matt started the slide show of the digital photos. The bodies outside of the truck were in very early stages of decomposition. The excruciating pain on one of the faces forced him to look away momentarily. Austyn glanced in the direction of the window again.

"It's getting worse," Matt said under his breath. "Looking at the pictures of the victims on that island in Maine… nothing was identifiable. But these…they're still human. You see it right there…what's happening to them."

"I'd like her to see these," Austyn told his partner.

"Are you sure?" Matt hesitated. "Especially if she's not Rahaf…"

"No amount of arguing will get the message across like these pictures. She needs to see them. I want her to know what's happening." He took his laptop out of his briefcase. "Load it onto this. I'll take it in to her."

Matt started booting up the computer.

Captain Adams walked in. She took a look at the window separating them from the prisoner before turning to them.

"Is it true?" she asked. "I just got word of another attack in the U.S."

"We don't know if it was an attack."

"Right," she said, skepticism lacing the word.

"We're only classifying it as an outbreak at this point. Both occurred in areas that are not exactly population centers. If they're part of an attack, the perpetrators are not trying to do any major damage."

The captain nodded. Austyn motioned with his head to the pictures on his partner's screen.

"We've just received these shots of the victims in Arizona. It's pretty ugly."

Adams moved behind the desk and went through the pictures, her face grim. "What's the number of fatalities for this one?"

"Five, as far as we know," Austyn answered. "It could have been a lot worse. But thankfully, those two police officers described the bodies with enough clarity that no other local emergency personnel were exposed."

He wondered if those poor souls really knew how painful and horrifying their deaths would be.

"Here you go." Matt handed the laptop to Austyn. "You've got it all, including the info we turned up on…uh, on the prisoner earlier."

"I hear Rahaf has shown more life in this past hour than she's displayed for five years," Adams commented.

They hadn't told Adams about Austyn's suspicions. There was no reason to muddy the waters until they were a hundred percent positive. The same went with their director back in the U.S. Austyn wanted to have proof first. His partner agreed. They had a suspect in custody. That was a start.

"The last pictures disturbed her. I'm hoping that these will upset her even more."

"I'm surprised. I didn't think she had any human feeling left. You might break her yet."

Break her. Nice term, Austyn thought ironically. He was

not exactly made for this side of the business. He certainly hoped she would open up to him, though he was only cautiously optimistic.

Austyn carried the laptop into the adjoining room and directed the guards to wait outside. Dr. Banaz gave no indication that she'd heard him coming in. He didn't bother with a chair and sat on the floor beside her, leaning his back against the wall and stretching his legs out in front of him.

Without saying anything, he studied the room from this angle. Whitewashed walls. The furnishings were the same as those she'd torn up in the other cell. He stared at the separating window. The overhead light cast a shadow on the glass and very little was visible from this angle. He barely made out someone backing away from the window. He guessed it was Captain Adams.

"Now I know what a fish in an aquarium feels like," he said under his breath. "Have you ever been to an aquarium?"

She didn't answer.

He turned to her. "Do you feel rested after meditating? Is it like getting a good night's sleep?"

He was surprised to have her open her eyes and look at him. Her gaze spoke volumes about how pointless she thought his questions were.

"I don't want to sign up for your Meditation 101 class, Professor Banaz," Austyn told her. "But I need your attention for a few minutes. We've just received some news that my partner and I believe you should be made aware of."

He didn't expect small talk and she didn't disappoint. Austyn opened his laptop and sat it on the floor between them. He brought up the pictures they'd just received.

She only looked at the screen for a second before turning her head away.

"You're making it way too easy for me," he said quietly. "Dr. Rahaf Banaz would look at these pictures."

"What do you know?" she murmured. "What do you know about anything?"

"I'm trying to know."

He waited, but she said nothing more.

"Rahaf Banaz would force herself to look at these photographs, gruesome and painful and unpleasant as they are, because she is a scientist, and her professional curiosity would take an upper hand. Her mind would ask a hundred questions. She'd want to know the specifics of where and how…the circumstances, the time of death. She's ask what lab work has already been done on the remains of the victims. She'd demand to know the results. Am I wrong?"

The woman still kept her eyes averted. She seemed to be focused on a crack in the wall opposite them.

"No amount of time in prison would shut down that side of her. As a biochemist, this is her field, the topic she spent a decade of her life researching. Someone else has done this, created the potential for an epidemic. She knows she is innocent. She knows that if her captors had any intelligence, they would recognize that, as well. She had a genetically compatible strain of this bacteria in her labs five years ago, but she didn't allow it to be unleashed. Not against the enemies of Saddam Hussein, even when they were knocking on her nation's door. She understands the danger of what is out there better than anyone else in the world, perhaps. That's why she'd care."

Her head turned. She stared at the screen. He had her. Rahaf *or* Fahimah. He was connecting, penetrating the thick veil of indifference that she had used to protect herself…or her sister…for so long. She was responding.

"Sedona, Arizona. Five people are dead," he said, paging slowly through the pictures. He watched the expression on her face. The green eyes were glued to the screen. "This happened today, only a few hours ago."

From the clenching of the muscles along her jawbone, he knew she was trying to hide her feelings, but it was an impossible task. The green eyes were expressive, and patches of color crept up her neck and into her sallow cheeks. She was clearly disturbed by the images.

"Do you know how far Arizona is from Maine?" he asked.

He expected no answer, but he waited a moment, anyway.

"Your sister would know that," he said.

"Some three thousand miles," she whispered. "I've been to both places."

Her answer caught him by surprise. They knew that Fahimah had never been to America, not as a student or a tourist. No visa had ever been issued to her. Rahaf could have been to both places. Nice try, he thought. The information was basic enough that an educated person could have come up with the answer. At the same time, if going along with her playing the role of Rahaf was the way to get her to cooperate, then he'd play along.

"The two outbreaks are three thousand miles apart," he said with a nod. "So far, we have found no possibility of contact between the two groups of victims."

She'd leaned her head back against the wall. Her eyes slowly closed. He wasn't sure if she was listening to anything he was saying or not. He wasn't used to being shut down like this. He thought they'd started a dialogue, albeit with his side a little more vocal than hers. He slapped the top of the laptop down.

"Back to meditating?" he asked thinly.

Getting no immediate answer from her, he decided to let her have it. "I'm not here to interrogate you, Dr. Banaz. I don't have any agenda other than what I told you. For most of your life, you've claimed to be a scientist. Well, that's what I am. It's what I do. I prevent bad things from happening. I try to stop the spread of illnesses that can hurt people. And I've read enough of your files to know that your facility was never tied in to any of the mass poisoning of Kurds or the Iranians during the Iran-Iraq War."

He laid the laptop aside. She was listening.

"Rahaf Banaz was involved with many humanitarian causes in New York. I'd like to think she hasn't changed, that we have a lot in common. I believe that it was Saddam's government and the estrangement between our governments that colored our view of what you were doing."

He let that sink in a moment before continuing.

"But we have a problem that could become an international disaster. It involves all of us, you and me included. You've seen the pictures. They're real. They…"

"I wasn't meditating," she interrupted him.

He had to reel in the rest of his lecture. He turned to look at her. She was staring at the window to the adjoining room. Austyn was happy to see that no one was standing there. He didn't want anything distracting her.

"I was thinking," she told him.

He waited for her to say more, but she was silent. "Are you thinking about helping me?"

She gave a hesitant nod. "Yes, I'll help you."

"I'm very relieved."

"I don't have any quick answers for you." She gathered her knees against her chest and pulled the blanket around her shoulders. "I've been a prisoner for too long. My work seems almost a dream to me now."

"We will change that," he said encouragingly. "We can show you all the laboratory results we have relevant to the victims. Naturally, we don't have the DNA sequence of the microbe from today's incident yet, but you can start looking at what we have from the Maine outbreak."

Minutes of silence dragged by. Austyn didn't care if she felt the need to rehearse her words a few times in her head first. The important thing was that this was the most she'd communicated with anyone since her capture.

"I was never told what was recovered from my lab after the bombing."

"Very little."

Her green eyes told him that she didn't believe him.

"We wouldn't be here asking for your help if any documentation had survived." He was telling the truth. "There were test samples that were collected, but all the files had been destroyed."

Austyn could have sworn that a satisfied expression crossed her pale features. Of course!

"But you knew that," he said. "You destroyed them yourself."

She didn't deny it. And this also explained how she'd survived the bombing. She'd been found in an office in the basement of the building, where she must have been shredding files. The section of the facility that housed the labs had been demolished by the bombing. Only a refrigerated safe in one corner of the labs had survived the devastation. It had contained a single vial of the microbe.

"Did anyone else live through the bombing?" she asked.

It was sad that all these years in prison and she'd never been able to ask these questions. Fahimah or Rahaf. Whichever sister she was, she'd been in that building. If she was Rahaf, she knew the people who worked there.

"No. You were the only one," he told her.

She showed no grief, but she looked away. Austyn saw Adams cross the window again. Fahimah's eyes flickered toward the glass.

"You are correct," she said. "I don't like fish tanks."

"You don't have to stay here," he told her. "Name the place, the facility. We'll take you wherever you want to work. Time is very important, though. We have labs available in this region or in Europe. We'll find as many people as you need to work with you. Some of the researchers in those facilities, you might even know."

He wasn't sure if this last bit of information was positive or negative, considering he still couldn't decide who she really was. She didn't look alarmed, however.

She rested her chin on the blanket covering her knees. She was silent again for a very long time. It was hard for Austyn not to push, not to encourage her to make a decision. Patience wasn't his middle name, but he had to allow her to set the pace. Whatever he'd done so far was working.

"There's not enough time to start everything fresh. To run new tests and wait for results," she said.

"I agree. That's why we're here. We have people in the U.S. working on this, but we don't have much hope for a quick solution there."

"You want an antidote…a serum to stop the microbe."

"We don't think standard antibiotics will work quickly enough."

"They won't," she said, a faraway look coming into her eyes. She seemed to be thinking about something else.

"What can you tell us?"

She continued to gaze into space for a moment.

"What I destroyed in the lab in Diyala wasn't all of my research," she said finally. "I have files."

She was lying now. Something in her voice…in her face…told him. Austyn was no fool. She had no reason to tell him the truth, and it would make perfect sense for her to send them on a wild-goose chase. Put out the decoy and go the other way. It worked for Osama bin Laden. It was the standard operating procedure in every peace negotiation in the Middle East, and had been for the past fifty years. Austyn could see it would be the same with the Banaz files. He could feel it coming.

Don't be such a cynic, he told himself. *Keep an open mind.*

"Okay, do you think your research files have been safe? Iraq has been a mess for some time. Where did you leave the files?"

Her silence was his only answer.

Austyn decided to change direction, to work on her empathy again. "The sample microbe we found at your lab. Did you witness the effects of the microbe on complex organisms?"

She nodded.

"Laboratory animals?"

"No," she said quickly. "I… I…" Her voice trailed off.

His mind jumped at the possibility. "Humans?" he asked hesitantly.

"One," she said quietly. "One person was accidentally exposed to the microbe."

Austyn saw her green eyes mist up before she looked away. She wasn't lying now.

"You watched him die?"

"I watched him suffer. But no, death did not ensue. There is a remedy. The microbe can be stopped."

Ten

"We need a specific location. Give me the sector. We're not mobilizing personnel without knowing *where* specifically we're going and *what* specifically we're after." General William Percy, commander of the multinational forces in northern Iraq, barely waited until Faas Hanlon was through talking before leaning in to object. "This is not some picnic excursion."

"I know that, General," Faas retorted in the same sharp tone. "I told you that we're operating by the seat of our pants. As of yesterday, fifteen Americans are dead. Thanks to the media, the American public has now seen images of those victims. We have no answers to give people, and with every passing hour the news reports are adding fuel to the fire. Fear is a very real problem now. If there is another outbreak, people could panic. We're talking about an entire terrified population with nowhere to run. People don't even know what they'd be running from. We have no choice but to pursue every option."

"All I'm asking for is a specific location," Percy barked. "We've lost enough troops. I won't move soldiers into any area unless I have some intelligence data."

"She's *not giving* us anything too specific," Faas Hanlon barked back. "Erbil International Airport. She's telling us to get her there, and then we'll get the next step."

"We can make her talk," Percy said matter-of-factly. "Even with the new directives."

"We've had her for five years under the old rules, sir, and she's said nothing," Faas argued. "She's in the custody of Homeland Security agents now. She's cooperating with us, and we intend to work with her."

"You don't even know if she's behind all of this or not. Your people aren't experienced enough to—"

"They obviously had enough experience to get her talking," Faas broke in, defending his agents. "The woman is not behind these outbreaks. She's been in black sites for five years. She's had no contact with the outside world. There's no way she could be running some biological attack on the U.S. long-distance from our own prisons."

"Your people have determined that the only known match for the bacteria was found in her lab," Percy reminded him sharply.

"We're getting sidetracked, gentlemen."

Everyone in the room swung around to look at the large-screen TVs at the far end of the room. President Penn's face was stern and he had the look of an annoyed schoolteacher.

Over a dozen top people from various branches of the armed forces filled the table in the room. The vice president was here as well. The head of the Joint Chiefs sat beside General Percy, and the commander of CENTCOMM—the Unified Combatant Command unit for the Middle East and Central Asia—sat on the other side of him. President Penn was on the center TV screen. The flanking screens showed the others gathered in the West Wing conference room. The director of the CIA sat opposite the national security adviser. The Speaker of the House and the head of FEMA were both in attendance. Faas looked at the director of Homeland Security seated beside the president. It would ultimately be President Penn's call, but the commander in chief's face was giving nothing away.

The meeting had a short agenda. Updates were provided on Reynolds Pharmaceuticals' ramped-up schedule for the DM8A antibiotic. The first batch was coming off the production line in five days. There were distribution issues that needed to be addressed—where, how many units, instructions and waiver information in the event of release and public consumption. They still didn't know if this specific antibiotic would have any effect on the strain of microbe that was producing the new necrotizing fasciitis they were facing. They couldn't afford not to pursue every option, though. Faas hoped the reports from the FBI labs in Phoenix, where the bodies had been moved, would be encouraging. A number of simultaneous tests were being conducted using DM8A on lab samples while the autopsies were being conducted. NIH was running those tests.

Another topic on the agenda pertained to how much of this potential disaster President Penn would relate in an address to the nation tonight. Reporters were acting more like wolves than usual. They were everywhere, hounding everyone.

The situation threatened to spiral out of control. The National Guard—already stretched thin because of deployments overseas—had already been called to Phoenix, Los Angeles and San Diego, in response to looting last night after the first of those photos showed up on the major networks. The government had made no other response except to call for calm. All questions would be answered tonight. Penn's advisers knew it was only a matter of time before the deaths in Maine would be tied to the outbreak in Sedona. They needed to head that off, but they also needed to have an emergency-response strategy in place that would help to calm the fears of the public.

Faas Hanlon had been running worst-case scenarios in his head for days now. An outbreak in an urban center. New York. L.A. Chicago. D.C. Preliminary reports were telling him that the super-microbe could possibly be transmitted by way of water supplies, though they were still working on the lifespan of the bacteria, as well as its susceptibility to heat and cold. Those worst-case scenarios, he knew, represented an international disaster that would make the plague look like a walk in the park. After all, the Black Death had only killed about a third of Europe's population. This plague could change the world in ways that were unimaginable.

Faas knew he was the only one in this room who was possibly holding a trump card. The phone call from his agents in Afghanistan had come late last night. Dr. Rahaf was admitting that she'd developed a remedy for this strain of bacteria years ago. She was willing to take them to where she'd saved a backup of the files that had been destroyed in the raid on her lab. Faas knew this was the biggest break they'd had so far. And that was why he'd insisted on speaking first at the meeting and putting everything he and his people needed on the table.

Austyn Newman and Matt Sutton were both competent agents. Austyn was upbeat about the prisoner's cooperation, but at the same time he'd voiced his concern that this could be a ploy on the part of Banaz. He told Faas that she could be using this simply as a way of giving them the runaround. Faas was willing to risk it, but Austyn would need to press her all the time. And if he decided that no files really existed, he was to cut the wild-goose chase short.

That trump card could still turn to shit in his hand, Faas knew, but he would hold it as long as he possibly could.

Austyn had also mentioned his suspicion that U.S. forces might have captured the wrong Dr. Banaz five years ago. Faas had directed him to keep this bit of speculation quiet, at least until they had substantial proof. If they didn't have Rahaf Banaz, then at least they had an important connection to her. And that was good enough for now. If Rahaf Banaz was still alive, and Austyn was escorting her sister around Kurdistan, then the wild goose might just come to them. Stranger things had happened.

"Specifics, ladies and gentlemen," Penn said. "Deputy Director Hanlon, you need to be as specific as you can be in terms of timeline, manpower needs and destination parameters. And you, General, need to decide how you can assist Deputy Director Hanlon's agents."

An air force general at the far end of the table leaned in. "Mr. President, Erbil International is a good-size airport. Our jets fly in and out of an airbase adjoining it daily. I can arrange for the transfer of the prisoner from Afghanistan to Iraq."

The commanding general of the marines in the Middle East chirped in, as well. "We have a special task force that is headquartered just outside of Erbil. We can arrange for an escort when they arrive."

Commander Percy looked across the room at Faas, his glare probing but a few degrees less hostile. "Dr. Banaz's lab was raided in Baquba, Diyala province's capital city, thirty-five miles northeast of Baghdad. Now she wants us to take her to Erbil. Why would a scientist keep backup files a hundred-and-sixty miles away in an area outside of Saddam Hussein's control, an area that has been closely monitored by the United Nations since the first Gulf War? Our intelligence never mentioned the possibility of a lab facility in that region. Doesn't the whole thing smell like a con job?"

"It does have a peculiar odor, General. We don't deny that."

Percy continued. "Even if these files exist, how could she have put them there and why? Even five years ago, it would have made more sense for this woman to tuck away an encrypted file in some corner of cyberspace, where she could access it from anywhere in the world." He shook his head and turned toward the TV screen. "This sounds like an exercise in futility, Mr. President."

"I understand your concerns, General." Faas thumbed through the file before him, forcing himself to keep a civil tongue in his head. "Mr. President, I don't have answers to all of the general's concerns, but I can shed light on some of them."

"Briefly," the president ordered.

"Yes, sir. The reason why we give any credence to the information Dr. Banaz has given us is because she is of Kurdish descent. She was born and raised in the village of Halabja in Northern Iraq. She lost her parents and all but one of her siblings in Saddam Hussein's Anfal campaign."

Faas looked around the room, contemplating if he should say more. He believed the Banaz woman's motivation to help them was based on what had happened to her family, but most of the people around the table were in the military and would know what Saddam's forces did to the Kurds. He was about to move on when the president broke in.

"And the Anfal Campaign is relevant to this discussion?" President Penn encouraged.

"Yes, sir." Faas glanced down at the page in his file to make sure he had the correct dates and numbers. "As you know, Anfal was an anti-Kurdish campaign led by Saddam Hussein's security forces between 1986 and 1989. The plans for the attacks were orchestrated by Ali Hassan al-Majid, a cousin of the Iraqi leader. Chemical Ali's trial in Iraq specifically described the use of ground offensives, aerial bombing, the systematic destruction of settlements, mass deportation, concentration camps, firing squads and chemical warfare."

Nearly twenty years had passed since the campaign against the Kurds, but from the expression on the faces of the people in this room, no one had forgotten why the world was a better place without Saddam and his henchmen. Of course, there were still some unresolved issues with what had happened back then, including American support of Saddam. Faas knew that some of the people who were present in this room may have played some role.

"The village of Halabja was the target of a poison gas attack in March 1988," Faas continued. "The estimated casualties in that village alone were seven thousand. In all, the Anfal campaign destroyed four thousand villages, killing more than one hundred thousand Kurds and displacing another million."

No one said anything. Faas didn't look at Percy, but he could feel that the general was about to explode. He quickly got to the point.

"Regardless of the fact that her education was paid for by the Iraqi government and that she returned to serve in the chemical labs of Saddam's regime, Dr. Banaz never severed her connection with her past." Faas Hanlon took out a folder and held it up. "In this recent CIA report on Rahaf Banaz, intelligence shows transfers of money that date from the very start of her service, up to the invasion of U.S. forces. In short, Dr. Banaz transferred the *majority* of her income to a number of institutions in the Kurdish region."

"What kind of institutions?" someone asked.

"Humanitarian aid groups?" the marine general chirped in.

"Our information comes from groups we have connections with," Faas told the room. "Some of the money was clearly intended for humanitarian efforts. Some of the money, though, made its way into the hands of Kurdish resistance groups. Naturally, we can't determine at this point how supportive she was of groups that opposed her boss, but what is clear is that she has never stopped identifying herself as a Kurd."

"She sounds like a loose cannon to me," General Percy said.

"I agree," Faas countered. "But right now, at least, she's cooperating with us."

"Does she understand the urgency of this matter?" the head of FEMA asked from the West Wing conference room. "It would be so much faster if she'd just give us the location of those files and let us get them for her."

"She has good reason not to trust us," Faas said directly to the camera feeding the images to the White House. "As I said at the beginning of this meeting, Dr. Banaz has spent five years in American prisons without any trial or legal recourse."

The marine general leaned forward. "This may be an erroneous assumption, but since she grew up in the village of Halabja, it is logical that Halabja would be her destination. The location of the village isn't particularly ideal for us, as close as it is to the Iranian border. But our patrols do go in and out of that sector regularly. If that's where she says she wants to go, we can arrange the escort…with General Percy's authorization, of course."

The air force general at the far end of the table spoke again. "Gentlemen, since the fall of Saddam's government, we've had only sporadic, isolated violence in Erbil…unlike most of Iraq. Of any region in the country, that one would be probably the safest to take her into right now."

A brief buzz of individual comments started around the room and then stopped abruptly when General Percy laid his meaty hands on the table.

"What's she bargaining for, Hanlon?" Percy asked gruffly.

"Her freedom," Faas replied, looking the general steadily in the eye.

"All right, then." Percy didn't blink. "But I won't forget who's putting the lives of American soldiers on the line."

Eleven

Brickyard Prison, Afghanistan

They had nothing to say to each other, and yet Captain Adams never ceased with the effort to engage Fahimah in small talk.

Thinking about it, Fahimah decided that it would be a difficult transition for anyone, especially an army captain in charge of a facility like this, seeing a detainee moved from dangerous "enemy to America" status to "we-depend-on-you-to-save-our-country" status in the matter of an hour or so. But the new status was exactly that, and Fahimah was being treated accordingly. The pendulum had swung completely.

Being able to move about without shackles or handcuffs or blindfolds made her feel immediately that she'd rejoined a world she never thought she'd belong to again. Receiving a change of clothing was another positive step. But none of this compared with the change in her jailors' attitude. She was given choices in food and even in the clothing she wished to wear, to some extent. She'd been allowed to take a shower in a private stall. She'd even adjusted the temperature and decided on the length of time she wanted to stay under the warm, cleansing water. This had been the most luxurious, the most stunning, of all her newfound freedoms.

Fahimah knew all of these were part of the ploy, of course. Another chapter in her long record of captivity. They could snatch it away at any time. Still, she was willing to go along with it all, even if it made the future more unbearable than the past had been. It bought time. It would give her a chance to find her sister. It was the only chance they had, and a small key opens big doors.

"You have good weather to fly in," Captain Adams said to her, moving around her desk to the window, where a small air-conditioning unit was working overtime, blasting only slightly cooler air into the room. Fahimah looked past the captain's shoulder. Two days in a row, she was getting a glimpse of blue sky. The captain's office was on the second level of the old brick-making facility. Two small windows overlooked a partially paved road with a view of mountainous terrain in the distance. Until yesterday, Fahimah didn't know what kind of building they were keeping her in. She'd heard someone say something about being in Afghanistan weeks ago, but she still didn't know what part of the country she was in or how many other people were imprisoned here.

She glanced at the table next to her, toward the magazines they'd given her that morning. Long ago, she'd locked up her mind, sealed her thoughts in an impenetrable bubble, but last night she'd made the decision to unseal that part of her. As a result, for the first time in perhaps years, she'd found herself starved for news. There was so much that had been happening in the world, so much that she had missed.

The news of Saddam's hanging had been a surprise, but not a shock. She'd figured that was only matter of time, anyway. There had to be a great deal more important news. She'd asked about a few things, but the Americans were clearly a little hesitant about how much they should tell her. When she'd been captured, half the world had been searching for a devil named Osama bin Laden, and a few were still looking for him. Arabs were a difficult lot, she thought, and the Saudis were the worst. Always stirring the pot of misery, and simply to drive up the price of their oil a few bloody pennies.

The few magazines they'd given her had offered very little of what she was after. Celebrity marriages between people she'd never heard of were breaking up, and a movie star was adopting what appeared to be a fifth or sixth child, but overall the magazines offered no perspective of what was happening in the world. Still, she had read the magazines cover to cover in the matter of a couple of hours.

"Do you have a home, a place where you can go back to, once this…this business is all finished?"

Fahimah was surprised by the question. She looked up. Captain Adams had moved to the front of her desk, her hip resting on the corner of it. The woman was looking directly at her. Fahimah had to remind herself that she should carry no grudge against this person. Governments and policies she could blame, but individuals like this one were only pawns in a larger and more complicated game. The same thing applied to Rahaf and Fahimah herself. They'd lived in a country that was run by a butcher. That did not make them *butchers*. In fact, they were just the opposite.

Still, despite this logic and the conscious desire to put animosity aside, it was terribly difficult to warm to a former jailer. Abuses occurred here; individuals were being denied the so-called inalienable human right to a trial, and Captain Adams occupied the top position of authority in this prison. Fahimah could not pretend to be friendly with the person holding the key to the shackles. She would play along with this pretense of freedom, but she would not forget that there were many others still locked in the cells below. If they were here, she guessed, they were in the same situation as she. No trial, no jury, no idea of what was going to happen to them tomorrow or next week or next year.

"I don't know," Fahimah shrugged. "I don't know what is left of my country."

Adams nodded with understanding, crossing her arms over her chest. Her expression became pensive. "This war has taken much longer than any of us thought it would. There are times I think the same thing about my own home and family."

Fahimah appreciated the candidness. From the horrible photographs she'd been shown by the agents, it appeared that people in the U.S. were under attack, too. Her thoughts immediately focused on what she'd promised Agent Newman. She hadn't lied. A remedy to the microbe existed. She'd seen Rahaf taking it. But if they were to find the remedy, then she would have to keep alive the hope that her sister was still living…and that Fahimah could find her. She rubbed the back of her neck. Thoughts of the plots she would need to hatch once they got to Erbil airport crowded her mind. There was so much that she still needed to figure out.

There was a knock on the door before the two American agents entered. She hadn't seen or spoken to either of them since last night. Each man gave her a long, hard look, as if he were seeing her for the first time.

Rather than a new pair of coveralls, Fahimah had borrowed some clothes from Captain Adams—camouflage fatigue pants, a white cotton shirt and plastic sandals. In spite of her very short hair, she didn't want to look like one of the soldiers. Of course, she thought, there weren't many American soldiers who looked half-starved. She'd been somewhat shocked this morning in the bathroom at how frail she looked.

"Captain Adams mentioned that you've been asking for some means of catching up on the news," the younger of the two agents told her.

Fahimah remembered that this man's name was Matt Sutton. From their interaction yesterday, she surmised that he had a lower rank than Agent Newman. Sutton was shorter by two or three inches, but with the exception of their height, the two men had the same athletic build. Both had short, dark hair, but that was where the similarities ended. Matt Sutton had boyish good looks. Newman's face, however, was too complicated to be summed up in a couple of words. *Handsome* and *ugly* did not really seem to apply. He had a nose that looked like it had been broken, piercing blue eyes and a moon-shaped scar on a strong chin. Already, Fahimah had been able to see that his moods had a great effect on his facial expression. That, she supposed, determined how he would come across to a new acquaintance. Yesterday, he'd sounded kind and understanding. That kindliness had been reflected in his face. Today, there was a dark cloud surrounding him that wiped out her first impressions of him. She turned her attention to the other agent as Sutton opened an oversize shoulder bag and took out a smaller leather case. Inside, there was a laptop.

"You're welcome to use this. I loaded a number of past issues of newspapers and magazines onto my laptop for the flight."

She stared at the proffered computer. It was a precious gem.

"The only thing is that everything loaded is in English. If you'd prefer some of the issues in Arabic…"

"No, English is fine," she said, reaching for the computer before he changed his mind. He handed her the leather storage case, too. She touched the piece of equipment, ran her fingers along the thin edge, already realizing that technology had changed a great deal since her capture. This machine weighed a tenth of the last laptop she'd handled.

"I guess you're ready to leave," Captain Adams commented, breaking a moment of silence.

"Do you have any personal belongings at all, Dr. Banaz?" Agent Newman asked, turning to her.

He was wearing sunglasses today, and that made his expression much more guarded. He looked older…and more threatening. She wondered if he still harbored the doubts he had expressed yesterday, or whether he had decided that she really was Rahaf. She also wanted to know if he'd shared that doubt with the people to whom he reported. If that were the case, then they were using her as a means of finding her sister.

No matter what happened, she wasn't going to lead the Americans to Rahaf, just to turn her over to them. The headache at the base of her skull was back. She would drive herself crazy thinking about all this. She looked up. He was waiting for an answer.

"No, nothing else." Fahimah shook her head. Her only belongings consisted of the clothing she was wearing and the new toothbrush that she'd rolled in tissues and wrapped inside a black Nike cap before stuffing it into the pocket of her pants. She'd refused the offer of more clothes. It might have been pride or stubbornness, but she refused to take anything more than was absolutely necessary. She put the laptop in the leather case and got to her feet.

"I'm ready," she said.

Captain Adams extended her hand. Fahimah decided against snubbing her and shook the other woman's hand. She stood a couple of inches taller than the captain. She gripped the woman's hand hard and kept her back straight.

"Perhaps we'll meet again," the captain said.

"I hope not," Fahimah said in all seriousness, not sure if they were talking about "meeting again" in the same context. But it didn't matter. She didn't care if she ever saw her again.

They ran into a soldier right outside of the captain's office. Fahimah thought the young woman might have been one of the guards who'd transferred her from one cell to the next, or slid a tray of food inside her door during her months here.

The soldier nodded to them. "Good luck, Dr. Banaz."

Fahimah was starting to hate this sudden civility. She

didn't want these people to be her friends. Matt Sutton went ahead of her down the stairs. Fahimah kept a hand against the wall going down. She'd had a meal last night. Another small one this morning wasn't sitting in her stomach exactly as it should. She wasn't accustomed to eating, so there was very little her stomach accepted. At the same time, she wasn't used to moving around, to standing. She didn't want to fall on her face going down the stairs.

Stepping out into the brilliant sunshine, Fahimah shielded her eyes with one hand. The outside air threatened to suffocate her with heat and dust. Figures of men and women in uniform and three closed vehicles were all that Fahimah could see when she was able to force her eyes open against the bright sun.

Fahimah was surprised that they weren't blindfolding her as they left this facility, but she wasn't about to remind them of it. There was no wasting time outside. She was told to climb into the middle vehicle in the caravan. Agent Newman climbed in after her. Fahimah moved to the far left to give him plenty of room. The other agent sat in the front with the driver. The air-conditioning was already set on high. The smell of leather and dust and recycled air caused her stomach to churn. She took a deep breath, willing her stomach to settle. The closed windows of the Humvee were tinted so that you could only see out.

Outside, everyone moved quickly once she was settled into the vehicle. She noticed a group of soldiers moving around the cars. They all had their weapons drawn. They were constantly watching the terrain around them. Fahimah looked out the window. There was nothing, just barren land and serrated hills. Rock and dust, as far as the eye could see. Her sister, Rahaf, had traveled to this country once for work, but this was Fahimah's first view of Afghanistan.

The radio in the vehicle crackled to life. The driver started talking to someone through a transmitter. She heard the loud roar of a chopper move overhead. She pressed her face against the window and looked up at the sky to see. The helicopter seemed to be hovering right above the car.

"Move this way," Agent Newman ordered, a split second before the door on her side of the vehicle opened. A large, powerfully built soldier wearing a bulletproof vest nodded and climbed in.

Instantly, Fahimah found herself sandwiched between the bodies of two large Americans. She moved the laptop to her chest to protect it.

"Couldn't you spare another car?" she asked quietly.

"No," Agent Newman said in a clipped tone. "Let's go over the rules now."

"I should have known that there would be rules."

Her response obviously surprised both men in the backseat. The armed soldier shot her a quick, amused look before turning his attention back to what was going on outside. Agent Newman's gaze stayed on her much longer.

There was nothing improper in the look he was giving her, but Fahimah suddenly felt very uncomfortable sitting so close to the man. She tightened her hold on the computer case and looked ahead as the caravan of cars started down the road. From the noise of the helicopter circling above, she knew it was part of their escort.

"All right, Agent Newman. What are the rules?" she asked, encouraging him to say something.

"Dr. Banaz, we believe your life is in danger. We have taken st—"

"My life was in danger back in that prison." She motioned over her shoulder at the facility they were leaving behind.

"Let me finish," he said in a sharper tone.

She shrugged, looking ahead. The driver and Agent Sutton gave no indication that they could even hear the exchange in the backseat. As the landscape sped by, Fahimah thought the vehicles were driving far too fast. Only an occasional glint of the sun off the rear window of the vehicle ahead of them was visible through the storm of dust they were raising.

"You've agreed to cooperate," Newman started again. "We're operating with the belief that someone who you might know, perhaps someone who worked for you or with you, could be responsible for the release of this bacteria in the U.S."

She couldn't argue that point. Rahaf must have feared the possibility of the microbe being used against humans when she'd asked Fahimah to go to her lab and destroy the documents having to do with her research. Her sister had always given Fahimah the impression that the purpose of her research was to find cures to horrible diseases, including those caused by microbes that could be packaged for use as weapons. From personal experience, they both knew how terrible biochemical weapons could be.

Fahimah wondered now if her sister had heard anything about what was going on in that country. Unconsciously, she tapped her fingers on the computer in her arms, wondering how much information about the outbreaks was known at all. Newman had never mentioned whether or not this terror had been made public.

"We also know that as much as we try, information leaks out from our bases." Fahimah felt the soldier beside her stiffen, but Newman continued without a pause. "So if our enemies don't already know about your existence, it will probably be just a matter of hours before the news will surface."

Fahimah looked up to Agent Newman's face. He was going with the assumption that she was Rahaf. That meant everyone else out there believed that, too, including, perhaps, whoever was behind the attack. That is, of course, if the outbreaks were even the result of some terrorist effort.

"Why should that cause you to worry about me, Agent Newman?"

"Your offer to help could ruin the plans of Al Qaeda…or whoever is engineering all of this. They'll try to kill you so that you *don't* help us."

The words should have been an icy steel spike of fear in her gut. He'd intended them to be frightening, she was certain. But after all she'd been through over the past five years, the words did nothing. Death was seen as the end by many, but for Fahimah it was only another realm of existence, the next stage in this experience. She'd wished death would free her from prisons so many times over the years.

"This kind of escort might work in Afghanistan," she said, pointing at the roof of the Humvee just as the helicopter roared across their path. "But once we're in Iraq, I think it will be too much. In fact, it will only draw unnecessary attention to you. An escort such as this one will tell whoever these people are that you have arrived. It is an invitation to be attacked, Agent Newman. You might as well have someone waiting at the airport and carrying a sign with my name on it."

"We'll have different security arrangements once we land in Iraq," he replied. "Perhaps now that we're under way, you wouldn't mind telling me where we are headed from Erbil airport?"

"We have discussed that before. I will tell you once we arrive." She looked out the window. "We have a saying, 'Stairs are climbed step by step.'"

"Well, that's great, Dr. Banaz. But we're not talking about an afternoon jaunt in the countryside for two. There are a lot of people who need time to prepare for this."

"That is your problem and not mine, Agent Newman," she said flatly. "I do not trust you."

"And I thought we were past that," he said in a mock pained tone.

"Neither of us is past it, as you say," she said seriously. "I am not in shackles, but I am still your prisoner."

"We're guarding you, protecting you. This is different than being a prisoner. I thought you understood that."

"Call it what you want," she replied thinly. "I believe what you have shown me with those pictures. I believe what has happened to those innocent people in America. I'll try to help you, but your past treatment of me has taught me not to trust any of you."

"Dr. Banaz, *I* didn't do anything to you. I've been honest with you from the first moment we met."

"There is no *I*, Agent Newman. You are here representing *your* government. That says everything about who you are."

"I don't carry a gun. I'm not a soldier or a policeman," he told her impatiently. "I'm a scientist."

"The same thing has always been true of me. I was a civilian, a scientist. If anyone had cared to do any research, they would have found that I never participated in any of Saddam Hussein's programs to develop biological weapons. There has been a great deal of good that has come out of the research I have done," she reminded him, not caring that there were others who were listening to this conversation. "But I was kept and treated with fewer rights than a prisoner of war. I was forgotten, lost. The rules of the Geneva Convention do not apply to me, according to America. So do not remind me of how little I care for you and your country. Do not ask for more than I am willing to give. I told you that I will help. I will remain true to my promise. I will tell you where to go once we reach Erbil. Leave it at that."

Fahimah looked straight ahead, finished with the discussion. It was a relief when he didn't argue more. She felt her cheeks and ears burning. Emotions had become foreign to her over the years, but now anger heated her blood. It had been so long since she'd allowed herself to feel and speak this way.

No one said anything. The noise of the helicopter overhead competed with the sound of the road, providing the only disruption to the silence inside the Humvee. Even the two-way radio remained quiet. She hadn't let anger overwhelm her during the years of her imprisonment, but she'd reached her limit. Like the long-trapped magma of a sleeping volcano, feelings about the injustices she had endured were suddenly erupting through the surface. It had begun yesterday, when in her fury she'd ripped through the room where they had moved her. She wished there was some physical means of venting those feelings now, but she knew she wouldn't get far with the two large bodies pressing her on either side. She had to find other means of calming herself.

Fahimah closed her eyes. She placed the computer on her lap and loosened her hold on it. She focused on her breathing. In. Hold. Slowly out. In. Hold. Slowly out. As she breathed, she felt the flow into each limb, joint by joint, muscle by muscle.

The shoulders of the two men on either side rocked against her. She lost her focus, anger and frustration pushing back into her consciousness. She focused again on her breathing, taking in the good…holding it so that it might spread through her…breathing out the bad. She was trying to relax her limbs with each breath, but it was difficult. There were so many distractions. So much noise. She tried to focus only on the rhythm of her breaths, to become separate from the body. In and hold and out. Again. Again. Trying began to give way to allowing. Awareness began to fade.

A sudden jolt caused the computer to fly off her lap. She opened her eyes, grabbing for it desperately. Agent Newman was the one who caught it before it was thrown against the front seat. He handed it back to her.

"Thank you," she whispered, trying to avoid eye contact. She tucked the leather strap under it and placed it on her lap again.

There was another jolt. She was crushed between the two men as they shifted and tried to regain their seat.

"You might want to put your seat belt on," Agent Newman suggested, reaching for his. There wasn't much room for him to maneuver.

"Sorry, sir," the driver said apologetically. "We're not far from the base."

Fahimah looked out the window at the group of Afghani kids running after the cars. The guns didn't deter them. Their bare feet, dirty faces, hungry bellies were reminders of what she'd seen before. She could hear their voices through the glass and realized that the helicopter had left them.

"Naan…naan…naan…"

They were asking for bread. Fahimah stared at the tents set up past the faces. This reminded her of the refugee camps that had been set up all over the Iranian border after Saddam's troops had destroyed all of those Kurdish villages, after he had killed so many men. Young children and women had been left to fend for themselves then, too.

The cars were slowing down. Fahimah saw security checkpoints ahead. The Afghanis were forced to stay on this side of the barriers. The radio came to life again, issuing instructions about driving through. Just before they reached the barriers, however, something hard hit the right side window of the vehicle.

Fahimah found her face shoved forward onto her lap by the soldier sitting to her left. Her nose hit the laptop hard.

"Speed up!" the soldier growled.

"It was just a rock," the driver replied.

"They're waving you through," Newman said. "Go."

Fahimah felt the vehicle speed up again. With her face still pressed against the laptop, Fahimah felt blood trickling down her face. She brought her hand up to her nose. The smell of leather from the computer case turned her stomach again. She tasted bile in the back of her throat. She took another deep breath as the weight of the soldier eased from her.

"Are you okay?" Newman asked, taking her by the shoulders and pulling her into a sitting position again.

"I warned you before. Your people are the ones who're trying to kill me."

She didn't know where the tissue came from, but he started patting her upper lips, holding her head up. She took it away from him and wiped her nose herself.

"Sorry," the soldier on her left said gruffly. "We can't be too careful."

"It was nothing," she replied quietly. "The bleeding has already stopped." She accepted another tissue that was handed to her from the front seat and wiped a drop of blood from the leather case.

In another minute or two, the Humvees began to slow again. At this checkpoint, armed soldiers looked into the vehicle and under it before allowing them to pass. After weaving back and forth through concrete barriers like a ski slalom, the road straightened and took them into the base.

The roads inside the base were busy, filled with military vehicles and Americans in uniform. A few Afghani civilians were visible in their turbans or caps and dark vests and their simple long shirts over white pants and sandals. They stood out among the soldiers in camouflage khaki and gray and green. Most were young men and boys. They appeared to be laborers.

"We have fifteen minutes before the aircraft is ready to board," Matt Sutton said over his shoulder after talking on the phone.

"Take us as close to the plane as possible," Newman ordered the driver. "Somewhere in or near one of the hangars, if possible."

The driver spoke to someone on his phone. They were stopping at another security checkpoint as they moved from one section of the base to another. Beyond the barrier, she could see the airstrips. Huge military cargo planes lined the side of one runway. Each vehicle came to a complete stop, and the driver and Agent Sutton both opened their windows. The driver passed some paperwork out to a soldier as two others circled the vehicle, looking under the car as they had at each checkpoint with a mirror on the end of a thin metal pole.

Perhaps it was the combination of the hot breeze outside, tainted with the smell of petroleum and jet exhaust. Perhaps it was the blast of air-conditioning on her face. It could have been anything, but suddenly she felt sick to her stomach.

"Can you open your window?" she asked in panic.

Agent Newman did as he was told. "You look kind of green. Are you okay?"

It was too late.

"Let me out," she groaned, reaching over him hurriedly for the door handle.

Luckily, he was quick and Fahimah scrambled after him. She barely had both feet on the pavement when her stomach emptied violently. Immediately, she went down on her knees as another wave of sickness hit her, making her retch as she emptied everything that was left inside of her. Her stomach was knotted with painful cramping, and she continued with dry heaves.

The air felt like it was on fire. The bare skin of her neck and her head sizzled under the stunningly hot sun, but Fahimah started shivering uncontrollably. Agent Newman was saying something into her ear, but she could not understand him. She felt hands under her arms, lifting her and moving her to the side of the road where she knelt, her eyes closed. It took some time before she could control her nausea.

As Fahimah sat there, she heard the Humvee that she'd been riding in back around to the side of the road, putting her in shadow. She took short breaths through her mouth, fearful of any smell or taste that might make her sick again.

There were noises of people moving around her. Someone was asking about doctors, about directions to the infirmary.

"No…no," she whispered weakly, forcing her eyes open.

Agent Newman crouched down next to her, his sunglasses pushed on top of his head, his expression showing concern.

"We're going to take you to the infirmary," he told her gently.

She shook her head and sat back on the warm road surface. "No. I am fine."

"You don't look fine to me," he told her.

"I've had two meals in the past twelve hours. My stomach is not accustomed to it."

"It could be something else. Perhaps food poisoning? Or something even more serious."

"No. It is nothing," she said sternly. He didn't look convinced. "You get sick occasionally, Agent Newman. After you vomit, then you feel better. Isn't that so?"

"No, not me. I never get sick."

She snatched the bottle of water that he was holding out to her.

"Please just give me a minute or two and I will be back to normal." She took a mouthful of water, rinsed her mouth and spit it out. She repeated it a couple of times more, unwilling to chance swallowing any of the water yet.

"You're shivering. This could be more than just food disagreeing with you. I can't have you dehydrate while we're on the flight out. I certainly can't have you die on me."

Her water bottle was already empty. He handed her another and took the empty one away.

His persistent worry was actually comical. "I'm thirty-six years old. I know my body. I always shiver when I get sick to my stomach, Agent Newman."

Someone else passed her some tissues. Newman slowly pushed himself to his feet. It took Fahimah a couple of minutes more before she was sure she was strong enough to prove her argument. She rinsed her mouth with the water again and took her time to stand up. The sun was bright. Everything around her was in a haze. The shivering, however, was already subsiding.

There was no way that she was not getting on that plane.

"The infirmary isn't too far away," Agent Newman said one more time.

Fahimah waved him off impatiently and looked at the open door of the Humvee. She shook her head. "No."

The other vehicles had pulled to the side, as well. The soldiers escorting them were looking out of open doors or standing next to their vehicles.

"I am not getting in yet. I want to walk around a little."

Half a dozen soldiers created a shield a few feet away from her. She was protected from view of others on the base.

"That's where we're going." Sutton pointed to a huge

corrugated steel building some five hundred feet past the barricades.

"I can walk there."

"I don't think that would be a good idea, sir," the soldier who had been seated next to her said to Newman.

"We are on an American base. If you do not trust your own people, then whom are you going to trust?" she asked before turning away. They were being so stubborn, she thought, raising her face to the sun. Now the heat actually felt good.

She didn't know what was said between them, but she must have won the battle, for the three cars drove around her, passed through the checkpoints and then continued slowly toward the building that Agent Sutton had pointed to. Giant doors on the side facing them were open, and on the runway next to it, a military aircraft was being fueled. She guessed this was the plane taking her back to Iraq.

Fahimah looked behind her. As she'd expected, Agent Newman and her protector, the burly soldier who'd given her a bloody nose earlier, had stayed behind.

"Ready to walk?" Newman asked.

She nodded, going around the cinder block barriers and toward the hangar where their caravan had headed.

Agent Newman fell in step beside her. The other man kept some ten feet away, walking behind them.

Getting rid of the food in her stomach actually made Fahimah feel much better than before. She didn't mind the heat and stretching her legs felt good. She hadn't walked this far outdoors in years.

"I'm glad we got one thing settled."

Fahimah glanced up at the agent. His sunglasses were again hiding his eyes.

"What have we settled?" she asked.

"Your name and your age. Dr. Fahimah Banaz, age thirty-six."

She stopped, looked up at him and snorted derisively.

He shook his head. "Don't waste my time denying it. I know the truth and you know the truth. That's enough."

She was now, more than ever, in their power. She knew that they could easily prove that she wasn't Rahaf. She tried not to panic, forcing her voice to remain steady. "What do you mean, 'That is enough'?"

He pushed the glasses down on the bridge of his nose, looking into her eyes. "You're taking us to your sister, to where we can get a remedy that will stop the microbe."

"I am *helping* you to get the remedy," she said, correcting him.

"Then you won't renege on your promise," he stressed.

"I will not go back on my word, if that is what you mean," she told him. "But I will not lead you to my sister." There was no longer any point in denying the truth.

"She might be behind the attacks."

"She is *not*," Fahimah said adamantly. "If you believe that, then you put our deal at risk."

"It doesn't matter what I believe. A court of law can determine her guilt or innocence."

She stopped and stared at him for a moment. Newman stopped, as well, but did not look at her.

"You have released me from my promise. My assistance ends now," she told him angrily. "I know my sister. I know what she went through to help people and to keep people from getting hurt. I'm telling you that she has nothing to do with this."

"I cannot change what my government might logically suspect. I know that they—"

"I have paid a thousand times over for your government's misplaced suspicion," she shot back hotly. "Go ahead and arrest me. Take me back to that prison. Shoot me if you want. I'm not taking another step to help you." She turned on her heel and started walking back toward the security gate.

Before she even reached their burly escort, a large hand caught Fahimah by the arm. Newman turned her around to face him.

"You have quite a temper, Dr. Banaz. I think you should consider doing a little more meditating."

Fahimah folded her arms across her chest, glaring up at him. "I have been in your prisons for five years, and I have never said a word, in order to protect my sister. I will gladly go back there for another fifty. I won't help you to hurt Rahaf."

"Look, I have no intention of hurting her or arresting her or prosecuting her. I'm looking for a way to stop people from dying. I can learn from her. The remedy might not be enough. If we can't stop who's behind the attacks, we'll be forever fighting against time. She might know the real people behind all of this. She knows so many people in this field. She could help us find them, stop them."

"But you believe she's behind these outbreaks."

"I was speaking honestly about what others might think," he said in obvious frustration. "When I came to offer you a deal, I had no idea that you might not be Rahaf Banaz. But now I *need* to find your sister. Innocent people are dying. I do not want anything to happen to her, and I will give you any guarantee you ask for that is within my power."

Fahimah knew that he would say anything. It was not the first time American agents had made offers in return for her cooperation. It was different this time, though. She had only one way to go, and that was forward. Now that they knew Rahaf was out there, the Americans would find her, with or without Fahimah's help. For the first time in five years, though, Fahimah was truly in a position to bargain. She would use it to save Rahaf.

"Let's go," she said quietly, starting again toward the hangar.

"Where are we going?" He fell into step with her.

"To Erbil."

"And from there?"

"I will tell you when we arrive."

"But what about your sister?"

"You have just asked me to trust you with the life and future of my only sister. I ask you to trust *me*. This is all I will say for now. It should be enough."

He fell silent and walked thoughtfully with her toward the plane.

Twelve

"**Y**ou can't talk us out of it. We're going, Mom," Josh stressed as he continued to stuff his backpack with the clothes he was taking on the week-long trip.

Arms folded across her chest, her shoulder leaning against the doorjamb, Sally Link wasn't ready to give up this fight just yet.

She turned and looked in the doorway of the adjoining bedroom. David was still packing. "David, you're the adult here. Talk some sense into him. You guys can go on this trip another time."

"No, Mom. There's a waiting list," Josh answered for his father. "We signed up for this trip three months ago. Please, this has been the one thing that I've been looking forward to all summer. I *want* to go on it."

Sally knew what her son was up to. He was trying to work on her sympathy. Josh's year so far had consisted of two chemo treatments and ten days in the hospital. It was a miracle that he felt as good as he did during this vacation.

"This isn't the best time for your father," she said to Josh. "He's got too much going on at work. They could need him at any time."

"Dad is on vacation," Josh answered.

She stared meaningfully at her husband. He'd talked with her for nearly an hour after dinner last night about the last-minute shuffling that they were doing with their key accounts because of some production crisis.

"David?" she urged, motioning for him to help her with this.

"They know how to reach me if they absolutely must." He shook his head and made a palms-up gesture, mouthing the words, "I can't disappoint him."

"It's not safe to go away," she said, blurting out her main concern.

"I told you not to read the newspaper," David warned. "It's all a lot of hype. They're making it all out to be much worse than it is."

"They have pictures of the corpses on the front page," Sally protested.

"They have pictures of the Loch Ness Monster and Bigfoot, too, Mom," Josh said, cracking a smile. He pulled a baseball cap over his bald head. "You really have to stop reading the *National Enquirer*."

"Honey, we'll be fine," David said, coming out of their room and putting an arm around Sally. "You're dropping us off at the pier. It's half a mile away. We'll only be gone for a week. You and Kate can pick us up right at the same pier."

Kate, still in her pajamas, took that moment to stroll into

the room. She looked around at the faces. "Did someone just use my name in vain?"

"Mom is being overly protective," Josh told his sister.

"So what else is new?" the nineteen-year-old said sarcastically just before the dish towel Sally had in one hand snapped her on the butt.

"Ow!" Kate yelped, hopping out of striking range. "Hey, that's child abuse, you know!"

"Save it for Oprah," Sally said. "Besides, you're too old to call it child abuse."

"Have you got everything, sport?" David said to his son.

"Yep." Josh zipped up his pack and slung it over his shoulder.

"David, seriously," Sally persisted. "Did you call them to make sure they haven't canceled the trip?"

"I called them an hour ago, when you asked me to. Like I told you, they said everything is going on as scheduled. The research boat is ready for us. The crew is all set. And they haven't had any cancellations from other parents."

"You see, Mom? You're the only one who's overreacting," Josh said, giving her a big hug.

Kate slipped past them. "Well, Mom, I guess it's just you, me, Oprah and the beach for the next week."

Josh grinned up at Sally and followed his sister to the kitchen.

"I'm all ready, Dad. Call me when you're ready to go," he said over his shoulder.

Sally sat down on the arm of the sleep sofa. This past week had been like heaven. With the three children around her and David staying here, too, it had been almost like the old days. Spending the days together on the beach, noisy dinners and arguments and laughter. Sally wished she could bottle that joy for the tough days that she knew they'd have ahead.

"Honey, what's going on? It's not like you to buy into these things." David rubbed her shoulders. "I know five people are dead in Arizona, but people die every day. It's been pretty quiet as far as big news stories for the past couple of months, so the press is making the most out of what they can."

"I'm not so sure, David," she whispered uneasily.

"There was nothing in the president's speech last night that made me want to grab all of you and hide in the basement. Think about it. We're going to be out on the open sea with nothing but clean salt air to breathe. And aren't you the same woman who let Jamie go back to New York City this morning? New York City, honey."

Sally smiled, remembering how upset she'd been when Jamie had taken a job in New York right out of college. She'd been afraid the big bad monster would eat up her baby alive. Two months later, their daughter was doing great and feeling right at home in the city.

"Come on. Tell me you're okay with this."

She knew her husband was right. Still, she couldn't kick the worry eating away at the lining of her stomach.

"Repeat after me. This…is…good…for…Josh."

"It *is* good for Josh," she repeated.

It was so difficult to shift one's perspective from what was best for your child over the long term to what was best for him today. The most crushing moment of Sally's life was when she'd been told of Josh's leukemia. She and

David both had been stunned. The twelve-year-old, though, had taken it well and had been a true champ through all of the tests and treatments he'd had so far. They weren't done, either. Josh still had a rocky road ahead of him. Sally had to teach herself to live today, enjoy today. She had to remind herself daily to do what was best for Josh *today*.

David had been the one who'd heard about this excursion at sea. Designed for teenagers who were at different stages of their cancer treatments, the research vessel only took ten students and one parent or caregiver each. The former fishing boat, which had been turned into a floating laboratory, was funded by a government Sea Grant. The American Cancer Society contributed additionally to fund these trips during the summer. From the literature Sally had read about the trip, the kids would work right alongside the graduate students and researchers. The boat's primary purpose was to monitor ocean disposal sites. The divers would collect underwater samples in specific locations, and the students would work with the crew, analyzing those samples on the boat's laboratory.

Fresh air, interaction with other kids their own age, learning in a hands-on atmosphere. The program was very well reviewed and booked long in advance. Josh and David were right. There was no way she could rob them of something this valuable.

She sighed and let her chin sink to her chest. "Get ready. I'll drive you two to the pier."

Thirteen

At the last minute, the decision was made to not use a military aircraft for the transfer of Dr. Banaz. The quickest flight pattern was over the Caspian Sea, north of Iran. With their ability to climb quickly to cruising altitudes, small commercial-type jets were frequently used for transportation between Afghanistan and Iraq. They provided a less-obvious target for some missile-wielding, half-wit freedom-fighter sitting in some mountain range in Turkmenistan or Azerbaijan.

Two air force pilots were being used to fly the ten-seat jet. Two of Fahimah's military escorts from the Brickyard and three more from the airbase at Bagram were accompanying them during the flight.

Austyn sat across the aisle, one seat back from Fahimah, on the plane. As they cruised, he watched her go through page after page of news on the laptop. Before getting on the flight, he'd called Faas Hanlon. He'd told the director about his certainty now that the wrong sister had been held in the CIA-run prisons for the past five years. The conversation had been brief and to the point. As far as Faas was concerned, the original plan remained in place. Austyn and Matt were to accompany Fahimah wherever she led them. At the same time, U.S. Special Forces in Iraq would be put on alert to look for the younger sister. The search was on, and Faas sounded satisfied with the turn of events. Now, Austyn thought, they had two lines of investigation to follow. Rahaf Banaz could potentially help them, or possibly she was behind the attacks. Either way, finding her could lead to a solution for the situation in America.

Austyn hadn't forgotten what he'd promised Fahimah. She wanted her sister to go free. A lot of that depended on what the younger sister's involvement in all of this was. Austyn guessed even Fahimah didn't really know. She'd spent five years in prison, and it was pretty unlikely that there had been any communication between the two.

No matter what happened, Austyn was determined not to allow Rahaf to become lost in one of the CIA's black sites like her sister. One way or another, he would make sure that she was treated fairly.

Austyn saw Fahimah close the laptop. There were so many questions he had for her. At the same time, he knew that only a very thin line of trust connected them. There was certainly no comfort zone.

He undid his seat belt and stood up. Matt had taken the last seat on the same row as Fahimah. He was constructing possible scenarios on Rahaf over the past five years, based on history of the fighting in Iraq and on possible identity changes she might have undergone. Upon seeing Austyn stand, the other agent shook his head. *Nothing yet,* he mouthed.

Austyn moved toward Fahimah. The leather case for the laptop was on the seat across the aisle where she'd placed it.

"Do you mind if I sit down here?"

She glanced across at the leather case before looking up. "Would it matter if I minded?"

He nodded. "Yes, it would."

"Then I mind," she told him.

Austyn nodded, forcing himself not to push it. She needed to be able to trust him. If he bullied her, they would never develop the rapport they'd need when they reached the Kurdistan region of Iraq. He took the step back to his seat. He was about to buckle himself in again when she turned her head around.

"Very good. You pass the test," she told him. "You may sit here."

"Just like a teacher," he said wryly. "I should have known there would be tests."

She said nothing and picked up the computer case off the seat. Austyn sat down as she turned her head away.

She had both hands resting on the computer, and she appeared to be looking out the small airplane window at the passing banks of clouds. He watched her profile for a few moments. In spite of all she'd endured, she was still very attractive. She turned and glanced at him. Those green eyes startled him, oddly disconcerting him when she looked at him.

"All caught up with your reading?" he asked, motioning with his head to the computer.

"Hardly at all," she replied. "I only read bits and pieces of things. Most of the headlines or the first paragraph or two."

"Can't stomach more than that?"

She shook her head. "I have missed a great deal." She paused. "But you have a valid point. It is a great deal worse than I could have imagined."

He wanted her to open up to him more. "In what way?"

"In every way. The world appears to be coming apart," she retorted. "To begin with, the war in Iraq. From these articles, it is clear that you have created a situation that has resulted in a civil war dividing my country. It seems that it has become a way of life for the Sunni to be killing the Shia and vice versa."

Austyn started to reply, but she waved him off.

"It is not just there," she said, continuing. "Look at what is happening in Africa. In half the continent, continuous genocide is being practiced. Even these Western journalists point to the role of self-serving financiers of the West in supporting these murderous regimes. And the Saudis play a huge part in that, as well. It always was and still is amazing to me how blind the people of democratic Western countries continue to be about the special interest groups that ruin countries in order to exploit them. So long as their gas prices are low, they care nothing about how these groups, with their government's support, put a murderer in power in a country. In my own country, so long as Saddam was fighting Iran and selling oil cheaply to America, he was a good friend." She looked at him. "I can go on and on. Would you care to debate any of this?"

"You're the political science professor. I'm not going

headfirst into any argument with you unless I have time to prepare."

A hint of softness touched her expression. She was obviously pleased to be acknowledged for the profession she had before.

She leaned her head back against the seat and looked out at the patches of clouds again. "And there is so much filtered news."

"Filtered news?"

"Of course, filtered. These are American publications…or funded by their interests," she said. "Before your people put me in prison, the censorship in your papers was so transparent. Nothing has changed."

Austyn wasn't going there. It wasn't censorship in the strictest sense of the word, but he knew sections of Homeland Security monitored what they called "sensitive information." It was no secret that mainstream news had adopted a new "sensitivity" about the way information was presented after the September 11 attacks back in 2001.

"I saw you doing some searches on the university where you used to teach."

Her gaze narrowed. "You were watching what I was doing?"

"You knew I was watching," Austyn said matter-of-factly, keeping eye contact. "You also know that we're keeping track of every search you do on that computer."

She shrugged and looked out the window again. "I was hoping you would not be so blunt about it."

"I thought we were dealing honestly with each other."

"You can think whatever you want."

Austyn enjoyed her quick tongue. It was admirable that after so many years of silence in prison, she hadn't lost it.

"Did you find anything useful about where you used to teach?" he asked.

She shook her head. "A report of bombings on the campus."

"The world thought you had died in one of the early attacks," Austyn told her.

"It seems that whatever parts of the university your missiles and troops didn't destroy in the initial attacks, the civil war and suicide bombings since have leveled." She reached out and pressed the back of her hand lightly against the glass window. "Who knows, but I might have fared better than many of my colleagues."

"I assume that your sister doesn't know you survived the taking of the lab," Austyn asked. "You had her keys. You were wearing her badge. She must have known that you were there."

Fahimah nodded slightly.

"After the bombing, reports were circulated that no one in the lab had survived. Do you think she believed them?"

She did not respond, keeping her eyes fixed on the clouds outside. The files indicated that Fahimah had been allowed no contact with anyone outside of the prisons over the past five years. Austyn wondered if he could trust those reports.

"It would be a nice surprise for her to hear from you," Austyn continued.

"I am sure she will be very happy," Fahimah replied under her breath.

"How do you know she's still alive?"

Her hands fisted and returned to her lap. "Faith. I would

have felt it, known it in here—" she touched her heart "— if she had died."

Austyn was a man of science. He didn't believe in those kinds of things. "I don't know anything about that, but I hope you're right."

The green eyes looked into his. "You don't *think* you're a believer, Agent Newman. That's fine. In time, you'll prove yourself wrong."

There was no reason to argue and explain that in his thirty-eight years of life, he'd relied on facts and figures to find his way. They were never going to be friends. She was only helping him to find her sister. The less she knew about him, the better.

"I do hope you have something more substantial than faith to lead us to your sister and her files."

"Don't ask any more about the details of our journey," she told him flatly. "I will lead you to what you want."

Fourteen

The steady diet of vending machine Twinkies and old coffee was making him sick. He needed some wholesome, high-protein nourishment. Something like a Big Mac and French fries.

Faas Hanlon crossed the parking lot, got into his car and put the key into the ignition. Glancing up First Street as he started the car, he could see the dome of the Capitol Building rising in the distance. The McDonald's was three blocks north to I Street and two blocks west to S. Capitol. *That's what you call fast food,* he was thinking when his cell phone rang.

"Crap," he muttered, flipping open the phone.

They wanted him back upstairs. The reports from Arizona were in.

Locking his car, he strode across the lot and took the stairs up rather than wait for the elevator. Food would have to wait.

Faas walked into the conference room and threw himself into his chair. It was still warm. The six agents were spread around the long table, working on their laptops just as he'd left them. Photographs of two of the Sedona victims were on the large screen at the far end of the room. Teenagers.

"Who do we have?"

"On the right, Leonard 'Lenny' Guest, age eighteen. On the left, Tyrone 'Ty' North, age nineteen. Both graduated from Red Rock High School in Sedona this past June. No criminal records, no arrests, no DWI. Normal, good kids. Always hung together. Described by friends we interviewed as being practical jokers. Lenny was supposed to start at Northern Arizona University in Flagstaff this coming September. Ty was headed to Los Angeles at the end of the summer. He had a job prospect to work at an uncle's body shop."

"What happened?" Faas asked.

"They spent the afternoon at Lenny's house next to the pool," one of agents explained. "They were supposed to go to a party at another friend's house, but they never showed up."

"Was anyone else home at Lenny's?" Faas asked.

"The mother came and went. She says the boys were fine when she saw them. Ty was fighting a summer cold, so they were taking it easy."

"From taking it easy to stealing a car, what happened?"

"The accusation about stealing the truck has been dropped," the same agent told him. "The owner of the red pickup was a friend of theirs that they were going to meet at the party that night. It seems that this was another one of their practical jokes."

"The owner hasn't come out and said it, but there's speculation that this is a regular thing, swiping one another's cars," another agent explained. "The two boys have done this before. They were driving the vehicle with the valet key."

"Drugs in the car?" Faas asked.

"Marijuana. It seems that they never had a chance to use it, though."

"Are we certain about that?" he asked. "We could be talking about some bad weed spreading the bacteria."

"There's nothing in the autopsy report about that." The agent to his left started typing an e-mail as he was speaking. "The chance that the two families in Maine were smoking pot is really slim, but I'll check back with our offices in Phoenix again for a toxicology report."

Faas looked up at the young faces. They were graduation pictures. What a waste of two lives. "I want to know how long they were unaccounted for."

"I have that right here." One of the agents pulled out a sheet. "Eleven-and-a-half hours."

"Twenty minutes to drive to where they were found. An hour or two to die." Faas was speaking to no one in particular. "Why the hell didn't they call someone when they first felt sick? Wasn't there a cell phone in that truck?"

"Yes, sir, there was. Each of them had one," someone offered. But beyond that there were no answers.

Faas leafed through the faxes and e-mail they'd received from Sedona. Lenny's home was under quarantine, as was every location that the boys had been and every person they'd been in contact with during the week prior to their deaths.

They had nothing so far. No one in the area was showing

any indication of the disease, including Lenny's mother, who had been in the same room with them the day they died. There was no sign of the bacteria anywhere, except in the corpses in and around that pickup truck.

It just didn't add up. Faas stared at the pictures, his appetite suddenly gone.

Fifteen

It was only midafternoon, but they weren't going any farther today.

Fahimah insisted that they stay the night in a hotel in Erbil. It didn't matter to her which one, and she wasn't telling them what they were going to do or where they were going tomorrow. Two army personnel joined their group at the airport, replacing the pilots. One of them, Ken Hilliard, had been stationed in this area of Kurdistan in Northern Iraq since the beginning of the war. He spoke the Kurdish language fluently and knew all the ins and outs of the place.

Rather than take the group to the Erbil Sheraton, officially the Erbil International Hotel, Ken directed the group to the smaller, far less conspicuous Shahan Hotel. Unlike the Sheraton, with its six-inch-thick concrete walls and armed soldiers searching everyone coming near the hotel, the Shahan simply offered security and clean rooms. Cen-

trally located in the city, the whitewashed building with the
tinted glass front had a growing reputation with foreign
business people, many of whom had started switching to
smaller hotels like this one.

Erbil was a dusty city that sprawled outward from a
mound of earth called the *tell*. As they rode in from the
airport, Ken played tour guide, informing them that what
they could see atop the *tell* itself was an ancient Ottoman
fortress, with its ancient walls dominating the city. Saddam's forces had completely destroyed the inside of the
fortress, but poor Kurds had rebuilt there since. While
Fahimah listened in silence, he told everyone that Erbil was
said to be the oldest continuously inhabited city in the
world, with some of the artifacts found there dating back
to 23 B.C. Erbil, in addition to being one of the larger cities
in Iraq, housed the Kurdish Parliament.

Austyn had been surprised to see, while they were still
in the air over this capital of Iraqi Kurdistan, that Erbil was
obviously in the midst of a construction boom. When they
landed at the International Airport, they were met with a
huge billboard—written in Kurdish, Arabic and English—
welcoming them to Kurdistan.

Driving toward the Shahan Hotel, Austyn could see the
new construction projects everywhere. The landscape was
peppered with them, and Ken told them that investors were
pouring their money in, eager to get a piece of the boom.

After Fahimah was given a room and two guards were
stationed on the outside of her door, Austyn and Matt met
with Ken for tea.

Chairs and tables were set up on the shaded sidewalk
next to the hotel. The afternoon air was still hot, but it was

almost comfortable here in the shade. Although it was too early for dinner, the smell of roasting lamb mingled with the normal smells of a city. The steady stream of people, cars, delivery trucks and an occasional horse-drawn cart kept the air vibrant with noise and activity. Other guests of the hotel, Iraqis and foreigners alike, were seated at the tables, drinking tea as well. There were no gates or dividers stopping pedestrians from weaving between tables as they went by.

Matt, inseparable as always from his computer, opened the laptop. "No signal here, either," he said.

"No wireless Internet at all, unless you're on the base. The cell service is shaky, too. From what I hear, the Kurdish government has had a hand in scrambling the signals."

"What about a dial-up connection?" Matt asked.

"Maybe. You'll want to check with the attendant in the lobby," Ken suggested. "And I'd be careful."

There were a few leads on Rahaf that Matt had told him about at the end of the flight. Austyn knew that the other agent was impatient to report the information they'd gathered back to the team in Washington and get someone working on it.

As Matt went back inside, Austyn looked around him. A white SUV with large, light blue UN letters on the hood and the side was parked across the street. A couple of peacekeepers wearing soft caps were laughing with a street vendor selling pistachios a few steps down the sidewalk. Austyn realized that the soldiers weren't armed.

"Your first time here?" Ken asked.

"My first time in Iraq," Austyn answered.

"You're lucky. This is a good place to start."

There were no questions asked, no menus brought out.

Not even a minute after they'd sat down, tea served in small clear glasses sitting on white saucers appeared before them.

"You have to tell them specifically if you want coffee," Ken told him.

"Tea is fine with me."

"And they won't bring out any sugar, either, since it's rationed, unless you ask," Ken continued.

"This is fine the way it is," Austyn said, taking a sip of the hot tea. It was strong. He noticed that the saucer under Ken's tea had a couple of sugar cubes on it. A regular customer, Austyn figured.

A cart carrying propane tanks on the back slowly went by.

"I assume those tanks are empty," Austyn said.

"No, they're probably full."

Every news report from Iraq, it seemed, had to do with some bombing and a rapidly growing number of fatalities. Austyn looked around them, thinking about security. Those tanks could cause a pretty good explosion.

"It's hard for outsiders to believe, but this is absolutely the safest area in Iraq."

Austyn decided he'd been too obvious. He leaned back in the chair, watching the bicycle-drawn cart take a right at the next intersection as a small car careened around the antique vehicle and sped off out of sight.

"From the images of Iraq that Americans see on television, you wouldn't know that there's even one place left in this country that isn't torn up."

Ken nodded with understanding. "Living here, I see and talk to the locals every day. Delivery guys say they're not worried about ambushes. Shopkeepers tell

me that security is not an issue. And they're not just
blowing smoke up my ass. You'll see for yourself. The
shops are open as late as people are on the streets…and
that's way after it gets dark. The restaurants are full. I
don't know how long we'll be here, but if we're here for
a couple of days, you'll hear it from the locals yourself.
None of the Kurds living and working in Erbil are
thinking war—they're thinking peace and prosperity.
Occasional violence or kidnappings are the result of
disagreements between Kurds about independence, but
that's a rare thing."

Austyn figured Ken was probably about fifty, maybe a
little older. Short red hair going gray, freckles, low-key. He
was easy to talk to and seemed like a guy a person could
trust. He'd first come over as an army reservist when his
unit had been deployed, but then his time here had continued to extend. Austyn could already tell that the other man
had a strong attachment to the people and this area.

"While life in the cities to the south—like Baghdad and
Falluja—is pretty much driven by the insurgency, Erbil is
part of the other Iraq, the region that stays out of the headlines and where life resembles something close to normal,"
he continued. "This is actually true for most of Iraq's north-
ernmost regions. This whole area forms a thin, peaceful
crescent around the upper rim of the country, extending
from Duhok to Erbil and Sulaimaniyah, cities that are less
familiar back in the U.S. precisely because they have
largely avoided the violence down south."

Austyn knew that was true. The media wasn't alone in
focusing on killings and disasters. The same went for the
general intelligence briefings they received at Homeland

Security. Reports were issued with the focus on trouble spots. Two tour buses drove slowly by.

"Tourists?" Austyn asked.

Ken smiled and placed one of the small sugar cubes between his teeth, then took a sip of his tea. "Yeah. The local businesses are promoting it heavily. They're trying to convince people that not all of Iraq is Falluja. They're trying hard to show that Kurdistan is safe. The new three-hundred-million-dollar international airport you flew into is just one sign of the changing times."

"Where do these tourists come from?"

"Turkey, Iran. There are some Europeans, too. And, of course, a lot come from south of the border."

"Border?" Austyn asked.

Ken laughed. "The Kurds maintain a hard internal border between what they consider Kurdistan and the Arab-dominated central and southern Iraq. They've had the border in place since the Kurdish uprising at the end of the first Gulf War."

"And they're using it to stop the violence from creeping in from the south?" Austyn asked.

"Seems to be working. Cars on the road heading north are stopped at a series of checkpoints. ID cards are checked. Vehicles are searched. Smugglers, insurgents and terrorists who try sneaking into Kurdistan through Iraq's wilderness areas are ambushed by border patrols."

"And that's enough? A few guards and there's no violence?"

"No," Ken said, looking around him at the faces of people on the street. "They have a second line of defense. The Kurds themselves. Out of necessity, these people have forged one of the most vigilant antiterrorist communities in the world."

"A kind of regional neighborhood watch, huh?"

"Exactly." Ken nodded. "Anyone who doesn't speak Kurdish with a native accent stands out. Kurds are famous for being hospitable, especially to foreigners…obvious tourists, contractors, the military. But if they think you're a problem, watch out. As a group intent on protecting itself, they can be pretty…uh, decisive. And then, there's the Peshmerga."

"I know about them."

"You should. They've fought alongside us since '91. Peshmerga means 'those who face death.' Not a bad name for their armed forces group. Peshmerga is really the group in charge of security. They do a pretty remarkable job of it."

Two fresh cups of black tea appeared before them. Again, Ken's had two sugar cubes on the saucer.

"This tastes good. What kind of tea is it?" Austyn asked.

"Whatever kind they're brewing today." Ken smiled. "I guess…today's tea is Ceylon…from Sri Lanka. That's what most of the hotels in the city seem to be serving these days."

Austyn sipped his tea and looked down the road. In the distance, mountains rose up, rugged and forbidding. His mind locked back on Rahaf Banaz. They needed to find her.

"How big is the region?" Austyn asked, feeling inadequate about his lack of knowledge of the area. But, he told himself, when he left Washington, no one could have foreseen that his mission would take him here. Luckily, Ken Hilliard was a walking encyclopedia, and Austyn was grateful that he was their escort.

The first tea glasses were snatched off the table by a boy

who couldn't be more than ten or twelve. He had the in-
credible ability to carry some twenty or so sets of teacups
and saucers, one stacked on top of the other, without a tray.
Wearing a long white T-shirt, pants and sandals, he flew
between the tables, taking care of everyone sitting outside.

"Iraqi Kurdistan covers about 36,000 square kilometers,
or almost 14,000 square miles, an area slightly smaller
than Switzerland. It's home to about 3.5 million of Iraq's
25 million people."

"I recall the president referring to Kurdistan as an
example of what has gone right in Iraq since 2003,"
Austyn commented.

Ken leaned back, looking around the street. "I thought
the same thing when I was first sent here. But after all these
years, I know better."

"What do you mean?"

"The relative peace they have here is not a result of the
U.S. invasion. This region has been self-governing since
the end of the first Gulf War in '91," Ken explained. "This
was all a no-fly zone patrolled by U.S. and British aircraft
after that war, and that pretty much freed the Kurds of
Saddam Hussein's grip. At least, north of the thirty-sixth
parallel. Since then, Kurds who fled Saddam's Iraq decades
ago have been returning to take posts in the government
and private sector, and in the universities here. They've had
time to stabilize and rebuild."

This explained what Austyn had read about Rahaf
sending so much of her income to this area. Homeland
Security didn't have a file on Fahimah, but he wouldn't be
surprised if she had been doing the same thing. It also
made sense why she would come here to look for her sister.

"Despite everything I've just told you, this area hasn't been entirely peaceful. We had a couple of attacks on the offices of Kurdish political parties in the city a few years back. I think about sixty or seventy people were killed. But that was it. Nothing compared to the rest of this country," Ken continued.

"That would be an average day in Baghdad," Austyn replied, frowning.

"Exactly."

The two men were silent for a moment, and Austyn watched the traffic and sipped his tea. The drivers in Erbil were as crazy as they were in any other city, and maybe a little more so. Surprisingly, nobody was laying on their horns the way they would be in New York or Cairo or Rome.

A street vendor selling watches came by, stopping at each table. When he came to their table, Ken spoke to him in Kurdish, and the man replied politely before moving along. Austyn put his glass on the saucer.

"It's more than just time or roadblocks or the Peshmerga or even foreign investors," he commented. "You can't buy this kind of stability, and God knows we've learned you can't really force it on people long-term, either. This comes by people making *all* of it work together. You've got to want it to work."

Ken nodded. "I agree. People are the main ingredient. I heard one of their commanders say that the Kurdish people identify with their regional government. They feel they have a stake in maintaining peace. He told me if you try to rule a country with oppression and force, you have to surround it with fortresses. But if the people are on your side, *they* become your fortress."

"Not a bad philosophy. Something we could keep in mind when we—"

Austyn stopped mid-sentence, surprised to see one of the guards he'd left outside Fahimah's room appear at the door of the hotel. Immediately behind him, Fahimah followed with the other guard in tow. She had pulled a Nike cap on her head, and she was still wearing the white cotton shirt and camouflage pants she'd put on back at the Brickyard. Although extremely thin, she drew everyone's gaze when she stepped out. Austyn realized that she was definitely a head-turner. Those green eyes in the pale face never ceased to startle him. She came directly to their table.

Ken and Austyn both stood up.

"I'm sorry, sir," one of the guards started. "She wouldn't wait in the room until we could ask you if—"

"I'm not a prisoner," she said in a low but clear voice before sitting down at the table with them.

Austyn motioned to the two soldiers to wait by the front of the hotel. He immediately saw the error in that. Everyone—from those at the tables to the people in the cars or on the sidewalk—was looking at the soldiers.

"There's very little U.S. military presence in the north," Ken explained. "People say they don't feel occupied. They're not used to seeing armed soldiers."

"I warned him of that when we were still in Afghanistan," Fahimah said.

Austyn wasn't about to let her sit out here without protection. He carried no weapon. Ken seemed way too relaxed to be counted on to draw the pistol he wore at his belt. Just then, an argument broke out across the street between a shop owner and the watch vendor who'd stopped in front of his store. For a few minutes, anyway, everyone's attention was focused in that direction.

He looked at Ken, who was studying Fahimah's profile intently. Interestingly, the red-haired soldier seemed to have a crush on her. Austyn noticed it at the airport, where Ken had met them. The British accent and the green eyes must have done it, he supposed.

The boy appeared with more tea. He put one in front of Fahimah.

"Supas...mamnoon." She nodded to him.

The boy shot her a surprised look, glanced at the men, and then asked something. She answered him. The boy smiled and walked away.

"What was that all about?" Austyn asked.

She didn't answer. He noticed that there were three sugar cubes on her saucer.

"What did he ask you?" Austyn asked Fahimah again.

She actually smiled and looked over at Ken. "Would you care to translate?"

Austyn noticed that the other man's face had blushed deep red. "I didn't get the whole thing. Something about the bathroom. And him showing to us..." Ken's voice trailed off.

"You are far too polite," she told him before turning to Austyn. "The boy asked me if he should pee in your tea."

"And you told him?" he asked.

"Not today. But maybe tomorrow."

Austyn looked suspiciously at the glass cup before him. It looked strangely lighter than the last one.

"Don't worry," she said, softly tapping his glass with a spoon she'd been given with her tea. "He's a good boy. He wouldn't do it unless I asked him to."

Austyn saw her drop the three sugar cubes in her glass and stir the tea.

"Did he recognize you?" he asked.

"No." She shook her head.

"Have you stayed here before?"

She looked up at the white cinder-block facade of the hotel. "Yes, I have. Many years ago."

"Then you could have run into him."

"No," she said with certainty. "I was detained for five years, Agent Newman. And I stayed here quite some time before that. No, this boy would have been too young to be working anywhere."

"Then how did he know you took three sugars in your tea?" Austyn asked.

"He didn't. I don't take any sugar in my tea. But I would have used whatever he gave me to make him feel appreciated. After all, in bringing me sugar, he was trying to make me feel special."

He couldn't help but notice how much more at ease she looked here. She seemed almost happy. Certainly, she looked at home. She turned her chair slightly so that she could watch the traffic going by. Ken was completely quiet now that Fahimah was here. Austyn noticed he was doing a lot of staring in her direction. The argument across the street had subsided, and the vendor had gone down the street.

"There's a place I need to visit today," she told him after finishing her tea. "I can't go there, though, escorted by your soldiers."

"What place?" Austyn asked.

"The prison."

"You feel homesick?"

Her gaze narrowed. "It is a little soon to be making such bad jokes, don't you think?"

He lifted both hands in defense. "You were the one who's planning the contents of my tea for tomorrow."

"That *maybe* just turned into *definitely,*" she warned him. "In fact, Agent Newman, I would not drink anything more at all while you are in Erbil."

"Which prison?" Ken intervened.

"Erbil Prison," she responded, turning to him.

"Do you need to see someone being held there?" Austyn asked.

"No, I simply need to visit the neighborhood."

"I know where it is," Ken told her. "In fact, I'm fairly familiar with the area."

The boy and the tea appeared again.

"Na," she smiled up at him. *"Supas."*

"What does that mean?" Austyn immediately asked.

"Na means no," she told him. *"Supas* means thank you."

Austyn looked at Ken first, making sure she wasn't telling him something totally off the wall. The other man nodded.

"Na, supas," he repeated to their server.

The boy smiled and dropped a sugar cube from his shirt pocket onto Austyn's saucer before going on to the next table.

"I think he likes me," he said cheerfully to the other two.

Another tour bus went by. A couple of young men stuck their heads out of the open windows and yelled something in the direction of the two soldiers standing guard on the street. One of them spit out the window. Austyn looked at Ken.

He shook his head. "Iraqis. Don't ask."

"I told you where I need to go." Fahimah turned to them, pretending what she'd heard hadn't affected her. "I will not accomplish anything if I go there followed by armed escorts."

"I can take you," Ken offered immediately. He turned to Austyn. "She's right. It's a lot safer to travel around the city if you don't bring that kind of attention to yourself. It's no problem. I'll bring her back."

There was no way she was going anywhere without him.

"Tell me who you're going to see. I want an exact street address," Austyn demanded of Fahimah. "Without cell phones and without knowing the language, there's no way I can get hold of you if I needed to."

She shook her head slowly from side to side. "I do not know who or where until I get there. I am acting on a…on a lead that is five years old."

Austyn was not about to be the one who would have to report Fahimah's disappearance to Faas Hanlon and the rest of them in Washington.

"We'll go," he said, standing up and putting an end to any argument she might have had. "The three of us."

Sixteen

In the east, a full moon hung low over the water. The research boat, *Harmony,* rolled gently on the calm rise and fall of the Atlantic. In the distance, lights from the cities and towns along the shore twinkled happily, offering a sense of direction to those unaccustomed to the broad black expanses of the sea. The kids, the parents and the crew were exhausted from the workday, but no one was ready to call it a night. Everyone was on deck.

David wished Sally could have been here. Josh and two other boys had immediately formed a friendship. The other seven kids on the boat were girls, but they were definitely not the enemy.

One of the guidance counselors played his harmonica while another one tried to match the melody with his guitar. The parents were happy just to sit and watch. Divided comfortably into various-size groups, everyone was sitting around, some with sleeping bags wrapped around them, enjoying this reprieve from hospitals and doctors and the day-to-day worry that was part of the illness.

"Ten hours into the trip and there hasn't been one medical emergency," a young father sitting next to David commented.

"That's a victory, isn't it?" he replied.

The younger man's name was Craig. His son was eleven and one of the boys that Josh had befriended right away. They'd come all the way from Virginia. Dan had the same type of leukemia that Josh did, except that he had been declared "cured" last month. The father and son were on this trip to celebrate. David thought that it was a good thing for Josh to see the full head of hair on the boy, the healthy-looking skin, the energy. Dan was a reminder that life could get back to normal.

No, David told himself. *Would* get back to normal.

A sore-sounding cough emanating from someone climbing the steep, narrow stairs from the galley drew both men's attention. Ever since Josh had been diagnosed, David and Sally had been very careful about keeping their son away from illnesses. The program director came out on deck. He was still coughing.

"*He* doesn't sound good," Craig commented under his breath.

"You would think they'd be sensitive about sending someone who was sick on one of these trips," David said.

"He's in charge of the trip, but he's also the lead diver, I heard," Craig told him. "A PhD candidate at Woods Hole. He does this in the summer. Real nice guy. I got talking to him for a while this afternoon when the kids were checking out the different instruments. He pretty much runs the show on these trips. I don't imagine they could have replaced him at the last minute. He doesn't think he's sick, though."

David snorted. "Really? What does he think is wrong with him?"

"He told me his allergies have been acting up, but it sounds like something worse to me, too," Craig said. "He was complaining of a sore throat. I have a bag full of homeopathic stuff that my wife packed for us. She's a distributor for a West Coast company that makes them. Maybe I'll ask him if he wants to try something."

"Well, I'm a walking pharmacy myself," David admitted. "He's welcome to whatever he needs. I've got a ton of stuff in my briefcase."

The young man was working his way along the deck toward them.

"Let's ask him," Craig said.

Seventeen

Having two people escort her was actually better than one, especially since one of them was so familiar with Erbil and the streets and neighborhoods.

The three of them took an unmarked white van from the hotel. Fahimah could no longer stand wearing the camouflage fatigue pants. And it was more than personal choice, she told herself. Dressed as she was, she didn't know how successful she'd be getting any locals even to talk to her.

"We are stopping there," she told Ken, who was driving the car.

"What is this place?" Newman asked, sitting next to her in the back.

"A woman's clothing store. And you are coming in with me."

The look on his face conveyed volumes about how

thrilled he was at the prospect of shopping for women's clothes. Ken pulled to the curb in front of the store.

"Out," she told him, reaching over him and opening the door. "Move, please."

He frowned at her for a moment, not moving.

"I thought you were in a hurry," she said.

"Maybe I should wait outside and send Ken in with you?" he asked as he climbed out. He stood on the sidewalk, eyeing the glass front windows. It could have been a shop in any Western city.

"No, you must pay for things. I have no money." She went past him into the store. Two women, who appeared to be the owner of the shop and her helper, were the only ones in the store. Their attention immediately focused on the American, despite the fact that Fahimah was obviously the customer. Fahimah decided his good looks might have something to do with it. Or perhaps her own clothes were the deterrent. The assistant spoke broken English.

Fahimah went quickly through the racks, picking up a couple of pairs of pants, some shirts, underwear and socks, and a sweater. She knew how cold this section of the country could get at nights. Near the register, she grabbed two head scarves. She didn't want to walk around wearing a cap. The store didn't have any shoes, so she had to do with the plastic sandals for now. She took her purchases to the counter to have the shop owner figure out the cost.

"You pay for them and I'll change," she told Austyn. The older woman was very pleasant, and after Fahimah spoke to her in Kurdish, she gave them a large discount on everything…without any bartering. Fahimah was directed to a curtained area at the far end of the small shop where she could change.

"Is she your girlfriend?" she heard the assistant ask when she headed that way.

"No…she's my wife."

Fahimah looked in shock over her shoulder. He had his back to her. She went around the curtain to change. She could clearly hear every word.

This area of the shop was almost half as large as the store itself. An old Singer sewing machine with a foot pedal sat on a table in the corner. Pieces of clothing in various stages of alteration and mending were draped on the tables and chairs around the machine. Yards of fabric were piled in a corner. Fahimah put her things on a nearby chair.

"What happened to her…*moo?*" Fahimah heard the woman ask the American.

"Excuse me?" Austyn asked. "I'm sorry, I don't…" His voice trailed off.

"Moo chee shodeh?" the other voice asked. She didn't know the word for hair.

"Ser…kelle…" The first one struggled.

"Oh. Head…hair," he said. "Her hair."

Fahimah figured she must have pointed to her hair or head.

"It's very sad," he said, lowering his voice.

Fahimah hurried to change, fearing what he was going to tell them as a way of explanation. He didn't understand their way of life. Still, he'd guessed correctly about the inappropriateness of a woman, even at Fahimah's age, to be going around with a boyfriend. When it came to dealing with women, Kurds were in most ways more advanced than the rest of Iraq. They educated their girls. The women worked. They voted. They played a public role in this open, liberal, peaceful society. At the same time, five years could not change the fact that Iraq was still an area ruled by conservative Muslim clerics. Correctness was a *must*.

Fahimah was pulling a shirt over her head. She'd missed what he'd said, but from the women's reaction, she guessed it wasn't good. The two were praying aloud, and she thought it sounded like one of them might even be crying. She hurried and folded the clothes she'd peeled off. She gave herself a quick look in the small mirror and draped the scarf over her head, wrapping one corner around her throat and tossing the end over her shoulder. She left the changing room with her arms full.

"Teflaki," the younger woman said with a sigh at the sight of Fahimah.

The older woman touched her chest with a fisted hand. *"Ghemgîn,"* she said as she came around the counter.

Fahimah looked suspiciously at Austyn. "What did you tell them?"

He shook his head. "It's okay that they know."

Both women reached her. The younger one took everything out of Fahimah's hands, taking her by the arm as if she was an invalid. The older one undid a pin and a charm from the neckline of her blouse and started pinning it on Fahimah. There was an Arabic prayer etched on the gold charm.

"Saratan…" The woman tapped her chest again.

"You told them I had cancer?" she asked, looking in shock at the agent.

"I told you it's okay. They understand," he said, looking contrite.

She was stunned to think that he thought he'd done her a favor. The older woman took Fahimah by the hand and took her back to the register. She tried to stuff all the money Newman had given her for the clothing back.

"Na, na. Mamnun," Fahimah said, thanking her. *"Ew zêngîn e. Mamnun. Mamnun."* She pushed the shop owner's register closed and took the bag of clothes from the other woman and grabbed Newman by the arm.

"What did you tell them?" he asked.

"That you are rich." She tugged on his arm. "We need to go. You have upset these poor people enough."

At the door, she remembered the charm and turned around to give it back to the shop owner. She was on Fahimah's heels and wouldn't have it. She had to keep it.

Prayers followed them as they left the store.

"That was very…mean, you know. They believed what you told them. You could see how it upset them so," she scolded when they were on the street. "How could you do that?"

"How else was I going to tell them why you're bald?"

"I am not bald," she said defensively, touching the scarf on her head. "I have very short hair. And you could have told the truth or given no answer. These women are innocent. They are really upset about this."

"Aren't you making too much of this?" he asked.

"No." She stopped and looked hard into his face. "These are Kurds. After Saddam's military poisoned the Kurdish people in Halabja in 1988 with their chemical weapons, the people's misery didn't just go away. Cancer and leukemia have been following the survivors of that horrible crime. I don't know what it is now, but before your people locked me away, we had one of the highest percentages of cancer in the world."

His expression changed. He touched her arm. "I'm very sorry about this. I didn't do that very well."

He had a kicked look. It flustered her. She felt the warmth of his fingers through the material of the shirt. She tried to focus on where she was, what she was saying.

"I'm sorry, Fahimah," he repeated.

She realized this was the first time he had called her by her first name.

"You do not lie to my people. Understand?" She got out the words before forgetting them.

The kicked look went away. He smiled.

"What are you smiling at?"

"You're defending them as if they were your family."

"They are Kurds. Of course they are like family."

He shook his head with amusement. "I can't believe you remained silent in prison for five years. You don't even consider yourself an Iraqi."

She was almost happy that he understood that there was a difference.

"I remained silent because I *am* a Kurd."

"And your sister?"

"She is a Kurd, too," Fahimah said shortly, turning and walking to the van. Before getting in, she noticed an SUV that was parked a couple of cars away behind them. She shoved the bag inside the van and marched down to the SUV. The windows were tinted and closed, but she had no trouble seeing the military uniform of the driver behind the wheel.

She stood on the sidewalk and knocked on the window. In the glass reflection she saw that Austyn had moved behind her.

"Tell them to open the window," she said over her shoulder.

"Open the window," he repeated.

The window rolled slowly down. There were four people inside the car. Her escorts. Matt Sutton was sitting nearest to her, looking out the passenger window.

"I am going to say this only once, and you all had better hear it," she said sharply. "You need my help. I am trying to help you. But you ruin my chances when you behave this way."

Fahimah pointed at the bustling street. "Do you see any foreign troops here?"

The four men looked around obediently. Agent Sutton was the one brave enough to shake his head.

"Now, do you see those people in uniform?" she pointed again. "Those two are policemen who direct the traffic. And the other three that you see in that intersection are Peshmerga. They are in charge of security. We saw them all through the city as we drove here. All I need to do is call or wave my hand to get their attention. They will not allow anything…*anything*…to happen to me or any other Kurd walking the streets."

They were all listening, as her students used to, so she continued.

"I'm in search of a person who can direct me to where I can get you some answers. Now, it is bad enough to have these two people with me." She pointed vaguely over her shoulder. "But I might manage to explain that. The four of you, however, is completely wrong. Other than frightening people away, you accomplish nothing."

"They might not know we're following you," Sutton suggested hopefully.

She shook her head. It was like speaking to children. "You are foreigners. You stand out more than aborigines in the House of Lords. Either stop following me or I shall just go back to the hotel. I will not waste my time."

The men looked at her, and then she saw Sutton's gaze shift upward, over her shoulder.

"Please tell them to go back to the hotel," she said to Austyn without turning around.

"Go back to the hotel," he repeated after a moment's pause.

Fahimah decided to stand there and wait. Sutton gave her a half salute and the windows rolled up. The SUV pulled into the traffic.

"Do you feel better now?" Austyn asked.

She turned around and started back to the van. "Thank you. I feel much better."

"My old Catholic nuns have nothing on you."

Fahimah nodded. "Thank you. I shall consider that a compliment."

She climbed inside the van. Again, rather than sitting in front, Austyn climbed in after her. Ken pulled out into traffic.

"Did you have them dismissed?" he asked, grinning into the rearview mirror.

"She did," Austyn told Ken. "Watch what you say or she might do the same thing to you."

Fahimah knew Austyn was trying to make light of everything, but her nerves were beginning to get the best of her. She didn't know if she was in the right city. She wasn't sure if her sister was anywhere around here or if she would be able get in touch with Rahaf. And if she did find her, could she trust these people to stand by their word? Suddenly, she was doubting everything, including herself.

"Okay, now it's only the three of us," Austyn told her. "How about telling us who you're looking for and how we can help?"

It would have been so much easier to deal with him if he were a louse, Fahimah thought. He annoyed her at times, but all in all he'd been cooperative and forthcoming. He wanted to achieve his goal; that she could count on.

Ken was battling traffic. The streets were packed with cars. She glanced at the clock on the dash. It was almost four o'clock in the afternoon.

"We are in Erbil since I believe my sister would have come to Kurdistan," she told Austyn. "But for five years, naturally, I have had no contact with her."

"Did she have a house here? Somewhere that we can take you to?"

"Yes…well, no. She lost me five years ago. She knew American troops would consider her an enemy just because of her work. She would not live where you, I or anyone else could find her."

"That makes sense, but we should try there to begin with, don't you think?"

"I already have. From the hotel. I rang up the city offices. Her house no longer stands. There is a new office building being constructed where she used to live. And as far as moving to some other address, I checked the telephone directory."

This was something new. With all the developments

in Erbil, obviously, came the modernization of many people having a telephone. And there would be a need for a directory.

"She'd be in the phone book?"

Fahimah could imagine how idiotic these agents would feel if they thought for all these years Rahaf had been listed in some directory.

"No," she said, wanting to put his mind at ease. "She would not be listed under any name that you would know."

"But you know how she would list her name."

"Yes, and as I suspected she's not there."

Ken looked in the rearview mirror at them. "I've seen that phone book. I'd say not even a tenth of the people living in Erbil are in there."

She shrugged. "That may be true, but it was worth a try. This city is too large to go door to door trying to find her." In phoning around, Fahimah had made sure to leave her name in many places. Her hope was that if enough people heard she was back in Erbil, Rahaf would hear about it and find her.

"So what's the next step?"

"I was getting there," she replied, hearing the impatience in her own voice. Fahimah glanced at the clock again. Erbil was having big-city problems. Traffic. Fifteen minutes and they hadn't moved far. She could see the sun's amber-colored heat rising in waves off the cars ahead of them.

"I'm hoping to find a man who, in the old days, would spread his prayer blanket at the foot of the street leading up to the prison," she told them.

The looks the two men sent her smacked of skepticism.

"A homeless old man?" Ken asked from the front seat.

"Jalal is not homeless," she explained. "He is a dervish…a holy man. Actually, he became a dervish after his only son was arrested by Saddam almost thirty years ago."

"By dervish," Ken explained to Austyn, "she is talking about members of an ascetic Sufi religious fraternity. They're known for their extreme poverty and austerity."

"I know a little bit about them," Austyn answered. He turned to Fahimah. "And you know this man?"

She nodded. "Many know him. He came from a village near Halabja. He is well respected."

"But he came before the trouble there?"

"Yes," she replied, looking out the window. "He came before that tragedy."

As the traffic moved a little, two Peshmerga came along the sidewalk. They looked at her as they passed the van and nodded. She smiled and turned back to Austyn.

"What happened to his son?" he asked.

She shook her head. "It was the way of the world then. He was arrested and never seen again. So different from my own situation, don't you think?"

He looked at her for a long moment, his face grim.

"Why did he come here, to this prison?" he said finally.

"After trying for several years to find out what had happened to his son, Jalal was told that his son was being held here at the prison in Hawler…I mean Erbil. Hawler is the Kurdish name for the city. Anyway, he left Halabja with a prayer blanket and the clothing on his back and came here."

Fahimah hesitated, hoping that she hadn't done the

wrong thing by mentioning Jalal's name. She reasoned that she was helping them, so there was no reason for the Americans to interfere with the old man.

"We know that you and your sister are from Halabja," Austyn said quietly.

"Of course," she said. "It is no secret."

Austyn paused for a moment. "And this Jalal is important?"

"In many ways. For all the years that the son has been missing, Jalal has kept his vigil on that street corner. Regardless of the season, he could be counted on to bring his prayer rug, where he sits and prays, asking any of the guards or prison workers going by if they know his son."

"How does he live?" Ken asked.

"People drop money on his rug. It is considered good luck to give," she told them.

It was difficult to explain to someone who'd been born and raised outside of this culture how curious and deep people's beliefs went.

"We have a saying, 'God finds a low branch for the bird that cannot fly.' What Jalal does is not begging," she clarified. "What he has done and continues to do is to take a stand for all the Kurdish people."

Fahimah looked from one man to the other before continuing. "That old man represents hundreds of thousands of people who never stop mourning their loved ones. He makes the younger ones remember, so that we won't allow the same thing to happen to us again."

Both men fell silent. The traffic was moving again, and Ken turned at the next intersection. In a few minutes, they were in a section that she knew well. Fahimah looked at all the new houses and shops that had gone up since the last time she'd been here.

Austyn broke the silence. "About the old man. The Kurds have been in control of this region for years. Why didn't anyone give Jalal information about what happened to his son?"

"I don't think there was ever any information to give him. In fact, I don't know if he was ever here. I don't know what has happened in the past five years, but before that, the Kurds were always finding the sites of more mass graves. The boy is probably in one of those graves, along with so many other Kurds who were shot in the back and bulldozed under in the killing fields."

Fahimah's eyes suddenly teared and she looked out the window again. Such thoughts were painful. She'd lost some of the men in her own family that way. Three brothers, two uncles and a cousin. Her youngest brother had been only twelve. He was tall for his age, and that was enough to collect him with the men, taking them where no one would ever hear from them again.

She blinked back the tears and focused on the low white-brick buildings and the people as they passed. She was glad they were moving again.

"Unless they give him his son's body to bury," she said finally, "Jalal will keep his vigil."

"And you think he might know where your sister is?" Austyn asked.

"No, he doesn't care to keep that kind of information. But many people talk to him. The Kurds respect him. It would be good for him to know that I have returned to Erbil. Through him, many will know."

She busied herself adjusting the scarf around her neck. She didn't want them to know she was upset.

"You haven't been back here for five years. Do you think Jalal still goes to the place by the prison?" Austyn asked.

His tone was gentle. She didn't want them to be nice to her. Not these people. She wanted it to be easy to walk away.

"I asked at the hotel where we're staying. People still see him there."

The van was now very close to their destination. She could see the high wall of the prison at the end of the street. Fahimah looked past the oncoming traffic at the sidewalk on the opposite side. Just ahead, she could see the stalls of an open-air bazaar that lined the far side of the street and spread up into several alleyways. There were crowds of people on foot in the area, but she spotted a group of men near one of the stalls, crouched and standing in the shade around someone sitting against the wall. It was the old dervish.

"Please pull to the curb and let me out."

"We're coming with you," Austyn reminded her.

"You can sit in the car and watch me walk across the street," she told him. "Jalal will not talk to me if he sees you. And even if he does speak to me, the news that will reach my sister is that I'm still under arrest. That is not the way to bring Rahaf forward to see me."

"You can pretend you don't know me," Austyn said more forcefully. "But I'm not going to let you go out there alone."

Ken pulled to the curb where he was directed. Fahimah considered arguing with Austyn, but glancing across the street, she saw Jalal starting to gather his things. A boy was helping him up.

"Keep your distance," she warned him. "After we cross the street, you go ahead and pass him. You can wait at that vendor's stall over there and watch me. Even if something happens, do not reveal that you know me."

She pushed her door open before he had time to disagree. For some reason, the traffic on the wide street had crawled to a halt. She began to weave through the cars across the concrete roadway. Behind her, the other door to the van opened and slammed shut.

Drivers were now beeping their horns and cheering out their windows, and she looked up the street in surprise at the sound of musicians playing. Beyond the line of cars and trucks, coming along the street at the base of the prison walls, she saw a procession of people. They turned onto their street.

"What's that?" he heard Austyn ask in her ear. He couldn't stay away from her.

"It's a wedding. People get married on Monday and Thursday nights. This is Thursday," she told him. "Now, get away from me."

The cheers were loud. The car leading the parade passed them. It was covered with flowers. The bride and groom were walking behind the car. The rest of the wedding guests followed behind, some on foot and others in vehicles. Musicians walked along the outside, singing and playing their drums, while women in traditional Kurdish costume followed behind and threw candy and rice on the heads of those standing by.

Everyone on the street, drivers and pedestrians alike, had come to a standstill, watching and cheering for the bride and groom. People shopping at the open-air market were now lining the street, as well, and Fahimah couldn't see the sidewalk. She was afraid that Jalal would leave. She made up her mind and made a dash across the street ahead of a truck carrying another mob of guests.

Arriving at the opposite side, she looked around and panicked, unable to see any sign of Jalal.

"Fahimah." She heard Agent Newman calling her name.

She turned around and saw him still in the middle of the street. He waved at her to wait for him. She searched the faces of the people on the sidewalk, looking for the older man.

Someone tugged on her sleeve. She looked down. It was a young boy.

"Hatin," he whispered.

Fahimah nodded, took his hand and followed him quickly into the throng of people.

Eighteen

Cathy Mittman, the office manager of the law firm Crandel and Smith, reached for the phone when her line buzzed at 8:59 a.m. It was the receptionist who answered external phone calls.

"Cathy, do you know where Leo might be? I have his girlfriend on the line, and she doesn't want to be put through to the voice mail."

Hired right out of Harvard Law School and moving quickly along the fast track, Leo Bolender was a newly made partner, working in the real estate group.

"I don't know where he is. But why don't you put her through to me?"

Cathy had only met Kimberly Cage a couple of times, at office parties. She worked in sales...some kind of rep. Cathy couldn't exactly remember. She seemed like a nice enough person, and very pretty. The two of them looked really cute together.

"Good morning, Kimberly."

"Cathy! Thank you for taking my call," the young woman said, sounding agitated. "By any chance, have you seen Leo this morning?"

Cathy glanced toward the young man's office. "Well, I know he's here. I can see his briefcase and suit jacket. And this morning when I came in, his office light was on. I haven't seen him personally, though."

"Oh, thank God," the young woman blurted, clearly relieved. "I've been so worried about him."

"Worried?"

"I'm in Seattle this week. But last night I couldn't get him at home. And I tried his cell, too, but he didn't answer it. I left half a dozen messages on his office line, too. I know he's been busy with the Dubai resort negotiations…."

Cathy put her hand over the mouthpiece of the phone and whispered *thank you* to one of the secretaries for bringing her a cup of coffee.

"And when I talked to him yesterday morning," Kim continued, "he said he wasn't feeling well at all. He was wondering if he should switch medicines."

Cathy logged on to her computer and checked Leo's appointment schedule. As the office manager, she had access to all the partners' appointment calendars, just as her phone could check their voice mail and pick up their lines.

"These young bucks just don't know how to take care of their health, do they?" she said brightly.

"I told him he should take the time and see a doctor. Do

you know if he went yesterday? He's been fighting whatever it is he's got for two weeks now."

Leo's first meeting of the day wasn't until eleven. She
noticed that there were eight messages left on his phone
line. He had to be around.

"I don't think so, hon. But I told him the same thing. He
was coughing and hacking all over us yesterday."

Cathy returned the wave of one of the summer interns
as he passed by her desk. She watched the young man go
down the hall toward the restroom. Dardo Saldano was
going to be a senior at Georgetown this year. This was his
second summer of working at their office, and Cathy really
liked the young man.

"Well, I'm not waiting for him anymore. I don't want
him to go through the entire weekend feeling miserable,"
Kimberly said. "Will you please tell him that I've made an
appointment with—"

Someone was shouting.

"Hold on a sec, would you?" Cathy took the phone
away from her ear and stood up. Everyone else in their
section of the office was looking in the same direction.

The bathroom door banged open.

"Call 911!" the intern called out, staggering out of the
bathroom.

He was as white as the tiled ceiling.

"Call 911," he croaked again before bending over and
throwing up into one of the office plants.

Cathy dropped the phone and ran toward Dardo.

"Do it," she shouted to one of the other assistants who
was staring in disbelief a couple of steps away from the
sick young man.

She crouched next to Dardo. He was gasping for air, crying at the same time.

"Get me some towels," she ordered a young lawyer who'd just arrived. She was standing with her briefcase in hand, watching.

"Towels?"

"In the bathroom," Cathy said. "There's a supply closet in there."

"No!" Dardo shook his head. "Don't go in there."

It was too late. The young woman had opened the door. "Oh, my God! What's that smell?"

When the young lawyer started screaming, she was loud enough to let everyone from here to the Capitol Building know the problem wasn't with the sick intern at their feet. Something else was lying on the floor in that bathroom.

Nineteen

Erbil, Iraq

She was standing there one minute and the next she was gone. Austyn shouted for Ken over his shoulder and pushed his way through the passing wedding celebration. When he reached the sidewalk, a sea of angry faces greeted him every way that he looked.

He didn't care. He couldn't see her. He strode to the place where he'd seen the dervish sitting, but he was gone, too.

Ken reached him. "Where is she?"

"Gone," he said angrily over the music and cheering of the wedding procession, which had stopped and formed a circle in the street.

He grabbed a wooden box from a stack next to a fruit stall and climbed on it. He scanned the crowd. Still, he could see no sign of her.

"I'll go talk to those Peshmerga," Ken told him.

Austyn saw the three uniformed Kurdish soldiers stand-

ing by the curb, enjoying the festivities. Based on what he'd
heard so far, he doubted they would help a foreigner at the
expense of a Kurd—no matter what the reason was. They
took care of their own people and their own problems.

Inside, he was kicking himself. He had somehow gotten
to the point with Fahimah that he actually couldn't believe
that she would do this to him…that she would just walk
away. Like a moron, he thought they'd formed a working
relationship, at least. They had an agreement. He'd
believed her when she said she was going to help them.

Austyn thought about the five years that she'd been held
in their prisons. What kind of grudge would *he* carry after
being treated like that? What a fool he was!

"Fahimah!" he shouted out, knowing there was no
purpose to it. He wouldn't answer if their places were
reversed.

A few people in the crowd near him turned around and
gave him a side look. They soon went back to watching the
wedding celebrations.

Ken was walking away from the soldiers. Austyn saw
the soldiers' attention turn to the dancers again.

"Anything?" he asked as he stepped down from the box.

Ken shook his head. "That was a waste of breath. They
haven't seen her. They don't have time to look for her. And
they didn't know what I was talking about as far as Jalal
goes. There's no such person, so naturally they couldn't
know where he lives."

Austyn kept looking beyond the crowds as he talked.
"We can spread out and check the side streets. Also, I need
you to get hold of Matt. I want him and the rest of our men
down here. Can we get help from your base?"

"I'll call them," Ken suggested. "But it will take time to round them up and get them down here. As I told you before, we have only a skeleton crew stationed in Erbil."

"I'll take whatever I can get."

"You know, maybe you should give her a little time. She might come back on her own. Fahimah did tell us that she wouldn't be able to get any answers if we were hovering over her shoulder."

"I'm not willing to risk that," Austyn told the other man. "She might have been abducted."

Ken shook his head doubtfully. "I know that's an everyday occurrence south of here, but you just don't hear it happening in Erbil."

Austyn disagreed. "If this is all connected to Al Qaeda, if the sister is behind the attacks, then the word could be out that Fahimah is here and that she could ruin everything. And even if Rahaf is not involved, she could hold the key to the remedy. If that's the case, then it doesn't matter which sister they get hold of. They'll know grabbing Fahimah is one way to stop any cooperation with us."

Suddenly, Ken seemed a lot more motivated in getting to a phone.

Austyn wanted to think of Fahimah as walking away of her own free will. He didn't want to think her life was in danger. It was so much easier to be angry at her than to think that he hadn't done a good enough job protecting her.

The truth was, though, that he'd failed miserably.

There was a tug on his sleeve. He looked down. A Kurdish boy, who couldn't have been more than six or seven years old, stuffed something into his hand and ran away. Austyn took a couple of steps after the boy, but the street urchin disappeared like a ghost into the crowd.

"What is it?" Ken asked over Austyn's shoulder.

"It's a scrap of paper." He opened the crumpled note, read it and looked in the direction the boy had gone. "It says, 'I'll see you back at the hotel.'"

Twenty

No one knew how the media got word of the debacle unfolding at the law firm.

Clearly, though, the phone call to 911 had not been the only call made from the law office of Crandel and Smith after Leo Bolender's rapidly decomposing body was discovered in the men's bathroom. By the time Homeland Security had moved in their ambulances, equipment and personnel to quarantine the people and the building, news vans were pulling up across Pennsylvania Avenue.

Before Faas even reached the office building, news stations were already reporting another outbreak similar to the tragedy in Sedona. The intelligence chief knew it could have been anyone at the law firm. One call to a family member would be enough to start a media avalanche.

It no longer mattered. What did matter was that the word *calm* no longer applied in D.C. In less than an hour, chaos had taken hold of the city. Telephone systems and cell phone lines were jammed. The highways were a parking lot. Emergency dispatchers were inundated with calls from hysterical residents.

President Penn had already called out the National Guard. Government offices were ordered to close by midday. A state of emergency had been issued for the District of Columbia, and the governors of Virginia and Maryland were about to do the same thing. Airlines, trains and buses were not running. All bridges into and out of the district had been closed and a perimeter was being set up, with Georgetown, Q Street, Florida Avenue and Benning Road forming the northern boundary. Police and troops would keep vehicles from moving into or out of the city at that point. A mandatory curfew was in place from 8:00 p.m. tonight, and people were being encouraged to remain where they were.

In short, the president had clamped a lid on the nation's capital. Assured by his staff and the director of Homeland Security that they weren't overreacting, President Penn had gone on television with the mayor of D.C. to explain the actions that were being taken. Their first priority, he'd told the nation, was to safeguard the well-being of the people of Washington. To do that, they needed the cooperation of everyone in getting off the streets and into a secure location. What the president didn't say was that there were no safe zones that anyone could be certain of, and until they knew how far and how fast the plague could spread, no one would be allowed to run away, only to carry the horror with them.

Faas leaned against the mobile command unit parked in

front of the building. The lines of vans and ambulances and police cars, four deep inside the police tape, provided some barrier to the news people. He crushed the cigarette he'd been smoking under his heel. He'd gone without one for eight months now. That had made his kids proud. Well, he thought, he'd just have to quit again.

The door to the vehicle opened. One of his agents held a phone out to him. "The president. He wants an update."

Faas took a deep breath and looked up at the windows of the law firm.

"Yes, sir. Only one dead. No other infection that we know of. It appears no one touched the body of the victim," he told the president. They'd already spoken half a dozen times this morning, and Faas was glad he finally had something positive to pass on. "Everyone on the fourth floor, where the law offices are located, has been isolated. They're being transferred to one of our nearby facilities for more testing and observation, but that will take some time."

"What about the two people who were in the bathroom with the body?" Penn asked. "How are they?"

"No sign of infection, yet. Our experts here think that the ventilation in the bathroom might have reduced the chance of infection," Faas answered.

"But the same ventilation may have exposed others in that building, or expelled the microbes into the city," Penn snapped. "Isn't that true, Mr. Hanlon?"

"Yes, sir," Faas answered, looking up at the roof of the building. He had personnel up there checking the HVAC units now.

There was no getting around it. He didn't know to what extent the bacteria may have spread. He didn't know who was infected and who wasn't. He didn't even know, for sure, how long the microbe was dangerous. That was why he had recommended the extreme emergency measures be taken in the city. "A suggestion was made a few minutes ago by NIH that a special quarantine area be set up in a two-block radius from Crandel and Smith offices."

"Do it," Penn ordered.

"Yes, sir. That puts us only three blocks from the White House, Mr. President."

"I know that."

"Yes, sir."

There was a pause on the line.

"Hanlon, do you have any of the DM8A serum for the people who have come in contact with the victim over the past twenty-four hours? I'm thinking specifically about the two who had the closest contact to this victim."

"Yes, Mr. President. I have NIH personnel here who are ready to use their test samples on these people if it becomes necessary," Faas told him. "Also, our liaison at Reynolds Pharmaceuticals told me twenty-five minutes ago that the company is doing everything in its power to push the first production quantities out."

"But we still don't know if the serum will work, do we?"

"No, Mr. President. We don't." So much for being the bearer of good news. "The lab tests so far have been inconclusive. The serum may only have a thirty to forty percent success rate."

He glanced down at his watch.

"I wish I had something better for you, sir. I know you're going on the air again in fifteen—"

"Mr. Hanlon, I've made the decision to be completely

forthright about what we know about the disease. I'm going to tell the people how important it is to avoid contact with anyone who may have been infected. But I'm also going to assure the public that very *few* cases have been discovered. I will stress that this is by no means an epidemic, and that our actions—and the cooperation of the American people—will keep it from *becoming* an epidemic."

"Very good, sir—"

"Mr. Hanlon, ignorance and rumor can breed far more fear than knowing the truth can."

"Yes, sir."

Faas hoped the president was right. There would be repercussions down the road, because the measures taken in Washington had not been taken in Arizona or Maine. And it was probable that what had happened in Maine would become news any moment. They had a total of sixteen deaths so far, but the president had not yet owned up to the ten bodies in Maine. The official position remained that the two outbreaks were unrelated. The American people would be extremely angry to think President Penn had kept such sensitive information under wraps for nearly two weeks.

"Not counting Maine, we have only six deaths to date, Mr. President," Faas said as a reminder. "Also, if I could make a suggestion, I don't think it would be a good idea to mention DM8A at this point."

"I agree."

Faas's fingers inched toward the packet of cigarettes in his pocket.

"You are to call me as soon as you have anything else, Mr. Hanlon."

"Yes, sir…and…well, good luck, Mr. President."

The phone clicked off. Faas turned toward the door of the command vehicle. As he reached for it, the door was pushed open from the inside.

"Bad news, sir." The same agent who had given him the phone poked his head out.

"Someone else in that office is infected," Faas guessed.

"Worse. We just had a call from Chicago."

"Another case?" he asked, dreading the answer.

"None of our agents are on the scene yet. But the cleaning crew going through a luxury apartment at a building called the Grand Plaza, right downtown, made the 911 call a few minutes ago. They found a decomposing body."

Twenty-One

Erbil, Iraq

Fahimah could have stayed the night at her friends' house and returned the following day. She had given Jalal's name to the Americans, though, and she didn't want to risk them going after the old man in the morning.

It was half past twelve when she had them drop her off at the corner, one block west of the Shahan Hotel. She wasn't about to risk exposing others. She feared that anyone who was connected with her—family, friend or whatever—would be considered guilty by association by Agent Newman.

She saw no pedestrians on the street, but there were still a few cars. Across the road, a small white car slowed down and the driver and a man in the backseat called out the windows at her. Realizing they were about to make a U-turn, she ran the remaining half block to the front door of the hotel. It was locked. Glancing back as she knocked on the door, she saw the white car coming slowly down the street toward the hotel.

"Come on," she murmured in Kurdish, knocking harder.

A sleepy doorman appeared and opened the door just as the car pulled up in front. Fahimah hadn't seen him that afternoon, but he let her in and locked the door.

As she gave the doorman her name, she looked out at the street and pointed to the white car. Two sets of eyes were watching her. The doorman looked out, and the car immediately pulled away from the curb.

"Mamnun," she said, thanking him.

The doorman told her that they were waiting for her. She didn't have to ask whom he was talking about. Thanking him again, she went up the stairs to the second floor.

All the rooms they'd taken were adjacent to one another. None of the soldiers were in the hallway. No one to guard, Fahimah decided.

She didn't know which room was Austyn's, so she tapped softly on both of the doors adjacent to hers before putting the key into the lock of her own room.

Her door opened before she could even turn the key.

"You're back," Austyn said, relief written all over his face.

His hair, though short, was standing on end, as if he'd been running his fingers through it. He was dressed in an old T-shirt and khaki shorts. As he stepped out and looked up and down the hallway, she thought he looked tense, weary, and somewhat worse for wear.

"I told you I would meet you back at the hotel," she said, going past him and into her room. "I suppose we need to talk."

He followed her, slamming the door shut behind him. "You're damn right!"

She glanced over her shoulder, surprised at the show of temper.

"How could you do that to us?" he asked, the look of relief completely gone. "Do you know everyone who traveled with us from Afghanistan is out searching the city for you right now?"

He needed to vent. She let him. She peeled the scarf off her head and threw it on a chair before walking to the bathroom.

"U.S. military barely has any presence whatsoever here in Erbil, and still they had to call every off-duty soldier they could find to help with the search," he continued.

Fahimah turned on the water in the sink, waiting for it to warm up. The temperature had dropped outside. She'd left the windows open in the afternoon. It was cool in her room.

"Would you mind shutting the window?" she asked.

Even as he shut the window, he continued to lecture. She tuned him out and looked at her face in the mirror. She wasn't used to this—actually seeing her reflection anytime she wished. She looked at the dark circles under her eyes. Her cheeks were almost sunken. She was too pale. She ran a hand across her head. Her hair had been reddish-brown for all of her adult years. She wondered what color it would be now that it had a chance to grow out. She noted a thin streak of gray on one side. She could live with that.

Her friend Banoo had told her that at first they hadn't recognized her. Banoo and her husband and son had been in a car waiting near the place where Jalal spread his rug. As big a city as Erbil was, word traveled fast. They heard that Fahimah had arrived that afternoon, and they had a good idea where she would be heading. It was

Banoo's son that had come to her at the open-air bazaar. The last time Fahimah had seen the boy, he'd been a mere toddler.

In the old days, Banoo and her husband had lived in Baghdad, and both of them taught at the same university as Fahimah. Now Banoo taught at Salahaddin University in Erbil, while her husband had given up teaching and was making a career for himself in real estate development. They'd taken Fahimah back to a beautiful, sprawling house on the outskirts of the city where she'd met the newest addition to her friends' family, a baby girl of two years.

Life hadn't stood still while she was away. Looking into the mirror, she realized that she, too, had once had dreams of her own. But that had been a lifetime ago, and dreams sometimes go to waste.

She bent over the sink and cupped her palms, filling them with warm water. She splashed her face again and again, trying to wash the saltiness of her tears away.

It was some time before she lifted her face and looked into the mirror again. Her eyes were red-rimmed. Her face was flushed. She saw Austyn's reflection in the mirror. He was leaning against the doorway, watching her, his arms folded across his chest.

"Are you finished lecturing me?" she asked.

"I wasn't lecturing. I was…reprimanding," he corrected. "There's a difference."

"Yes, I know. But I wanted to give you the benefit of the doubt."

He raised one eyebrow.

Fahimah took a towel off the shelf and dried her face. "You lecture someone out of concern, worry. You reprimand a person if you think they have done something wrong. Now, which is it?"

He didn't answer. She turned around and saw the struggle so plainly reflected in his face.

"You didn't have to come back," he said, his tone much more gentle.

"I know. But I told you I would."

"I should have trusted you," he said quietly.

"You should have trusted me," she repeated.

He turned and disappeared inside the room. As she hung the towel on the rack, she heard him talking to someone on the telephone. He was contacting the others to call off the search.

Fahimah took her time. She wanted to be composed, have her emotions under control. When she stepped out of the bathroom, he was sitting on a chair near the window. Other than the bed, the only place to sit was a bench by the same window. She grabbed a blanket from the foot of the bed and went to the bench.

"You must be hungry. I ordered room service."

"This is Erbil," she reminded him. "We're not in London...or New York."

"Really?" he said with a straight face. "Well, whoever answered in the kitchen said he'd brew us some tea."

"He's going to add hot water to the tea from this afternoon."

"That's okay with me, so long as he brings up the five lumps of sugar I asked for."

"Five?"

"Sure, I'm learning how to drink tea here. You just put a cube between your teeth and drink your tea through it."

"And you need five for that."

"Well, you said yourself that the tea was going to be strong."

Fahimah smiled and shook her head. "You're going to rot your teeth before leaving Iraq."

She opened one of the windows a little and then sat on the bench, wrapping the blanket around herself.

"You did just ask me to close that, didn't you?"

"Yes, I did."

They said nothing for a while, and she was thankful that he let her just sit. A cool, dry breeze wafted in and Fahimah closed her eyes, breathing in the familiar smells. Everything she'd heard tonight played back through her mind. The news of a mass grave they'd found on the road to Halabja. The news of their other friends. The fate of the few family members Fahimah and Rahaf had left behind. The names of all those who had died during the years of senseless violence that was ripping their country to shreds.

The American soldiers might have been fooled the day they took Fahimah, but Banoo and her husband knew soon enough about them arresting her instead of her sister. They suspected immediately, but Rahaf had told them about it not long afterward. No one knew where to look for her, though.

Her peace and quiet was short-lived.

"Are you going to tell me where you went?" he asked.

"No."

"Why not?"

"I won't tell you where I went because it has nothing to do with what you're after."

"Did you see your sister?"

"No."

"Do you know if she's in Erbil?"

"Yes…no."

"Which is it?"

"I know she is not in Erbil."

"Are you going to tell me on your own what you found out, or do I have to keep asking questions?"

"Yes, I will tell you on my own," she said, realizing that she'd been taunting him.

There was a knock on the door.

"It must be your old tea," she said, starting to get down from the bench.

"You sit. I'll get it."

Fahimah watched him reach under the back of his T-shirt. That's when she saw the gun tucked into the waistband of his shorts.

"You're armed," she said, as if that should be news to him, too.

He made a hush sound at her and went to the door. There were no security peepholes. He put his foot and shoulder to the door before opening it a crack.

"*Chai*," someone said from the other side.

"Uh…*mamnun*." Austyn opened the door and took the small tray from the doorman's hand.

"You're learning the language," she told him, putting her feet down so that there was room on the bench for him to put down the tray.

"I only know *tea* and *thank you*."

"That's very good for half a day. If you learn the word for *food*, you'll be ready to apply for residency."

He put the tray down next to her and sat down on the bench, as well. She touched one of the glasses. "It's cold.

He must not have had any hot water in the samovar, so he just added cold water to the afternoon tea."

"No big deal. Beggars can't be choosers."

"At least he didn't forget your sugar cubes," she commented, picking up one of the glasses of tea. She drank half of it down in one gulp. She hadn't realized how thirsty she was.

"I had a telephone call from the U.S. before you got back tonight."

His tone was once again serious.

"There's been another outbreak of the bacteria," he told her.

Fahimah wished it would go away. She wanted this to be like the anthrax scare that she'd watched on the news back in 2001, but obviously it wasn't going to be.

"More casualties?"

"One confirmed dead," he told her. "But this time the attack was in Washington, D.C. In a very populated area. The chance of it spreading is huge. Whoever is behind this is getting bolder by the minute."

"Rahaf isn't behind it," she reminded him again, to make sure he hadn't forgotten.

"Do you know where she is?"

Fahimah nodded, debating with herself how much to tell him.

"Will you take us to her?" he asked.

"Your soldiers in American uniforms can't go where she is."

"Where is she?"

"In the mountains."

"Which mountains?"

"The Zagros Mountains."

"Zagros…" he repeated, thinking. "But isn't that a huge mountain range?" he asked.

"More than fifteen hundred kilometers. They run from Kurdistan down through northwestern Iran to the Persian Gulf," she explained, putting the glass of tea back on the tray. "But we don't have to search the entire length of the Zagros to find her."

"Do you have a specific location?"

She nodded halfheartedly. "I know the general area. Rahaf is working in the refugee camps on the Iranian side of the border with Kurdistan. There used to be four camps…Sahana, Pavana, Saryas and Jwanro. I'm told she goes between them as needed."

Fahimah knew that it would be a problem for U.S. soldiers to get there. After five years in prison, she'd needed to read only a handful of headlines to know that relations between the Iranian and American governments were as hostile as ever.

"What's she doing there?" he asked.

"The people I met tonight told me my sister is working there as a doctor."

"But she didn't go to medical school, did she?"

She stared at him for a long moment. "Over the past three decades, five thousand villages have been destroyed by the Iraqis. When you're forced to pack a lifetime of belongings onto the back of a truck or a mule and cross the mountains to escape the genocide that is happening to tens of thousands of your people, when your home for more than a decade has been a tent on the side of a mountain and you rely on others' generosity to eat or clothe your children…you are not so foolish as to ask for the credentials of the doctor who is caring for your sick child. Especially when that doctor is one of your own people."

Fahimah and Rahaf had lived in those camps themselves after the horror at Halabja. Even back then, with thousands of people being in dire need of medical assistance, real doctors had been a rarity.

He watched her silently for a few heartbeats. "Is that where Rahaf has been for the past five years?" he asked.

"Yes," she told him. "And I will take *one* of you to her."

Twenty-Two

The research vessel Harmony
In the Atlantic

Standing at the railing, David could actually see the outline of the squall to the west.

The rain was moving toward them quickly, and the edges of the storm—a single patch of low dark clouds—were distinct against the clear blue sky beyond. To the right and left of the squall, he could see sunlight glistening on the ocean surface. There was no question in his mind that the rain was going to sweep right over them. He shook the folds out of his waterproof parka and pulled it over his head.

This was the first sign of any disagreeable weather since they'd boarded the ship. Everything about this trip had been perfect. Everyone's mood, especially the children's, was riding high. The staff couldn't be more helpful. There'd been no emergencies.

Once again, he wished that Sally, his wife, could be here. She would have loved to see this. David didn't remember seeing Josh this happy and consumed by any activity…ever. The teenager was already campaigning to come on this trip again next year. David knew that Josh had been resisting any thoughts or planning about anything down the road since learning of his cancer. This was a huge breakthrough.

More than anyone, he thought wistfully, Sally should have been here to hear it.

"You got the word, I take it, that our esteemed program director wants to talk to us here," Craig said, joining David at the railing.

"It's going to be pouring any minute now."

The other man looked out at the approaching storm. "Looks like it." He shrugged. "He wants to keep us informed about the news, without bothering the kids."

Parents were beginning to approach them. The kids were all belowdecks, busy doing lab work with the samples they'd dredged up from a couple of test sites earlier this morning. David had a good idea what Philip Carver's "talk" was going to be about. No television, radios or cell phones were allowed on this trip. In fact, no electronic equipment of any sort, including iPods and laptops, were to be brought on board the *Harmony*.

A few times since the beginning of their trip, however, David and Craig had gone up onto the bridge to chat with the ship's skipper. It was during one of those visits this morning that they'd heard a Coast Guard report over the ship's radio warning all vessels, commercial and private, that river traffic on the Potomac and Anacostia was banned north of Alexandria, Virginia. Another weird case of flesh-eating disease had been discovered, apparently—this time in Washington, D.C. David had said nothing about it to Josh.

He looked out again at the water, watching the dark cloud moving in closer. It looked as if it was raining sideways.

Having worked in pharmaceuticals for his entire career, and with a background in chemistry, David wasn't terrified by these kinds of things the way the average person might be. There were many instances of people dying across the country of unusual causes. This could be one of those. A rare disease that would have never caused a stir if the media hadn't gotten hold of some pictures and blown the whole thing out of proportion.

David turned around to see the program director joining the group. All ten parents and caregivers had assembled on deck.

"I'm going to make this quick," Philip announced as they all formed a circle around him. "I have just two things to say." He took a handkerchief out of a pocket and blew his nose.

"I don't want to create hysteria, but some of you might have already heard whispers. Now, I know nobody here is from Washington, but I want to keep you all up-to-date. So this is what we know…. There's been another outbreak of this flesh-eating disease, this time just a few blocks from the White House. I just talked to the Coast Guard station at Indian River, and they said there's been only one fatality. Now, I believe our young crew downstairs has been exposed to enough stress and bad news in their short lives, so that's why I wanted to keep the news of this to the adults for the remainder of the trip. How you handle this with your children is, of course, your own business."

There were some nods. No one seemed horribly shocked by the news. David figured word of what was happening had reached all the adults.

"Now, the reason for this get-together…" Philip paused. It sounded as if he was losing his voice. He took a long sip from a water bottle—blew his nose again.

David wondered if the young man had taken any of the medicine he and Craig had passed on to him. Although he kept his spirits up, every day Philip's cold or flu or whatever it was seemed to be getting worse. It definitely wasn't allergies. They were lucky none of the kids were showing similar symptoms.

"Where was I?" the program director asked.

"The reason for the get-together…" someone repeated.

"Oh, yeah. I wanted to get a feel from everyone as far as what our next step should be," Philip explained. "My crew and I are perfectly content to continue with this excursion as originally planned. But if there is any consensus that we should get back to port right away, then I'd like to hear it. This is your trip."

The members of the group were silent for a moment, and then a few people began to comment.

"This is probably the safest place we could be…." one of the parents noted.

"It's not as if our families are infected with the disease. It seems to be rare," was one woman's opinion.

"And isolated," someone added.

"My feeling exactly." David had to put his two cents in. "There's no epidemic to speak of. We don't have entire communities of people coming down with this disease as far as I know."

"I can't think of anything more stressful for our children than to have them exposed to the hoopla that the news people are creating about this," a young mother told Philip. "I was glad to get away from the business in Arizona or New Mexico or wherever that was. My vote is to stay on course. I'm sure the crisis will have passed by the time we get back."

There were many nods of agreement.

"Perhaps you could just continue to keep us in the loop of any other news that comes by way of the radio," Craig suggested. Philip was fine with that.

Like a slap in the face, the first drops of rain hit them, carried on a sudden gust of wind.

"Then it seems that we *do* have a consensus," Craig summarized, looking around at the circle of people. "So, if you can tolerate your cold and put up with us for a couple of more days, we should continue the trip as we originally planned."

Philip gave a satisfied nod before saying, hoarsely, "That's all I needed to hear. Now we'd better get under cover before the rain really starts."

Harmony rocked against the buffeting winds. As if taking its cue, the rain began to come down in sheets. People cut in front of one another in their rush to get out of the weather. Craig and David brought up the rear of the line with Philip.

"How are you feeling?" David asked the young researcher.

"Hanging in there." He blew his nose. "I'm usually better at kicking this kind of thing, but having to dive every day doesn't help."

As one of the two divers on the research vessel, Philip went into the water every morning to collect samples and take photos of different sites. The other diver was also a grad student.

"Do you have enough medicine to get you through?" Craig asked.

"I used some of those throat lozenges you gave me. They taste horrible but they sure work."

"My wife swears by them," Craig told the young man.

Philip made no mention of the bag of stuff David had given him. David started down the ladder ahead of the other two men, feeling very annoyed.

Don't be defensive, he told himself, trying to shake it off. He should be used to this new wave of homeopathic, all-natural, tree-hugging crap. It all went back to Al Gore and company. Synthetic drugs were bad. Drug companies were evil. Those who worked for them were the spawn of Satan. He should have known that Philip Carver, grad student and program director of the Ocean Research team, would be one of those. Go ahead, Philip, be a jerk. Go ahead and brew up some tree bark, he thought. There's a reason why Americans are enjoying longer, healthier lives. And Josh and the other kids on this boat are a testament to the success of modern medicine, critics be damned.

He descended the steps and turned to watch the other two men come down. Craig was giving advice to Philip on some vitamin-packed powder he'd given him.

"Dad… Dad!" Josh ran over and gave him a big hug. "Hey, you're wet."

"It's raining up there." He hugged the twelve-year-old back, happy that Josh still didn't find anything wrong with showing affection, especially with him.

"Guess what?"

"Tell me."

"My shrimp is pregnant," Josh said excitedly.

"No kidding!" A hundred different options ran through David's mind as to what the correct response should be.

Congratulations?

When will the joyous event take place?

Hasn't anyone talked to you about using condoms?

Or something equally inappropriate. The almost comical thing was that, as the father of a nineteen-year-old and a twenty-two-year-old daughter, pregnancy was one of the announcements that he'd most worried about.

David's mood was starting to improve.

"That's wonderful news, Josh," Philip said hoarsely, stepping down from the bottom rung of the ladder. "Do you know what this means?"

"That means the site isn't dead," Josh answered. "In fact, there's going to be a tomorrow."

"Exactly." Philip put a hand on the boy's shoulder, and they started for the lab area. "We got the samples today from that ocean disposal site. Now we'll constantly monitor those areas to make sure humans aren't destroying the…"

"I take it all back," David whispered under his breath.

"Take what back?" Craig asked, standing next to him.

"The stuff I was thinking about Philip. He's not a jerk. In fact, he's okay."

As David turned away, he realized Craig was looking at him as if he'd sprouted two heads.

Twenty-Three

The White House, Washington, D.C.

"I'm not sure, Mr. President, that it's a good idea for us to be in the same room as you," Faas said cautiously.

"Your people have investigated five sites now. Isn't that correct, Director Hanlon?"

"Yes, sir."

"And what were they?"

"Moosehead Lake in Maine. Sedona, Arizona. The law firm here in Washington. The Grand Plaza incident in Chicago. The fifth was the two bodies found last night at the bakery in Boston's South End."

"And have any of your agents been infected?"

"We've taken every precaution, sir."

"So none have been infected?

"No, sir."

"Then I consider myself safe."

Faas Hanlon would not have wished this mess on John

Penn. He was a decent man and a pretty good president. But if being the first African-American president wasn't enough pressure in itself, Penn had taken office during a major scandal created by the former president, an election scam that had threatened both national security and the faith of the people in the whole electoral system. He'd quickly restored faith in the country's leadership, and for that alone, John Penn deserved four trouble-free years. Penn was popular with the people and with the elected officials in both Houses of Congress. As a result, for the first time in more than two decades, things were getting done in Washington. Congress was finally earning its salary, producing results for the people who'd voted the individual members into the office. Health care reform was being addressed. Education programs were formulated. The economy was on an upswing.

Unfortunately, not everything was going smoothly.

Troop reduction. Troop increase. Reduction again. Iraq had become a self-inflicted wound that wouldn't heal. America was too deeply entrenched in the troubles, not only in that country but in the entire Middle East. Aside from the ongoing civil war in the south of Iraq, Afghanistan had never been settled, and the Taliban continued to cause trouble. The Western world still depended on oil, and no one had an answer how to get out of the mess. There seemed to be no end in sight.

This outbreak, though, was potentially the greatest challenge John Penn's administration would face.

"What have you got for me?" Penn asked the group gathered before him.

Faas glanced at his boss, the secretary of Homeland

Security, who had okayed them bringing along Bea Devera. She was just back from Sedona and, having worked the site there, she was a perfect candidate to offer constructive feedback. But they weren't the only ones on the hot seat. Cabinet Secretary James Abbott of Health and Human Services was there with the current NIH director, Rich Judson. NIH had been tasked with coordinating and interpreting all data on the victims. The EPA director had also been asked to attend this meeting, since every one of the sites where the disease had surfaced had to go through an equivalent of a toxic-spill cleanup. The press secretary had joined them a couple of minutes into the meeting, and assistants were hovering behind those at the conference table.

"It would not be inappropriate, Mr. President, to call this an epidemic, at this point," Dr. Judson admitted.

Faas and the NIH director had started this discussion on the phone before they all had arrived here. Including Chicago and Boston, the number of casualties had risen to twenty-four. Unlike the early outbreaks, though, when ten days had passed before there'd been another incidence of the disease, the outbreaks were coming at shorter intervals.

"I am sure that will make the American public feel much more secure. Maybe we should color-code it, too. Make use of some of the millions we spent a few years ago after 9/11," Penn said sarcastically. They were all used to his direct, no-nonsense approach. He turned to the Secretary of Health and Human Services. "Do you agree with that, James?"

"It's a mess, sir. I think that, at this point, it would be wise to put the fear of God in people."

"The fear of God is already in them," Penn commented.

"Not all of them, Mr. President," Judson replied. "Look at both Chicago and Boston. The casualties should have been limited to one at each site, but instead we had multiple deaths because of people arriving on the scene, discovering the bodies, and not taking the correct precautionary measures. I think most people still treat this as some sort of media invention."

The Secretary of Homeland Security chimed in. "A position that is understandable, considering we lose more people than this every day to car wrecks and cancer. But this situation is far different, and I don't know that finding the right words is enough to get this message across. Recent history has taught us to be wary of what is put in front of us. People have forgotten that they sometimes need to trust those in charge."

Faas knew Penn understood where the Homeland Security czar was coming from. During President Penn's reorganization of Homeland Security, Faas had been privy to conversations between his boss and the president. Several of those conversations had focused on how to regain the public's trust. For too many years, the color-coded Homeland Security Advisory System had been used too carelessly and with motives other than the national security. As a result, the general public had become numb to it. Several members of Congress had said publicly that the system had outlived its effectiveness. Faas agreed.

"I'm going to continue with my daily news conference until we have this situation under control," Penn told the group. "We won't keep any new incidents secret from the public. In fact, we'll announce that the incident in Maine has now been connected to this same outbreak. We'll increase the number of confirmed casualties, too."

"That was our largest blow as far as deaths," Judson reminded everyone.

"I don't want the focus to be on fear," Penn responded. "The truth is our best ally right now."

No one was about to disagree.

"What's happening with the DM8A production?" the president asked the HHS Secretary.

"The first production lots are out and distribution is going according to schedule," Secretary Abbott replied.

"Is it doing anything for us?"

"We don't know," the NIH director jumped in. "We think so. We have all the people who have had any contact with the victims on the serum now. There haven't been any more outbreaks, so we'd like to think the antibiotics are working, at least as a preventive measure with those who have had direct contact."

Faas knew it wasn't like Judson to be so vague, but there was so much that they didn't know about the disease and there'd been so little time for any serious research.

Penn rocked in his chair a few times, considering the situation. "Now, let's get to a more important issue. What's causing it?"

Faas felt as if he were back in high school. He didn't know the answer. None of the people in the room knew the answer and they were trying not to make eye contact. For his part, he'd heard very little chatter in the terrorist circuits about the attacks. Just as the health guys were working blind, the investigative effort was also operating in the dark.

"You must have something to tell me," Penn persisted. "How are these people contracting the disease?"

There was some shuffling of the papers. The president's stare was directed at the NIH director.

Rich Judson shrugged. "We know they're contracting it through something taken internally. At least, that's the situation with the first victim on each site. But we don't know what that substance is. We've ruled out any number of possible subst—"

"We know who the first victims were in each incident?"

"Yes, sir. From the autopsies, we've been able to determine the time of death, and in each incident, one victim is clearly more severely decomposed than the others. Our conclusion is that the initial victim contracted the disease prior to passing it on."

Faas saw Bea Devera take out a file and leaf through it.

"Also, there's the destructive path of the disease," Judson added. "It's clear that the first individual had contracted it internally. In these individuals, there's much more damage to the internal organs than to the external tissue."

"Okay, so then we know the primary victim must have contracted the infection by eating, drinking or inhaling the microbe," Penn summarized.

There was a general agreement.

"We have a wide age group here, ladies and gentlemen," Penn reminded everyone. "What would be a substance commonly ingested, whether we are talking about a teenager or a man in his seventies?"

"The substance is obviously not very common," Faas added, "as there have been only twenty-four deaths so far."

"The number of deaths is irrelevant, Mr. Hanlon," Penn

shot back. "We've had four instances of this outbreak in the past forty-eight hours. At this rate of increase, we could be talking about twenty-four *hundred* deaths by next week."

Faas nodded. "Point taken, sir."

"Whatever this substance is, it has a nationwide distribution," Penn told them. "It's out there for the public to use. We seem to have a time-release bomb that is only starting to go off."

"They all had a cold," Bea Devera said in a lower voice.

This was the first thing she had said since the meeting began, and it took a few moments for the agent's words to register with everyone.

"What did you say, Agent…?"

"Devera, Mr. President. I said that one victim at each site had a cold or the flu. They were sick," she explained, leafing through her files and pulling out individual sheets of paper.

Faas noticed that the room had become totally quiet. All eyes were on Bea.

"Continue," the president encouraged.

"Moosehead Lake, Maine. One witness reported that the fourteen-year-old, Lizzy Hansson, was fighting a cold when they arrived for their vacation," Bea announced.

Faas noticed that one of Judson's assistants was taking notes. Another was leafing through her files.

"Rich, how does that match with the autopsy reports?" Penn asked.

Rich Judson's assistant slid a sheet of paper in front of him. "Lizzy Hansson appears to have been the first fatality on that site," the NIH director announced.

Penn looked at Bea again.

"Sedona, Arizona. Lenny Guest, age eighteen. He was

fighting a flu or cold the day of his death. That was why he'd stayed off work and was hanging out with his friend."

Judson was looking over his people's files and gave a thumbs-up.

"Washington, D.C. Leo Bolender, age thirty-two, had a cold."

They all knew Leo was the only fatality at that site.

"Chicago, Illinois. Herman Ogden, age seventy-seven, had been fighting a cold for a week," Bea continued.

There was another nod by Judson.

"Boston, South End Bakery. Tasha Giles, age forty-nine, had returned to work after being out two days with a cold. She wasn't really improving, either, according to a boyfriend."

"This agrees with what we have," Judson said, nodding again.

Penn leaned back in his chair. "Very good, Agent Devera," he said. "This could be a breakthrough, ladies and gentlemen, don't you think?"

The energy in the conference room had definitely picked up.

"I don't need to tell you what to do next. You each have your own jobs to do. But start with pulling any prescription or nonprescription medication these people might have taken. Test the hell out of anything that was left over in their cabinets." Penn turned to Faas. "Do you remember the cyanide injected into Tylenol bottles…what was it… twenty, thirty years ago?"

"That was 1982, sir," Faas answered. "Seven people in the Chicago area collapsed suddenly and died after taking Tylenol capsules that had been laced with cyanide.

Five females and two males, all relatively young. They were the first victims ever to die from product tampering."

Faas had been working for the FBI back then. Just out of college and the academy. A wave of copycat tampering had followed that original incident. They never caught the Tylenol killer. A somewhat bumbling suspect who had attempted to cash in on the unprecedented publicity was arrested and charged with extortion, but not with the murders. The police concluded he was merely an opportunist.

Faas considered the possibility of terrorists using this method to spread the microbes. No one was taking credit. Nothing was showing up on Al Jazeera. Nothing.

He wondered if their search in Iraq would turn out to be futile. What if someone here in the U.S. was responsible for the epidemic…just another case of product tampering? He almost hoped that was the case, but he wasn't willing to stop any part of this investigation.

"For a change, I can pass on some good news in my address," Penn told them.

"I would not advise that you be too specific, sir," the NIH director reminded the president. "We have billion-dollar industries that could be affected by this."

"Yes, pharmaceutical companies. Their lobbyists and lawyers will be all over us. I won't forget," he assured Judson. "I'll be vague but I'll make sure to hint at positive news in the ongoing investigation."

"Mr. President," Faas added. "If you could, continue to stress the importance of respecting the quarantine perimeters to impede the spreading disease."

"Point noted." Penn scribbled something on the pad of

paper in front of him. "Another thing. I also want to talk about a Federal Bioterrorism Rapid Response Card."

"New York and a couple of other states have had cards available for a while, sir," the HHS secretary said.

"Yes, I have it here." The president took a multifold card from a staff assistant standing nearby. He pulled open the information card and tossed it onto the conference table. "I want the federal government to distribute one of our own. A card put out by New York isn't going to help people in Maine or Arizona or Montana…or wherever this thing hits us next."

Faas had passed New York State's Rapid Response Card on to the president's secretary this morning, and it was good to see Penn bring it out here in this meeting. When he'd sent it over, Faas had suggested that copies be requisitioned from New York and passed out in the D.C. area. The small brochure consisted of tables of information on recognizing and diagnosing illnesses possibly caused by bioterrorism, along with treatment and prevention measures for first-responders. Everything from inhalational and cutaneous anthrax through viral hemorrhagic fevers to smallpox was included. Naturally, there was nothing about any fast-acting flesh-eating disease.

"Combine the best of whatever is included on existing information cards, update it to include this situation, and make it available at every government office and distribute it through the schools and any other venue you can think of," the president ordered. "Aside from English, I want it printed in Spanish, Chinese, Japanese, Hindi, Arabic…whatever. And I want that out yesterday."

James Abbott signaled for one of his own staffers, who left the room running.

"People feel better when they have clear instructions," Penn said. "It lets them know that we care…and that each person has a stake and a responsibility in this time of crisis."

The president ran through his list of agenda items.

"Oh, yes. This brings me to a very important issue. This thing is getting big enough that it needs a name. In the past, we have dealt with SARS…Severe Acute Respiratory Syndrome…AIDS, avian flu and a hundred other conditions, all of which have a recognizable name or acronym. When we can put a name or a face to an enemy, that enemy becomes a little less frightening. We still respect it as a foe, but it is no longer the faceless monster in the dark. Am I making my point clearly?"

There was definitely a general agreement.

"The media has been calling it the flesh-eating disease," the president's press secretary said. "My office actually got a phone call asking if there were cannibals attacking people in D.C."

"I hope you told the caller that only happens on Capitol Hill," Secretary Abbott deadpanned.

There were a few chuckles.

"Flesh-eating disease syndrome," the NIH director mused out loud. "The acronym would be FEDS."

Faas shook his head as others laughed.

"I don't think that would exactly send the message we're looking for," Penn responded.

"Necrotizing fasciitis *is* a mouthful," said the press secretary.

Rich Judson wasn't giving up. "I do think that initials would serve to identify the condition without being a constant reminder of the horrific manifestation of the disease. Perhaps just using the initials of necrotizing fasciitis infection," Judson told them.

"NFI," Secretary Abbott said, jotting it down as he said it.

"NFI." Penn echoed as he leaned back in his chair. He considered that for a moment. "I say we go with that."

Twenty-Four

Erbil, Iraq

At first, it was hard to swallow the fact that Fahimah was in charge and that they had to follow her suggestions or nothing would happen. Once Austyn decided not to dwell on minor details, though, or allow his ego to come into the equation, life became much more bearable.

She had come back, he kept reminding herself. This said something, at least, about her commitment to the mission. She was going to help them. So be receptive to what she wants, he told himself.

"I just got a report from Washington of another outbreak," Matt said in a low voice as he caught up with Austyn in the hotel hallway. He had his bag slung over his shoulder.

"Where?"

"New York City."

"Terrific," Austyn said, shaking his head. "They really need that. How bad?"

"I don't have any details yet."

"Okay. What else?"

"Not much."

"No holding out on me, Sutton."

"NFI," Matt said.

"What?"

"They're calling it NFI. Necrotizing Fasciitis Infection. It's now important enough to earn its own initials." Matt had a peculiar look on his face. "I actually used to be a member of NFI."

"What was that, the name of your garage band?" Austyn didn't know Matt's exact age, but he figured it couldn't have been too many years ago since he was in high school. "I assume the initials didn't stand for the same thing."

"No, I was a junior member of the National Fisheries Institute. I was about eight. Got an official membership card and a newsletter and everything."

"Great, Sutton. I think this heat must be getting to you." Austyn shook his head. "National Fisheries Institute."

"I'm sure the current members aren't going to be too happy with it."

"Probably not," he said, adding wryly, "but hopefully they'll understand."

Austyn stared at Fahimah's door. She was supposed to pack and meet them right here, outside her hotel room. They were all going to meet here.

How long could it take her? he thought. She owned two pieces of clothing and a toothbrush, for chrissake. It wasn't like she had to fix her hair.

He shook off his impatience. "Okay. Anything else from Hanlon?"

They'd come up with a new plan and sent it on to Homeland Security in Washington. They weren't about to risk taking any of their military escort across the Iran-Iraq border. The consequences would be too great if the mission tanked. They didn't need to ignite an international diplomatic crisis in the midst of everything else that was going on. With the new arrangement, Matt would stay behind in Erbil and handle communications with Washington. The escort would remain here, as well. If they needed an airlift from the border, he'd arrange it.

Austyn was staying with Fahimah. He wasn't in the military. If they got caught and the Iranians started digging, they might consider him a spy. But Matt was going to make sure no files would show up on him and figure out a new identity for himself.

Austyn knew he was putting his life at risk. But it didn't worry him. Once they crossed the border, Fahimah could blow the whistle on him, but in his gut, he had a feeling she wouldn't.

After all, she'd come back.

Ken would drive them the 150 miles to Halabja, which was only a stone's throw from the Iranian border. Fahimah still had family there, and she hoped she could find more details on Rahaf. Perhaps they would even know which camp she was working in now. From Halabja, Fahimah and Austyn would have to go up into the mountains to sneak across the border to the refugee camps.

Fahimah had assured him that crossing the border wouldn't be a Von Trapp Family ordeal. Though it could be dangerous, there were actually quite a few roads that crossed into Iran. Of course, some roads were more used than others. After all, she said, smuggling was a profitable business. She told him the Kurds went back and forth on a daily basis. The two of them could do it, too.

Sutton was talking, all seriousness again. "They're going with the hypothesis that some kind of product tampering is being used as a means of spreading the microbes. The first victim in each outbreak was fighting a cold or something."

"That's a big step."

Matt nodded. "But they've yet to identify the specific medication that might be involved. They're cross-checking for something used by all the victims. So far they've ruled out prescription drugs. And they've narrowed the search to the possibility of a cold medicine that could be bought over the counter."

Austyn thought of the cabinets and drawers of cold medications that every household in America kept. The victims were spread across the country, so the tampering couldn't have been done at a purchase point, like a grocery store or pharmacy. Also, there'd been no cases reported outside of the U.S. He figured that should narrow their search to a national distribution center, one that possibly served both Arizona and Maine.

If he were back in the States, he'd be involved with the day-to-day investigation of it. This was the jurisdiction of his department. He reminded himself that he *was* working on this case.

"Boston could have been a mess," Austyn said with a frown. "It's a good thing none of the baked goods were contaminated."

He hadn't been able to get hold of Faas Hanlon last

night, but he'd spoken with one of the special agents working directly with the intelligence director, so he was reasonably up-to-date on all the new cases. Austyn had passed on the information Fahimah had given him. He'd been contacted soon after with a curt message from Washington. He had authorization to proceed according to his own discretion. The mission was now solely in his hands. And Fahimah's.

"New York could turn out worse than Boston," Matt commented. "Eight million people within three hundred or so square miles."

Austyn agreed. "New York could be one serious…"

His voice trailed off as the door to Fahimah's room opened. *Finally.* She came out carrying a small duffel bag.

For a second, Austyn forgot what they were talking about. She looked different, healthier. There was color in her cheeks. Austyn knew she'd sent one of the hotel workers that morning to get her some things. He noticed that she was wearing a pair of leather walking shoes that were definitely better than the plastic army-issue sandals she'd been wearing.

"I overheard you saying something about New York City," she said. "Has there been another case reported from there?"

"We don't have all the facts and figures yet," Matt told her.

She nodded, but Austyn could see the news upset her. She looked at Austyn.

"You didn't shave," she told him. "That's good."

He ran a hand over his face and jaw. He didn't have time. After everyone returned to the hotel last night, he'd been up with the rest of them planning what needed to be done. He'd grabbed only a couple of hours of sleep and taken a quick shower this morning to help him wake up.

"I've been thinking about how to explain you, in case we get caught by an Iranian border patrol."

Austyn was glad she was thinking about it.

"I have some ideas, too. We'll talk on the way."

He looked at Matt, hoping that the younger man was okay with that. Matt gave him a reassuring nod. Ken came down the hall.

"I assume everyone is ready," he said, looking at Austyn's and Fahimah's bags. His eyes lingered on her face. "I'd say you're getting back to normal very quickly, Dr. Banaz. In fact, I'd say you look beautiful this morning. Austyn, I don't think it'll be safe to let her out of our sight again."

An immediate blush colored her cheeks.

"Don't forget," Ken told her comfortably with a nod toward Austyn. "There's still plenty of time to ditch this one, you know."

"Thanks for your input, soldier," Austyn said curtly.

Ken pretended to ignore him. "Seriously, I can cross the border with you. I even speak the language. It would be so much easier to pass me off as a local than this red-blooded American boy standing here."

Austyn was starting to become annoyed with the man. He should have checked to see if Ken was married or not. Sometimes these guys needed a reminder…like a call from the wife and kids. In this case, Ken needed a knock on the head with a two-by-four.

"You speak Kurdish with an American accent," she told him, shaking her head. "I much prefer him not speaking at all."

Austyn took Fahimah's bag off her shoulder.

"Let's go, partner," he said, giving her a wink. She was

so fair-skinned that every emotion poured right into her complexion. The word *partner* seemed to almost fluster her.

A crack-of-dawn departure had been out of the question, so Austyn had settled for anything before noon. They weren't going to leave through the front door of the hotel and have the dozens of people having tea on the sidewalk witness it. The van Ken was going to drive had been parked in the back, accessible through the kitchen door.

Coming out into the alley, Austyn saw they had a different vehicle from the van they'd driven last night. This one had a number of large dings in the front and sides. He glanced at Ken questioningly.

"I wanted to make it more authentic. Up here, along the border, they either drive a brand-new, hundred-thousand-dollar European car, like a Mercedes or BMW, or they drive some old shitbox that's on its last legs."

"How do you know that?" Fahimah asked in surprise.

"I saw it at Zahho, on the Iraqi-Turkish border. I was passing through about a month ago. Big money and abject poverty all mixed up in one big bag."

"Smuggling money?" Matt asked.

"Construction money," Ken told him. "Rebuilding projects and new construction everywhere you look. Some are cashing in and some aren't."

Austyn eyed the beat-up van. "I see that we aren't."

"Things have changed since I went away," Fahimah said, climbing into the backseat.

Ken sat behind the wheel. When they were all in, Matt handed Austyn a bulging envelope from his bag. He opened it as they pulled out of the alley.

"You're now from Argentina. You have a passport with

your picture and a phony name on it. Most of the South American countries have tourists who travel in Iran. There are also maps, Iranian money—*rials* and *toman*—and a couple of pocket dictionaries for appearance. You have English, Spanish, Kurdish, Arabic and Farsi. There are some other travel documents…paper visas into and out of Iraq and Turkey. Also, postcards friends supposedly sent to you from Argentina."

"You've been busy." Austyn opened the flap of the envelope and looked inside. "Argentina?"

"Is that a problem?"

"No, that's actually good. I've been there before."

"I know. And you speak Spanish."

Austyn figured that there was nothing in anyone's personnel files that Matt couldn't access if he wanted to. That was his thing. He probably knew more about Austyn's background than he could remember himself. He pulled out the passport.

"We've put in entry and exit stamps from a dozen different countries. You like to travel."

Austyn looked deep in the envelope. There was something that looked like a badge at the bottom.

"What is that?" He reached in for it.

"You're a writer. Freelance and novels. You don't have a press visa, though, because this project is your own idea. You hope to sell it afterward."

"The badge?" Austyn asked, pulling it out.

"*Buenos Aires Herald.* That was your last newspaper job. The badge has a hole punched in it, meaning it's no longer valid. You kept it for a keepsake, though."

Matt handed him another bag.

"And what's this?"

"Camera. Everyone who goes into the refugee camps takes plenty of pictures. If you're going to write an article or a book, you'll need a ton of pictures," Matt told him. "Also, there are chocolate bars, some canned goods, first aid stuff. I called one of the American reporters who's in Erbil and tried to get an accurate account of the stuff they carry with them. He's the one that reminded me about the camera."

"You've thought of everything, haven't you?" Austyn asked, impressed.

"For your sake, I hope I have," Matt said.

"Now, what about Fahimah?"

"She has everything she needs."

"What do you mean?"

"I duplicated her old papers and printed all the documents she would normally carry with her. She's got a somewhat beat-up booklet that's the Iraqi equivalent of our birth certificate, her university ID card, travel permits issued by the new government."

"But she was presumed dead after a bombing at the university," Austyn reminded his partner.

"There's no way for them to know that. So many people die every day in Iraq that they're about two years behind in issuing death certificates, and a lot will never be issued. And you saw what we checked online. There isn't even a reasonably functional Web site for the university. I tried to call the university yesterday. There's no place to check information at all there. And why should they check, anyway? She's a Kurdish woman. No threat. Kurds are mostly respected in Iran. You're the dangerous one."

Austyn realized that Matt was right. She'd probably be

safer across the border than she'd been in the past five years, if not longer.

"And she has those documents."

"I gave all of them to her this morning. We went over them. She should be all set," Matt told him. "By the way, she returned the laptop to me. She didn't think it'd be safe where you two are headed."

"The laptop isn't safe but we are?" He smiled.

"No," Fahimah interrupted. "We won't be terribly safe, either."

Austyn nodded his thanks to the other agent and stuffed the envelope into his bag. He and Ken each had a couple of DOD satellite phones on them. They had been given the three phones yesterday by the special units group in Erbil. These phones had their own dedicated gateways, so there was no out-of-service area anywhere. The decision whether they should take the phone across the border or not would wait until they got closer to their destination. Austyn figured he'd keep the one he had until the very last moment, even if he ended up chucking it.

"Okay," Matt said. "This is where I get out."

"This is the Brayati section of the city," Ken told him, pulling over. "See that mosque there?"

"Yeah."

"On the far side of it, you'll find a bazaar where you can pick up a taxi. He'll charge you a fortune, but he'll get you back to the hotel, anyway."

"Don't worry about me," Matt said. "Good luck to you guys. And don't lose contact with me."

He climbed out and crossed the intersection without looking back at them.

The day was warm, and the new vehicle had no air-conditioning. Fahimah already had her back window open. Rather than staying in front, Austyn moved into the backseat with her before Ken pulled out into traffic.

"You don't mind playing chauffeur so that we can get some work done back here, do you?" Austyn asked Ken.

"It doesn't matter if I mind or not. You're going to do it, anyway," the other man grumbled.

"Exactly." He patted him on the shoulder.

"We have a hundred fifty miles to go before we reach Halabja," Ken told them as he settled into the flow of traffic. "There will be a number of roadblocks between here and there."

"Who's manning the roadblocks?"

"Mostly Peshmerga, the Kurdish armed forces," Ken explained. "There might be some others set up by individual villages. I told you, the people here are sick of violence."

"How about Americans?" Austyn asked.

"There's one roadblock, but that's not a concern," Ken said. "They know we're coming. Most likely, we'll be waved through."

"What do the Peshmerga look for at the roadblocks?" Austyn asked.

"Mainly Arabs." Ken looked in the mirror at them. "I'm not exaggerating. There's racial profiling to the max around here. The Kurds hate Arabs."

Austyn saw Fahimah look out the window. She wasn't contradicting anything Ken was saying.

"And what else are they looking for?" he asked. "Weapons?"

"Maybe. They might search the car for God knows

what…maybe something else that they'll like and decide to keep."

"Will they check papers?" Austyn asked.

"You never know, but that's a possibility. They might want to know what you're doing here, where you've been and where you're going and all that. They could be as tough as the Iranian guards you'll face crossing the border. So you have to get your stories straight before we get to any of these roadblocks."

Austyn pulled out the envelope Matt had given him and emptied the contents on the seat between him and Fahimah. She looked over, watching what he was doing.

"Do you know what you're going to tell them?" he asked her.

She nodded. "I am a professor of political science at the University of Baghdad. My name is Fahimah Banaz."

"What are you doing here?" Ken asked her from the front seat.

"I'm visiting family at Halabja. That's where I am from originally," she said. "Of course, I'll answer all of this in Kurdish, and they'll have no problem with it. My Argentinean colleague here could have a problem."

"Only if you tell them to pee in my tea," Austyn said under his breath.

She smiled and Austyn found himself distracted.

"How about crossing to Iran? What are going to tell them if they stop you?" Ken asked.

"The same thing. And I'll tell them I'm looking for some family members that might be in one of the refugee camps across the border," she said. "I'll tell them I want to take them back to Iraqi Kurdistan with me."

"That's the magic word," Ken said. "I've heard they're so overcrowded in the camps that any time you're going there to bring someone back, they have no problem with it."

"What about if they ask for the name of your family?" Austyn asked her.

"I can give them three dozen names…perhaps even more. I have many family members who went missing during Saddam's campaigns of terror," she said quietly. "I will also be speaking Farsi with them, so that's another feather in my cap."

"That works for me," Ken commented.

Austyn replaced his own passport and documents with those establishing his Argentinean identity. "Where do you want my real passport?" he asked Ken.

"There's a slot that leads to a compartment under the rug behind your seat."

Austyn made sure there were no cars tailing them or anyone to see what he was doing. There was an advantage in leaving when they had. There wasn't too much traffic and the neighborhoods were beginning to thin out. He looked over his shoulder and found the spot Ken was referring to. He deposited the extra papers there and pulled the rug back over the slot. He opened the passport and studied his new name and information, which he went over with Fahimah.

"Someone might ask what you are doing with this guy." Ken said when they were finished. "What will you say?"

"He contacted me through the university because I teach political science. He's writing a book about Kurdistan and the refugee camps. I was going to Halabja, anyway, so I offered to bring him along."

"And going over the border?" Ken asked.

"The same thing. I'm serving as his translator. He doesn't speak Kurdish or Farsi," she answered simply.

Austyn was impressed. She spoke with such authority that it was difficult to challenge what she said. He guessed she was an excellent teacher.

"Won't they find something majorly wrong with the fact that you're an unmarried woman and traveling with a foreign male?" Ken asked.

"No, not at all," she said confidently. "We are in Kurdistan, and I teach at the university. This will stop anyone from asking such a frivolous question. The Islamic fundamentalists don't have so much influence on the way people live in the north. At least, they didn't five years ago. And based on what I saw on the streets last night and heard from my friends, I'd say things are—"

"Well," Ken said, interrupting. "This came up sooner than I thought." He slowed the van.

Straight ahead, the traffic came to a standstill. Past the half-dozen cars, armed Kurdish soldiers were checking every vehicle going in either direction.

"They usually do this when people are coming into Erbil, not leaving it," Ken commented.

"What are we doing traveling with you?" Austyn asked Ken.

"I'm giving you a ride."

"Why?" Austyn asked.

"I'm on leave for forty-eight hours. Sightseeing. Met at the hotel and, rather than let the two of you travel by bus, I offered to give you a ride."

"U.S. soldiers are instructed to travel in groups when on leave," he pressed. "What are you doing alone?"

They inched forward.

"My girlfriend is stationed in Sulaimaniyah," Ken said smoothly. "I'm going there to meet her. I don't need a crowd with me."

They moved ahead a little more. The soldiers were checking the car ahead of them.

"Your girlfriend? Aren't you married?" Austyn asked, testing.

"I'm making up stories, remember?" Ken replied.

The car ahead of them left the checkpoint, and a Peshmerga soldier waved them forward. Ken stopped where he was directed. The soldier looked in the van at Ken's uniform and nodded.

"IDs, please," the soldier said in a thick accent.

Austyn handed over his fake passport and Fahimah's university ID to Ken, who handed them to the soldier. Another armed Peshmerga fighter circled the van, looking in.

The soldier looked briefly at Ken's and Austyn's documents and handed them back. He glanced at Fahimah's next and tapped on her window. She opened it. He looked at her ID again and stared at her face a couple of seconds.

"Jawerrwani," he said, walking away and taking her identification. The soldier waved to two other soldiers, who moved in front of the car, blocking them.

"What did he say?" Austyn asked.

"He said to wait," she answered.

"We're not starting out too well, are we?"

"I don't know what the heck this is about," Ken grumbled, taking the phone out from under the seat.

It wasn't like Fahimah to get nervous, but Austyn saw her tuck her hands under her legs. She looked anxiously in the direction the soldier had gone. He was now talking to someone sitting in a car across the road. Whoever it was, he seemed to be in a position of authority. The other man took the ID from the soldier and looked at it, too. He yelled out something to the two Peshmergas blocking their path.

"He said we need to pull to the side," she explained, translating for them in a thin voice.

"I heard him," Ken said. "Shit, what do they want?"

"Do you have any idea what this could be about?" Austyn asked her.

She shook her head. "Pull over to the side," she suggested. "The traffic is backing up behind us."

"I don't give a damn about traffic," Ken said.

The Peshmerga in charge walked across the road to them. He was a younger man and had the strut of a bantam cock. He was wearing no uniform but was dressed in the traditional Kurdish garb of baggy trousers and a plain jacket with a colorful sash. His shoes set him apart. He was wearing new Reebok sneakers. Ken stepped out of the car.

"What's wrong?" he asked.

Austyn didn't know if this was by choice or if Ken had forgotten to speak to them in Kurdish. He quickly got out of the car, as well.

"Both of you...inside your vehicle," the man said in fairly good English. He pointed to Fahimah. "But you, *khanoom,* you come with me."

Twenty-Five

David Link had spoken to the main office at Reynolds Pharmaceuticals before he'd come on board the *Harmony*. The 10,000-unit shipment of Strep-Tester was ready to go out on Monday. On the phone, he'd given his input about suggested late changes in the regional shipping numbers. He was sure the numbers he'd okayed had been sent out by e-mail to the sales force by now. There was, no doubt, plenty of grumbling going on across the country. This was a good time to be away and incommunicado.

"I think they should follow this trip with a weeklong excursion providing scuba diving instruction."

Realizing one of the mothers was talking to him, David turned away from the railing and focused on what was going on around him. Kids and parents were gathered on deck, helping the divers get ready to go over the side for the next collection.

"That's true," David agreed, watching the buzz of activity.

Doing chores was clearly a treat on the *Harmony*. The kids fought over the opportunities to take responsibility for what was happening. Right now, half a dozen kids were working together, doing the last-minute checks for the two men who were supposed to go down.

Only one of the divers was on deck. Philip had not appeared yet.

One of the boys was connecting the underwater video camera to the cables. A lanky blond girl wearing a Phillies cap was loading cassettes into the handheld cameras that the divers took down. Baskets and nets for the samples were tagged and nearly ready to go. Flags were bundled together. Other tools were put in a mesh bag and placed on the deck.

Philip had explained to everyone over breakfast that they were collecting samples this morning at an active ocean disposal site. Apparently, there was currently some controversy between the EPA and the Army Corp of Engineers whether or not this specific location should stay open. The researcher had told everyone that he would be submitting a report with their findings about this location to both agencies. He was also going to include the names of all the people in the crew who helped with the report.

The comments had definitely made everyone feel like professionals, including the parents and caregivers, though they had nothing to do with the actual work.

David looked around. He hadn't seen Philip come up yet, but he knew he would. He'd looked better during breakfast and seemed to be over the worst of whatever he was fighting.

"Is there any way I can go down with them?" Craig's son asked him. "I can hold the camera or be in charge of carrying the nets."

Every teenager on deck picked up on the request and started asking the same question. The woman next to David gave him a "didn't I tell you" look.

Craig's firm "no" was to everyone. The scuba diving was to be left to the divers. Period.

David realized that his son wasn't one of the kids asking to go down with the divers. He moved away from the dive station, looking for him.

Sally always said that she knew their children were getting sick before they got sick. Or she knew they'd be getting a fever before their temperature went up. David, the girls and Josh always laughed at her, but she was always right.

On the far side of the boat, in sight of the divers' station, Josh was sitting by himself on a bench, tying some ropes.

David had woken up this morning with this feeling that he couldn't explain—like there was something wrong with Josh. He figured Sally's parenting skills must be rubbing off on him, finally. Of course, the twelve-year-old had denied feeling sick.

David made a mental note to check Josh's temperature, take a look at his ears and listen to his lungs. The leukemia made Josh susceptible to illnesses. To help them keep track—and to help them stay calm—their pediatrician had armed them with all kinds of diagnostic tools. Of course, they'd had to learn that every cold or sore throat didn't have to mean the child's death was imminent. Still, the doctor agreed that in Josh's case it wasn't a bad thing for David and Sally to stay on top of his health and make sure they caught everything early.

Kirk, the other diver, was pulling on his oxygen tanks with the assistance of a dozen willing hands. The wet suit he was wearing today had a hood, and he was wearing gloves and foot protection, too. It had been explained that because this was an active dump sight, the divers would have to use extreme precautions to keep from exposing themselves to dangerous substances. There was still no sign of Philip, and Josh didn't seem interested in what was going on.

David worked his way toward his son. So far during the trip, he'd tried to give the twelve-year-old some space. He didn't want to baby him, the way they usually did at home. Josh wanted to be one of the kids, to be normal. There was nothing David wanted more.

He sat down on the bench next to his son, making sure there was a manly amount of distance between them.

"A little bit chilly today, isn't it?" David asked.

The boy nodded.

The boat had tied up to the yellow special-purpose buoy that marked the site, but the gusts of wind were kicking up whitecaps and making the vessel rock. David looked up at the flags snapping in the wind.

"Do you want me to go and get you a thicker sweatshirt?"

"No."

"I wonder where Philip is?" David asked.

Josh looked up from the elaborate knot he was making. "He should be up any minute." He cleared his voice a couple of times. "I was talking to him downstairs before I came up."

"You're starting to sound kind of hoarse."

"It's not too bad."

"Josh," David drawled. He didn't have to say more. The boy had been told many times the importance of being honest about how he felt.

"It's my throat. It's sore."

The immediate panic of thinking how far they were from the closest hospital shot through David. He forced that fear to the background, though, and did a quick mental check of the medications the pediatrician had sent along with them. Josh had a ten-day supply of antibiotics, in case he needed it. They would be back on shore long before that ran out. David and Sally had been warned not to use the medication unless it was absolutely necessary. They needed the twelve-year-old to fight the viral illnesses himself. Antibiotics weren't the answer to everything. David knew that as well as anyone, from all his years of working in pharmaceuticals.

David remembered the two Strep-Testers he'd brought along. He'd given one of them to Philip. He didn't know if the program director had used it or not. But they still had one left, anyway.

"How about if we go down to the fo'c'sle and I do a quick swab of your throat?" David asked. "How's that, eh? Sounding pretty nautical, ain't I there, matey? Fo'c'sle… I'll be saying 'shiver me timbers' next. Come on. It'll just take a minute. I've got these new testers, not even on the market yet."

"No, Dad. I'm fine."

"Josh, if you have strep throat, things will only get worse. The sooner I test it, the sooner we'll know."

Josh looked around the deck reluctantly. "Not yet. In a little bit. Maybe after the dives are over."

Kirk was ready to go, sitting on the railing and waiting for Philip. With the help of the kids, he started lowering the video camera cage and the nets carrying their tools into the water.

Just then, Philip went past them without saying anything. He was already dressed in his wet suit with the hood up and the gloves and boots on. David thought he was walking awkwardly.

"It must be tough coming up that ladder with all that gear on," he said confidentially to his son.

"I think I have what Philip has," Josh said out of the blue. "He's doing pretty well without all the drugs. I'll kick it myself, too."

David decided there was no point in arguing with the twelve-year-old now. Perhaps the downside of this trip, what with hanging out with people like Philip and his crew, was that Josh would naturally be influenced by their alternative-medicine attitudes. Another week and he could have a complete natural-healing nut on his hands. The past two nights Josh had refused to have any kind of meat with dinner, just because he heard Philip say he was a vegetarian.

Whatever, David told himself. Just so long as Josh got everything he needed now. He could fight the rest of it out with his mother when they got home.

"Are you okay?" David heard Kirk ask the other diver. "You don't look too good."

Philip was pulling the oxygen tanks on his back with the help of one of the parents. David saw him wave at Kirk to go in.

The younger man waited until Philip joined him at the railing. A few words passed between them that David couldn't hear from where they were sitting. There didn't seem to be any reason for concern, though, as the two flipped backward into the water together.

Some of the kids rushed to where a small TV hung on a portable mount next to a cabin door.

Josh was shivering.

"Come on, Captain Jack," David joked encouragingly. "Let's get it done before them there barnacles grows on us."

The boy looked at him and shook his head. "I think there's something wrong with *you*, Dad."

David laughed. "You're probably right, but we can do this before the video feed comes up. We run inside, you get another sweatshirt, and I'll take a second and check your throat."

"Okay," Josh replied, reluctantly pushing to his feet and following David downstairs.

Twenty-Six

Erbil, Iraq

The shouting match between the two Americans and the Kurd in charge would have been comical, if it weren't for the fact that the little Peshmerga kept tugging gently on the handle of the pistol in a holster beneath his coat. If Ken even reached for his pistol, Fahimah had no doubt someone would be killed.

"La darawa." The first soldier, who'd taken their papers, spoke to her in Kurdish and motioned for Fahimah to get out of the van.

"Dabe safar kayn bo Halabja," she replied, telling him they were traveling to Halabja. He nodded, but motioned again for her to move. She decided to do as she was told. She didn't like the look of the other soldiers who had joined the leader. They were holding their guns on the two Americans, and they looked as if they would just love to blast them away.

"Na tirsinok." Don't be afraid, the soldier told her quietly. *We just want to talk to you.*

He looked older than the rest of the Peshmerga. She hesitated, but he nodded reassuringly to her.

She turned around to the argument that hadn't eased at all.

"I'll be all right," she said loudly over the hood of the van to Austyn. She called out a second time to get their attention.

Austyn spun around and started back toward her. The Peshmerga leader was now screaming at him to stop. Ken was looking at her, as well, and ignoring the little Kurd. The Kurd pulled out his pistol, and Fahimah knew he would shoot Austyn in the back.

"Stop," she said to Austyn, holding up her hand.

He stopped.

Fahimah looked at the Peshmerga leader. "If you want to talk with me," she said in English, "I will. But there is no need to hurt these Westerners." She pointed to Ken. "You do not want to fight with an American soldier, do you, with all these people watching?"

She nodded with her head at the line of cars that had stopped by the checkpoint. The little man stared at her for a moment, then swaggered a little as he put his pistol back into its holster.

"You are a woman of great wisdom," he said in Kurdish. "But we *will* talk to you."

She pointed across the way. "I'm only going with them that far."

They both seemed reluctant…especially Austyn, who tried to come around the car to her, but the barrel of an AK-47 against his chest stopped him in his tracks.

"Will you stop?" she said to him directly. "I'm a Kurd. They won't hurt me."

Fahimah believed what she said. She turned to the soldier.

"Aya?" She asked where she should go to.

The man looked at his superior, who in turn nodded toward a small building behind the man's car across the road. The soldier next to her then directed Austyn and Ken to move the car farther off the road. She was thankful when Ken got behind the wheel and did as he was told.

"Hatin," the little leader told her.

She gave one last look over her shoulder at the van. Ken was already on his phone. Austyn had one hand on top of the van, his eyes glued to her as she crossed the road. She had no doubt that if she showed any sign of fear, he'd come charging across that road, gun or no gun.

The leader was no more than twenty-five, but he had regained his composure and again exuded authority in the way he walked and talked.

A rustic, white-brick building, no larger than three meters square, sat on the side of the road. One small, un-shuttered window and an open door faced the roadway. Remembering the frigid winters in Erbil, she decided this had to be a very popular place for the soldiers manning this checkpoint during the cold months.

Fahimah followed the Peshmerga leader. There was no one else inside. A couple of chairs and a table stood against the far wall. A large flag of Kurdistan had been pinned to the wall above the table.

"I am Ahmad," he told her in Kurdish, with far less bluster than he demonstrated outside. He left the door open. "And I know who you are."

He was holding on to her ID, so naturally he would know who she was. She didn't bring that to his attention, though.

"You are Firishte's sister."

Firishte meant "angel," but he used it like a name.

"You know Rahaf?" she said, relieved.

"Yes, I know her very well. I worked alongside her at Saryas and Jwanro refugee camps. You are brave, like her."

She shook her head in modesty, never comfortable about receiving compliments.

"How is my sister? I'm on my way to find her, to see her. It has been so long. Do you know where she is now?" Fahimah had hundreds of questions, but she had to give Ahmad a chance to answer the ones she'd already asked.

"We have no time," Ahmad said. "The American soldier is calling his people. In ten minutes, a truck full of them will swarm around here. We have to get you out."

"Get me out where?" she asked, perplexed.

"Rahaf told me in strict confidence that you were in their jails." He motioned to her hair. "You suffered in taking the place of your sister."

"She was innocent. I could not let them find her. She was very sick when I was captured, and they would not have understood. But those two men outside—"

"They are still holding you prisoner," he interrupted her. "Yesterday, the word spread quickly that Firishte's sister was in Erbil. I heard also that American soldiers were guarding you. When I heard, I knew I had to act. I owed that to Firishte."

Yesterday, she made sure to use her name every place she'd called and with everyone she'd seen at the hotel. She knew how the news traveled in Kurdistan. It was more effective than any modern communication system.

"I thank you, Ahmad," she said. "But I am not their prisoner."

He wasn't listening to her. "We can bring a car to the back and have you taken away before their soldiers arrive. We can have our people drive you to the border."

Fahimah shook her head.

"That won't be necessary," she said more forcefully. "I want Rahaf to meet the younger American. It is important for her to meet him."

Ahmad looked at her blankly.

"He needs my sister's help. He is a scientist, as she is. He is the one that saved me. He freed me from the prison," she explained.

She looked out the window at the van across the road. Austyn was standing straight as an arrow beside the vehicle and staring across at the building. Ken was still speaking on the telephone. She turned back to the Peshmerga leader.

"A terrible disease has struck America."

"This is nothing to us. We have disease here, as well. I like the Americans, *khanoom,* do not misunderstand me, but what of it? They have many doctors in America."

"Ahmad, this is the same disease that caused Rahaf to lose her leg. But in America, people are perishing every day. Children are dying painfully. I know my sister, my friend. Rahaf would want to help."

"They did you wrong," he reminded her, still not sounding completely convinced.

"Yes, they did," she replied. "But they did that wrong to me. And I have not forgotten that it was because of the Americans that our own people were not wiped from the face of the earth by Saddam Hussein."

"Nothing will ever destroy the Kurdish people. The Peshmerga have—"

"The Peshmerga have had Americans fighting at their side since 1991."

Ahmad said nothing for a moment, so Fahimah took advantage of his hesitation.

"That man out there had nothing to do with my imprisonment…nor did the people who are dying," she said passionately. "You call my sister an angel. Do you think she would want to see anyone die when she has the knowledge to possibly help them?"

Fahimah could tell she had him. The man's dark gaze looked out the open door at the van across the road. A Peshmerga soldier with his weapon drawn still guarded the two Americans, but the traffic was once again flowing. Fahimah could not believe that these people would go to all this trouble to find her…to free her. For so many years, she had felt so alone.

"What about the American soldier? Why do you need him?" Ahmad asked.

"He is only driving us to Halabja. From there, Austyn Newman and I cross the border into Iran on our own."

"He is American. How will he cross the border?"

"His passport is forged," she said, deciding on honesty. These were her people. They were here to help her.

He looked across the road again. Ken was out of the van now and looking anxiously down the road. Fahimah knew he was hoping his reinforcements would arrive soon.

"If you are no prisoner, then the Peshmerga will take you to Halabja," Ahmad said adamantly. "You will not travel with the American soldier."

Fahimah thought about that for a moment. She'd feel safer traveling with these Kurdish soldiers over an American soldier anytime. She'd already learned that Americans were a target across Iraq, regardless of the region. And in going with them, the Peshmerga leader would save face.

"Very well…but Austyn Newman comes with me," she reminded him.

He agreed. "We will take both of you there. And in Halabja we have contacts with some of the Iranian border guards. We will arrange for you to cross over when there will be the least trouble."

It was all too good to be true.

"Okay?" he asked in English.

"I want to say yes, but let me talk to them first," she told him.

He shrugged. "Firishte never asks anyone's permission. She is in charge. She does what she thinks is right. You should do the same."

"I am not asking their permission, I'm going to tell them," she told him. "But I do not want American helicopter gunships chasing us through the mountains."

He smiled. Fahimah noticed his top four teeth were missing. This close, she could also tell that the unshaven face hid old scars. He was a young man, but he had obviously earned his position of authority.

The Peshmerga forces had been around since the advent of the Kurdish independence movement in the early 1920s, following the collapse of the Ottoman and Qajar rulers who ruled jointly over the area always known as Kurdistan.

Being a Peshmerga, "those who face death," was a great honor, but it was an honor that was not easily won. The

Peshmerga did not lead easy lives. Many fought and died young. Many had suffered brutally at the hands of Saddam's torturers. From what she had gathered from Ken's words and from what she read on Sutton's laptop, many of the Peshmerga had only left the mountains and their long decades of guerrilla warfare after Saddam's fall.

She started out the door, and he walked out behind her.

"I need to talk to them alone—as you wanted to talk to me alone—so they do not feel that you are pressuring me to do this."

He smiled again. "*Baleh*, Dr. Banaz," he said with a salute.

It was touching, in an odd way, to have so tough an individual as this young fighter be so respectful.

Fahimah crossed the road, weaving between the cars that were stopping at the roadblock security check on their way into Erbil. Both Austyn and Ken ignored their armed guard and met her in front of the van.

"What was that about?" Austyn asked.

"First, let's get out of here before they change their mind," Ken suggested. "We're so short-handed around here that no backup to speak of will be coming."

"There is no need for backup, as you say," she said to Ken before turning to Austyn. "Some new arrangements have been made for us."

She explained the reason for the stop and how Ahmad and others believed she was still their prisoner. She also told them about the offer to have Peshmerga fighters escort them to Halabja and from there to arrange for them to cross the border.

"That's crazy. We don't need their help," Ken said, stunned by her words.

"But we are better off with it," she said flatly. "The Peshmerga are worried about me. Considering my past treatment at the hands of Americans, they have every right to be concerned."

"I don't like it. I was given the task of taking you both to Halabja, and frankly, I don't—"

"Ken, this is nothing personal against you, but we will be safer with them than with you."

"How do you know they're not going to drive you into the mountains and cut your throat?"

"How many years have you been here?" she asked him quietly.

Ken looked over his shoulder, avoiding her gaze.

Fahimah spoke gently but firmly. "These fighters see it as their duty to *protect* the Kurdish people. You know that. They stopped us because they were worried about me."

"Yes, but—"

"Besides, you were taking us only as far as Halabja. We still need to find a way to cross the border. This man, Ahmad, will take care of that second leg of the trip."

Ken didn't say anything more. She looked at Austyn.

He shrugged. "You trust them. That's good enough for me," he said. "Did he tell you that he knows where Rahaf is?"

"He mentioned two of the camps where he worked with her," she told him. She thought for a moment. "Another thing. The last time I crossed the border, I was a teenager. There is so much that I don't remember. It will be a relief to have a guide who knows the area."

Austyn patted Ken on the shoulder once and went to the van to get their bags.

"You're still upset," Fahimah said consolingly. "I appreciate your concern, Ken. And I am grateful for your help. But Austyn is in charge and he does not seem to have a problem with this change in plans."

"That's fine. I follow orders." He shrugged.

He looked at Austyn and then kicked the dirt a couple of times with the toe of his boot. He finally looked up at her.

"So, will you come back with him or are you going to stay in Halabja?" he asked, looking a little like a teenager.

The realization was slow in coming, but she finally got it. Ken was attracted to her. Fahimah didn't know how she should feel about that. She couldn't really decide if she liked him or not…as a romantic interest, that is. Sometime during the past five years, all thoughts of this kind simply disappeared. She never thought anyone would ever look at her this way again.

"I haven't had time to think what I will be doing or where I will be going. Up to a few days ago, I would not allow myself to think of tomorrow or next week or the week after. And since my release, other matters have been pressing."

"If you decide to come back to Erbil, will you let me know?" he asked.

She frowned. "Pardon me for saying this, but you never answered Austyn's question about being married."

Ken actually blushed. "No. No wife."

"So you're *not* married?" Not that it made a difference, but Fahimah sensed that he was not being entirely truthful, and she found herself getting some enjoyment out of seeing him squirm.

"We're separated."

"Naturally," she said. "You are here, and I assume she is in the United States."

"No…no… We were separated before I came over here. It just works better this way, as far as benefits and all that."

"I have our bags," Austyn said, joining them.

Fahimah was relieved. She shook Ken's hand and thanked him repeatedly before crossing the road and allowing Austyn to make whatever arrangements he needed to make with the other man.

The peculiar feeling of having someone show this kind of interest in her tugged at something within Fahimah. The last time she'd actually dated someone had been when she was twenty-four years old and in graduate school in England. Her last offer of marriage had been when she was twenty-eight and teaching at the university. A Kurdish physician who worked in Toronto, and whom she'd never met, had asked for her hand in marriage by sending a delegation to her house. The delegation had consisted of his mother and sister, who was a student of Fahimah's at the university. Fahimah's answer had been no, and that had been the extent of her love life.

She was past that stage of her life, she thought, reaching the other side of the road and looking for Ahmad. She had another path to travel now.

Twenty-Seven

Bagram Airbase, Afghanistan

Airman First Class Joseph Sawyer had yet to get a letter from his mother, but he didn't really blame her. A single mother, she worked two jobs to put food on the table. She just stunk when it came to picking husbands. Twice now, she'd been dumped with an infant and no child support or help of any kind. Still, making a mistake like that twice in her life, almost fifteen years apart, wasn't too bad.

Joe and his friend Ron Miller, members of the 455th Air Expeditionary Wing, came to Bagram together in the summer of 2006. The 455th served the Central Command Air Force, providing strike, rescue, survey and airlift capabilities to U.S. and Coalition forces, and they had been here since the beginning of Operation Enduring Freedom. They both shipped over from Goodfellow Air Force Base in Texas, where they'd met the first time. While Joe had left only his mother and his teenage brother back in Mobile,

Alabama, Ron came from a very large family in northern New Jersey.

Naturally, Ron got mail almost every stinking day. Besides the almost daily letters, he got a care package sent to him at least once a week from his mother, or one of his sisters, or sisters-in-law, or some PTA people in his niece or nephew's school.

The Miller family's generosity was, of course, a sweet deal for Joe. Ron got too much of everything, and after he went through the gifts himself, he let Joe have first dibs on picking what he wanted.

Paperback books were a frequent gift, as were CDs and personal hygiene items. Cookies, Joe could do without. Even though they were homemade, by the time they arrived they were rock hard. Salsa and chips fared better. but Ron usually invited a whole bunch of guys over, and they attacked that food like a swarm of rats.

The bars of dark chocolate were Joe's absolute favorite. And since he'd included a thank-you note in with one of Ron's letters home, he could always count on his friend's family to add a few for him.

A couple of hours ago, Joe had seen Ron walking back to the containerized housing unit they called home, along with the four other guys in their squadron they shared it with. The housing units were better than tents, but they were nothing like what they had at Goodfellow back in the U.S.

When Joe saw him, Ron had another package under his arm.

Both of them were off duty this morning. Usually, they'd spend the time in the gym. This morning, though, Ron was feeling worse. He'd been fighting a sore throat for a few days now, but he never was one to go to the infir-mary, and Joe knew better than to bug him about it.

The door to the unit was ajar, a big negative with all the dust in Bagram. It was as hot as summers in Mobile, but dry as hell and dusty as the inside of a Shop-Vac.

Joe went in, sure his friend would be feeling better. A care package from New Jersey always seemed to do the trick.

"Hey, Ron, you in here?"

The room was dark. The shades were drawn to keep out the unbearable sun, but it was still stifling in the unit. The fan wasn't running, which meant the electricity was out again…for the third time this week.

"Christ, it stinks in here," he muttered. "Ron?"

The way it smelled, Joe figured his buddy was using the crapper. At one end of the rectangular room, a faux-wood panel partitioned off the small bathroom. Six cots and built-in lockers lined the wall. There was no shower in these housing units; the showers were in a special unit down the row.

Joe's gaze focused on the open mailer sitting on Ron's cot. He crouched down next to it.

"Ron, you alive in there?" he asked over his shoulder. "Jeez, boy. You should get your folks to send you some of that potpourri shit. Man, you're killing me out here."

It looked as if Ron had already sorted through the box. New paperbacks were stacked against the wall. Joe's bars of chocolate were sitting in front of them, and there was an envelope in front of the chocolate with his name on it.

"Bless you, good people," he murmured, opening the envelope and reading the note. It was from Ron's mother, inviting him to stay with them when he and Ron came stateside for their two weeks' leave in the fall.

"Boy, you must have been adopted or something," he called to his friend, pawing through the items on the bed. "Your folks are too good to have birthed a shithead like you."

Ron's mother had sent cold medications—bottles of over-the-counter stuff, vitamins and samples of all kinds of things. Joe noticed that Ron had already opened a couple of the boxes of cold medicines and vitamins. The wraps and cotton balls were next to the carton.

Out of habit, Joe gathered up the trash. Being in the air force had turned him into a neat freak.

"Are you coming out of there?" he asked. The sealed package of chocolate chip cookies at the bottom of the carton was still untouched.

A piece of trash had been dropped back into the box, on top of the cookies. Joe reached in and picked it up. It looked like the wrapper for a Band-Aid, but it wasn't. He smoothed it flat between his fingers. The words Sample and Not for Sale were printed all over it. He read the back.

"'Reynolds Strep-Tester Home Kit.'" Joe remembered that one of Ron's sisters was a sales rep for a pharmaceutical company. "Huh! Good idea."

He pushed to his feet. It occurred to Joe that he'd gotten no response from Ron since coming into the housing unit.

"Hey, Ron. You in there, boy?" he asked, walking toward the bathroom door. The smell was horrendous.

Each unit had its own self-contained sewage tank, with water brought in through a flexible hose. One problem with these units was that the small tanks under each unit had to be pumped out regularly, and it seemed like every day one bathroom or another along the rows would back up.

Joe walked toward the bathroom. The door was cardboard thin, made out of some kind of pressboard designed to look like wood. He knocked on it.

"Ron?"

He tried the door. It wasn't locked. When he pushed, it gave slightly and then closed again. It felt like a weight was propped against it on the inside. Unless someone was in there, that wasn't too likely.

"Ron?" he called louder.

Again there was no answer.

Joe pocketed the trash and put both hands on the door. He gave a hard shove. The door opened a couple of inches and slammed shut. There was no doubt in Joe's mind that someone was leaning against it. Most likely, that someone was sitting on the floor, since the top of the door gave easier than the bottom.

"Shit, man. Open up. You need help?"

Joe stepped back and looked at the door. Moving across the small living space, he yanked open his own locker and pulled out a small mirror he had taped to the door. Going back to the bathroom, he put a shoulder to the door, holding it open at the top and sliding the mirror through the opening.

He angled the mirror and saw Ron on the floor, his head tipped forward onto his chest.

"Ron? Christ, Ron? Say something."

Joe knew the right thing to do would be to run out and call for help. Instead, though, he gave the door a couple of hard shoves. The fake-wood outer panel of the door buckled. Sliding his fingers into the opening and putting everything he had into the next pull, he ripped the outer panel halfway out of the door.

Punching through the inner panel was easier, and in a moment Joe had created enough of an opening to put his arms through.

When Joe touched him, Ron slumped sideways, his head cracking on the toilet on the way down.

"Christ, boy! What happened?" Joe didn't know where the extra burst of energy came from, but the next thing he knew, he was ripping the door off its hinges.

"What's all that racket in there?" a voice called jokingly from the doorway.

Joe recognized T.J.'s voice. T.J. lived two units down. "Get in here and help. Something's wrong with Ron."

Instantly, the man was beside him. A moment later, the door was lying on the floor by a bunk.

"Pull him out," Joe ordered. "Grab that leg…. Watch his head!"

Each man took hold of a leg, and together they gently pulled him out of the small bathroom.

"I never knew how goddamn heavy he was."

They laid him flat on the floor.

"What the hell…?" T.J. blurted out, immediately backing away.

Joe looked at Ron's face for the first time. His skin had a purple hue. There were raw, open sores on his neck, on his face. A foul-looking fluid was oozing from his nose and mouth. He smelled like a week-dead dog.

Even as Joe looked at him, the skin seemed to peel right off Ron's flesh.

Twenty-Eight

Kurdistan, Northeast Iraq

Austyn was perfectly happy with the new arrangements. As he'd discussed with Faas Hanlon, he would need to put more control of the mission in Fahimah's hands once they reached Halabja. Traveling with the Peshmerga just meant the transition had started a little earlier than planned.

Ahmad turned out to be a better ride and escort than they'd had before. Two cars were taking them to Halabja. Four Peshmerga soldiers were split between the cars. The vehicle Austyn and Fahimah were riding in—along with two of the fighters—was an older SUV, a 2002 BMW X5, and much nicer than the old van Ken had been driving. This one also had working air-conditioning. The other car leading the caravan was an old military four-wheel drive that looked like it had risen from the ashes of some scrap heap.

Austyn had been told that one way of going to Halabja from Erbil was through Kirkuk. But because of the daily violence in that city, they were going from Erbil to Lake Dokan to Sulaimaniyah to Khurmal to Halabja.

Fahimah had translated for him that this was slightly longer but more scenic…and safer. So far, Austyn whole-heartedly agreed. The view was beautiful. The well-paved road snaked through mountains carpeted with touches of green.

His only complaint was the driving. If it weren't some-what bloodcurdling, the entire situation would be comical. Both of the Peshmerga fighters liked to gesture with their hands as they spoke. There had already been a few in-stances of the driver talking and gesticulating energeti-cally. They would be off some cliff by now if the soldier in the passenger seat hadn't reached over to hold the wheel or make an adjustment. He did it all calmly, though. Ob-viously, this was the way everyone drove a car. Luckily, there weren't too many cars coming along the opposite side of the road.

"What are they saying now?" Austyn asked, seeing the Peshmerga fighters smile as they talked.

The two sitting in front only spoke Kurdish, and they never seemed to stop talking. The man behind the wheel was older. Fahimah said he was the one who had told her at the checkpoint not to be afraid. Austyn liked both of them. They were very pleasant and polite…now that they knew he was no threat to Fahimah. Anytime they said something over their shoulder to Fahimah, they'd follow it with the word *tarjomeh*…which she told Austyn meant "translate."

"One is telling a joke to the other," she whispered. "I need to wait for the punch line."

The two men burst into laughter a moment later. Austyn saw Fahimah smile and shake her head.

"Tarjomeh, tarjomeh!" they both called to her.

"You need to realize that jokes in Kurdish are quite different than what you Westerners are accustomed to," she told him.

"How different?"

"They are racist. They are slanted against whatever ethnic group that they dislike."

"So I assume this one was an Arab joke?" he asked.

She nodded.

"Tell me."

"Tarjomeh," the driver encouraged, looking in the mirror at her.

"He's taking his eyes off the road," Austyn reminded her.

"Okay. But remember, I am just repeating it," Fahimah reminded him again.

He could understand her reluctance. Her extensive education, her years abroad, the time that she'd spent teaching, all must have reinforced her innate sense of tolerance.

She shook her head one more time, as if she couldn't believe she was actually relaying the story.

"All right. Two policemen in Baghdad…they were Arabs…came on duty and went out on their usual route through the city. A short time later, while they were in a park eating their lunch, before taking their naps, they found two American Tomahawk missiles that had never exploded. One said to the other, 'We should take them to the American base and get the reward.' So the two policemen loaded the missiles into the backseat of their squad car and drove toward the base. After an hour of driving, the second Arab said, 'Tell me something, what will we do if one of these missiles explodes in the car?' His friend thought for a few minutes and said, 'I've got it. We'll say we only found one missile!'"

Austyn couldn't help but laugh. The two men in front, although they didn't speak English, were in stitches at what appeared to be the end of the joke.

"Okay," she whispered. "Don't encourage them."

"Why?"

"Because they probably have a hundred Arab jokes each up their sleeves."

As if on cue, the younger Peshmerga started another one. This one was a short one, and both men burst into laughter afterward.

"Tarjomeh," they chanted at Fahimah.

She tapped the driver on the shoulder and said something to him sternly.

"Baleh, khanoom."

"What did you say?" Austyn asked.

"I said that this will be the last one."

"There's no harm in this," he said, smiling at her.

"Right now, maybe not. But when they start telling jokes that are otherwise inappropriate, I'm the one who turns eighteen different shades of red."

He nodded in understanding, holding back the comment that she was already turning eighteen shades of red. And actually, he thought, she looked quite beautiful in all those shades.

"Okay, tell me this last one."

She gathered her hands on her lap. "Two thieves broke

into an Arab's house. The Arab woke up and asked them, 'What are you looking for?' The thieves told him, 'Money.' Hearing that, the Arab jumped out of bed and responded, 'Wait a second, I'll help you.'"

Again, there was a burst of laughter from the men in front.

The passenger made another casual grab at the wheel since the driver was laughing so hard that he'd closed his eyes. Austyn looked at the thin, foot-high guardrail that was the only barrier between them and what was probably a thousand-foot drop off the side of the mountain.

He tore his gaze away from the road when an argument broke out between the two fighters and Fahimah. Austyn didn't think it was anything too serious, though, as they were smiling and Fahimah had her teacher's voice on.

They started chanting. *"Yek. Yek. Yek."*

"What do they want now?" he asked, totally entertained.

"Yek. Yek. Yek."

"They are reneging on their promise."

"They want to tell another joke?" Austyn asked.

"No, they want you to tell them an American joke."

"Okay, I can do that."

"Oh, God," she said, rolling her eyes.

"Seriously, I'm a good joke-teller."

"Only one," she agreed reluctantly.

"Yes, ma'am," he told her. "Give me a second to think of one."

"Keep it clean," she warned him.

Austyn decided to use some one-liners. "This is all one joke. Just translate after each line."

She nodded.

"Do you know what a redneck is?" he asked.

"A redneck." She thought and then nodded. "No education. Lives in the woods. Not very bright."

"Right. Okay, here we go…you know you're a redneck… *Tarjomeh,*" he reminded her.

She did as she was told. Her translation of *redneck* took a couple of minutes, and the two men in front nodded politely.

Austyn continued. "You know you're a redneck if the only tooth you've got left is the one you're wearing on a chain around your neck."

She simply stared at him.

"No, wait a minute," he said. "I'm not remembering that one right. It had something to do with your hound dog's tooth."

She looked at him. "You know, most of these people live in the mountains. They've never seen a dentist in their lives, and if they ever have seen one, it was for the sole purpose of having their teeth pulled."

"I'm sorry. That was insensitive," he said, feeling the heat rise into his scalp. "Okay, try this one for them. I've got it. You know you're a redneck when your dad walks you to school because you're in the same grade."

Fahimah smiled and translated. There were some nods and polite smiles. She didn't have to say anything more.

"Okay, I'm done," he said quietly.

The two men in front started making noises, motioning to him to continue. "Come on, you can come up with more." She spoke to him gently, as if she wanted to make sure his feelings weren't hurt.

"You know you're a redneck when you keep your food stamps in the icebox."

She shook her head. "I don't know what a food stamp is."

Rather than explaining it to her, he decided to try a new line. "You know you're a redneck when you and your wife get divorced and you're still cousins."

Fahimah shook her head again. "There are a lot of marriages in the same tribes and families among the Kurds. They won't find that funny." She lowered her voice. "In fact, you might insult them."

"I'm not doing too well, am I?"

"You're doing great," she said encouragingly. "It's just a different humor."

"Do Kurds love their mothers-in-law?" he asked, remembering another line.

"No. Not always. There are a few jokes about that."

"Then try this on them. You know you're a redneck when you're always hoping to find your mother-in-law's picture on the back of a milk carton."

"Why would they put anyone's picture on the milk carton?" she asked.

"Missing people's faces…" He shook his head. "If you have to explain it…it's not funny anymore. Guess I won't be going on the comedy circuit anytime soon."

She bit her lip, trying to hide a smile. "Well, perhaps not in Kurdistan, anyway."

Jokes forgotten, the driver pointed straight ahead and said something to Fahimah. The other man said a few words as well. Looking in the same direction, Austyn caught a glimpse of blue waters ahead.

She turned to Austyn when the two men finished. "They were telling me about this famous resort at Lake Dokan."

Along the way, Fahimah had told him about Dokan being a beautiful resort town northwest of Sulaimaniyah.

The man-made Lake Dokan was a large water reservoir that supplied drinking and irrigation water to many towns and agricultural areas in the region. In addition to that, the dam's turbines generated enough power to provide electricity to a large area.

"The Ashour Hotel is a luxury accommodation. It has been around for a while," she told him. "The place has absolutely stunning views of the lake. It has terraces with pools and stone walkways that wind through beautiful gardens with flowering trees. It's really one of the most striking places in Kurdistan to stay."

"Did something happen to it?" he asked.

She shook her head. "They were telling me that American troops rented the entire hotel a couple of years ago for a few months. No Kurds were allowed to use it or even step foot on the grounds. I guess the people weren't too happy about that."

Over and over, Austyn was hearing the message. The Kurds loved Americans, so long as they didn't act like an occupying army.

"Do the Americans still have the place?"

"No." She shook her head. "The owner must have made a great deal of money, though. They say he's done some major renovations. Now it's open to the public again."

Austyn saw her look in the direction of the lake again. "Did you ever stay there?"

She smiled, nodding. "After I came back from England and Rahaf was back from America, we would try to go away, just the two of us, for a week during Norooz."

"Norooz?"

"The first day of spring. That's what the Iranians and Kurds celebrate as the new year," she told him. "We always took a week off and came here. Kurdistan is prettiest in the spring."

"How was it that the two of you ended up going to different countries for your education?" he asked. He knew the source of Rahaf's educational funds, but he had no idea how Fahimah had gotten to England.

"Our parents died in Halabja during the bombings," she explained. "Our brothers, all three of them, were taken away a few months before that. They were killed by Saddam's soldiers."

Austyn saw her chin quiver slightly. She looked out the window for a minute or two, obviously trying to compose herself.

"Rahaf was fifteen and I was sixteen. We packed our bags and made our way with some of our cousins across the mountains to Iran. We stayed in one of the camps where Rahaf is working right now."

This explained why Rahaf went across the border. Austyn had been a couple of years older than Fahimah back in 1988. He remembered when the news of the killing of the Kurdish civilians hit U.S. newspapers and television screens. The aftermath of the massacres had been photographed and reported, and he'd studied the events in his training as an epidemiologist. Still, none of that affected him as much as sitting next to Fahimah, a victim of that tragedy…right here, right now.

"We both got our high school degrees while going to school at Paveh. That is a city in Kermanshah province in western Iran."

"Did you go back and forth between the camp and the city while you were going to school?" he asked.

"No, an Iranian Kurdish family took us in. They were wonderful people. They had three girls about our age." She smiled, obviously remembering their kindness. "Paveh is a great ancient city that dates back three thousand years. They say the name of the city has something to do with Zoroastrianism, the past religion of its people. In fact, there is still a fire temple that tourists can visit."

Austyn thought that it was sad that so much of the history of that region was lost to Westerners because of politics.

"One of the most amazing things about Paveh is the housing. The homes of the people are built in the shape of many long, wide stairs climbing the foothills of the mountain."

"Stairs?"

She smiled. "The buildings have been built in such a way that the roof of one house actually serves as the balcony of another house, built just a few meters above it."

"I wish someday I could see it," he said.

"So do I," she told him. "I would love to go back there. Anyway, after 1991—the First Gulf War, I understand you call it…"

He nodded.

"After the U.S. and its allies established the no-fly zone to protect the Kurds, many of us felt much safer about returning to Iraq. So Rahaf and I, with our high school degrees in hand, went back to Kurdistan."

"Did you go to Halabja?" Austyn asked. He looked at the two men in the front seat who were laughing. They were paying no attention whatsoever to the discussion in the backseat.

"No, that was far too painful for us. It was just too

soon to return there. We went to Erbil. We needed jobs to make a living."

"Did you have anyone to stay with in Erbil?" he asked.

"We did. That is the wonderful thing about the Kurds. They help one another. They are generous in their hearts. They throw open their doors to others," she said proudly. "The word went around that Rahaf and I were in Erbil, and we had dozens of offers from people who either knew our parents or considered themselves related…something like fifth cousins thrice removed or perhaps a little more distant. We stayed with a family whom we knew from Halabja."

"Now I really understand how inappropriate my joke would have sounded to these guys," Austyn said.

The driver must have been in the middle of another joke, because the passenger was again steering the car. Austyn turned his attention back to her.

"So what happened after that?"

"We were in Erbil for only a few weeks when a cousin who lived in Baghdad contacted us about a fund the Iraqi government had set up to educate promising Iraqi women overseas. Rahaf applied for it and took the tests. Despite being Kurdish, she was accepted. Three months later, in the fall, she was on her way to America."

"What about you? How come you didn't apply for it?"

"I was a year older than my sister. As soon as we arrived in Erbil, I found a job working in the office for a British organization. I was their translator."

"You could speak English?"

She nodded. "I wasn't as fluent as I am now, but I could do the job they were asking me to do."

"What was the organization?"

"The Kurdistan Children's Fund. They were one of many volunteer organizations that came to the region then. They were trying to somehow help all these parentless children. There were so many children," she explained. "They were truly good-hearted people that I worked for."

"Do you know who was funding the organization?"

"I didn't know then, but later I found out that the donations came from individuals and some large annual funding from the British government."

Austyn knew there were many programs like this that flew under the media radar. Sometimes they were fronts for funding resistance groups—like the Peshmerga—and sometimes they were legitimate.

"The man I was working for—Dr. Whittaker—was a retired British government official," she continued. "He was extremely kind to me. It was with his encouragement and recommendations that I applied to continue my education in England."

"But not to just any university," he teased. "You went to Oxford."

"Yes. To this day, I believe he had a lot to do with that. He was very proud to call himself an Oxford man."

"He paid for your education?"

"No. The Kurdistan Children's Fund paid. Somehow they convinced me that even as a nineteen-year-old, I qualified for their grants. They paid all of my traveling and living expenses, and my first four years of education. Beyond that, I became fairly self-sufficient."

Until she stepped in and took the rap for her sister.

"Can I ask you something?"

She shrugged. "I don't think there is very much I haven't told you yet."

"What were you doing in Rahaf's laboratory the day of the bombardment? Why *exactly* were you wearing her badge?"

Twenty-Nine

The research vessel Harmony
The Atlantic

"First tell me how this thing works," Josh told his dad.

There was no *let's do it and get it done* with Josh. Tests and medications had become part of the twelve-year-old's life. He was curious and worried about every X-ray, every needle, every microgram of drugs injected into him. He wanted to be part of every decision. David and Sally encouraged their son's curiosity. They wanted him to be involved with his own care. They both knew that cancer was a chronic disease, so Josh would have to be aware of what was going on with his body for his entire life.

David sat down next to him on the bunk.

Their room was in the bow of the boat, on the starboard side. They shared the cabin with two other boys, their fathers, and two Sea Grant lab instructors. The port cabin was occupied by the females on the trip. The skipper and the mate shared a cabin farther aft. The large galley where everyone took their meals was also used as a lab, and David knew a couple of the men from the research center had berths there. The whole experience made for close quarters, but no one complained.

Josh and David were the only ones who'd come below deck. Everyone else was hanging around above, either waiting for the video feed from the divers or hanging over the railing in anticipation of the samples that the two men would send up.

"You put on that sweatshirt and I'll tell you," David said.

Josh tugged a hooded sweatshirt out of his bag and pulled it on. It was a new one that he'd gotten as part of the cost of the trip, and David smiled at the words on it. *I've gone off the deep end. Cape Henlopen Ocean Research Experience.*

"This is not like one of those giant Q-tips that they stick in your throat and make you gag, is it?" Josh asked.

"No, nothing like that." David opened his briefcase and grabbed the medicine bag out of it. "This is very simple. In fact, anybody can do it themselves."

"I can make myself gag?"

"No gagging involved, I promise you. That's the beauty of it." David dug out the one sample tester he had left at the bottom of the medicine bag. "I'm telling you, Josh, the company is going to sell a million of these things in a little while. There isn't going to be a household in America that doesn't have a stash of these."

The twelve-year-old sat on the edge of the bunk looking

at him with a bored look. "Dad, can you just read me the instructions?"

"No formal instructions needed. It has just three simple steps. But to keep us from getting sued by every moron with a lawyer for a brother-in-law, the three steps are written inside, on the tester itself."

To the sales force, the five-hundred-piece sample lot— made individually in the prototype lab—had been pure gold. Each person was instructed to give out only one sample to each of their top clients. Nothing had been said, but David had expected that each sales rep probably kept a few for themselves or their families. David had done that, too.

"Okay, this is how it works…" He put the Strep-Tester in Josh's palm.

"It looks just a like Band-Aid," Josh commented.

"Exactly." David nodded with a grin. "Except you can't say 'Band-Aid' or Johnson & Johnson will sue us. The ads will say 'small, flexible, disposable, individually wrapped' or something like that."

"That's actually pretty cool."

"Thanks. Okay, this is what you do. You tear open the outer wrapper. Then you just peel the shiny clear membrane away from the gauzy side until a pink circle in the middle is exposed. It'll look like a little bubble in the middle. Then you stick out your tongue and press the pink circle onto the middle of your tongue…."

"Does it taste disgusting?"

"No. It's strawberry-flavored." As Josh shot him a suspicious look, David gave him a Scout's honor sign. "Besides, you're not going to eat it. You just press it on your tongue."

Josh had yet to open the package. "I thought it's supposed to check your throat?"

"It is," David explained. "This Strep-Tester is so sensitive that it recognizes the strep bacteria from anywhere in your mouth."

"Does this mean I can just touch my teeth with the tester?"

"Yes, you can. But that might be a little bit more complicated than it needs to be."

David thought his son had a career in the FDA. Josh's tenacity in getting all the answers was superior to anything the Food and Drug Administration had put Reynolds Pharmaceuticals through.

"Okay, then what?"

"You just press the clear membrane back over the pink circle and hold it for ten seconds."

"So the bubble is on the inside," Josh pointed out.

David nodded. "We can go through the steps as you're testing yourself," he suggested.

"No, not yet." Josh held on to the strip, not ready to give it up yet. "Do I need a stopwatch for counting ten seconds?"

"No. All you have to do is count. 1001, 1002…you know how to count."

"Then what happens?" the twelve-year-old asked.

"After ten seconds, if you have strep, then the clear membrane turns bright blue," David explained.

"And if I don't?"

"If you don't have strep, it stays clear and you can still see the pink circle. If you don't have strep now, you might be fighting a virus or it might be too early to show up positive. But either way, you can still check it again later with another Strep-Tester."

Holding the strip's edge, Josh raised it to the light as if checking to see what was inside through the wrapping. "What do you do with it after you're done? Save it for your doctor to see?"

"No, the company recommends you flush it down the toilet. They're water soluble," David told him. "This doesn't replace what the doctor might want to do in his office. Most likely, in a couple of months, they'll be using these Strep-Tests in their offices, too. It'll save them a lot of money over the traditional tests."

"If I have to go through it all over again at the doctor's office, then what's this good for?" Josh complained.

"This will eliminate unnecessary trips for parents or for people who think they might have strep throat but then find out when they go to their doctors that it's only a viral infection and they have to wait it out."

"Won't the doctors lose money on this?"

Josh's intelligence always amazed David. At his young age, he was aware of how businesses worked—especially when it came to the medical field.

"The loss to them will be minimal. Doctors are mostly swamped with patients. Besides, this is something we're doing for the patients. That's the group that will be benefiting from it."

"And you can buy these in any store?"

"Pretty soon you'll be able to. Come on, try it out."

Josh looked at the Strep-Tester again. "How many of these do you have?"

"This is the last one I have with me. I had two of them, but I gave one to Philip a couple of days ago."

"Did he use it?" Josh asked.

"I never asked him. He might have."

"If this is your last one," Josh persisted, "what happens if someone else ends up needing it?"

"You're the most important person on this boat, pal. You come first."

"Sure…after Philip," the boy drawled with a crooked smile.

The voices of kids could be heard from the deck above them.

"Okay, wise guy." David gave him a gentle shove and snatched the strip out of his hand. "You've put it off long enough. There's all kinds of excitement going on upstairs, and you're missing it, grilling me with all these questions."

"Seriously, Dad. What happens if Mom needs it next week?"

"I'll have tons of these by next week." David ripped the wrapper off the Strep-Tester.

"I might do it wrong and ruin it. It might be too early for the testing. Maybe we should wait another day…."

Strip in hand, David looked into his son's face. "You're nervous about this. How come?"

Josh shrugged. "I don't know. I just don't have a good feeling about it."

David tapped the rim of his son's baseball cap. "Considering everything that you've been through…after all the needles and tests, after how brave you've been through it all, this is nothing. It's just a simple test."

David held it out to him. He didn't want to force Josh. He wanted his son to do it himself.

Josh nodded. "Okay. I'm sorry, Dad."

The boy took the Strep-Tester out of David's hand and very gently peeled back the clear paper.

"It looks like a zit," he said, looking at the pink circle. Both of them burst out laughing.

"Okay, now press it on your tongue."

Thirty

"**W**hy was I in the lab with Rahaf's identification card? That's not an easy question to answer—"

"*Emeriki,*" the driver announced, interrupting them. A roadblock ahead captured everyone's attention. Fahimah didn't get the chance to answer Austyn's question.

There were many words that she didn't have to translate for Austyn. As she took out the ID that she'd gotten back from Ahmad, she noticed that Austyn wasn't taking out his forged Argentinean passport.

"They should let us go through," he told her. "Ken was taking care of communicating with all the American patrols along this road."

The two cars ahead seemed to be moving through. There was no major holdup. Their escort reached the American barricade and, after a couple of questions, was waved through. Their driver approached the soldiers, rolling down the window and handing out everyone's papers and documents.

The soldier receiving the documents looked inside the car, specifically at Fahimah and Austyn. He leafed through what was handed to him.

"Pull to the side," he told the driver. He waved someone over from the pair of Humvees and the covered truck at the side of the road.

"Come on," Austyn mumbled.

The driver cursed under his breath but did as he was told. Fahimah was relieved that Austyn didn't ask for a translation.

"I hope they're not planning on doing another switching of drivers," Fahimah told him. "Would your bosses in Washington order that?"

"I hope not."

Two soldiers approached the car this time. Austyn and Fahimah both rolled down their windows. The air-conditioning continued to blast. One of the men poked his head into the window. He was holding on to their documents.

"May we speak to you, sir?" he asked Austyn.

He got out without having to be asked twice. One of the soldiers remained by the car, and the other walked with Austyn to the back of the truck parked on the other side of the road.

The driver opened all the windows and shut off the engine. A soft breeze swept through the car, smelling like water and hills. It was a sweet smell, one that Fahimah remembered from years back.

Fahimah told herself she wasn't worried about Austyn. This had to be very much the same type of inquiry she'd undergone with Ahmad. An American in the car with three Kurds. They probably wanted to make sure that they weren't being double-crossed. Perhaps they were concerned that Austyn was being kidnapped. The articles she'd been given to read on the laptop told of how kidnapping foreign personnel—military and nonmilitary—was the latest rage in Baghdad. It bothered her to think about what had become of the city where she'd taught.

She looked at the mountains. More of the lake was visible from here. The farther they got away from Erbil, Fahimah's anxiety grew. She had so many memories connected with Halabja and with the road leading into it. Every time she went there, or even passed through, her sadness would get the better of her. She'd lost so much there. So much…

Fahimah had to remind herself that she should focus on the happiness of this journey. She was going to see her sister after five years. She wondered how adapted Rahaf had become to having only one leg…whether or not she had been fitted for a prosthetic leg. Whatever she had done about it, Rahaf lived in the mountains and traveled between the refugee camps, so Fahimah doubted the loss of her leg had slowed her down any.

They would both need to make decisions now, once they were together again. Once they were free. A lot of those decisions would be hard. Where would they go? What would they do? Rahaf was the only person in this world that Fahimah had left. She didn't want to be away from her sister anymore. She'd be happy living wherever Rahaf chose to live. She'd teach at the camps if that was her sister's decision.

But a feeling kept gnawing away at her, a feeling that

she'd had ever since talking to Ahmad, the Peshmerga leader. It was as if there were something that she didn't know. She'd read it in Ahmad's eyes, the way he would look away when they were talking about Rahaf.

Tears welled up in her eyes and she closed them tight. A headache pulsed at her temples. Fahimah wished she still had the concentration she'd mastered in prison. She tried to meditate, to make herself leave this moment and all the anxiety that was building up, burying her. She wanted to drift off on the warm breeze brushing her face and be carried on the mountain air to Rahaf.

Fahimah heard the BMW start up again. She opened her eyes and looked across the way. Austyn was crossing the road toward them. He'd pulled on his sunglasses. A car going in the opposite direction, leaving the blockade, beeped at him. The backseat was packed with teenage Kurdish girls. They all screamed with excitement as they went by. Austyn was a very handsome man. But what stood out in him, as far as Fahimah was concerned, was the mixture of confidence and gentleness that defined his actions and his words. A couple of the girls poked their heads out the window and continued to scream as the car drove away.

Fahimah didn't remember ever being that free.

Austyn seemed oblivious to it. He said something to the soldier standing by their car and then got in.

"We can go," he told her.

"Boro," she told their driver.

"Chashm," the man said, and pulled out into the traffic. The other car that had been part of their escort was waiting at the side of the road just ahead of the roadblock. They pulled out, too.

"What does *chashm* mean?" he asked.

"It is another way of saying 'yes.' A polite way. Like 'yes, sir,' or 'yes, ma'am.'" Fahimah motioned over her shoulder at the barricade they had left behind. "What was that about?"

"I've kept the cell phone off. Matt couldn't reach me, but he knew we would be traveling on this road."

"More bad news?" she asked quietly.

"There's been an outbreak at Bagram Airbase in Afghanistan," he told her.

"Isn't that where we flew in from?"

He nodded.

Fahimah felt an uneasiness grip her middle. She'd been there. They could accuse her of infecting the people at the base before she'd left. But how could she? She'd been in their prisons for five years. But there'd be no trial. Like before, they could just lock her away.

She was surprised when his hand closed over hers. It was warm and strong. Her fingers were freezing, and she hadn't known until now that she was shaking.

"This has nothing to do with you. No one is accusing you of having anything to do with it."

"How did you know what I was thinking about?"

He gave a shrug. "There's not much that you think about that isn't reflected in your face."

"In your face, either."

"We're both pretty transparent, I guess," he said softly. "What a pair."

"How bad is it?" she asked. He was still holding her hand. She fought the urge to pull away. Such human comfort was foreign to her. But now, receiving it, she felt flustered and calmed at the same time. How was that possible?

"Two dead. A third death is imminent. They don't know how many more are infected," he said gravely. "They pack them in that housing like sardines, so this could be the largest outbreak yet. I don't even know how they'd start setting up parameters for any kind of quarantine. I don't know if they're equipped for cleanup or testing."

"And they have no idea how they contracted the bacteria?"

"A box mailed from the U.S. is their only clue. The airmen were fine until they consumed something that was in the box," he told her. "That's all Matt knows so far. He told me he'd keep us abreast of what's going on. Which reminds me…"

Her hand felt cold again when he took his away. He reached into a duffel bag by his feet, took out a satellite phone and turned it on. "I want to make sure we leave this in Halabja. The last thing I need is to have Iranian border soldiers find it among my belongings."

She nodded in agreement, tucking her hands under her legs.

"Rahaf had nothing to do with what happened in Afghanistan." Fahimah felt the need to remind him again and again, or at least anytime he got fresh news of another outbreak.

He nodded but didn't say anything. She knew he trusted her, but there was so much about her sister that he didn't know. Rahaf had the knowledge, the motivation, and for the past five years she'd been free to act, as far as the Americans were concerned. This would be enough for them.

"You asked me a question before we reached this last barricade," she told him.

He pulled his sunglasses off. His blue eyes focused on her face. "I asked what you were doing in Rahaf's lab."

She nodded. "I was sent there by my sister, with her badge and her keys, to destroy all the documents for this research."

"Why did she want to destroy them?"

"Americans were attacking. Saddam was capable of anything. She was terrified of Saddam or his supporters getting hold of what she'd discovered."

There was disbelief in his expression. "Why work on something that you know you need to destroy?"

Fahimah shook her head. "I don't know every single thing about what she was doing. She can explain that to you much better and in detail. But my understanding was that she was working on something completely different. Finding this microbe was not her intention. Once she had it, though, she knew she had to destroy it."

"Her facility was supported by the Iraqi government," he reminded her. "Wouldn't it be a feather in her cap if she passed on the information of this deadly strain?"

"She is my sister," Fahimah said passionately. "We lost both of our parents in the chemical attack on Halabja. She would *never* give them anything that could destroy people, regardless of who was paying her."

"She worked for *them*," he said stubbornly, making it clear that he wasn't convinced.

"I worked for them, too, at the university. Half of the professional positions in the city of Baghdad were somehow funded by the government. That is the way things were. But that doesn't mean we were all terrorists," she told him.

"You taught. She worked in a chemical lab."

"How many pharmaceutical research labs are there across the United States? Couldn't every one of them be called a chemical lab? How about the research facilities at the universities? Aren't most of them funded by government dollars? Even the clinics where there are experimental programs for cancer or mental illness or for different kinds of dependencies." She didn't wait for him to answer. "You can call people whatever you want. Everyone's job and the interpretation of them stand at the mercy of some political power. If you go back and really spend the time and study everything that Rahaf presented at all the conferences she attended around the world…if you read the papers she has published…you will see the truth. But you cannot just select the facts that suit your argument."

"What was her area of interest?" he asked.

"Cancer in survivors of chemical warfare. Detection, treatments, cure," Fahimah told him. "I told you before. Halabja is not behind us. The survivors are the ones who are facing the greatest battle right now. But she couldn't spend all of her time on that, so there was other work she did, depending on the latest funding for her lab. Never, though, did she work on building bombs or anything that could be used for biological warfare."

Fahimah realized the two Peshmerga soldiers in front were quiet, with the driver every now and then sending a nervous glance in the mirror at her.

"They think we're fighting," Austyn commented.

"Aren't we?"

"No, we're not," he said. "I'm trying to understand the truth about your sister."

"I will tell you the truth about my sister," she told him. "But believe it. I do not lie."

"She's your sister."

"Do you think I would have wasted five years of my life

in prison if I thought Rahaf was responsible for making weapons that could be used on our own people?"

"Sometimes we're blind to the faults of those closest to us."

"You haven't heard anything I have been saying, have you?"

"Of course I have. Make me believe in her innocence," he shot back as sharply. "Why did she send you to destroy her files? Why not go there herself?"

He knew everything else. As well, he needed to learn this last bit of the truth.

"She was exposed to the strain in her lab by accident. She told me a vial fell and broke. A very small amount of the contents touched the skin on her right leg where the broken vial had left a cut. As you already know the bacteria spreads through the body with great speed. She had some remedy, but it wasn't enough." Fahimah would never forget that day. "She called me. Asked me to find a surgeon, to convince the person to come to my house. She told me she was hurt, but no matter how much I pleaded she wouldn't go to the hospital."

"Why not go to the hospital?" he asked.

"I didn't understand it myself until later, when she came over."

"How did she get to your house?"

"By cab," Fahimah told him. "I called a friend of ours who was a doctor. He called someone who knew someone else, and by the time Rahaf arrived at my house, the surgeon was there, too."

"Did she know she was exposing you to the microbe, too?" Austyn asked.

Fahimah shrugged. "I believe everything was new to her, too. She wouldn't let me near her. You said it is a similar strain to what you see in the U.S., but I think it must have slightly differences. She had a little more time to act, and what she contracted seemed to be less contagious. I was never infected, but then again, she would not let me touch the wound or dress it. Even the remedy was a solution that had been passed on to her from a friend for some other illness. As far as how effective it would be, she could not be sure. It had something to do with counteracting the bacteria in the bloodstream, before it infected cells."

"What happened?"

"She asked the surgeon to amputate her leg. But he wouldn't do it at the house. Rahaf was in excruciating pain." Fahimah found herself shaking again. "The surgeon convinced me that we should at least take her to a nearby clinic. The wound was growing on her leg. He agreed that the leg had to be amputated. Rahaf kept injecting herself with this solution, too, which seemed to make her horribly sick to her stomach. But she believed it was helping her."

"Did you take her to the clinic?" Austyn asked.

"Yes. And when we got there, the surgeon amputated the leg," she said, feeling chilled to the bone. She was no scientist. No physician. But she'd been in the room with her sister when her leg had been amputated. She'd gladly have given any part of her own body to relieve her sister's pain. A tear dropped down her cheek. She reached up quickly and dashed it away.

Austyn took her hand in his. "She did the right thing. The antidote obviously worked. The amputation saved her life. And no one else was infected?"

"No one."

"What happened next?"

"Rahaf was upset because the people at the clinic, even the surgeon, were asking too many questions. No one had seen this kind of flesh-eating wound. The surgeon knew Rahaf was a scientist. So she asked me to take her out of the clinic before more people started asking questions."

"Right after the amputation?"

"The next morning, at dawn, before the nurses came to check on her. She was still bleeding. I took her back to my house. She wanted to hide in the basement. I wasn't to tell anyone that she was staying with me. She was afraid."

"Of what?" he asked.

"Of how people could use this to their advantage. The wrong kind of people. The country was in chaos. No one seemed to be in charge. Every day, bombs were dropping on Baghdad. Saddam's people were fighting back. Kurds were fighting alongside of the Americans, but that didn't mean we could trust them, either." They'd been crazy to stay in Baghdad. Both of them should have left as soon as things got worse with the war. "Rahaf knew the nurses and doctors at the clinic might talk. The surgeon would, for certain. And she would have no way to stop them."

"Did she ever say how she discovered this strain of bacteria?" Austyn asked.

"She told me they were doing research on different types of streptococcus bacteria. It was during tests on the microbes that she discovered this monster."

"While she was recovering from the amputation, that was when she sent you to her lab?"

Fahimah took a deep breath. The events of those two days were as clear in her mind as yesterday. "Yes. She sent me there with specific instructions on what to do, what to destroy, where the files were, what was important and what was not worth my time."

"Weren't the other people who worked there suspicious of what you were doing there?" he asked.

"There were only a few there on that day, and they knew me. I stopped there occasionally and picked up Rahaf on the way to dinner. I used the excuse that Rahaf was under the weather and I was taking some files home for her. In reality, I was taking the printed files to the basement and putting them through the shredder."

"None of the other people who worked in the lab were around when she had the spill?" Austyn asked.

"No," Fahimah said. "She'd been there all alone when that happened. None of them knew anything about it."

"Is that when the bombing started?" he asked.

Fahimah nodded. "I was in the basement. I had all the files she'd told me to get. I was almost done shredding them when the first of the bombs hit the building."

"You didn't stop, did you?"

She shook her head. "I'd promised Rahaf I would finish it. And I did. When the power went out, I burned the last of them."

"And when the American soldiers poured into the building?" he asked, concern reflected in his face.

"I never lied to them. They assumed I was my sister. I had the badge around my neck, all of her keys. We look similar enough. No one else seemed to have survived the attack, so there was no contradiction. I made the decision to say nothing and let events play out as they did."

"You had no idea how long your imprisonment would be."

She shook her head. "I thought perhaps in a day or two or a week they would realize they had the wrong person. By then, Rahaf would have heard of my arrest and would have gone to Kurdistan to hide." She smiled bitterly. "After that, I imagined there would be a trial and the truth would come out."

"But there was no trial."

"No, there never was. They moved me out of Iraq and the chain of subsequent moves eventually brought me to Afghanistan."

"You never said anything, even when you were interrogated."

She could feel his distress in the pressure of his fingers on hers.

"No," she said, looking at their joined hands. How easy it was to get comfort by the mere touch of someone's fingers. How she'd missed human touch. "But they were never abusive to me…not in the way that I read in those articles on Agent Sutton's laptop. No, they asked questions, and by not answering, I let them believe what they already thought they knew."

"A month later, six months later, why didn't you tell them the truth and try to get them to free you?"

She shook her head. "If you had seen your own sister the way I'd seen Rahaf, you would have done the same thing. No, I could not do that. I did not know if she would be strong enough to avoid capture, if they were looking for her. I did not know if she could escape to Iran or anywhere. I only knew that if they freed me, they would go after her. No, I could not do that in a thousand years."

She was shocked when he brought her hand to his mouth and pressed a gentle kiss on the back.

Thirty-One

The research vessel Harmony
The Atlantic

Just as Josh raised the Strep-Tester to his tongue, his new friend Dan burst into the cabin breathlessly.

"Mr. Link, my dad says he wants you to come up right away. It's an emergency. There's something wrong with Philip."

The strep test completely forgotten, David and Josh followed the other boy up on deck. Most of the students were standing around the small television. The crew and the parents were bending over the railing, some manually helping haul in the thick rope and others watching and waiting to help.

"What's going on?" David asked one of the crew who was reeling in the cable for the camera cage.

"There's something wrong with Philip. He seems to be in a lot of pain. He isn't able to come to the surface on his own. Kirk is motioning to have him pulled up with the ropes."

Josh moved to the front of the television and stood beside
Dan. David took a look that way. The water was murky, as
it was expected to be; this was an ocean disposal site. Beyond
a few shadowy shapes, there wasn't much anyone could see.

"Just now, Philip ripped his mouthpiece off and tried to
yell. He swallowed a lot of water," one of the girls was telling
Josh. She was crying. "He looked like he was drowning."

David moved to the railing, to where Dan's father was
waiting. "Craig, what's going on?"

"There's something wrong with Philip."

"How come they're not up yet?" David asked.

"I guess they were at the bottom. I don't know their depth,
but Philip was in trouble. We couldn't see Kirk on the monitor
when it all happened. I guess he was collecting samples."

"Shouldn't someone go in there and help bring Philip up?"

"One of the crew members just went in with an extra
air tank," Craig said. "She's down there now. That's what
we're waiting for. We're hoping they're coming up."

David tried to think of what kind of injury Philip could
have sustained. He was no diver himself, but after a few
days on this boat, he was learning the basics. "Did he bang
his head going over?"

"No," one of the mothers standing near them said. "He
was motioning to the kids when he reached the ocean floor.
He seemed fine, and then something just…happened."

David was just about to go and get the emergency kit,
but one of the mothers who was an RN was already coming
back with *Harmony*'s skipper, who was carrying it.

Something broke the surface. Two of the crew members
bent over and fetched the net. It was the divers' tools and
flags and camera.

Everyone else continued to wait.

"The TV was disconnected," one of the kids called from the monitor.

"They're coming up," the crew member who was reeling in the cable announced.

Someone else arrived at the railing carrying an armful of towels. The air was cold. David was impressed that no one was panicking. He wondered if anyone had contacted the coast guard, but realized that until they knew what was wrong with Philip, there was no point in jumping the gun.

Three heads surfaced together some twenty feet from the vessel. Two still had their tanks on. The third one was being held up by the other two and had a rope connected to him.

"He isn't breathing," Kirk yelled as he tore his mouthpiece out.

The two started swimming toward the side of the boat, and Philip's body turned around. The two divers pulled him behind them and the crew members hauled in the rope looped around Philip's chest.

Hands reached over the side to help. David and Craig took hold of the line to pull up Philip. The divers brought Philip to the very edge of the vessel. The two fathers reached down and grabbed the scientist by the arms, dragging him up over the railing.

The RN took charge. "Lay him flat here," she said. The part of his face that was visible was purple "He isn't breathing. I'll give him CPR."

"Call the coast guard," Kirk told the skipper as soon as he climbed aboard. He turned to the woman crouched over Philip. "I think he took in a lot of water before we got to him."

Everyone wanted to help. At the same time, they knew enough to give the woman space to do her job.

The nurse put her hand under Philip's neck and lifted, gently pulling off the hood of the wet suit. She drew back suddenly.

"What's that?" she asked.

Crouched on the other side of the diver, David had a clear view of what she was talking about. There was an open wound on Philip's chin that spread across his cheek and down his neck and disappeared under the wet suit. It looked deep and, despite the fact that Philip had been in salt water, it was already oozing.

Kirk had pulled off one of the diver's gloves and was checking Philip's pulse.

"There's no pulse," he said.

Everyone was trying to get closer and see what the nurse was talking about.

"Stay back," David shouted forcefully, feeling panic course through him. "Take a step away from one another. *Back up!* We need to have everyone who had any contact with Philip separate yourself from everyone else."

"We all had contact with Philip," someone responded.

"I mean since he came up," David said, pointing to Craig, the two divers and the nurse.

"Yes. I agree," the RN said, her voice cracking. "He thinks…he thinks Philip might have the flesh-eating disease."

"Back up," David ordered again. His gaze rested on Josh's terrified face.

The nurse crawled backward a few feet from the body.

"He has it," she whispered. "We might all have it now."

Thirty-Two

Office of Homeland Security, Washington, D.C.

Faas moved the phone from one ear to the other and rubbed a spot in the center of his chest. With the diet of fast food he'd been on, the pack-a-day smoking again, the lack of sleep except for ten-minute catnaps here and there, and the steady stress that had his ulcer acting up again, having a heart attack would be the next natural thing.

He reached into the drawer of his desk and took out a couple more antacid pills, popping them in his mouth and downing them with the cold black coffee left at the bottom of his mug.

"Sir, I have Austyn Newman on the line," his secretary told him through the intercom.

Faas clicked over from the president's line to speak with Austyn. Penn had him on hold, but Faas was certain he'd understand.

"Okay, I know you're en route to those camps, and we

haven't given you enough time to get there…" Faas started without any greeting.

'That's correct."

"But I called to tell you that we're in deep shit."

"That's what I've been hearing," Austyn said from the other end through the static.

"You heard about Bagram Air Base. That's a total mess. But now, on top of it, we have cases reported from six more goddamn cities across the country. At this point, we don't know what's real and what's hysteria. Are you there?" he asked as the static subsided.

"Yeah. I'm listening."

"Good. Then listen to this." Faas grabbed a list off his desk. "Every government health organization is now involved in this. We've got Centers for Disease Control, the FDA, the FDA for Kids—whatever the hell that is—NIH and the World Health Organization. And you know what?"

"None of them have any answers?" Austyn asked.

"You got it. None of these big-budget, highly paid directors has been able to get their people to produce shit. And on top of it all, the Secretary of HHS is breathing down my neck every five minutes…like I report to him."

"What about the connection with all the victims having a cold?"

"Not conclusive," Faas snapped. "They can't tie it to a single product. No, wait, what am I talking about? They can't tie it to anything. They have no fucking idea how these people contracted the damn disease."

"They really haven't had much time for their testing," Austyn replied.

He *would* say that, the director thought. Austyn was a

research scientist, first and foremost. He'd been recruited to work for Homeland Security by Faas. The files on the young man had been beyond impressive. Ivy League education, excellent track record in NIH. Later, he'd worked in the private sector as a top manager. He had the knowledge, intensity and work habits. He was the kind of person they wanted at Homeland Security.

"Quit defending them," he growled. "You work for us and not them. They're all lazy bastards. Idiots!"

There was a chuckle from the other end of the line.

"I don't know how the hell you can laugh in the middle of this."

"Nobody's laughing here," the other man lied. "But I will find Rahaf. I think she has the answer, but that's no guarantee that if she does have it, she'll cooperate with us. Still, I'm almost positive she has nothing to do with what's going on over there or at Bagram."

"And how do you know that?"

"She contracted this disease herself, lost a leg to it, and for the past five years has been doing humanitarian aid in refugee camps on the border of Iran and Iraq. I personally can't see someone who spends her life helping others that way being filled with vengeance, can you?"

Faas was silent for a moment. "You just made me a very happy man."

"And how's that?"

"You said she had the disease and that she's alive today, five years later," Faas said, thoroughly pleased. This was the first break he'd had. "Who gives a shit about losing a leg? We can't keep these people alive long enough to get them to a hospital."

"Don't build your hopes up. The possibility exists that there's a difference between what she had and what we're facing now. What she contracted doesn't seem to have been as contagious, for one."

"You told me the DNA of the microbes were virtually the same."

"*Virtually* the same…but mutations can occur over five years. Be prepared for complications."

"Don't be a wet blanket, Newman," Faas told him. "Accept it—you're our only hope."

"Stop harassing me."

"You haven't *seen* harassment yet," he corrected. "Now, what do you need?"

"Nothing. I have what I need for now."

There was a knock on the door, and Faas's secretary poked her head in. He motioned her inside. "This woman only brings me bad news. Is it bad news?" he asked her.

She nodded gravely, dropping a message in front of him.

"What's happening?" Austyn asked.

Faas read the message. The pain in his chest was back.

"We've got another circus on our hands." He looked up at his secretary. "The president will be on the phone any second. Put him right through to me."

She nodded and left the room.

"We have a research boat in the Atlantic carrying a bunch of kids with cancer. The head of the expedition has come down with NFI. The coast guard is on its way, but news helicopters are already overhead and they're broadcasting live footage."

"How the hell did news crews get there before the coast guard?" Austyn asked.

"Depends on how many channels they used to send their Mayday signal." Faas read over the message again. "A boatload of sick kids. What a nightmare."

A light appeared on his phone set. His secretary's voice rang through. "I have President Penn on the line."

"Put him through. You know what you have to do, Austyn," Faas said before switching to speak to the president. "And I don't care if you have to put a gun to her head."

Thirty-Three

The outskirts of Halabja, Kurdistan

Austyn ended the call and dropped the phone into his bag on the backseat of the BMW. Both vehicles had stopped in the middle of the dirt road. The four doors were open, allowing the breeze to blow through. Their Kurdish escorts were huddled together near the front vehicle. There was no other car in either direction as far as he could see. While he'd been on the phone with Faas Hanlon, he'd seen Fahimah reach over and tell the driver something in Kurdish. Shortly after, they pulled off the main road onto the winding dirt path that took them here.

Austyn didn't know why they were here, but he trusted Fahimah. She'd been robbed of her homeland for five years. Despite the crisis that everyone at home was dealing with, he would not rob her of the right to take a few minutes to herself.

He looked straight ahead. Fields of green grass were

bisected by the two worn dirt tracks of the road. Across the flat landscape, in the distance he could see the Zagros Mountains. Fahimah had been generous in answering his questions, and as a result he had a good sense of the geography of the area.

Planting one elbow on top of the BMW, he watched Fahimah moving inside a fenced-in area in the distance. He saw her crouch down. Two large tricolor Kurdish flags had been planted in the ground by the opening in the fence. Even from here, Austyn could see the broad horizontal stripes of red, white and green, with the golden sun in the center. The two waving flags stood in bright contrast against the increasingly clouded sky. He knew this place had to be a memorial of some sort.

The wind whipped at his shirt, pushing the open door of the car against him. Though the breeze earlier had been comfortably warm, there was now a chill in the air that he hadn't felt since arriving in Kurdistan.

The place had an eerie feel to it. It was lonely, with nothing in sight but the mountains and the sky. Even so, there was a stark beauty here. He remembered the saying that he'd heard a few times since arriving here. *The Kurds have no friends but the mountains.*

Austyn saw their driver step away from the other three in his group and walk over to him. He wished he spoke Kurdish.

The driver said something in rapid Kurdish. Austyn shook his head. He searched in his pockets and took out a piece of paper. He'd asked Ken to write some must-know sentences down for him.

"Ez ji te te nagehim." Austyn looked up. This was

supposed to mean that he didn't understand. He hoped Ken had been right.

The driver nodded encouragingly. "Okay…okay…" he said in English. He pointed to where Fahimah was. "Bra…Bra…" He held out one hand and counted off three fingers.

"Brothers?" Austyn asked. Suddenly, the reality of this place came through to him. He remembered what she'd told him about losing her three brothers before the Anfal campaign.

The driver nodded gravely.

This was one of the killing fields. One of the mass graves that Saddam's people used to bury scores or hundreds of innocent victims.

He looked at her in the distance, crouched on the ground, one lone human being against the mountains. Austyn felt his throat close. There was something extremely sad about this scene, about what her life had become.

"Boro," the man told him.

Austyn looked at him in confusion.

"Boro." He tapped Austyn on the shoulder and motioned to where Fahimah was. *"Hari."*

Austyn decided he was telling him to go to her. He didn't have to be asked again.

Against the majestic backdrop of the mountains surrounding them, with each step Austyn felt smaller. His past, his life, all seemed so insignificant. The beauty of the place was magnificent, and the tragedy that these hills had witnessed was devastating.

He remembered reading that new mass graves had been discovered almost on a daily basis after Saddam's fall. Some sites contained hundreds of bodies, while some were so full of human remains piled on top of one another that no one could keep count of the victims. The broken bones and skulls, the scraps of clothing, told a horrifying story. The Kurds said 300,000 had died during Saddam's twenty-four-year rule. Some said there were more, others less. Austyn couldn't understand those who argued numbers. One life lost was too many.

She didn't see him until he reached the opening of the fence. She'd wrapped a scarf around her head. When she lifted her face to the wind, the edges of the scarf fought to fly free. He saw the tears.

She didn't move. He went to her and crouched down next to her.

There were no headstones. No individual names, only a small plaque with writing in Kurdish.

He pointed to the plaque. "What does it say?"

"Killing field. The bodies of one hundred and twenty-two men from Halabja were found at this site. The plans for a monument are in progress."

"I'm sorry," he said quietly. "When did you find out about this place?"

"The friends I saw in Erbil told me that while I was away this mass grave had been found. My three brothers' remains were among the hundred and twenty-two bodies that they'd found."

Her fingers continued to take fistfuls of the dirt and hold it up into the wind. Austyn watched the clouds of sand fly off.

"How old were your brothers?"

"Twenty, eighteen and twelve when they were taken," she said. "Aref was the eldest. He was smarter than all the rest of us. Studying extra hours on his own, he skipped three grades. He was hoping to save enough money and perhaps someday go to the university."

Austyn understood her need to talk about them. She'd never had closure. He thought of his own family. He still had his parents, had never lost a sibling, and had enjoyed a comfortable life for all his thirty-eight years. He'd never felt inclined to marry and have children, because that constituted too much responsibility. How different and privileged a life he'd led, compared to how Fahimah had lived.

He looked at her profile. "What did he do?"

"He was an electrician. He could fix anything. That was another thing that he'd taught himself. Later on, he made good money doing odd jobs for people. Many hired him." More tears fell on her pale cheeks. "Then came Mohsen. He was eighteen. He liked to play the part of big brother to me and Rahaf. He always worked well with his hands. He would never say no to someone needing his help. He was loved by everyone who met him, even if they'd had only one meeting with him. People remembered him. Rahaf and I were very close to him. He took great enjoyment in watching over us. He was a great joker, too."

A gust of wind threatened to steal her scarf. She grabbed it and tied it around her neck.

"Of the five of us, many thought Mohsen and I were twins. We had the same eyes, the same color hair. We were only two years apart in age. Mohsen wasn't much of a student, so we were even in the same grade." She touched her left ear. "We even had a mark in the same place."

She wiped her eyes with the back of one hand. Austyn

searched in his pockets, but he had no tissue. "Tell me about your youngest brother."

"Arsalan." A gentle smile broke across her lips. "He was destined to live the meaning of his name."

"What does Arsalan mean?" he asked.

"Lion, brave. At the age of twelve, he was taller than all of us. He had the build of a man and the courage of a lion. He felt he was the protector of all of us."

"They took away a twelve-year-old?"

Fahimah sat up straight, bent her head back and lifted her face to the sky. Austyn watched her eyes close as tears rolled down her cheeks. No sounds came out of her throat. She displayed no anger at the hand fate had dealt her family.

He never remembered a time that he'd felt more useless than at this moment. He wanted to gather her into his arms, comfort her, but he knew she needed this. After a moment, though, he couldn't stop himself. He reached out and gently touched her arm.

"Tell me about it," he said, hoping that the more she talked, the easier it would be later.

She struggled to bring her emotions under control. Austyn waited, finding the patience that he'd been missing for all his life. He sat next to her, realizing he could sit here with this woman for a very long time, perhaps for the rest of his life.

"It was a winter day," she started raggedly, "when the Iraqi soldiers swept through some of the neighborhoods in Halabja. We'd heard about the arrests, but our corner of the world in Halabja had never been a target for anything… until that day. Rahaf and I were away with our parents, visiting a cousin. One of the houses the soldiers raided was ours. Their instructions were to collect all men between the ages of fifteen and fifty for questioning. But there was no rigorous check of identity documents. A neighbor, who was taken away with my three brothers, later escaped. He told us when they shoved Arsalan in with everyone else in the back of the truck, our two older brothers spoke out, saying he was only a child of twelve. Arsalan denied their words. He told the soldiers he was old enough to carry a gun for Kurdistan and insisted on being taken away with his brothers."

She tugged at the scarf at her neck and wiped her face with it.

"We never saw them again."

"Did you know they were dead?" he asked.

"The same neighbor told us that all of them were taken to a detention center where trucks rolled into a central courtyard. He called it the parade ground. Other trucks would come in with women and children. The process was brutal. The men would be divided by age. Small children would be kept with their mothers. The elderly and infirm were sent off to their own corners."

She wiped at a new wave of tears.

"Men and teenage boys considered to be old enough to use a weapon were herded together."

Austyn watched her take a deep breath. She was having a hard time talking without becoming overcome with grief. So much of what had happened during Saddam's Anfal campaign had been little more than a news flash that ran across the screen for the people of the West. At the time, in 1988, he doubted that more than a few people in the U.S.

realized the extent of this genocide, which included ground offensives, aerial bombing, the systematic destruction of settlements, mass deportation, concentration camps, firing squads and chemical warfare. All of it created to kill innocent people, simply because of their ethnic background.

"Our neighbor told us that the male detainees were hustled into an overcrowded hall, where they were exposed to constant beating and torture for several days. And then, without an exception, the men were trucked off to be killed in mass executions." She broke down again.

Not able to stop himself, Austyn gathered her into his arms. She was shivering violently but forced herself to keep speaking.

"Our neighbor saw my brothers taken away in the truck ahead of him. He told us he heard the sound of the gunshots, people screaming. The truck he was in carried him to another site. There was a long trench there filled with dead bodies, like sardines. He was made to stand up with the others, shoulder to shoulder, next to the trench, before Iraqi soldiers fired their guns at them. The bullets wounded him badly, but he didn't die. He was one of two men who crawled out of the mass grave after being buried alive. It took him a long time to be well enough to return to Halabja. By then, we were all gone."

He could feel her tears soaking into his shirt. He rested his chin on her head, gathering her against him with all of his strength. She'd been suffering with the pain of this loss for too many years. And even here, at this sacred site, he knew this ground was only a symbol of all the other places where people had lost their lives.

Austyn knew why there were no names on that plaque

or on so many others like it. Many people remained unaccounted for.

Still, people needed closure. Fahimah needed it, as well.

Thirty-Four

The research vessel Harmony
The Atlantic

A tarp was pulled over Philip's body. Weights were used to hold the corners down. No one wanted to get too close to where the program director lay. Even pulling that plastic over him, with the wind whipping around, had seemed like madness.

Josh crouched on the deck, his knees to his chest, his back resting against one of the storage places that held the life jackets on the boat. A helicopter continued to circle overhead. From down here, he could see the TV station's markings on the side. He wondered if his mom was watching them on the news right now. She'd be worried, and he felt sad about that. But he didn't want to stand up and wave or doing anything stupid that would send him downstairs with everyone else.

One of the mothers had been really bossy and had

gathered all the kids like a herd of sheep. Everyone who
had not touched Philip had gone downstairs—the parents,
too. But Dan and Josh had refused to go. Their fathers were
on deck, and no one could force them. They'd promised to
keep their distance from the people left on deck. Josh
wouldn't let his dad out of his sight. From here, he could
tell there was nothing wrong with him yet. There didn't
seem to be anything wrong with any of the five people
who'd been close to Philip.

He wasn't sure how he felt about seeing Philip dead.
He'd never seen anyone dead before. He'd never even had
a pet that had died.

The way people treated him after he was diagnosed with
cancer, Josh knew they thought he'd die. He didn't like
pain. He hated feeling sick to his stomach, the way he did
after some of the treatments. He hadn't been too crazy about
losing his hair. The missing-school part wasn't too bad, and
he'd actually liked the attention he got from everyone the
few days that he was allowed to go to class. But beyond that,
he hadn't really thought too much about dying.

He looked at Philip again. He wondered if Philip had
parents, or a wife, or kids. They'd be really sad. Josh knew
that, more than dying himself, he'd hate to lose anyone in
his family. Definitely, he'd hate that more than dying.
Philip didn't seem to be in any kind of pain.

Josh saw his friend Dan come up on deck. He'd sneaked
down there a couple of minutes ago to get something. Josh
wondered if Dan had been afraid and wanted to get as far
away as he could from the dead body.

"They're all gathered in the girls' bunk room," Dan said,
sitting down next to Josh.

"What are they doing?"

The other boy shrugged. "I don't know…holding hands and praying, I guess. I didn't go in there. The door was closed."

Josh looked at his dad again. He was sitting against the railing, talking to Dan's father. Josh's mom made them do some praying as a family and that wasn't too bad. Especially at first, when he'd been told he had cancer. Josh thought it always made her feel better, and that was what was important. When she was happy, Josh was happy.

Dan took something out of his pocket.

"What did you get?" Josh asked.

"Our digital camera," the other boy said excitedly.

"What are you gonna take pictures of?"

"Everything. Everyone. Philip's body. Your dad and my dad. The divers. The helicopter up there. When the coast guard shows up, I'm taking pictures of them, too. I think I'll be able to sell these pictures later for a ton of money. You know…to magazines and stuff."

"Maybe I should take pictures, too," Josh said.

"Why not? I think there'll be lots of money to go around. If you want, we can sell them together and split the money."

Josh paused for a minute, wondering if he should feel guilty about taking pictures. But it wasn't like he could do something other than just sitting there. He looked at his dad. He was still fine, and he was still talking. His mom always said it was the salesman in him. He was never short on conversation.

"Okay, I'm sneaking down to get my camera, too."

"Hurry back."

Josh tried to not bring any attention to himself as he slipped through the door and went downstairs. Dan was right. The door to the bunk room where the girls stayed was closed. He tried to be especially quiet going by that door. No way did he want to get dragged in there. Once in the men's cabin, he had no trouble finding their digital camera. He liked to take pictures, so there were already some hundred or so photos on there.

He stuffed the camera into his sweatshirt pocket and his fingers brushed against something else. He pulled out the Strep-Tester that his dad had been trying to get him to use before. Josh had forgotten all about it. He must have stuffed it in his pocket on the way upstairs. He looked at the thing. The pink circle part of it had burst. It was covered with lint from his pocket now.

"Guess you're a goner." He crumpled up the tester.

Funny, he thought, with everything that was going on upstairs, he'd totally forgotten about his cold. He convinced himself that his throat was better, too. It didn't matter; the coast guard would probably be picking them up soon, anyway.

He threw the tester into the trash bin attached to the bulkhead. As he did, though, his gaze caught on something else at the bottom of the bin. It was another Strep-Tester. He crouched down next to the garbage can. He didn't want to touch it. His mom had drilled into him forever about germs, and he'd seen how nervous everyone was about touching Philip. He went and got a pencil from his father's bag and used it to move a couple of pieces of tissue from around it. The Strep-Tester flipped over. It had turned blue.

"Philip did have strep."

Thirty-Five

"I'm sorry," Fahimah told him again. "This is not what you bargained for when you decided to accompany me."

"Yes, I did," Austyn said. "Stop apologizing."

They had just passed a memorial welcoming visitors to the city. The memorial included the shells of bombs that had been used in the chemical attacks. Black ribbons hung from a sign where name after name of the victims had been listed. Going by it had brought on more tears.

"This is a poor town, he says." She continued to relay what the driver was telling her. "Only twenty percent of the people who lived here in 1988 still live here. Those who stayed were too poor to find a place elsewhere in Kurdistan."

She looked out the windows. The road needed repair. She'd been told that there was a shortage of clean water and electricity.

"There is a great deal of animosity between the people

remaining here and the city government," she told him.
"The driver says that back in 2006, there was a massive
demonstration in Halabja on the anniversary of the
bombing. He says the demonstrators burned the memorial
that was dedicated to the victims of the attacks in the city.
This is the second memorial they have erected."

"That's sad. I would think that memorial must mean so
much to people."

She nodded. "They were young people without jobs, he
says. They were restless and angry. This city hasn't seen
any of the rebuilding that has been going on in the rest of
Kurdistan."

Fahimah looked at the neighborhoods they were
passing. Young children playing in the remains of what
were once buildings stood and stared at her as she went by.

"Why do you think this area has suffered so much
more?" he asked.

"Probably the major reason *this* area has suffered is its
location near the Iranian border," she told him. "But to
understand why the Kurds suffered so badly, one must go
back to the black shadow of American foreign policy. In
1975, the Algiers Accord, endorsed by Dr. Kissinger, determined the border between Iraq and Iran. One part of the
agreement was that America and Iran would cease their
support for the Peshmerga. It was an event that became a
defining moment of disaster for the Kurdish independence
movement. The Kurdistan Democratic Party, or KDP, collapsed immediately. Mustafa Barzani, the nationalist
leader, was forced to flee the country. The socialist Patri-
otic Union of Kurdistan continued to fight, which is why
Saddam's regime targeted this area in the 1980s."

Fahimah stopped short, realizing what she was doing. "I'm sorry, I'm lecturing."

"I asked. I'm learning," he said cheerfully. "So am I correct to assume Kissinger's name is a curse word in Kurdistan?"

Fahimah nodded. "Yes, for those who know the history. And you would be amazed how many people in this region do know their history. The Algiers Accord is the one topic that can cause a Kurd to become quite anti-American. But when Westerners consider the highlights or lowlights of Kissinger's career—and the lowlights include places like Cambodia, Chile and East Timor—Kurdistan does not draw much attention."

"Until you consider the massacres that followed."

Fahimah bit her lip to calm the satisfaction that she felt in having him understand. He was an American government agent, but he listened to her. He didn't try to think of everything in life simply as a matter of absolutes, in categories of black and white, right or wrong. People made mistakes. Leaders had faults. One had to travel though life with one's eyes open. This was what she had always preached to her students.

It was getting late in the day. They had made one stop just outside of Halabja to have some food. Their driver thought it was better to eat outside of the city.

"Things look worse than they did when I last passed through here."

"When was the last time you were here?" he asked.

"About six years ago."

"Do you know where we're staying tonight?" he asked.

Fahimah saw a machine gun mounted in the wagon of a white Toyota pickup. Peshmerga soldiers were standing next to the truck. The two vehicles making up their caravan beeped their horns at the fighters as they went by.

There used to be a couple of small hotels in Halabja, but she was no longer sure if they still were in operation. She'd told herself she didn't want to get any of her friends involved. That was the reason for the secrecy in leaving Erbil. Now, though, she felt different about introducing Austyn to people she knew. Odd as it was, she trusted him.

"My friend in Erbil told me that a second cousin of mine is living in Halabja only for this summer. She was going to contact her, in case we decided to stay with her."

"What do you think?" he asked.

She was happy that he left the decision to her. "I think it would be okay. She teaches biology at Salahaddin University. But for the summer she is working with an American doctor who's doing some studies in Halabja."

"Do you know what the study is about?" Austyn asked.

She nodded. "They're collecting clinical data about the population. I suppose the study is trying to confirm the links between exposure to chemical weapons and the rates of disease."

"After that lecture you gave me in Erbil, are you telling me that nothing has been done on this before?"

"Of course. This is one of many studies." Fahimah leaned toward the driver and gave him the address that Banoo had given her for the cousin.

"By the way, I don't want to build your hopes up, but I had an idea," she said to Austyn.

"Okay. Shoot."

"I told you about the family Rahaf and I stayed with at Paveh," she told him. "Now, I don't know if they are still living there or if I can get hold of them, but I was thinking of calling them when we get to my cousin's house."

He brightened. "Do you think they might have a more exact address for Rahaf?"

She shrugged. "I don't know, but perhaps. We always tried to stay in touch with them. And I cannot imagine Rahaf working on that side of the border and having no contact with them."

"I think that's a great idea," he said, putting his hand on top of hers.

Fahimah had to fight a sudden flutter in her stomach, and she felt embarrassed about her own reaction.

He squeezed her hand and released it. "So what's your cousin's name?"

"Ashraf," she said. "Dr. Ashraf Banaz."

"Another PhD?"

Fahimah nodded.

"Does every woman in your family have a doctorate?"

She thought about that for a moment. "I don't know. I lost contact with all of them when I was put away. But I do believe we may have a couple of engineers mixed in there."

"Every family has a few black sheep."

"Exactly."

Thirty-Six

A coast guard cutter, a smaller boat, three boats marked Department of the Interior, and two coast guard choppers…in addition to the news helicopter. They were all around them, talking through megaphones, giving instructions, dropping them suits that they had to change into. But no one had yet boarded their vessel.

David was relieved that none of them had, as yet, shown any sign of what Philip had died from.

"So, do you think the worst is behind us?" Craig asked as he zipped up what looked like a plastic space suit.

"I don't know. I don't feel any different, so maybe we're in the clear."

The only one who continued to show signs of distress was Rene, but that was emotional. She was the diver who had gone down to help Kirk bring Philip to the surface.

There hadn't been time to put a wet suit on, so she said straight out that she'd had the greatest chance of exposing herself to the open wounds on Philip. As yet, she didn't show any outward sign of the disease, but at the same time, albeit quietly, she hadn't stopped crying.

David couldn't help but wonder if feelings for the dead researcher might have been the real reason. The two of them, he heard, went to school together and worked on this project and others during the summer. If there was a romance going on between them, they'd kept everything professional in front of the children. But romance or no romance, Philip's death must be a difficult blow for her.

"I wish I'd paid closer attention to everything on TV about this disease before we came on this trip," Craig said. "I don't remember hearing anything about incubation times when they reported finding those five bodies in Arizona. Did they all die at the same time?"

Maybe it was because of what he'd gone through with Josh, but David had no fear about what was going to happen to him today, so long as Josh didn't get it. That's all he cared about. He shook his head at his new friend. "I don't really remember anything specific about that, either."

Josh took a picture of them from near the stairs. David zipped up the suit and made a face at his son. It was fine with him that their boys had decided to stay on deck, as long as they didn't come close to them. No one knew what place was safe or how Philip had contracted this thing. There was nothing saying that something he'd touched or eaten downstairs wasn't responsible for it. At the same time, he'd gone diving at an ocean disposal site. The most likely scenario was that something down there had caused the immediate infection. But Kirk hadn't been affected by it.

Josh took another picture, and David thought the cameras were a great distraction for all of them.

Sharon, the RN, was communicating with the rescue vessels surrounding the *Harmony*. David thought the young mother had done an excellent job of regaining her composure after the initial discovery. She'd been clear in telling all of them what they had to do. She walked toward them now.

"This is how they want to evacuate everyone," she began, motioning Rene to come closer, too.

The young grad student wiped her face and came over. She had already changed into her space suit.

"The smaller coast guard boat will approach and the children will go off first. Then the parents and crew...with the exception of us. They'll take the other parents and crew to the cutter. The coast guard boat will come back for us, but they won't transport us to the cutter. On one of the Department of the Interior boats, there is a special group that will board the vessel to see Philip. I think they're going to use one of the choppers to airlift him out. Less chance of spreading contamination."

All of them glanced in the direction of the dead researcher. The tarp had been a good choice. David didn't want to know how bad the scientist's wounds were getting. He'd heard something about an incredibly quick rate of decomposition.

And to think how skeptical he'd been of everything they'd heard on the news. He'd blamed media of making too much out of it. What a fool, he thought.

"Okay, I guess they're getting started," Sharon told them.

The designated boat was approaching the *Harmony*.

"Josh and Dan, why don't you tell everyone downstairs to come up," Sharon called to the two boys.

"Do we know where they're going to take them?" David asked, suddenly realizing he was about to be separated from his son. "I want to be sure they contact my wife right away."

"I'm sure they'll contact everyone," Sharon told him.

David had to remind himself that he wasn't the only parent there.

The teenagers, the parents and the crew all came up. The boat approached and the two vessels lined up side by side. The transfer began very smoothly. David saw Josh working his way toward them. A couple of the coast guard personnel blocked his path.

"I need to tell my dad something," he told them.

David took a step closer. "What is it?" he asked.

"Philip had strep, Dad. His Strep-Tester was blue. I saw it. He tested positive."

David tried to make some sense of the significance of Josh's news. Josh thought he had what Philip had. So did this mean that Josh thought he had strep, too? Or something worse?

No. Josh was obviously fine.

"They'll take care of you when you get ashore," he called out. "If your mom is not waiting for you, make sure you call her right away."

David frowned, watching his son move toward the line of kids transferring onto the other vessel.

So what if Philip had strep? He obviously had something worse. And if Josh had strep, he'd survive it.

Yes, he'd survive it.

"You'll be fine," he murmured as Josh waved to him.

Thirty-Seven

Halabja, Iraq

Ashraf Banaz and her colleague shared a newly repaired five-room house in an old neighborhood of Halabja. Clara Hearne was a physician at San Francisco General Hospital. She was in her thirties and eager to tell another American about everything she was involved in here.

Austyn had already heard about the collaboration between the American and Kurdish doctors from Fahimah. As the young physician repeated some of what he already knew, he found his mind drifting back to the moment when Fahimah and her cousin met earlier.

There had been laughter, tears, a million questions, while neither would stay quiet long enough to give the other one a chance to answer. Then the two of them had escaped to one of the rooms off the living room where Clara and Austyn were sitting. There had to be so much the two wanted to catch up on.

"Would you like another beer?" she asked.

Austyn looked down at the half-full bottle in his hand and shook his head. "No, thanks. I'm fine."

Clara had told him before that strict Islamic laws were enforced in Halabja, but only in public. People did what they wanted in their homes. He was also told that the two women bought the beer in Ankawa, a Christian town near Erbil.

"Where was I?" she asked.

Austyn couldn't remember, but he figured Dr. Hearne was the type that never forgot anything. He was right.

"Oh, yes, I was telling you…this work in Halabja is showing me one of the basic differences between American and Kurdish doctors. In New York City, research is a foundational feature of medical education. In the aftermath of September 11, doctors enrolled 60,000 patients from the city in prospective trials. Everything that happens to them is being recorded, and additional data will be collected on them as they age." She took a sip of her own beer. "In Kurdistan, there is no such research infrastructure. Medical education is antiquated. Skill sets like research that are considered an essential part of modern medical education have not yet entered the curriculum at the universities here. The result is a group of intelligent, clinically skilled doctors who are ill-equipped to collect data and publish their findings about the patient population."

He didn't entirely agree with this, as both Fahimah and Rahaf had published. But he remembered she was talking about the medical profession in this little corner of Iraq. Considering what these people had gone through, compared with the environment Clara was most likely from… well, there was no comparison. Austyn told himself that he didn't have to get defensive. He took a long swig from the bottle, amused by his own reaction.

Austyn decided to change the subject. "So, Clare…I'm curious. You two don't mind living in this house when two-thirds of the houses on the street are in ruins?"

"Not at all." Clare shook her head adamantly. "The manager at the hospital didn't want me to stay in Halabja. He claimed he couldn't guarantee the safety of an American woman. He wanted me to stay at Sulaimaniyah, where there are hot showers and clean drinking water. He said he'd have me be escorted here a couple of days a week to check on the data the nurses are collecting. But I said, *no way.*"

"Is that how you and Ashraf connected?" Austyn asked.

"We knew each other before. So I told her what I was doing. She got an okay from her university. They tied a grant to it, and here we are."

Austyn was certain things couldn't have been as simple as that, but he appreciated her enthusiasm.

She took another sip of her beer. "You mentioned the rubble. In the morning, you'll see it yourself. There is a real charm in this place, set as it is into the foothills of the mountains."

"Still, the fighting and the poverty must get to you."

"That's true. The disconnect between the setting and the recent history makes it an emotionally taxing environment to work in. But enough about me. Ashraf wouldn't give me a straight answer about you or her cousin Fahimah. Where has she been? I heard her name mentioned before, many times, but I thought she was dead."

"Obviously she's not," he said, not wanting to reveal

anything more. He didn't know how much of the truth Fahimah was telling her cousin.

"I hear she used to be a political science professor in Baghdad. I was premed all the way as an undergrad, but I loved poli-sci."

Austyn nodded.

"All of them—everyone I've met in their family—they're so wicked smart."

He nodded again.

"Another thing that Ashraf was vague about was about your job. What is it that you do?"

"I'm an epidemiologist. I work specifically on the spread of rare diseases." He looked around the living room. There was no TV. He wondered if these two women knew anything about the outbreaks in the U.S. and Afghanistan.

"So you're an MD?"

"No, just a researcher with a master's degree. I work on the investigative side of things. On how to stop epidemics."

She moved to the edge of her seat and her eyes narrowed. He almost laughed.

"Are you CIA?" she said in a low voice.

"No. No guns. No spying. No tricks." He thought Homeland Security might sound too much like CIA. "I work for NIH."

He did work for them at one time, so that was close enough.

"Oh, yeah. Sorry, but NIH can be a real pain in the butt sometimes."

"I hear that a lot."

Clara finished her beer, put the bottle on the coffee table and sat back.

"So what's your connection with Fahimah?"

"She is taking me to her sister," he said, assuming if Clara had heard about Fahimah, then she must know about the younger sister, too.

"You mean Rahaf?" she asked, frowning.

"Yes. I'm hoping that she can help us in some research we're doing," Austyn told her. "Have you ever met her?"

"No. No." She stood and picked up both of their bottles before walking to the kitchen. She looked disturbed.

Austyn looked at the doorway Fahimah and Ashraf had gone through. He thought he heard a noise, like Fahimah crying. He stood up as Clara came back into the room with two open bottles. She handed him one. He didn't want it and put it on the table.

"You know, I'm pissed off," she said, starting to pace the room.

"At what?"

"I'm pissed at their friends back in Erbil. After they called her, Ashraf was really worried about this."

"She was worrying about what?"

"That they wouldn't tell her," Clara muttered. "That it would be left up to Ashraf to break the bad news."

"What bad news?" Austyn asked.

"Rahaf has cancer. She's dying."

Thirty-Eight

"Fourteen *individual* cases, Mr. President. Fourteen different infection sites. Each is considered a separate incident," Faas said into the phone. He sat on the edge of the bed. With his free hand, he rubbed his chest.

The big guy obviously does not sleep, Faas thought. He looked at the clock next to his bed—1:03 a.m. Not that he'd been sleeping himself when some perky voice had told him that the president was on the line.

"Total fatality number is one hundred twelve, sir," Faas said, answering the next question. He stood up and padded barefoot to the bathroom.

He knew he was on a speakerphone. Penn had kept his staff together to prep for the morning press conference. Nobody had bothered to tell Faas who else was in the room with the president. He'd recognized some of the voices, though. Tomorrow would be a big media day at the White

House, and the president obviously wanted to make sure they were ready. They were planning on skipping the daily press secretary's briefing. Instead, the president would be going in front of the cameras himself at about eight in the morning.

"Yes, sir. The hundred twelve includes the boat with the cancer kids."

He took out a bottle of antacid out of the cabinet. He opened it. Empty. He tossed the bottle in the trash.

"On the research vessel *Harmony,* there has been only one fatality so far," Faas said, then listened. "Yes, sir. Considering the circumstances and how many people were in contact with the victim, it's quite unusual."

There was another bottle of antacid on the shelf below. He shook it first. There was nothing in this one, either. He tossed that bottle into the trash, too.

"The NIH people think the salt water might have been a factor," Faas said.

He pulled out the drawer that Betty used to keep all her personal stuff. With the exception of some cotton balls and lots of hairpins, she'd emptied it. She'd taken his kids, his paycheck, and left him a house that he didn't want or need. Shit, the least she could have done was to leave her prescription-strength meds. A couple of years ago, Betty had a problem with acid reflux. She kicked the shit out of the thing with her diet and had no need for the medication the doctors had given her.

Faas, on the other hand, really liked those blue-and-white pills. They worked magic at handling his ulcer. He was too busy to have his stomach checked out and get his own prescriptions. So Betty had continued to be the drug pusher for him. He thought maybe he should have her arrested for that.

"Yes, sir. It seems that we may have learned something from the *Harmony* incident." He sat down on the edge of the tub. The pain was really getting to him.

"No, sir. As far as we know, none of those kids are going to be on *Oprah* tomorrow. Everyone on the *Harmony* was taken to the VA hospital in Maryland where we have them quarantined. They'll be kept there for at least forty-eight hours for observation. But there's no telling if Oprah won't be storming the place. Who's going to say no to her?"

He heard some laughs from the conference room. He slid the drawer out a little more to check the back of it. The whole thing came off the drawer slide and went crashing to the floor.

"Yes, sir. Everything is fine. I was stumbling in the dark and kicked something with my foot," he lied. "Yes, sir. I will turn on the lights. Thank you for the recommendation."

Here he was, bent over with pain, and Penn was thinking he was being a wiseass. Faas wished he had enough breath left in him to be one.

"I'll call you with any news, sir. Absolutely. I'll talk to you before the eight o'clock press conference." He ended the call.

Faas sat down on the toilet seat. *Shit, this hurt.*

Looking across at the gaping hole left by the missing drawer, he thought he spotted something. Edging forward, he reached inside. Two blue pills, still in their wrapper.

"I knew you wouldn't leave me totally high and dry, honey," he said out loud as he tore off the paper backing to get at the pills.

Thirty-Nine

Halabja, Iraq

Through the door, he could hear Fahimah crying out in anguish. She said something in Kurdish that he doubted was intelligible even to her cousin.

She knows about her sister.

Propriety be damned, he thought. He rapped his knuckles on the door. Ashraf must have been standing just next to it, as she immediately pulled it open.

"Can I talk to her?" Austyn asked.

"Yes, please," the young woman said tearfully, sliding past him and disappearing into the other room.

Austyn walked in, closed the door and leaned his back against it. She was crouched in the corner, her arms wrapped around herself, rocking back and forth, sobbing. The guilt he felt was overwhelming. The fact that he personally had nothing to do with robbing her of five years of her life, of time she could have had with her sister, didn't matter. He stood for the black hole that sucked the lives out of people who were innocent, as well as those who were guilty. There were no checks or balances, no chances to defend yourself. You were lost in an abyss, sometimes forever.

He knew the rationalization for the prisons. It was a dirty world. The government's duty was to protect its own people…and businesses. There was no place for idealism in that world. Austyn remembered reading in college something about idealism increasing in direct proportion to one's distance from the problem. Well, he was standing in the middle of the problem, on the border between Iran and Iraq, and he wasn't feeling too good about the business.

She said something again in Kurdish, one fist striking her chest again and again.

Whatever lid he was trying to keep on his emotions popped. He walked toward her, crouched down on the floor and gathered her in his arms.

"I'm so sorry," he told her. But no words were enough. Nothing he could say or do could take away the pain of losing this loved one, this sister, this last family member left…this one person you sacrificed your own life to protect.

Austyn didn't know how long he held her like that. Her sobs subsided, but the tears never stopped.

Large pillows made out of rugs were the only furniture in the room. At some point he leaned against one and took her with him. His shirt was soaked with her tears. Austyn wished she would get angry, the way he'd seen her do at the Brickyard prison. He wanted her to unleash her anger on him. But she didn't, and that made him suffer even more.

He didn't know how long they sat there like that before she started to talk.

"Rahaf is in a hospital in Kermanshah," she whispered. Kermanshah was a major city in the western part of Iran.

"What kind of cancer does she have?" he asked. His mind was already racing with arrangements that he could make to get Rahaf to the U.S. With the latest cancer treatments, there had to be something that they could do for her.

"It started as leukemia…some eight months ago. But she refused treatments…and now it has spread everywhere. They're keeping her sedated…so she can tolerate the pain."

She pulled away from him. Her eyes were swelled to slits, her nose was red. She reached for a box of tissues and blew her nose. He was relieved when she moved back and sat next to him.

"Who's with her?"

"A couple of the people she worked with at the camp," Fahimah said. "They took her there last week. The doctors say there is nothing more that can be done. They're just making her comfortable until she dies."

The Peshmerga soldiers who'd dropped them off were coming back tomorrow around midday to drive them to the border. They knew the Iranian guards who were on duty at that time. "We have to arrange for a faster way to get to Kermanshah," he told her.

She nodded. "Ashraf is going to make some calls. There's a small plane that occasionally flies between Halabja and Kermanshah to transfer patients to the hospital. She's going to speak to the manager of the hospital and see if they can fly us over there in the morning."

He was relieved that she was talking, thinking, planning.

"Rahaf's cancer was the reason my cousin Ashraf

became interested in helping with Dr. Hearne's study," she said quietly. "I did not know."

"You and Rahaf were both here during the chemical attack, weren't you?" he asked, dreading the answer.

She nodded, looking straight ahead. "Including my parents, Rahaf and I lost twenty-six relatives that day."

He took her hand. "Do you want to talk about it?"

She didn't immediately answer. Austyn didn't know if it was helpful or not thinking of another loss right now. But that was where the root of Rahaf's cancer lay. He looked at her, wondering, wanting to know more. He was fearful to think the same illness could haunt her, too.

"Halabja was already battered by war when the chemical attacks came. Iranian troops and Kurdish Peshmerga guerrillas backed by Tehran had taken over parts of the city. The two days prior to it, we had suffered attack by planes and shelling by the Iraqis. The noise was horrendous." She gathered her knees into her chest. "We were still in mourning because of my brothers, so there was nothing being done about Norooz. There was going to be no celebration of the new year, the first day of spring, that year."

Austyn said nothing, trying to visualize the situation she and her family had faced.

She continued. "That was March 16 in the Christian year 1988."

There seemed to be no tears left in her. She rested her head against the rug, still looking into space.

"I remember it was Wednesday morning. Because of all the bombing, no one was going to school. We heard planes going overhead, but there were no blasts afterward. It seemed strange that they'd dropped no bombs. Rahaf and

I went out. I counted seven, but Rahaf kept swearing that there were ten Iraqi planes overhead. They were dropping smoke bombs and pieces of paper." She took another tissue and wiped her face. "We didn't know that the Iraqis were checking which way the wind was blowing."

Austyn gathered her to him, and she leaned against him willingly.

"But it wasn't long before they come back."

"Yes. It was around noon. Maybe a little after noon," she croaked. "Other children were amused by those little pieces of papers, but my parents forced Rahaf and me to stay in a shelter that my father and brothers had built in our dugout basement maybe ten years before that. There were no windows, no clocks. My mother kept coming down and checking on us. We just assumed there would be more bombing like before. We never thought…never even imagined…the Iraqis were going to drop chemical bombs on us."

Austyn remembered reading that the Halabja attack involved various chemical agents, including mustard gas, the nerve agent sarin, tubin, VX and hydrogen cyanide. The most authoritative investigation into the Halabja massacre had been conducted by the Stockholm International Peace Research Institute. They had concluded that Iraq had been responsible and not Iran, as the U.S. administration had wanted reported. According to Iraq's report to the United Nations, the know-how and material for developing chemical weapons had been obtained from firms in the United States, West Germany, the United Kingdom, France, China, India, Egypt, Netherlands and a Singapore company affiliated with the United Arab Emirates.

There was plenty of blame to go around for supplying the gun, but Saddam Hussein and his henchmen had been the ones to pull the trigger.

"They came back," she continued. "It wasn't too long after that we heard the thunder of Iraqi planes overhead again. But again there was nothing. No missiles, no shattering explosions, no screaming…just silence. I remember Rahaf saying that maybe they were spreading more paper over the city."

"How long was it before you suspected something was wrong?" he asked.

"Not long. Minutes, perhaps. I remember spending the entire time arguing with Rahaf, trying to convince her not to go up, to wait for our parents to come and get us. But then, shortly after the bombing, we started hearing the sound of people shrieking and wailing. We stared at each other. We didn't understand. Then, just as abruptly, the noise of voices just…stopped."

"Did you two go up then?"

She nodded. "I still remember fighting with Rahaf. I had this feeling that something horrible had happened. But despite being younger, she was bigger than I was. She went up there, and I had to follow."

Fahimah closed her eyes. The tears weren't too far away. Austyn wanted to tell her to stop talking about it. He'd seen pictures of streets littered with the dead. Men, women, children. So many children. Many victims had a grayish slime oozing from their mouths, their frames contorted, fingers grotesquely twisted in pain. Most of the victims probably died within minutes. For those affected by nerve gas, death was instantaneous; their breathing stopped so abruptly that people simply dropped to the ground as if frozen. They were the lucky ones.

He had seen the pictures, and that was horrifying enough. Fahimah had been there.

"We found our mother in the kitchen. She'd been cutting beets. She was dead. Our father was sitting in the doorway. His face was frozen in a scream. There was a sweet smell in the air. I got gas in my eye and couldn't breathe. Rahaf started vomiting. It was green." She grabbed a couple more tissues, blew her nose, rubbed away the tears. "Rahaf and I and thousands of other refugees fled the city that day. We were not there for the burial…not even the burial of our parents."

The tears overwhelmed her again.

"I'm so sorry," he said once again.

She looked up at the ceiling, and they sat for a few minutes in silence. A few more tears escaped, but she dashed them away. Austyn could see her slowly regaining her composure.

"No more," she said finally. "I cannot cry anymore. I have cried enough. I need to pull myself together. I need to be strong for Rahaf. We will see each other tomorrow."

Forty

In his entire life, David had never been checked as thoroughly as he was in this hospital during the past twelve hours. Blood test after urine test after physical. All done twice by two separate teams of doctors, each checking the same things, asking the same questions. Having an endoscopy while he lay there awake, though, was a bit much. He hoped he only had to go through that once.

He ran into Craig in a waiting area. They had quarantined a section of the hospital just for the five of them. They were told the rest of the people on the boat were in this same hospital, but they were on a separate floor. David had spoken to Sally. She was allowed to join Josh. Their son was doing just fine, and his only worry was David.

"How did you make out?" Craig asked.

"Okay," he said. "I hope I don't have to do another one of those plumbing checks again…ever."

"Is it that bad?" Craig asked. "I have to go in for it next."

"No, not at all," he lied. They hadn't had time to do the proper fasting. David could feel the cramping aftereffects of that now. "But when the scope popped out of my ear, I told the doctor I thought he'd made a wrong turn somewhere."

"Great," Craig replied with a wan smile. "Well, that coffee is for us, if you want it. And we can use that computer to check e-mail or whatever."

"Did they say how long they're going to keep us here?"

"No. I really don't think they have any idea," Craig told him. "Just reading the headline news, though, it's a mess out there."

"More outbreaks?"

"They're not sure. There were so many calls to 911 in all the major cities that they're saying the emergency system is breaking down. There are some people who they think they have the disease. Others who think their neighbor has it, or their dog or cat. There's even an idiot or two out there calling and taking responsibility for it. It's total chaos."

The nurse came out to get Craig. He pointed a finger at David.

"Stay away from headline news. It's not worth it…I'm telling you."

Sally said she'd talked to Jamie and Kate. They were both doing fine. He knew where Josh was. There was no reason for David to check the headlines.

There was also no point in calling the office in the middle of the night. Knowing his secretary, she'd already answered all the calls and made whatever decisions needed to be made. He decided to check his e-mail instead.

Thank God for the Internet, he thought. The entire country could be in total disarray because of this NFI plague, but nothing slowed the Internet. Grabbing a cup of coffee, David settled into a chair in front of the computer, hoping that the doctors and nurses were done with him for a while.

He had over four hundred e-mail messages.

Browsing through the list, he deleted a ton of spam. Despite the company security filters, junk e-mail still managed to get through. Of course, some important e-mail—like family news or forwards from his daughters—never got to him.

As he started thinning out the list, David started seeing the notices.

Death in the family. Death in the family. Death in the family.

One of their sales people in Arizona was going to be out next week because of a brother's funeral. Another similar notice sent out from the Washington, D.C., office where the fiancée of a sales rep there had passed away. Two more like it. None of the e-mails mentioned the cause of death.

What Josh had told him as he'd left the boat flashed in his mind. *Philip had strep.* He picked up the phone next to the computer and dialed his wife's cell phone. Sally answered right away.

"Is Josh sleeping?" he asked.

"Are you kidding? He's wide-awake."

"Can I talk to him, honey?"

"Is everything okay?" she asked, sounding worried. "Do they have any of the results back?"

"Everything is fine. I just need to ask him something."

David looked at the e-mails again. He jotted down the

names of the four sales reps who'd lost a family member. He read each e-mail again to make sure he'd written down the names of the deceased, in case they had a different last name.

"Hi, Dad," Josh said from the other end. "Everything okay?"

"Everything is great. How are you holding up?" David opened a new browser.

"This is easy. Hospital room, watching TV with Mom. I'm a pro at this."

"I have a question for you, Josh." He Googled Lenny Guest's name.

"What is it?"

"Did you ever use the Strep-Tester I gave you on the boat?" David asked. His heart climbed into his throat as he read the screen. Lenny was one of the victims of the NFI outbreak.

"No, I didn't," Josh said. "By the time I got back to the cabin, the tester was all dirty, and I thought it'd be worse if I…"

"It's okay that you didn't use it," David said quickly. The answer to his next search on Leo Bolender made him break out in a sweat. There was something terribly wrong here.

"What's wrong, Dad? You sound upset."

"No, I'm not," he lied. "What did you do with it?"

"I threw it in the trash in the cabin."

"Good."

The other two names on the e-mails didn't show up as NFI victims, but after doing a couple more searches, David realized not all of the victims' names had been released yet. Most of the outbreaks had occurred over this past weekend. There hadn't been enough time to notify some of the families.

"Remember when you were leaving the boat, you told me something about Philip having strep. How did you know?"

"When I went down to get the camera, I realized I still had the Strep-Tester in my pocket. It was ruined, so I threw it away. That's when I saw Philip's tester."

"But you didn't touch that one, did you?"

"Of course not."

"Good boy. What did you see?"

"The Strep-Tester he must have used was in the trash. It had turned blue. I knew that meant he had strep. Didn't you say that's what the blue meant?"

David slumped back in his chair and gazed at the monitor. He'd brought up the online ad for the Strep-Tester. He stared at the screen, watching numbly as the pink circle turned blue.

"Yes, Josh. It turned blue because he had strep."

Forty-One

"Have you ever flown into Kermanshah Airport?" Austyn asked.

Fahimah shook her head. The pilot in Halabja had told them that the airport was northeast of the city, and that they could easily find a cab to take them to the hospital. It was amazing that Ashraf had been able to manage this flight in such a short period of time. Fahimah knew the rest of arrangements would be up to her. She looked down. They were approaching the airport.

"My only time here was when Rahaf and I were staying in Paveh. On one of the school trips, they brought all the students to Kermanshah to see some of the historical monuments. Some of those sites date back to the Achaemenid and Sassanid eras."

"What was the favorite place that you saw?" he asked as they descended.

"Rahaf and I were both impressed with a place called Tagh-e-Bostan. It was there that one of the Sassanid kings chose to have beautiful reliefs carved into the rock. There is a sacred spring that gushes down from a mountain cliff and empties into a large reflecting pool. We were there in the spring, and the entire place was clouded in mist."

Fahimah closed her eyes for a moment and evoked that image in her mind. She'd replayed that scene so many times when she'd been in prison. She could use some of the discipline she'd exercised during those days now. She wouldn't allow herself to be weepy when she met Rahaf.

"Was there a place you didn't get to see and wanted to?" he asked.

She knew what Austyn was doing. He was trying to keep her mind busy. She smiled at him in appreciation. She'd never imagined that he would be the one she would lean on during this time of sadness.

"I wanted to see Darius the Great's inscription at Behistun. But the site is thirteen hundred meters up into the mountains, and there was no time to go there. That day, Rahaf and I promised each other that someday we'd come back and hike up there."

He reached over and took her hand. "Perhaps some-day you will."

Fahimah leaned her head back against the seat as the plane's wheels chirped and settled onto the runway. She wasn't willing to give up hope. She wanted Austyn to be right.

The plane taxied toward the terminal. They were the only passengers. She had no clue what kind of customs or immigration restrictions they would face. The documents

Matt had collected for her would have been good enough if they'd crossed the border at Halabja, but she had no passport. She hoped it was the same thing at the airport. Much more so than herself, she was worried about Austyn. She didn't want to imagine what the complications could be if they decided his passport was fake and that he was an American agent.

She began to hyperventilate just thinking about it.

The plane came to a stop near one of the doors. She looked out the window at the long building of sand-colored stone and glass as they unbuckled their seat belts.

"Please let me do the talking," she told him.

"I'm not nervous. You shouldn't be, either. Not about me, I mean."

Fahimah looked at his unshaven face, the kind blue eyes. It scared her how attached she was beginning to feel toward him. It was terrifying.

"Let's go," she said quietly. Ashraf had given her a shawl in Halabja, and she now draped it over her head. The pilot had the door open for them. There were no formalities. They each only carried a duffel bag. He pointed out the door they had to walk to.

An Iranian policeman opened the door for them as they reached it.

"Khosh amadeen," he told them.

She was about to tell Austyn that the man was welcoming them.

"Motashaker," Austyn replied to the officer.

Fahimah looked at him, surprised. The policeman directed them toward the line where they had to go. Inside, the terminal area was crowded with people. She hadn't realized until the pilot had mentioned it that flights from all the major cities in Iran came into this airport.

Other policemen were standing around, but the line moved freely. There was no checking of passports. The realization came to her suddenly.

"This is not an international airport," she whispered to him. She didn't have to say more, and he understood.

He looked straight ahead and she followed his gaze. People ahead of them were leaving the terminal through double doors.

Fahimah was relieved. Luck was on their side. She couldn't believe that arriving in Iran could be as easy as walking out on the street and getting a cab to the hospital.

"Now, don't look at anyone, especially the policemen," she told him. "Please don't act like a tourist."

"*Baleh,* Dr. Banaz."

She sent him a quick look. He'd been practicing a few Farsi words.

"If anyone asks anything, don't answer. I will do the talking."

"Is my accent terrible?" he asked, smiling.

"Dreadful," she whispered back. He was still smiling, so Fahimah figured she hadn't hurt his feelings too badly.

The line of people was moving. Straight ahead, she could see the doors leading into the brightness of outside.

She was wearing a raincoat that reached her knees. Ashraf had told her that the coat and the shawl she'd used to cover her hair served as what was called a *ropoosh* in Iran. In the pocket of the raincoat, Ashraf had given her some *toman*. Fahimah needed to use that money for the cab ride to the hospital.

They were close enough to the door that she could see the line of cars waiting by the curb.

"Dr. Banaz."

Fahimah practically jumped out of her skin. She turned to the man who'd called her name. One of the policemen was moving across the floor toward her. She should have known things wouldn't go this smoothly.

"*Baleh.*" She nodded.

"*Ba man biah,*" he told her flatly, and started moving away.

"He wants me to go with him," she told Austyn quickly. "You go to the hospital, and I'll meet you there."

"No, I'm coming with you," he said under his breath.

"You are *not,*" she stressed. "You must bring no attention to yourself, remember?"

"I'm *not* leaving you here alone with them."

"This is no time for chivalry."

Realizing she was not following him, the policeman stopped and threw his hands up in the air.

"*Doe tatoon beyayeen,*" he said impatiently.

"He wants both of us to go with him," she said to him, defeated.

"I wouldn't have it any other way."

Fahimah was angry. He'd had a chance to get out of here. Now they would be subjected to scrutiny, especially Austyn. He didn't look like an Argentinean. Not that she knew anyone from Argentina. But they'd know he was American and then...

"Dr. Banaz," someone called from behind her. It was Austyn.

Fahimah hadn't realized it, but while she was arguing

with herself, she hadn't watched where she was going. She turned around. Austyn was standing next to the policeman. They were chatting about something and both were smiling. So much for not saying anything.

"Een dar," the policeman said when she started walking toward them.

"This door," Austyn translated for her, motioning to a door leading out.

She could have hit him.

The policeman opened the door and motioned to a van with the hospital's name on the side.

"Have a good stay," the policeman said in English, shaking Austyn's hand.

The two of them went out. The driver of the van came around and opened the door for them. On the way to the hospital, Fahimah turned to Austyn.

"What were you telling that policeman?"

"Nothing important."

"You two were talking and seemed to be enjoying yourselves."

"I just told him a couple of jokes."

Forty-Two

Faas did *not* get sick.

He didn't take care of himself, either. But he didn't get *I just want to crawl in bed and die* sick. He couldn't ignore the feeling of pressure just above his rib cage anymore, though. There were no more medications in the house for him to take. What he'd taken had no effect. He was starting to think it wouldn't have mattered if Betty had left an entire pharmacy for him.

He was sitting on the edge of the bed. He couldn't bring himself to lie down. There was something wrong with his breathing. It hurt when he took a full breath, as if he had a broken rib.

He grabbed the phone. It was getting light outside. He looked at the clock—5:13. He figured on a Monday morning Betty was lying in bed but awake. Probably just getting ready to get up. In their twenty-two years of marriage, she'd always been an early riser.

He was happy when she answered right away.

"Faas?" she asked before he said anything.

"Morning," he said.

"I was sleeping."

"Sorry. I didn't know who else to call."

"What's wrong?"

What was wrong? he asked himself. He'd screwed up his marriage, that's what was wrong. They'd been divorced for eight months now, and he missed her. He missed having a house full of his kids and their teenage friends. He missed the smell of something always in the oven. He missed Betty's smell. He missed the way she talked to him like he was one of the kids. The way she looked after him, took care of him, snuggled against him...no matter how late he got home and crawled into bed.

"I'm going through remorse," he managed to say. He tried to lean back against the headboard. The pain was bad. It was spreading to his shoulders, neck, jaw.

"I couldn't take it anymore," she told him for the umpteenth time. "If I'm going to raise our kids alone, I might as well be a single parent."

She was right. His job was demanding. But during the times between crises, he'd taken advantage of her. Baseball games with his friends, poker, golf and fishing trips. There had always been opportunities to do things without his family. He'd been stupid. He'd taken advantage.

They had four children, from eleven to seventeen. When Betty had asked for a divorce, there hadn't been any question who the kids wanted to live with.

"Are you still there?" she asked.

"I'm here," he said.

"I'm going back to sleep," she told him.

He nodded. It hurt too much to talk.

She didn't hang up. A few seconds of silence went by.

"Are you okay, Faas?" she asked gently.

"I think…I think I'm dying, Betty."

The phone slipped through his fingers to the floor. Faas slid from the edge of the bed and hit the floor hard.

Forty-Three

David's frustration was growing with every person he spoke to.

The nurse on his floor looked at him like he'd lost his mind, but she said she'd pass the information on to one of the doctors. The 911 call had been useless. They'd taken his name and number and said someone would get back to him. He'd tried a direct number to the police station. Also a waste. He'd been put on hold for so long that he'd hung up. He'd tried the special emergency response numbers. All circuits were too busy. Tried 911 again. No use.

He wasn't a hundred percent certain that the Strep-Tester itself was the cause of the spread of the NFI disease, but this couldn't be a coincidence, either. There were a total of five hundred of these samples that had gone out. He wished he had the breakdown of where every one of those testers had gone.

David felt the blood drain out of his face. The ten thousand Strep-Testers were being released this morning.

"Shit." David looked at the clock. It was 6:20 a.m. No one would be in the office yet. He called the number, anyway, leaving detailed instructions for his secretary to call every regional sales manager as soon as she got in. He'd do it himself if he had their home numbers with him. They had to stop the distribution of those testers.

As soon as he hung up, he realized he might not have been too coherent. He called back, and this time directed her to call him at the hospital if she didn't understand what needed to be done. He made it perfectly clear that it was urgent.

One of the nurses going by gave him a nervous look.

"Can you get hospital security for me?" David asked her.

"No, I can't," she replied. "This wing is under quarantine. Nobody is allowed to go in and out of here…and that includes the staff."

She disappeared inside one of the rooms before he had a chance to argue.

David found himself staring at the clock again. The first five hundred pieces had been intended to wave in front of the clientele's face. Some of those testers were probably still sitting in reps' briefcases. And medicine cabinets.

He wasn't the only one who would be checking e-mail this morning. Rushing back to the computer, he quickly began to hammer out an e-mail for mass distribution to the employees. His fingers paused over the keyboard. He couldn't make a statement that might be wrong and destroy the future of the product. He was only going on a hunch. Less than a handful of deaths that might actually be a coincidence. He rewrote the e-mail, directing the sales force not to distribute or use any more of the Strep-Testers until further notice.

He could already be too late, though, David thought. They weren't too much of an "on-time" company. The pieces could have gone out Friday and already be in the hands of the consumers.

In panic, he remembered the two Strep-Testers he'd given Jamie and Kate. He dialed his wife's cell phone again. The recorded message came on that all circuits were busy. David dialed his daughter's number. The same thing. Suddenly, no cell service was going through.

The feeling of helplessness washing through him was cold and numbing. But he'd been here before, David told himself. This was the same feeling he'd experienced when the doctors had told him and Sally that Josh had cancer.

Reading about so many other children like Josh and hearing their stories had provided a turning point for him. There was power in knowing that they weren't going through that crisis alone.

Knowledge was power then, he reminded himself, and knowledge is power now.

David's fingers flew over the keyboard. He e-mailed his daughters first. They were from the generation of PC junkies. They checked their e-mail more times during the day than anything else. He then started a search on who was running the NFI investigation. There was no point in chasing his tail at the bottom of the ladder. He had to go to the top, and the Internet was magic. He had the name in less than one minute.

Faas Hanlon.

Forty-Four

Taleghani Hospital, Kermanshah, Iran

There were nine regional hospitals tied into Kermanshah University of Medical Sciences. Taleghani Hospital was one of their smallest, but it was the best. Fahimah had heard this much from her cousin Ashraf.

The van that had met them at the airport reached the hospital and pulled up to the front door of the 1970s-era brick building. They both thanked the driver and got out.

Fahimah's nerves were getting the best of her. She could feel her knees shaking. Putting one foot in front of the other was a major feat.

"Your cousin mentioned that Rahaf was being kept sedated," Austyn reminded her. He had grown serious the moment they'd left the airport.

Fahimah nodded. She would have to be happy with whatever time she got with Rahaf, even if it were only a chance to look at her. To touch her hand, her face.

They reached the door. A doorman opened it for them. In the lobby a balding, distinguished-looking man wearing glasses and dressed in a suit and dress shirt, but no tie, came toward them.

"Welcome, Dr. Banaz, Mr. Newman." He greeted them in English. "I am Dr. Mansori."

Fahimah realized that Ashraf had called and made all these arrangements. She wondered if Austyn minded that this man knew his real name. He didn't seem to as he shook his hand.

Dr. Mansori was the director of the hospital. Fahimah knew Austyn had been surprised by what he'd seen in Halabja, but he betrayed no surprise with anything that was happening here. Dr. Mansori was in charge of the hospital, and yet he was a working physician, visible and available day to day. And he spoke excellent English.

"We're so glad you have come," Mansori said, speaking directly to her. "Since they brought your sister here a week ago, she has declined steadily. I believe she knows it is her time, but she is trying to make life easier for all those around her."

Fahimah willed herself not to cry, to stay strong. "Is she heavily sedated?"

"She was," Dr. Mansori told her, "until I received the call from Halabja last night. We have cut the morphine. She is in pain, but when I saw her an hour ago, she was gaining consciousness, recognizing people around her. She would want it this way…to see you."

"Does she know I'm coming?" Fahimah asked.

The physician nodded. "I told her this morning." Behind the thick glasses, his eyes were welling with tears. "I have

known and worked with your sister on many different occasions over the past few years. Frequently, she has contacted me to accept patients that she felt needed to be
hospitalized from the refugee camps. I do not know if you
have heard the nickname the people have for her."

Fahimah nodded. "*Firishte*...the angel."

"And she truly is an angel." Dr. Mansori smiled. "I must
tell you, though, that I have never seen your sister as happy
as today, when I told her you were coming."

Fahimah's eyes burned with unshed tears. "Will you
take me to her?"

The doctor stretched a hand in the direction that they
should go. He led them up a set of stairs. Austyn and Dr.
Mansori talked, but Fahimah didn't hear a word of their
exchange. She was lost in a different time.

Two girls, holding each other in their mother's kitchen,
staring out over the body of their father at the sea of dead
friends and neighbors on their street.

She and Rahaf were two lonely souls who only had
each other left. This had been the story of their life. Only
fifteen months apart, they were each other's shadow, each
other's soul. There were two hearts in their bodies but they
pulsed as one.

"This is it, *khanoom*."

Rahaf's door was open. Two people and a nurse who
were inside saw Fahimah and quickly came out. They each
said something kind to her as they passed, but again she
couldn't hear.

Fahimah stepped through the doorway. She looked at
the bed, and her tears began to fall.

Rahaf lay on the high hospital bed. She, who had once

been so young and vibrant and full of health, was now a mere skeleton. The missing leg created a void that was visible under the smooth white blanket. Her green eyes tried to focus as she lifted her hand.

"Fahimah?"

She didn't remember taking the steps, but she was there, next to her sister, holding her in her arms.

They'd spent a lifetime apart, but they were one again.

Forty-Five

VA Medical Center, Maryland

Cell phone lines were jammed. Some of the regular telephone exchanges seemed to be working, but it was hit and miss.

Finally, David got through on an 800-number for Homeland Security in Washington. Could he speak to Faas Hanlon? He was unavailable. Was the next person in charge of the NFI investigation available? No, no one else in charge of that investigation was available, either.

"There's got to be someone there to talk to. I have critical information about the situation."

"Mr. Link, we have no one available to talk to you right now, but if I could take a number where you can be reached, an agent connected with the investigation will get back to you."

"I've been doing just that at a number of places over the past two hours, and *no one* has called me back yet."

David was disgusted. "Fine, let me leave a message for Faas Hanlon."

He had been right about the e-mail, at least. Both of his daughters e-mailed him back within an hour. They wanted to know what the heck was going on…and yes, they still had the Strep-Testers.

The company-wide e-mail he'd sent out was creating some questions. But no one was jumping in and offering anything useful. Both Bill and Ned Reynolds had their "I am away" messages on, and the VP of Sales hadn't opened his e-mail yet, either.

His secretary had e-mailed him that she was making the calls to the sales force, but that she wasn't able to get through to a lot of them because of clogged phone lines.

He decided that leaving a message for Faas Hanlon wasn't enough.

David e-mailed and then phoned the White House. He couldn't get through. He e-mailed the FBI. He was getting to be a master at it. The same text was copied and pasted in each e-mail. Name, phone number where he could be reached, the company he worked for, identifying himself as a survivor, so far, of the NFI research boat incident, indicating that he has information that might tie the source of the infection to new sample Strep-Testers that his company had released.

One of the residents came out in the hallway, and David pounced on him.

"The nurses are becoming very concerned about your behavior, Mr. Link," the young man told him.

"Good," David said, frustrated. "Call Security. Call the police. Call the FBI."

"We can't do any of those things right now." He started into a long speech about the procedures for the quarantining of the patients.

David cut him off. "I'm trying to give you information that could save thousands of lives. I work for the company that makes a new product, over-the-counter home Strep-Testers."

"Oh, I've heard of them. That's an interesting idea. But they haven't hit the market yet, have they?"

"Five hundred of them are in circulation. And there are ten thousand that are going to be distributed this morning…unless we can stop it," David said, trying to keep any hint of fanaticism out of his voice. "I believe the Strep-Testers are causing the infections."

"And why do you think that?" he asked too casually, sending David's blood pressure a notch or two higher.

"Four of our sales people who had these samples had a death in the family from NFI," David told him, exaggerating a little. He wasn't certain for two of the cases, but he decided it was a safe assumption. "They might have used these testers."

"They *might* have," the resident repeated doubtfully. "Are you sure they used them?"

"I'm pretty sure they did. I *know* that Philip Carver, the program director on our ship, used one, because I gave it to him."

"You know, sir, every investigator in this country is working on this disease. Don't you think they would have found that information, if it were a common link? And that's only four or five cases out of how many? I've lost count of the total number of fatalities. What about the rest?"

"Yes, you're right—" David looked at the resident's badge "—Dr. Niles. You're right to be dubious. But don't you think this information needs to be brought to someone's attention?"

"Have you called the FBI…or the police department?"

David told him about all the phone calls and e-mails he'd sent.

The young doctor shrugged. "Sounds like you've done everything you should be doing. I don't know what else to tell you. But I still think it's highly unlikely that your theory is correct, since your company had to go through all kinds of testing with the FDA to get the product approved. If there was any question about the tester's safety, don't you think it would have shown up then?"

"Does the name Vioxx mean anything to you?"

"Well, that's not exactly the same thing, but I believe they're still fighting that out in court."

"Who wins in court is not the issue. People could be dying because of *this* product."

The resident shrugged again.

"Even if the product that was tested is viable, it may very well be that *this* product lot was infected. Who knows, maybe some *terrorist* planted something in our lab."

"I still don't know what to tell you. You've done everything you can. Now wait and see. I'm sure they'll get back to you." He glanced at his watch. "Sorry, I have to go."

David rubbed the back of his neck. The muscles were knotted. He wasn't overreacting. What happened if he was right?

He couldn't believe how close he'd come to making Josh use the strip.

A cold sweat washed down his back. Anyone could be using one right now.

He made up his mind. He dialed the number for the White House again and got through. He punched numbers until he was speaking to a living human.

"Yes. This is David Link. I am the terrorist behind the NFI outbreak.... Yes, you heard me correctly. The NFI outbreak... No, I don't want you to put me on hold. I've just been taken off the research vessel that had all the kids on it, and I'm being held in the VA Medical Center.... That's right, the VA Medical Center in Maryland. Yes, I am behind every single one of the outbreaks. Yes, David Link. I work for Reynolds Pharmaceuticals. Okay...now listen to me, because I'm only going to say this to you once. Are you ready?"

David definitely had the White House operator's attention.

"As we speak, ten thousand infected products are being shipped all over the country. Ten thousand. That means the number of NFI deaths so far is *nothing* compared to what will happen tomorrow if you don't get someone over to this hospital *now.*"

Forty-Six

Austyn couldn't have felt more welcome.

After asking him a couple of questions about his background and realizing their visitor's interest in science and research, the physician gave him a complete tour of the hospital. He talked about the staff and their publications. Dr. Mansori had been here since before the Iranian revolution, and his thirty-year tenure gave him the air of a proud parent.

Austyn didn't want to stray too far and for too long away from Fahimah, though, so after a couple of hours they made their way back toward the wing where Rahaf was staying.

There was a nurse outside the door, and she told Austyn that Fahimah was looking for him.

He knocked on the door and Fahimah opened it.

Austyn had to keep from putting his arms immediately around her. She had a look on her face that he could only describe as one of gain and loss. She had found something that she knew she was about to have torn from her.

"I told Rahaf about you," Fahimah said softly. She drew him into the room.

Austyn looked at the bed where Rahaf lay. The absurdity of imagining she could be responsible for the terror in the U.S. would have been comical if it were not for her condition. She was beyond frail. The years and her illnesses had been very hard on her. She looked so much older than her age. Her intelligent green eyes, though, were very much alive.

"Mr. Newman," she said hoarsely.

"Please, call me Austyn," he said, approaching her. The head of the hospital bed had been raised and a couple of pillows were propped up beside her. There were no IVs or any other monitoring devices hooked up to her. His gaze went over the place where her leg should have been.

He saw, pinned to her hospital gown, a gold charm. He recognized it as the one the woman at the clothing store in Erbil had given Fahimah.

"My sister tells me that she owes her freedom to you."

Now he was embarrassed. He looked at Fahimah and shook his head. "All I can say is that I'm sorry, though I know that will never be enough."

"Let's not discuss politics," Rahaf said, wincing. She was sounding very tired and short of breath. "We all are victims…every one of us."

It was obvious that she was in a great deal of pain. Dr. Mansori had mentioned that, other than shots of morphine to ease her suffering, she wouldn't allow treatment that would needlessly prolong her life. She moved slightly and motioned to a chair near the bed.

"Please sit down," Fahimah said, repeating her sister's gesture.

Austyn did as he was told but not before Fahimah brought another chair that was by the window closer to the bed, too, where she could sit.

"Fahimah tells me you are facing an epidemic in America."

Austyn summarized the situation, focusing first on the strain of bacteria they'd never seen before—with the exception of what had been discovered in Rahaf's laboratory. He gave her as much background information as he had on the cases discovered since that first outbreak. He also mentioned the latest suspicion that some kind of cold medication might be infecting the victims.

Rahaf listened to everything he said. Despite her pain and obvious discomfort, Austyn could see she comprehended every word.

"My study initially started on a family of Panton-Valentine leukocidin," she began softly, "which, as you know, is toxic to cells. They can cause leukocyte, or white blood cell destruction, pneumonia and necrotizing fasciitis…."

Austyn pulled out a pen and paper and scribbled her words as fast as he could. She told him the details of the study that she'd been doing prior to the discovery of something unexpected, the mutation of the bacteria into a super-microbe. Despite her illness and physical frailty, her mind was sharp and clear. She had no trouble remembering anything.

"Although MRSA…methicillin-resistant staphylococcus aureus…has traditionally been seen as a hospital-associated infection, MRSA strains have begun to appear outside of hospitals and clinics in recent years. This specific strain is definitely a community-associated one," Rahaf told him.

"As you know," she continued, "MRSA strains are resistant to the usual antibiotics, but a curious interbreeding with community staph has led to the genetic acquisition of a PVL factor, which in turn has produced a series of changes that make these strains particularly invasive, as well as resistant."

"My understanding," Austyn said to her, "is that staphylococcal infections are an issue only when the individual has suffered a skin break or an open wound, but this isn't always the case with these victims."

Rahaf closed her eyes for a moment, and Austyn looked at Fahimah.

"There is no need to do this now," he said. "I don't want to tire—"

"No, Austyn," Rahaf said. "Just give me a moment."

Fahimah kept her eyes on her sister's face, and Austyn could read the sorrow there. Rahaf drew in a deep breath and looked at him.

"What you say is true." She nodded. "My laboratory experiences were in a controlled environment. But my contention is that, in the real world, this strand can colonize in the mouth and the throat. You see, it is in the genetic combination of these three microbes: staphylococcus, carried by thirty percent of healthy adults in their nose, the strep infection that must be present in the throat, and an outside staphylococcal cassette chromosome, introduced separately that forms the basis for the creation of the deadly new strain…you have a name for it."

"We just call it NFI," he said. "Necrotizing Fasciitis Infection."

As she continued to explain, it became clear that outside

of a laboratory environment, the victim had to have a strep infection for the NFI microbe to mutate. Austyn thought of all the cold medications they were testing in the U.S. This narrowed the field down to medications relating to a sore throat where the victim actually has strep throat.

Fahimah gave her sister some water.

"If this is too much for you, we can stop and get back to it later," he told her again.

"No," she said adamantly. "You see…I was so frightened of this NFI…that I destroyed everything. Not only what Fahimah did for me at the lab…but any documentation I had outside, too." She touched her head. "What is left is here."

Austyn understood now the need to remove the bacteria through the amputation. "Can you tell me about the remedy you took to survive?"

Rahaf motioned to Fahimah and sipped some more water first. "Most classes of antibiotics were discovered in the 1940s and '50s. You know that they work by blocking synthesis of the cell wall, DNA, and proteins within the bacteria."

Austyn knew this. "And I know that most of today's antibiotics are simply a variation on that original concept."

"Exactly. The fact that they work in similar ways may be one reason why bacteria are developing resistance," Rahaf told him. "Now, this remedy was not something that I discovered. It is a product presently under testing by one of your pharmaceutical companies. The antibiotic was discovered by isolating a certain microorganism from a sample of soil from southern Africa."

Austyn wrote down the information. She told him the name of the company and how successful the product had been so far on mice. She said she heard it might be a decade before it became available for humans. Rahaf had gone to school with one of the lead scientists working on the project at the time, who had given her a sample of the product.

"If the compound passes clinical trials it will become only the third entirely new antibiotic developed in the past four decades."

"Do you know how this antibiotic works differently from the others?" Austyn asked.

"It acts to block enzymes involved in the synthesis of fatty acids, which bacteria need to construct cell membranes."

She had to stop again. Fahimah gave her sister more water. The burst of energy Rahaf had gathered to give him this information was draining from her body. He hoped she would bounce back. But he could see the pain was too much.

"I need the nurse, my love," she told her sister.

Fahimah ran for the door, and Rahaf beckoned to Austyn.

He went to her and held her thin hands. The green eyes met his. "She has suffered."

He nodded.

"You make good on that suffering. You make sure she is taken care of."

"She will be," he promised her.

Forty-Seven

Washington Hospital Center, Washington, D.C.

They were calling it a mild heart attack. At least, this was what the initial ECG and blood tests indicated.

Faas was far from being out of the woods, but he'd made it clear that it was a matter of national security for him to take a call from Agent Newman. Considering everything that was going around the country, none of the doctors or nurses had a problem with it.

One of the nurses handed him a phone as soon as they rolled his bed into a curtained-off area. They told him he was only between tests. This was a rest stop only.

"Pressure of the job getting to you?" Austyn asked.

"No, I'm faking it. It's a good way to get my ex-wife's sympathy back." Betty had been the one who'd called 911. She was at the hospital by the time the ambulance had brought him in. Now she was talking to the doctor in the hall.

"Great idea. How is it working?"

"So far, so good," he said. "What have you got?"

"Some very good things," Austyn said. "But first of all, you should know that you're the third call I've made. NIH already has this information, and so does our department. So you don't have to leap out of bed and try to do everything yourself."

The curtain opened and Betty walked in. She frowned at the phone in his hand. He made a sign that it would only take one minute.

"Tell me. Make it short."

"All the initial victims at each site had to have strep throat, and they had to have an outside staph infection introduced, probably orally. So NIH is checking the inventory of the drugs these people had that might have something to do with that. Once that initial person became infected and decomposition began, the bacteria could spread in any of three ways: direct contact, airborne particles and insect transmission, depending on environmental conditions."

"Interesting. Go on."

"But there's something else. I was talking to Bea Devera at the office. She said they've been getting about a dozen phone calls from some pharmaceutical company executive who claims he knows what's going in. In fact, he's already made a call to the White House claiming he's behind the attacks, and that it's not over."

"Shit. Is anyone checking him out?"

"Yeah. Bea said the guy was on the research vessel with all those kids. She's on her way to the hospital where he is, along with about a hundred other agents."

"Okay."

Faas took his wife's hand when she came closer to the bed. "I'll talk to you later," he said, handing the phone to Betty.

"What's going on?" she asked.

"They're all jerks. I have to have a heart attack for them to get their act together. They might just have the case cracked."

She smiled. "See? This is what I've been telling you for all these years. You need to delegate more."

Forty-Eight

Taleghani Hospital, Kermanshah, Iran

Fahimah held her sister's hand as the nurse gave Rahaf a shot of morphine. One of the doctors had stepped out only moments before. He'd whispered to Fahimah that these could be her sister's last moments.

She placed a kiss on the fragile fingers. Once again, there seemed to be no end to her tears. She had no will left to fight them. The sorrow was overwhelming her.

"We're at the reflecting pool," Rahaf breathed. "Do you see the hanging mist?"

Fahimah looked at her sister. Her green eyes were distant. She had a smile on her face.

"Yes, I do, my love. We are at Tagh-e-Bostan."

"Do you remember her poems?" Rahaf asked. "The Saint of Basra?"

Fahimah didn't need any book of verse. For five years the Sufi poet's words had carried her. She recited them softly, as she remembered them. As she wanted to remember them.

"'Oh, my joy, my dream, my support. My friend, my precious one, my intention. You are the soul of my heart, my hope. You are my comfort—your desire sustains me.'"

Rahaf's lips kissed their joined fingers. She closed her eyes.

"So many blessings you have given me, my sister. Now your love is my desire and my heaven. It clears the path to my captured heart. Now, so long as I live, I will not be apart from you. You are my strength when I despair. If you are pleased with me, then—my heart—my happiness has begun."

The fingers relaxed in Fahimah's hand. She reached out and touched Rahaf's face. She was gone.

"I will not be apart from you," she whispered. *"Firishte."*

Forty-Nine

Reynolds Pharmaceuticals
Wilmington, Delaware

Federal agents, local police, representatives from practically every health-related branch of government swarmed the buildings and grounds of Reynolds Pharmaceuticals. David Link's suspicions were confirmed. Out of sixteen individual cases that were reported and the victims who'd already been autopsied, all had had strep throat, and a piece of the Strep-Tester—be it the outer paper or the tester itself—was found in all but one case.

Bill and Ned Reynolds were already going back and forth between the facilities. The packaging phase was identified as a probable source of the problem. Agents were focusing on a possible heat-induced chemical reaction between the clear plastic strip and the tester ingredients.

The important thing was that the shipment of the ten thousand testers had been halted, and an emergency announcement had been made regarding the initial five hundred.

At noon on Monday, however, 273 of them were still unaccounted for.

Fifty

"They should tout you as a national hero," Sally told him on the phone.

"I'll be happy if I don't end up in jail," David answered. A great weight had lifted off his shoulders when he passed on his suspicions to the Homeland Security agent who'd interviewed him though a glass partition at the hospital the day before.

"Come on, now. They would never do that," Sally protested.

"You never know. I called the White House and claimed that I was behind it all."

"You explained to them that you were only trying to get someone's attention," Sally protested.

David could tell where this was going. She already had the mother's voice on. The gloves were off and the claws were out. His wife was ready to take on the world for her family.

"I know. And I'm not too worried about it." He smiled, leaning back against the chair in the lounge area.

They'd given the run of the floor to him and Craig and Kirk. It looked as if they were done with the testing for now. So far, none of the tests had turned up anything wrong with any of them. But still, not a word had been said about when they'd be releasing them. Josh, at least, was supposed to go home tomorrow morning.

"Here it is," Sally said. "They're running it again."

Kirk had gone back to his room to sleep and Craig was reading a magazine in one of the chairs. Craig and David had gotten sick of watching the same news, so they'd turned off the TV. David got up from the sofa and quickly switched it back on.

On the screen there was an aerial view of Reynolds Pharmaceuticals with cars and people swarming like ants around the building. A bright banner scrolling across the bottom referred to sixteen individual sites of the outbreak with 154 fatalities. The rest of the Strep-Testers were now accounted for.

"There goes my job," David said to his wife. "Reynolds Pharmaceuticals can say goodbye to any more government contracts, and I'd say it's a guarantee that they have their asses sued off for this Strep-Tester. I guess it's a safe bet that I'll be standing in the unemployment line next week."

"We'll manage," she said with all her positive attitude.

David felt that he and Josh had missed taking the bullet by inches. Still, the magnitude of how close he'd come to killing his own son with the Strep-Tester made him go ice-

cold every time he thought of it. There were so many
people out there who weren't so lucky.

He and Sally finished talking for now and he hung up.
Of course, he knew before the hour was up, one of them
would find a reason to call the other. It was strange to be
in the same hospital but not be allowed to see each other.

"Are you really worried about your job?" Craig asked
when David put the phone on the side table.

"I'm more than worried about it. This is going to bury
the company."

"It'll be tough with Josh still going through his treatment," Craig commented.

David nodded. A national disaster had been minimized.
But he hadn't given any thought yet to how to take care of
the personal disaster that was brewing.

"This is one negative thing about working for the same
company for so many years. You don't have your résumé
ready to go out."

Craig looked at him for a minute. "That's no big deal.
I can help you with that."

David appreciated the thought, and he said so.

"Have you considered getting out of pharmaceuticals?"
Craig asked.

"After this past week, I'd say yes. I'm more than considering it."

Craig seemed to be thinking about something, so
David picked up the magazine from the table next to
him. Before he found anything worth reading, though,
Craig nodded to him.

"What would you think about getting into the homeopathic line? With your sales contacts, I know my wife's company would be interested."

David didn't have to hear another word.

"Do they offer health insurance?" he asked.

Fifty-One

Austyn was told that Kurds got together for only two formal social gatherings—weddings and funerals.

People had arrived from other camps, from Iranian villages and from Iraqi Kurdish villages. People had come all the way from Turkey. As he watched what seemed to be thousands gather on a green hillside to celebrate the life and mourn the death of the woman who'd worked courageously and tirelessly to help them, he was only interested in one.

As he watched her, he could see the resolve in Fahimah's face.

Wave after wave of people approached her. Austyn didn't understand most of the words spoken to her. But the signs of gratitude, affection and condolence were unmistakable.

Austyn was certain that Fahimah now understood the magnitude of the gift she'd given, not only to her sister, but all these people during the five years that she had been imprisoned.

Two men played the *ney,* a smaller version of the flute, while another played a stringed instrument called the *tanbur.* The melody was heartrendingly sad. A woman sang. Austyn recognized the names of Rahaf's family members mentioned in the song.

Dr. Mansori came from Kermanshah and attended the funeral. He stood with Austyn and explained the customs as the ceremony proceeded.

Rahaf's body was shrouded in white. She had been placed on a flat board that was like an open casket. Flowers covered her. Sometime around midday, a group of young men approached the corpse and lifted the casket onto their shoulders. They started a procession that wound through the crowds. People threw flowers at the body and then joined the line of mourners. Fahimah led the group to the small burial ground on the hill. In the distance, the rugged peaks of the mountains pierced the clear blue sky.

Austyn was in awe of Fahimah's strength. For one burying the last member of her family, she displayed tremendous courage.

He had to leave today. The same private plane that had brought him over from Halabja was taking him back. He would drive back with Dr. Mansori to Kermanshah to catch the plane. Fahimah knew he was leaving.

Austyn had spoken to a number of top officials in the U.S. Every kind of arrangement was being made possible. From a teaching position at Salahaddin University in Erbil to financial settlements so that she could start her life again in Kurdistan, he was leaving no stone unturned for her. He had even cleared the way for her to go to America, though he knew she would never accept that path. When they talked, she told him her wish, for now, was to stay in Kurdistan.

After the funeral she stayed with him at the cemetery as everyone else moved down to the tents that had been set up to feed the crowds.

"Thank you," he told her, taking her hand and placing a kiss on her palm.

"If it were not for you, I would never have seen Rahaf before she died," she told him, smiling sadly at the spot where fresh flowers covered the dirt where her sister had just been buried.

"I'm sorry. It didn't have to be like this."

She nodded. "As Rahaf said, we are all victims of the actions of those who govern our countries. The past is behind me. Now I have to decide where I want to go from here."

"I told you that you can come to the U.S.," he immediately offered again. "I know you will get an invitation from the president if you choose to come. You can teach…or do whatever you want to do."

"No. My place is here…for now, at least," she said gently. "These are my people. We are only starting the fight."

"What fight?" he asked.

"The road to independence," she said. "I cannot act the part of a physician like Rahaf, but perhaps I can be my people's voice."

Austyn was honestly happy for her. She'd already found a purpose. He told her that. About the sadness he was feeling for himself, he said nothing.

A car horn beeped at the foot of the hill. They were waiting for him.

"You need to go," she said encouragingly.

"Do you think our paths will ever cross again?" he asked.

She smiled, looked up at the blue sky above. Her green eyes startled him still.

"I cannot say. Perhaps not." She raised herself on her toes and brushed a kiss against his cheek. "But we have a saying…. No matter where you go, your destiny follows you."

Austyn's climb down that hill to the waiting car was the hardest path he had ever traveled. Reaching the road, he looked back.

At the top of the hill, Fahimah stood in the breeze…alone, strong, her clear eyes fixed on the distant peaks.

Author's Note

We hoped you enjoyed reading *The Deadliest Strain*. We found this to be a very emotional book to write; many of the references to the genocidal Anfal Campaign that killed and displaced hundreds of thousands of innocent people in Kurdistan are sadly, painfully true.

We would like to thank our aunt and uncle and cousin, the Rahimian family, for it was the pride they carry for their Kurdish heritage that planted the seed in us years ago to write a book set in that region. We are also grateful to Kurdish filmmaker Bahman Ghobadi for his inspiring films—especially *Turtles Can Fly*—and for bringing attention to the children who are left behind after every war.

We are also forever indebted to our many loyal readers. We hope you enjoyed this visit with President Penn, who was originally introduced in *Silent Waters*. Once again, characters never go away in our books…they only take short breaks.

As always, we love to hear from you. You can write to us at:

JanCoffey@JanCoffey.com
Nikoo & Jim McGoldrick
P.O. Box 665
Watertown, CT 06795
or you can visit us on the Web at www.JanCoffey.com

The Deadliest Strain, by authors Jim and Nikoo McGold-rick (writing as Jan Coffey), is a thriller that will have you turning the pages into the night. But it is also the compelling story of a woman's journey home to her country and family after surviving terrible losses. We invite you to explore the themes and characters in *The Deadliest Strain* with the following discussion questions:

1. What strength of character allows Fahimah to survive five years in the "ghost prison"? She muses, "God finds a low branch for the bird that cannot fly." What does this Kurdish proverb reveal about her outlook on life?

2. What makes Austyn suspect that they have the wrong sister? How does this affect the way that he proceeds with his mission?

3. "Stairs are climbed step by step." Fahimah and Austyn are each on a journey. In what ways are their journeys different? In what ways are they similar?

4. Why does Fahimah agree to help the two agents? Why doesn't she run away at the first opportunity?

5. David and Josh's weeklong trip on the research vessel *Harmony* is supposed to be part of a journey of healing. How does irony play a part in the unfolding

events on the boat? How does irony play a part in the novel's later action?

6. As we learn more about Fahimah's background, we learn more about her situation as an Iraqi and as a Kurd. Discuss the ways that the distinction between the two comes across in the novel. Why is it important?

7. Discuss your perception of the Kurdish city of Erbil. How is it that the city has escaped so much of the violence and destruction found in the rest of Iraq?

8. "When it came to dealing with women, Kurds were in most ways more advanced than the rest of Iraq." How is the role of women different in Kurdish Iraq? Is the portrayal of women in the novel surprising?

9. Jalal is referred to as "a dervish…a holy man." Discuss how he might be symbolic of the Kurdish people.

10. The attack on Halabja was a major formative event in Fahimah's life. Discuss how other tragic events form our perspectives on the world and on our personal lives.

A stunning sequel from
DEANNA RAYBOURN

Fresh from a six-month sojourn in Italy, Lady Julia returns home to Sussex to find her father's estate crowded with family and friends—but dark deeds are afoot at the deconsecrated abbey, and a murderer roams the ancient cloisters.

With a captivating cast of characters in a remarkably imaginative setting, *Silent in the Sanctuary* is a marvelous sequel to the evocative *Silent in the Grave*.

SILENT *in the* SANCTUARY

"Fans of British historical thrillers will welcome Raybourn's perfectly executed debut."
—*Publishers Weekly* on *Silent in the Grave*

Available the first week of January 2008 wherever paperbacks are sold!

MIRA®

www.MIRABooks.com

MDR2492

REQUEST YOUR FREE BOOKS!

2 FREE NOVELS
FROM THE ROMANCE/SUSPENSE
COLLECTION PLUS 2 FREE GIFTS!

YES! Please send me 2 FREE novels from the Romance/Suspense Collection and my 2 FREE gifts. After receiving them, if I don't wish to receive any more books, I can return the shipping statement marked "cancel." If I don't cancel, I will receive 4 brand-new novels every month and be billed just $5.49 per book in the U.S., or $5.99 per book in Canada, plus 25¢ shipping and handling per book plus applicable taxes, if any*. That's a savings of at least 20% off the cover price! I understand that accepting the 2 free books and gifts places me under no obligation to buy anything. I can always return a shipment and cancel at any time. Even if I never buy another book from the Reader Service, the two free books and gifts are mine to keep forever.

185 MDN EF5Y   385 MDN EF6C

Name _____ (PLEASE PRINT) _____

Address _____ Apt. # _____

City _____ State/Prov. _____ Zip/Postal Code _____

Signature (if under 18, a parent or guardian must sign)

Mail to **The Reader Service:**
IN U.S.A.: P.O. Box 1867, Buffalo, NY 14240-1867
IN CANADA: P.O. Box 609, Fort Erie, Ontario L2A 5X3

Not valid to current subscribers to the Romance Collection,
the Suspense Collection or the Romance/Suspense Collection.

Want to try two free books from another line?
Call 1-800-873-8635 or visit www.morefreebooks.com.

* Terms and prices subject to change without notice. NY residents add applicable sales tax. Canadian residents will be charged applicable provincial taxes and GST. This offer is limited to one order per household. All orders subject to approval. Credit or debit balances in a customer's account(s) may be offset by any other outstanding balance owed by or to the customer. Please allow 4 to 6 weeks for delivery.

Your Privacy: Harlequin is committed to protecting your privacy. Our Privacy Policy is available online at www.eHarlequin.com or upon request from the Reader Service. From time to time we make our lists of customers available to reputable firms who may have a product or service of interest to you. If you would prefer we not share your name and address, please check here. ☐

Jan Coffey

32406 THE PROJECT	___ $6.99 U.S.	___ $8.50 CAN.
32319 SILENT WATERS	___ $6.99 U.S.	___ $8.50 CAN.
32057 FOURTH VICTIM	___ $6.50 U.S.	___ $7.99 CAN.
32192 FIVE IN A ROW	___ $6.99 U.S.	___ $8.50 CAN.
66859 TRUST ME ONCE	___ $5.99 U.S.	___ $6.99 CAN.
66919 TWICE BURNED	___ $6.50 U.S.	___ $7.99 CAN.

(limited quantities available)

TOTAL AMOUNT	$ _____	
POSTAGE & HANDLING	$ _____	
($1.00 FOR 1 BOOK, 50¢ for each additional)		
APPLICABLE TAXES*	$ _____	
TOTAL PAYABLE	$ _____	

(check or money order—please do not send cash)

To order, complete this form and send it, along with a check or money order for the total above, payable to MIRA Books, to: **In the U.S.:** 3010 Walden Avenue, P.O. Box 9077, Buffalo, NY 14269-9077; **In Canada:** P.O. Box 636, Fort Erie, Ontario, L2A 5X3.

Name: _____
Address: _____ City: _____
State/Prov.: _____ Zip/Postal Code: _____
Account Number (if applicable): _____

075 CSAS

*New York residents remit applicable sales taxes.
*Canadian residents remit applicable GST and provincial taxes.

MIRA®

www.MIRABooks.com

MJC0108BL